THE FIVE ANGELS

Book One
of
The Five Angels Trilogy

KIMBERLY M. RINGER

Kisy Kane Publishing, LLC

Contact Information: www.kimberlymringer.com

ISBN Hardback: 978-1-7373358-0-1

ISBN Paperback: 978-1-7373358-2-5

ISBN E-Book: 978-1-7373358-1-8

First Edition: August 2021

DEDICATION

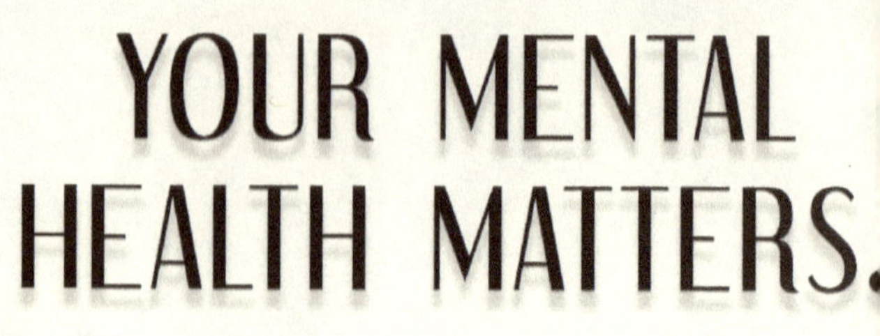

YOUR MENTAL HEALTH MATTERS.

If you or someone you know may be struggling with suicida[l] thoughts, you can call the U.S. National Suicide Prevention Lifeline by simply dialing 988 or the full phone number: 800-273-TALK (8255) any time, day or night, or chat

Crisis Text Line also provides free, 24/7, confidential support via text message to people in crisis when they dial 741741.

Content Considerations

Family Death
On Page Death
Emotional and Physical Violence
Politics
Religion
Profanity
Sexually Explicit Scenes
Torture
Misogynistic Society
Narcissistic Persons
Car Accident
Hospitalization
PTSD

CONTENTS

AUTHOR NOTE TO READERS:

THE FIVE ANGELS HAS been a heart project of mine for longer than I care to admit. Megan and CJ's story has always been on my mind and begged to be told. Once it was down on paper the entire Nalrin family started screaming. I hope you have enjoyed the story, and are looking forward to the next two books. If you enjoy this trilogy you can pick up in the Nalrin world with the Ashridge Duology which takes place 40 years after the end of book 3 in the Five Angels Trilogy.

Please post a review on whichever platform you have purchased this book from. Indie Authors live by your reviews.

I could not have done this without support in so many forms. I can in no way name everyone who has helped, loved, supported, or inspired me through writing this trilogy. Thank you to: Catalina Ringer, Thom Jones, Marshall Hundemer, Barbara Wright, Barbara McLeary, George McLeary, Alan and Sandi Brown, Ariel Mann, Patrick McLeary, and of course my amazing husband.

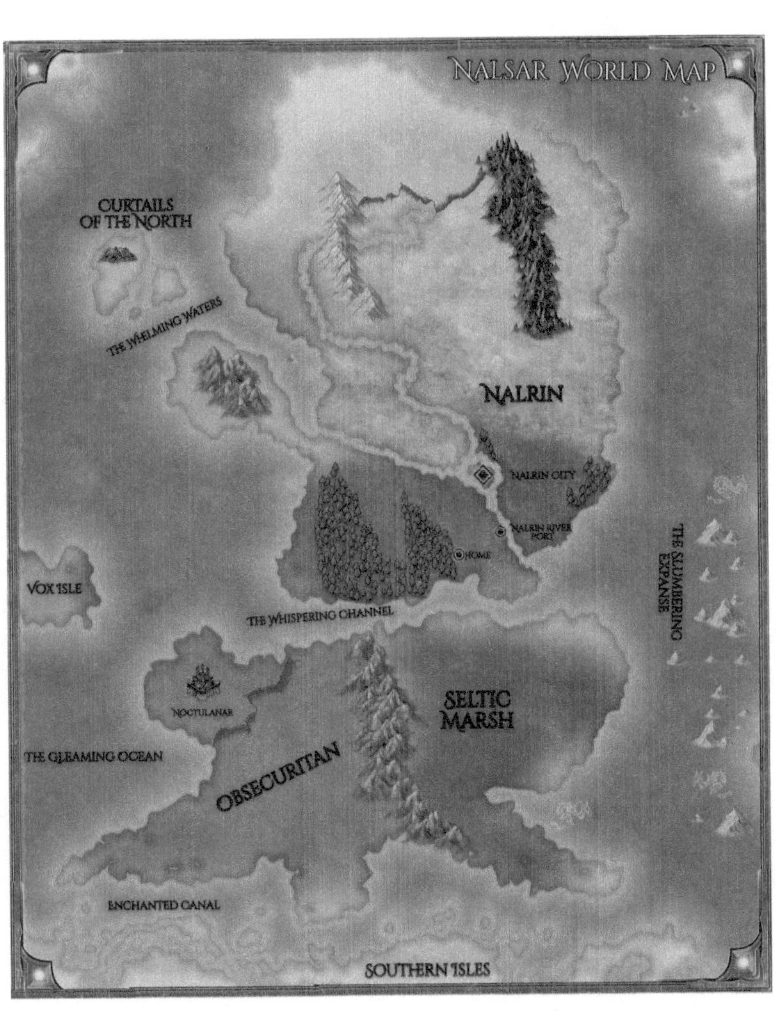
NALSAR WORLD MAP
CURTAILS OF THE NORTH
THE WHELMING WATERS
NALRIN
NALRIN CITY
NALRIN RIVER PORT
HOME
VOX ISLE
THE WHISPERING CHANNEL
THE SLUMBERING EXPANSE
NOCTULANAR
SELTIC MARSH
THE GLEAMING OCEAN
OBSECURITAN
ENCHANTED CANAL
SOUTHERN ISLES

CHAPTER 1

EVERYONE WANTS TO BE special. They want to fly, have x-ray vision, see the future. That is, until they actually have them. When the beings that controlled the worlds dished out specialties to newborn babies, they made me one of those very people. They decided that I should dream of things that happen in the future, whether I wanted to or not.

My life wasn't horrible per se. I had a few great friends. I got good grades and even scored multiple scholarships that paid most of my way through college. I had a decent paying job, a roof over my head, and food on the table. Not to mention the fact I could just get up and go to the beach whenever I wanted. There was a reason why people paid so much to live here on the Monterey Peninsula.

So, what was the problem, right? Those visions were the problem. I'd see things in my dreams that would come true way too often to just be deemed déjà vu. Then there were the things that couldn't be from this world. Creatures. Wisps of shadow.

Things that to others would be on the fringe of their vision, but I would see clearly. All the time. Usually, they left me alone, and I ignored them. But, when they would acknowledge me, it was usually a tip of a hat, or a snide grin and it scared the shit out of me every time.

The visions however, never provided me anything useful like those perfect numbers to win the California State Lottery. Usually, I just dreamt someone would call, a situation in day-to-day life, or that someone was coming to visit. If that were all it was, they would be nothing more than common annoyance. The problem lied in seeing your best friend's girlfriend cheat on him or seeing your family die or knowing when your friend's grandmother was going to die from the cancer she had been fighting for years. You know, the life-altering kinds of visions. Those were the problem.

Two and a half years ago, I started having visions of my brother Matt, dying in a horrific car accident. I told him about it, only because he noticed I had been extra clingy to him when we saw each other. He hid his distress from me well, but I had dreamt of the wreck for *months* before it actually happened.

Roughly four months after Matt died another vision started. I was standing in my parents' house in Seaside, a bright light would flash, blinding me, but just as the light would go out, I'd wake up. It never *really* worried me, and I didn't know what it was until it happened a year later, and they died in an explosion that destroyed the house.

So here I am a year later, 24 years old, working my ass off each and every day. I worked a full-time job as a Paralegal in a law firm, so that usually meant overtime in abundance.

"It's been a long day. Why haven't you gone home yet?" Janeen said as she came around the corner. She looked through the stack of files that I completed earlier that afternoon and added, "You've been busy."

"Just trying to finish the pleadings for the Sanchez case." I said hitting print on the interrogatories response. "They have to be filed Tuesday. I'll call the process server to take them and file them at the court. Brad still needs to review and sign them."

She studied me for a long moment while waiting for the document to finish printing. Concern filled in the deep lined wrinkles around her eyes as she said, "You okay? I noticed you didn't eat lunch." She readjusted the legal files she picked up off my desk against her bright red button-down shirt, the sleeves rolled up to her elbows, and placed them against her full hips. The black slacks bunched underneath.

"Yea. Just a headache. Didn't sleep well." I said rubbing my temples. The fact of the matter was that all night I had the same vision over and over again.

"Brad won't be in tomorrow, no clients either, so no dressing up. Come in sweats for all I care." She said, "Now go home. I order a glass or two ... or three of wine before bed."

"Thanks. See you tomorrow then." I smiled at her. She was by far my favorite here. Janeen was the firm's manager, and she ran a tight office, but she was fair and considerate.

I put the response on the file and handed it to Janeen to put with the others for Brad's review tomorrow. Once my desk was cleaned up and I shut off the computer, I loaded up my things and headed out to the parking lot where my car, Betsy sat waiting for me. The payment stretched me pretty thin, even with the $20,000 down I put on her, but Betsy was my dream car. Ford Shelby GT350 Mustang. There was just something about the 526 horsepower that instantly got the adrenaline pumping. She was worth every fucking penny.

I ran a finger along the hood, climbed in, and shut the door with a firm thud. Betsy roared to life, and a small grin twisted across my face. Again, worth. Every. Penny.

All day I had been thinking about that damn vision. I couldn't take my mind off it. I didn't usually have the same one on repeat all night. That was what made it so strange. I shook my head and decided some good old-fashioned saltwater therapy was what I needed and headed down to the beach.

Forty minutes later, after enduring a shit ton of traffic, I pulled into the parking lot at Seaside Beach. I was so tired that I leaned my head back and took a deep breath inhaling the salt air. It washed over me, and it helped calm my mind.

The sign at the gate indicated that US Airways Flight 2073 to Monterey, California was boarding as a voice over a speaker called for passengers Cory Mathewson and Melanie Sankton to please come to the gate for immediate boarding. A moment later, Cory Mathewson was handing the attendant his boarding pass, rolling a bag behind him, with a small duffle slung over his shoulder.

"Sorry. Last minute flight." He said sheepishly. "I need to gate check this please."

The attendant took it from him and told him to go ahead and take his seat on the plane. Cory Mathewson looked around quickly, stared a long moment down the hallway, heaved a heavy sigh and walked on down the path, and faded away.

CLUMP. CLUMP.

I startled awake at the sound of the seagull landing on my hood. SHIT! The sun had gone down and I had fallen asleep. I rubbed my face. How long had I been asleep? I rubbed my face again to clear my head. It was the same vision that kept me up all night.

Sighing, I got out of Betsy and went to the trunk of my car. Luckily, I had a change in clothes with me left over from my trip last weekend to Marin, so I changed quickly out of my work clothes into a pair of jeans and a t-shirt. Sighing as I slipped some shoes on, I walked down to the water, inhaled the cold briny air, and instantly felt the tension in my shoulders start to loosen. The fog had set in heavy tonight, as it always did this time of year in Monterey, I couldn't even see the lights from the Aquarium.

The beach had always been my place of comfort. It was one of the few places, I could just let my thoughts wander into the expanse of the big blue, and let the rolling, crashing waves carry it all out to sea. My feet in the sand did it every time. I could spend forever here.

I wandered down by the water and kicked my shoes off to ensure the grainy sand was there to calm me. It was too cold to walk in the water, but I just wandered along the water line until

I found a little spot a way down from the entrance to sit and watch the waves. This was my little bit of heaven in my life.

Today's vision obviously, wasn't anything devastating. Well, at least no one was dying. The boy boarding the plane was Cory James Mathewson, CJ for short. We've been friends forever, though a friend may not be the best description for him. Yes, he is my friend, my absolute best friend. He knew everything about me. I was also totally and completely in love with him. Not that I would tell him that. Taking that step, was not something I was willing to risk our friendship on.

He had always been there for me. He was always the first one to step in when something was wrong and always the first one there to comfort me when shit hit the fan. Our friends sometimes wondered about his protective nature, but I had seen him be protective of them too. They just seemed to think he was more protective of me. I've shrugged it off. The most I've ever seen him protective of me was one night a couple of months after Matt died, at Starlight, a club downtown when he almost got kicked out for protecting me against a creep that just would not take no for an answer. The creep had grabbed my ass, and when I turned and slapped him to get him to back off, he grabbed my hand and pushed me against a nearby wall. The next thing I knew he was laid out on the ground and CJ was wiping a cut on my cheek asking me if I was okay.

Amber had taken a picture of us as he stared at me, and framed it. It was hanging in her living room, and she swore it was her favorite picture of us. I was pretty sure that CJ thought of me more as a little sister than as any kind of romantic interest and I was honestly okay with that. If he wasn't going to be my man, then I wanted to keep him as my best friend.

CJ often flew out here to visit. That wasn't a big deal. It's just not often that I get the same vision on the same day or even week. A smile crossed my face as I thought about how much he hated that I usually knew when he was coming. He had tried so many times to make it a surprise, but he had only been able to pull it off once. Granted I never knew exactly when he was coming, but because I'd *seen* it, it wasn't much of a surprise when he did show up. He was also the only one who knew about my visions. That was only because when we were in high school, I had had a vision of his girlfriend cheating on him, and I warned him about it. Of course, it happened exactly as I had described. He accepted it so thoroughly that that may have been the point my heart first fell for him, not that I knew it at the time. Even after all these years, he never judged me for them. He trusted them completely. I almost told Amber once, but I backed out at the last minute and changed the conversation.

I pulled out my cell, intending to call him to apologize for a fight we had had earlier this week when it rang in my hand. The number on it didn't look familiar, but it was local. "Hello?"

"Betcha didn't expect it would be me calling did ya?" the voice said on the other end, "Come pick my ass up at the airport."

I shook my head and laughed.

"Ceej! What are you doing in Monterey? Aren't you supposed to be at work right now? And why are you calling me from a local number? What happened to your cell?" I asked without giving him time to answer.

"WHOA! Stop with the twenty questions Megs. My phone died so, I'm using the airlines. I'll explain later about work. Now, get out of bed and come pick me up."

"I'm not at home. I'm at the beach. I... I needed to clear my head. I dreamt," I shook my head and continued, "I was just gonna call you to apolo–"

"What did you dream?'" he asked cutting me off.

"Just that you were on a plane out here." I said quickly. "I'll be there in 15 minutes. US Airways?"

His soft rumbling laughter filtered through the phone, "Bet you even know what flight number then, huh?"

"2073 from Phoenix. Anyways, I just gotta get to Betsy. Be there in a few minutes." I hung up on him, his voice still coming through the speaker, and headed back down the beach to the parking lot.

When I got back to the car, there was a cop making his rounds, and of course he was standing at Betsy.

CRAP. I can't afford a ticket right now.

"I'm just leaving officer." I shouted.

"Beach closes at sunset ma'am." He said as I walked up.

"I know sir. I was just walking along the beach. I wasn't in the water. See I'm completely dry." I tried to explain. I know it's a safety thing. Riptides here are some of the worst in the world.

"Regardless." He said looking me over and then behind me where a couple was walking down the path looking quite disheveled.

"Like I said sir, I'm leaving now to pick up a friend at the airport." I said trying to be as innocent as possible.

"And this is your car?" The officer asked me a little suspiciously.

I beamed. "Yes sir. Betsy's beautiful, isn't she?" I unlocked the doors and stood at the driver's door.

"That she is ma'am." He said looking her over appreciatively. "Taken her to Laguna Seca?"

"Nah, but I took her to Buttonwillow last year. That was wild." I ran my hand over the roof and smiled at the memory.

"Ok. Well, drive safe." He said still looking her over. "Have a nice night ma'am."

"Will do, sir." I said climbing in.

Sighing in relief, I jumped in and started the engine. The cop jumped a little as she fired to life. He smiled and then turned toward the couple that was coming down the path. A mischievous grin spread across my face, as I backed out and headed to the airport.

When I took the exit from Highway 1 onto 68 toward the airport, I hit the gas and felt the back end holding on with everything she had as I made the turn. As a friend once said to me, "*If you're gonna have a car like that, you better drive it like you stole it.*"

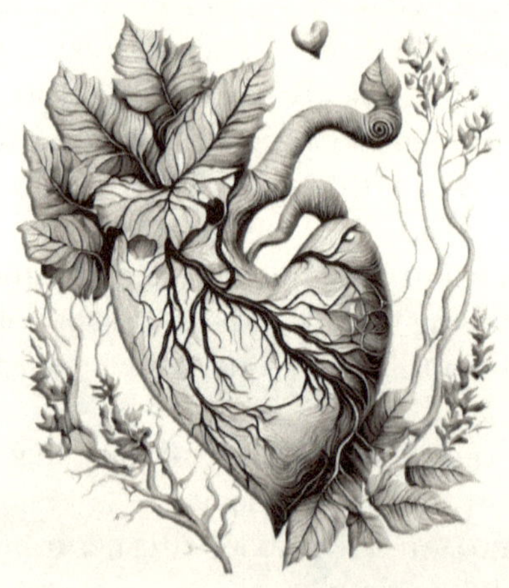

CHAPTER 2

I PULLED UP TO the passenger loading zone, CJ's six-foot-two, well-built frame was leaning against the wall as a tall brunette shamelessly flirted with him. I laughed at his reaction. I could tell he was trying to be nice, but anyone who could read body language could tell he really wasn't interested. As his eyes met mine, a bright smile lit up his face and he shoved off the wall, almost knocking down said brunette.

I warmed a little inside as he reached down, picked up his bag, and ran his hands through his chestnut hair, which was just long enough to reach just below his green eyes. I cleaned off the sand as much as I could from the passenger seat and got out of the car to meet him at the trunk, popping it open with click.

He had mentioned he'd been working out, trying to drop some fat and gain some muscle, but I didn't expect it to have such an effect on me. He was smiling and it lit a fire in my stomach that no one else could. The sight threw me a little off guard. What was wrong with me today? I looked him over, trying not to be a creep about it, but when my eyes met his, there was something else there. Hesitation?

"Hey." He said nervously.

"Hey yourself." I said trying to sound nonchalant. "Impromptu visit?"

"You could say that." He said throwing his bags into the trunk.

When I closed the trunk, he pulled me close and hugged me tight, lifting me up off the ground. I could feel his heart beating through his lightweight sweater, and it felt as if it were beating a million times a minute. Over his shoulder, I could see the brunette that had been flirting with him give me a look that made me very grateful that looks did not, in fact, kill. I couldn't help a small smile against his shoulder at the thought of her jealousy.

"I'm starved, let's go get some pizza. We need to talk." He said lighter and more relaxed now.

"Sure. Is everything ok?" I asked walking back to the driver's side door and getting into the car.

"Yea. Yea. Fine." He said as he put his seatbelt on. Then his stomach growled.

"Food first."

"Pizza first." He said with a smile and then clarified. "Russo's Pizza."

"Well, okay then."

As we headed to Russo's, we apologized to each other for the fight that neither of us could remember the cause of, but he fell silent the rest of the way. He stared out the window and occasionally I thought I would see him flick his eyes toward me, but it was so fast, I wasn't sure if he really had. It wasn't awkward, but it wasn't our usual silent understanding of each other either. I blamed him of course. He was the one wound up tighter than a three-dollar violin.

Once we got to Russo's, he took a deep breath which he released slowly as he got out of the car. I furrowed my brows and shook my head. When we met at the trunk, I turned to face him.

"What did you want to talk about, and then we will eat." I said crossing my arms across my chest, daring him to challenge me. In his eyes was a flash of light I couldn't place.

"Can't we eat first?" He said, almost whining.

"No. Now. I haven't seen you like this since you got your acceptance letter for college and you had to tell me you were moving 2,000 miles away. Hell. This is worse. You won't even look me in the eye, Ceej."

He nodded and then took one step toward me. Just one step and froze. I stared him down. His mouth opened, then closed. He still wouldn't look at me.

"Cory. James. Mathewson." I said and his eyes popped up to meet mine as he heard the worry in my voice.

"It's fine Megs. Let's go get our table and get some food. We have lots of time to discuss it." He said as he wrapped his arm around my waist and moved me toward the door.

"You get a table in the back room. I'll get our pizza." CJ said, then he headed to the counter leaving me to glare as his back.

They were swamped tonight. Pacific Grove High School must have won their game judging by the amount of celebrating high school students along the back wall. Jealousy rippled through me as I thought of how carefree they were. No worries. No loss. No burdens to carry. I remembered back to when I used to be that carefree in high school, even with my visions.

I sighed and found a corner table in the back room. There was a couple that was sitting a few tables over, but the room was mostly empty, so it would be easy to talk without having to shout over the celebrations.

"Root Beer m'lady." CJ said when he found me a few minutes later.

"Thank you, kind sir." I said mirroring his regal tone.

He sat down and clasped his hands around his glass, still refusing to meet my gaze.

"Ceej?" I asked tentatively.

"So, what has been going on the last week?" He said as if he weren't strictly avoiding something.

"Nothing. Everything's the same." I said as lightly as I could but there was a trace of skepticism in my voice.

"Amber ok?"

"She's fine." I said sighing. "She's out with David. Again. She said she may move in with him in the next couple of months if things keep going well. She really likes him, but something is off about the guy."

"Like what?" He said finally meeting my gaze before his eyes fluttered to look out the window.

"CJ. Are we really going to do this?" I asked sitting back in my chair.

"Do what?" He looked down at his glass and took a big gulp of his beer.

"Make awkward small talk. Geez, it's like a first date with someone you just met. We have known each other forever, so you can't just avoid talking to me about whatever it is that has you all worked up." I looked at him pointedly until he finally kept my stare.

"Ok. You're right." He took another big gulp of his beer and sighed heavily again. "Megs. We've been friends for a long, long time."

"Yes." I said drawing the word out slowly, not knowing what that had to do with anything. The color was draining from his face and he kept moving to wipe his hands on his jeans. Ok, now he's scaring me.

"What is it? What's wrong? You know you can tell me anything." I said putting my hand over his and looking him over. He looked healthy. Hell, he looked fantastic.

He chuckled, finally understanding why I was starting to panic. He slipped his hand from under mine and ran his fingers through his hair. Then with a laugh said, "Yea, I'm fine. Healthy as a horse. It's just I ran through all the right words the whole flight, and now with you here, I can't remember my well-rehearsed speech."

"Speech? What speech. What in the world are you talking about?" He looked so conflicted. "Ceej. This is me. You know you can tell me *anything*! What. The. Hell. Is. It?"

"Megan calm down." He finally met my eyes and then let out another big long breath through is nose, then he said, "Megs, why have we never ... why haven't we ever gone out on a date?"

My heart stopped.

I blinked.

There is no way I'd heard him right. He couldn't possibly be saying...

"I'm sorry?" I said as I blinked again.

"Why haven't we ever gone out on a date?" He said slowly, emphasizing each word.

"I... I..." I was stammering like an idiot. I just sat back in my chair and blinked at him. The couple next to us were very consciously not looking in our direction finding the wall very, very interesting.

Then he started talking really fast. "I don't want to jeopardize our friendship. It's just that, well, we get along so well, and we know each other better than anyone else in the world."

"That we do." I managed to say. The corners of my mouth wanted to twitch up in a smile, my heart was racing faster than Betsy on a straightaway, but my brain was having a hard time processing anything coming out of his mouth. I really wanted to blurt out how much I love him, and that I've wanted to tell him that for a long time, but I still couldn't do it. Instead, I took the chicken way out.

"I just never thought you would have had those kinds of feelings for me. I thought you always just thought and protected me like your little sister..." I trailed off with a small voice playing with my fingers and now unable to look at him.

"Megan. Seriously? We went to prom together. You're my best friend. You're beautiful and smart. There is no one in this world I could say I care for more than you. Then we fought." He shook his head and continued sternly, "We never fight. I miss you when we aren't together Megs, and three days ago I couldn't even remember what that stupid fight was even about. I don't know what it was, but something clicked inside me and I realized at that point, I had to come out here and take the chance to ask.

So, I put in for a transfer and booked the flight, packed my shit, threw it in Mom and Dad's garage, and well, here we are."

I could feel my cheeks getting warm and sore from the smile that had at some point spread across my face. He was about to say something else, but the pizza showed up, and he stopped with his mouth half open.

"Pepperoni, extra cheese." The server said putting the elevated tray down and taking our number from the table. It allowed me just enough time to calm my insides and slow my heart rate down to something resembling normal.

"Thank you." CJ said before turning back to me and meeting my gaze. "So how about tomorrow night? Our official first date. I'll take you out somewhere nice when you get home from work, and we can go down to one of the pullouts and listen to the waves crash until the cops kick us out."

"It sounds kinda perfect." I said finally lifting my gaze from my lap as I studied his face. This wasn't a trick, was it? His shoulders and chest were tight, and his leg was bouncing quickly. He was nervous. "Are you dead serious?"

"I'm serious." He said meeting my eyes and holding them. His voice was calm and held determination. When I looked into those green eyes, I saw hope for a future I never thought I would ever have.

I must have been holding that gaze for longer than I thought because he gulped before asking again, "Is it a date?"

My nerves suddenly vanished with something in that final question. This was CJ. The one person in the whole world, who I had no secrets with, save this last one. This last one that, ... that could actually be a possibility. A future with CJ. Well, a date at least. A try at a future. If it didn't work, it didn't work.

"Ok, Ceej. It's a date." I said, then I heard his stomach growl. I giggled, "but only if we eat now. I think your stomach has waited long enough."

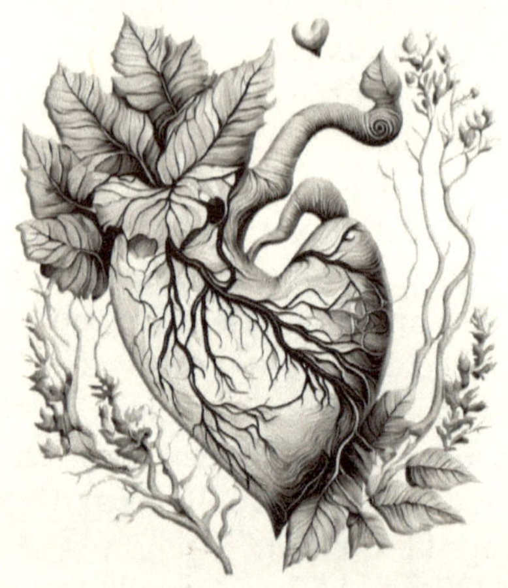

CHAPTER 3

THAT NIGHT HE REFUSED to share the bed like we had been doing for years. He said that if we were going to try, that he was going to sleep on the couch's pull-out bed. Sharing a bed with me now was different than how we had shared my king-sized bed before. I didn't really think about it that way. To me, it would just be normal.

I had to admire his chivalry though. It was just weird knowing he was in the house, but not lying beside me. Since we had graduated college, we had always shared the bed when he stayed here. There had been nothing romantic about it. There was just so much bed that we could easily share it without it being that way.

I laid there for hours with my mind racing but finally got to sleep sometime around 2:00 in the morning. When my alarm went off at 5:45 am, I glared at my running clothes, then at the clock, and reset it for 6:30 am. When it went off again, it took every ounce of my being not to just call in and go back to sleep.

Brad wasn't going to be in. I had stayed late to get the most critical of things done.

"Don't be irresponsible Megan." I told myself and threw the blankets back and jumped in the shower.

When I grabbed my keys to leave, CJ was still asleep on the couch. He hadn't even pulled out the bed. Just crashed out on the couch. I smiled as I leaned against the door jamb, watching him sleep. His hair was going in every direction, and with his t-shirt lifted up like that I could see he really had been working on his stomach.

I let out a long breath of appreciation at just the hint of abs and grabbed a blanket from the closet before putting it over him. He had at least kicked off his shoes before falling asleep.

I sighed and tip-toed by him to leave, not wanting to wake him up. Who knows what time he fell asleep. While the couch is great for hanging out on, it wasn't the most comfortable for sleeping. I often had woken with a sore back after sleeping on it overnight.

I reached down to move his shoe from the walkway when he mumbled and grabbed my hand.

"Cory ..." I said screaming like a little girl, cutting my words off and snatching my hand back from him.

He laughed himself awake and looked up at me. "You were going to leave without saying anything? Trying to run away just to get out of tonight?"

"I thought you were sleeping you jackass. I was *trying* to be considerate." I said.

He reached over and took my hand again. "Sorry I scared you."

I looked down at him and there was so much softness, that I was surprised I didn't melt into a puddle right then and there. This, us, had already changed. Whether it worked or not. We had already changed.

"You didn't answer my other question. Are you having any second thoughts at all about tonight? I'm serious about not wanting to mess things up between us." He said running a thumb over my hand. Damn him.

"Well, if you don't want to mess things up, then you better wine and dine me right tonight Mr. Mathewson." I said trying to sound serious. His face lit up and I let a smile cross my face. I squeezed his hand and continued, "Seriously. I'm looking forward to it."

"I'm so relieved to hear you say that." He gave me a quick kiss on the back of my hand. "Now, go to work. I'll see you about six."

The joy in his face had me rooted to that spot. It isn't that I hadn't seen CJ this way before, because I had with his ex-girlfriends, but it was very, very different having his affection placed toward me.

"Megs? Are you ok?" There was a small smug smile on his face. Did he know what effect he was having on me? Does he know that tonight is exactly what I've been wanting for so long?

"Yea. Sorry." I said shaking my head to clear it. "Tonight."

"Tonight." He said his eyes sparkling.

I don't know how I did it, but I pulled myself from that spot and just as I was going to close the door, I turned toward him and said, "Make sure to shower. You smell like a dead camel."

He roared with laughter.

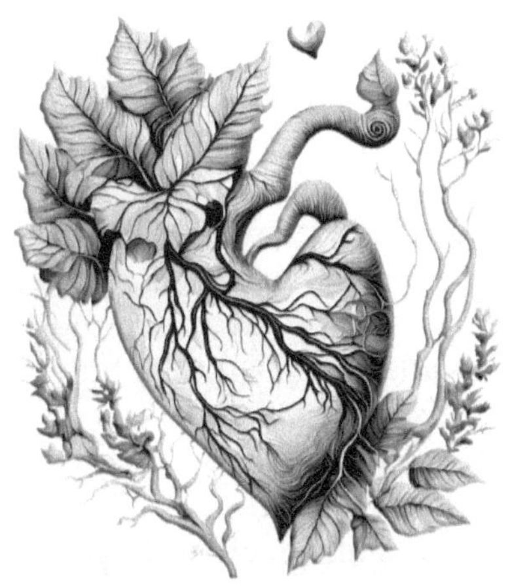

CHAPTER 4

MY STOMACH WAS TIED up in knots all day worrying that we would go to dinner and it would be that classical awkward first date. I worried that he and I would sit there, not knowing what to say, or how to act. There was none of that. In fact, when we got to the parking garage and started walking toward the restaurant, he naturally took ahold of my hand and it was just so easy to interlace our fingers together. As we walked toward the restaurant out of the garage, I stopped short seeing movement off to the right.

"What is it?" CJ said.

"I could have sworn I just saw Becca duck around that corner." I said hesitantly as he pulled me along toward the restaurant.

"Well, if it was, it won't be long before the cat was out of the bag anyways." CJ said shrugging and smiling broadly. "Let them see. It isn't like they haven't been wondering why we haven't started dating anyways. For years. Years, Megs."

I rolled my eyes and stared at him. He wasn't wrong. Our friends *had* thought we should be together, but I just said, "Not the point CJ."

"It is the very point." He said, and when I didn't say anything, he raised an eyebrow, "Come on. You know as well as I do, that they have been secretly taking bets on if either one of us was going to step up."

I blushed because I did know, and then said, "Well then. I guess you really should make sure this goes well then. Wouldn't want them to lose out on too much money." There was a ray of hope that danced through his eyes that make me smile. "Come on, let's eat. I'm starved." I said.

Dinner was amazing. Even though it was officially our first date, it was comfortable, happy, and well, lovely. The only thing that was different from any of other dinner outings, was that we were dressed up and we weren't just grabbing a pizza or hitting up some cheap place to eat.

Two hours later, after we had our fill of steak and chocolate volcano cake, we were sitting shoulder to shoulder on a boulder at the beach. It was one of our favorite places along the coast in a large pullout next to the Pacific Grove Golf Course.

I sighed and rested my head on his shoulder looking out toward the ocean. This. This was familiar. Normal for us. He reached his arm around my waist and pulled me close. I sighed content. Tonight had been perfect. It was dark and foggy, so we couldn't see the waves crashing, but the sound of the waves crashing against the rocks was soothing and cemented the familiarity between us.

"Remember when Becca and James were running through here and that wave came up and drenched her?" CJ said.

I laughed. "She was so pissed."

"I thought she was going to kill James. Like he had planned it or something."

"Because apparently, James has control over the waves." I said rolling my eyes and laughing. I turned to look at him and when he turned to face me, he was so close that I could feel his breath.

I froze. I couldn't bring myself to breathe. My stomach tightened and I just stared into his eyes. I let my thumb rub his thigh in a small motion as his repeated the motion on my hip. We sat there like that for a long, long moment. His eyes moved down to my lips, and then his eyes met mine.

"I love you, Megan." His words were a whispering caress against my heart, which shuddered, then beat faster. There was a flash of fear in his eyes, but as soon as he realized what he had said, it was quickly replaced with resignation.

I felt my eyes instantly swell with tears and I tried to tell him that I loved him too, but I couldn't speak.

My mind started to spin and I felt that lump in my throat grow bigger. I blinked and I thought I felt a tear run down my cheek. I opened my mouth again but then closed it. Where were my words? Why wouldn't my voice come to say them back?

He lifted his hand and slowly cupped my cheek in his hand. I leaned into his touch, just that little bit, savoring his gentleness. His thumb wiped the tear from my cheek so caringly.

I just sat there gapping like a fish. GODS! Where was my voice?

"I have for years. It's always been you." He continued with a ting of hurt in his voice, as he pressed his forehead to mine. "If you don't feel the same way, it's ok. We can go slow."

He leaned away from me and let his hand drop from my face. There was disappointment on his face.

He didn't know.

He really had no idea that I had ever felt for him the way that I do.

"Ceej." I finally said sternly grabbing his chin to make him look at me. He looked at me questioning the tone of my voice. This time I'm the one who took a deep breath, and said, "You don't know how long I have waited to hear you say that."

Then before I could chicken out, I leaned in and kissed him with every ounce of the love I had been keeping bottled up. He was so shocked, that when my lips met his, he just froze, a moment later when his mouth opened to mine, we weren't gentle. There was genuine desire and wanting in every touch of our tongues. He explored every inch of my mouth and then without warning, he broke away from me. He slid off the edge of the boulder and stood in front of me, putting my face in his hands.

"Wait, you've been waiting for me to say it?" He said incredulously.

I just nodded blushing as bright as a baboon's butt.

"But last night when I mentioned us even going on a date, you seemed shocked. I thought it was because you didn't feel the same way. I thought that maybe you were just humoring me tonight." He said, a smile on his face, but shock still in his eyes.

"Humoring you? I *was* in shock! I thought you were just fucking with me. I honestly believed you have always thought of me as a little sister, and I was fine with that. I would rather have you in my life as my best friend than not at all, but at the same time been waiting for you. I've had these little girl fantasies of being more than just your friend." I was babbling. I knew I was babbling, and so before I could second guess myself, I told him. "CJ, I love you."

My words were cut off as he kissed me again. He shuddered and pulled me close. I wrapped my legs around his waist willing him to get closer to me. There was nothing but the two of us. The apocalypse could have been raging around us, and I wouldn't have noticed.

When I felt tears slid down my cheeks, I wondered for the briefest of seconds if they were mine or his. It didn't matter. The feel of his lips on mine, the way our tongues danced together, the heat of his hands that burned through my clothes, down to my bones.

Not breaking the kiss, he lifted me and spun me around.

He pulled his head back slightly and whispered against my lips, "Well tonight has gone way better than expected. Some first date. Huh?"

I smiled at him but froze when a movement over his shoulder caught my eye. It was large and made the shadows under the tree look like a dark deep pit leading to nowhere. He set me down, "What's wrong?"

"Something was moving in the shadows. By the tree." I said carefully.

"The fog is so thick. How can you see anything? It was probably just a raccoon or something heading for the trash." He said winking trying to reassure me.

"No, I don't think so." I watched the unlit area closer. There was something black and branchlike there. Holding his hand tight, I walked around the boulder we had been sitting on to get a better look. In the blink of an eye, it burst out from within the branches straight for CJ and me.

I gripped his hand harder, screaming. I felt a strong breeze lift us off the ground, as we were surrounded in blue smoke. I held onto CJ tight and closed my eyes.

When I felt my feet on solid ground again, CJ's arms were still tight around me. Slowly I opened my eyes, staring at his chest. Blinking at the brightness around us, panic rose in my chest, and I took deep huffing breaths to keep it at bay.

"Megs. Where are we? What did you just do?" CJ said trying to stay even and calm, but failing miserably. The quick rising of his chest betrayed his worry and distress.

"I don't know. I'm not sure I did anything." I said trying not to bite his head off as I turned to look at our surroundings. We were not in the pullout. We were not in Pacific Grove anymore. Betsy was gone. It wasn't even night anymore. It was warm. The sun was high in the sky and we were standing in a beautiful garden. The air smelled like a forest after a light rain.

"Something was in the shadows. I saw it lunge. You screamed a slew of words I couldn't understand, then next thing I knew, we were here." He said, but he didn't make sense. I remember screaming, but CJ continued, "Seriously Megs, where is here?" He held me tight. Every muscle in his body was alert.

I looked around the garden to see stone benches along a pathway that lead to a very intricate stone archway at the end of the walkway. The garden was filled with vines, oversized orchids, lilies, and tulips, but they moved. I stared at one of the lilies. The petals moved to curl in on themselves and then seemed to exhale as they unfurled the petals.

Something tickled at the back of my memory. I've seen this before. No. Not seen, but I could almost hear my mom's reverent voice as she described it to me one night trying to get me to sleep. "It looks almost exactly as Mom had described Grandma's garden when trying to get me to bed at night as a kid. How was that even possible? Where are we?"

A voice from the right answered. "*Vitus Sancitum de la Gardina mis Amigos* known to the Keller Family as *The Friends Garden*, Ms. Megan Keller."

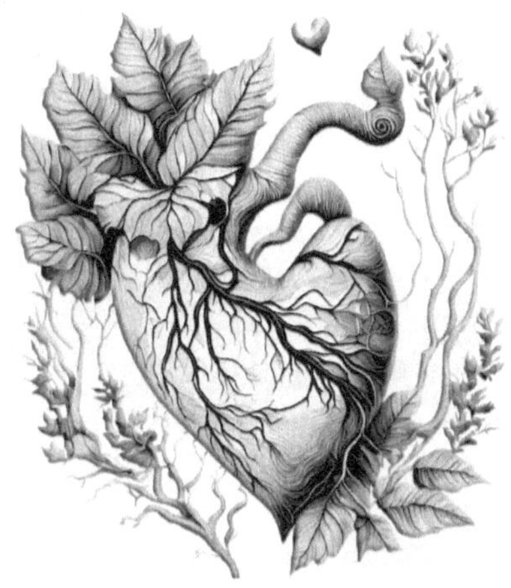

CHAPTER 5

LONG WAVY JET-BLACK HAIR flowed behind a mid-30's looking woman as she sauntered through the archway at the end of the garden. She couldn't have been more than five feet two inches tall. Her boots thudded on the ground, and she stopped and stood wide-legged and arms crossed. She had blue jeans on with a royal blue shirt covered by a black fitted coat that stopped mid-thigh. Something glimmered there in the sunlight, and I narrowed my eyes at her.

"You must have been scared to death to be able to bring someone with you, considering you are completely untrained." She said concern in her voice, and then she looked to CJ snapping. "And exactly who are you?"

"Ahh...CJ Mathewson." CJ answered hesitantly as he moved to stand between me and the woman.

She looked at him a minute, then turned toward the gate. "Come on. I will explain everything inside."

"WAIT!" I yelled, panic rising. "What the hell just happened? Who are you? How do you know my name? Where are we? How did we get here? And what in the hell was it that jumped out at us?" I spewed the questions out not waiting for her to answer. CJ's hand tight around mine was likely the only thing holding me back from screaming in her face.

She turned around and saw the frightened look on our faces and sighed. "You're right. I'm sorry. I can forget my manners sometimes."

That sauntering walk she had was a little unnerving as she strode to one of the stone benches just a few feet from where we were standing. She stood there for a moment, and I saw her lips move before three figures came through the gate, all dressed exactly like she was.

She eyed me closely again and as if she got the answer she wanted, she said, "Please sit down. My name is Jean. These three are Lindy, Owen, and Clarice."

I raised my eyebrows as if I were going to say something, but CJ cut me off. "Again. Where are we?"

"Nalsar in the Nalrin providence. Now, are you physically alright?" She asked. Her eyes had softened just a little bit, but the muscles in her body were taught.

CJ looked me over and then with a quick kiss to my temple, he pulled me close and said, "Yes."

"Good. Now you need to understand Megan, the world you know is not the world that you were born to be in." I started to interrupt her, but she held her hand up to stop me. "Please, I will answer all your questions, but there are things you need to know first." I looked to CJ and his face mirrored mine. We were lost.

"You will have many more questions after I tell you this, and I will answer them, but you first you must know where you are and some background information." She took a deep breath and looked over to the other three. The one male of the group, Owen, came and put his hand on her back in what appeared to be a reassuring gesture before she continued.

"There are things that haunt your world, which came from ours, ... and others. Your stories and mythologies call them demons, but there are many different kinds. Some are dangerous, most aren't. They are not from your, umm dimension, I guess you could say. We call yours the Manusia."

"Our dimension?" CJ asked slowly.

"Yes. There are threads that run from here to the Manusia, which we can access with the use of our inner power to an infinite number of different dimensions." She said pausing, ringing her fingers together, and studying us. Scientists have theorized for eons that there may be multiple dimensions, but is this really what they meant?

"What triggered you bringing yourself here?" She asked carefully.

I looked to CJ and said, "I saw a shadow creature jump out and straight to us. It wasn't one of the fuzzy shadows though. It was more angular. Stick like arms and legs, and a pointy head. Next thing we knew we were here."

She thought for a moment and said, "It was probably a *Bakta*. It runs in the shadows and would have only fed on your happiness. The only effect humans would have felt is the joy slowly slipping from the situation, and then they would have run off and continued with their day. Normal humans never would have seen it."

"Normal humans?" I asked my eyes flicking to CJ, "but CJ and I did see it."

"Yes, you could see it Megan because you are a hybrid. You are Sangra."

I looked to CJ and back at her, my eyebrows pinched in confusion. When I looked back at CJ, he had the same look on his face. Did she just say...

"I'm not human?" I said in disbelief. "Did you seriously just say that I am not human?"

"That is what I said. You are Sangra." Jean said again.

"You're crazy. Of course, I'm human. What is this some kind of joke? A TV show or something?" I said, my voice sounding sturdier than I felt.

"I assure you that I am not crazy. We are Sangra and so are you. Well, technically you are part Sangra, but that is neither here nor there at the moment. There is the question of why CJ could see the Bakta?" She trailed off, pondering that for a moment.

She completely blew over the fact that she had just told me that I wasn't human at all like it was the most normal thing she had ever said. This woman was completely insane if she thought I would just accept that as if she said that my t-shirt was purple.

One of the other women, Lindy, Jean said her name was, leaned her 5'7" frame in close to CJ to study him. Her auburn-streaked brown hair was done in a way that reminded me of retro 40's glam. Her muddy brown eyes crinkled to meet her high cheekbones as she studied him.

"Yes, why did you see it? That is a good question. What is your name again?"

"CJ Mathewson." He said tightened his arm against my waist.

"Mathewson. I haven't heard of any Mathewsons'. Have you?" She said as she turned to the others, who were shaking their head.

"I haven't seen them before tonight, though." CJ said as if he was trying to cover up something, "I've always just tried to convince her it was a flicker of light, or her eyes were playing a trick on her."

"When I first mentioned it, he thought it may have just been a raccoon or something headed for the trash can?" I said.

"Hum, very interesting." Jean said.

I waited a moment trying to be patient, this was obviously a point of confusion. Frankly though, I didn't really care. My nerves were getting the best of me, and I kept digging my nails into CJ's hand. He didn't say anything, but there may be blood involved. I wanted to know WHERE I was, and most of all are we safe?

"Can we worry about that later please? What's a Sangra? Where in the hell we are?" I said then biting off, "And HOW IN THE HELL DID WE GET HERE?"

"Oh right. As I said, you are in the Nalsar dimension in the Nalrin providence. This is your grandmother's garden." Jean said. I thought I saw the other whom who must be Clarice eye her carefully.

"My grandmother's garden? My grandmother died when I was 3." I said. Jean is crazy.

"Actually, No. She came back here. She died when you were about 13 or 14. Years get a little warped between Manusia and here. Even though we try to keep the same monthly calendar due to business interests, it's ... well off. The days are longer here so it's a little harder. It was very painful for her to be away from you and your mother," There seemed to be a slight resentment to her voice. "However, it was a Tulainar that actually killed her. Don't worry. It was just like going to sleep, so she was never in any pain."

Clarice's face made a look that clearly thought this should have been information that I received later. I sort of thought the same thing, as my head was starting to spin. I leaned against CJ. I suspected he will ask to be sent home as soon as he can.

"We are Sangra. Humans in form, but we all have an inner power." Clarice said trying to get us back on track.

"Like magic?" CJ asked, looking at me with wonder then back to Clarice. "Like a witch, wizard, or warlock?"

"It's not magic, per se. With magic, you need a device in order to focus your power. We do not. There are incantations and movements that channel the power into what we would like for it do. After you have practiced enough, most can channel the power non-verbally, and on occasion, without the full movements. Sometimes just flick your fingers. Though that usually only works on the most common of incantations.

"As for how you got here? The fact you were able to transport at all, and to bring CJ with, it's very impressive. Jean assumed because you had not been trained and because of your age, that you would have lost any ability to perform. We never expected to meet you" Clarice said.

"My age? I'm only 24." I said feeling a little insulted. It isn't like I'm old. There was a giant bird that screeched overhead, and when I looked up it reminded me of a condor. The massive wingspan circled the garden and then with a quick couple of flaps, flew off into the forest.

"Yes, but in this world, if left untrained, powers usually retreat and diminish by the age of 15. It's only with the constant usage of powers that we retain them afterwards. Here we are trained from the age of 6, and usually finish training at about age 16. It's a *tough* 10 years. At 16 you receive your Maltal, a tattoo of sorts that protects and centers your power and your first syth." Lindy said, picking up where Clarice left off.

Clarice pulled out a golden dagger, about 8 inches long, thin and curved up at the point. It reminded me of a Jambiya dagger, but it had an intricate pattern that ran along the blade, and it glowed faintly in the sunlight. She whirled it around in her hand expertly and then sheathed it back at her thigh. The motion made me jump a bit and there was a hollowing in my stomach. She cocked an eyebrow knowing what had just gone through our heads. She moved it with such ease, it left no doubt she knew how to use it.

"There is still much to discuss. First of all, how you knew the incantation to get here, then we must figure out how you were able to bring CJ and why he has the sight." Jean looked to CJ. "You are of course welcome to stay with us as long as you wish, or should I say as long as you have Megan's protection."

Jean stood and turned from us in a motion that was so fast, she almost blurred. In the corner of my eye, I saw someone else walking into the garden. I stood, turning to face him, but CJ tried to put himself in front of me, but only managed to get about halfway before he stopped.

Five feet tall at most, he looked like a child. He had all the proportions of an eight-year-old child, but he had a full black beard that hung down to his chest and carried a silver bow on his back. He was dressed in the same jacket as Jean and the others, only in white. Everyone but CJ and I stood up tall, almost as if they were standing at attention in the military.

"Hello, Naggle. To what do we owe the pleasure of the Council's visit today?" Jean said as she bowed deeply. The bow was formal and elegant, extending their left leg and foot, bending parallel to the ground, right hand outstretched, and head low.

CJ and I just stood there gawking. Ok, I was gawking, CJ was hiding his reaction much better than I was, still trying to get me to stand behind him.

"Jean, my lovely woman! I know you just arrived back from Nalrin, but I must speak to you and your cadre immediately. There have been more reports of their activity in the north." His eyes flicked to CJ and me and a bright engaging smile crossed his face as he clapped his hands together. "Oh, you have visitors."

"Yes, Naggle. Megan and CJ. They are from the Manusia. Megan saw what I believe was a Bakta and brought CJ and herself here." I could see Naggle's head jerk in my direction and there was curiosity in his eyes as Jean continued.

"We have been slowly explaining our world to her," I didn't think it was so slowly. I felt like I had been thrown up against a brick wall repeatedly. "They need sleep. It's late at night in the Manusia. I can explain why there was no clearance."

"Let us all go inside for tea. We will get CJ and Megan a room set up so they may rest while we talk in private Naggle." Owen said sternly with another bow. While his voice sounded polite and formal, it was laced with hidden meaning.

Thoughtfully Naggle replied, "Yes, let's have tea."

CJ's arm around my waist was the only thing keeping me standing at this point, but my mind was racing. Trying to absorb all of this was exhausting. I looked at CJ, who wrapped both arms tight around me as he stared at Naggle intently. I knew that look. It promised death if any harm came to those who he cared for.

"Ceej?" I said in a tone that was all warning.

"Do you want to stay?" He said quietly in my ear. To anyone else, it looked like we were just having a private moment, and I put my hand on his cheek as I looked at him, searching his eyes for the answer.

"One night. Let's see what they have to say." I said barely above a whisper after a moment's thought. My head was reeling. He nodded, accepting my decision.

As we walked through the garden again, I was shocked at how perfectly it matched my Mother's descriptions as a child. Through the archway, at the edge of the garden we turned toward the house, and I stopped in my tracks.

"Megan." CJ said carefully.

"How is that possible?" I said barely above a whisper.

The house, which was more of a cottage, had stone at the base and worn wood siding around the top. On the far side was an uneven stone chimney, a black chimney crown with purple smoke that slowly flittered out the top. It was an exact real–life version of a cottage I had been drawing since I was four years old. I had one of them framed and hanging in my dining room back home.

"I don't know." He pulled me closer.

"Mom never told me about, and never said anything in all the renderings I did."

"Megs. It's the exact same. Right down to the purple smoke. I always thought that was strange, but being a kid, you draw what you imagine."

"You would think as I grew up, it would change to grey, but I never saw it that way. It was always purple." I said a small smile crossing my lips, but an uneasy feeling went through me. It was a mix between awe and fear.

The others were almost to the door, and we hurried to catch up to them. We entered through the kitchen, where a wood set of worn table and chairs, wood counters, and cabinets that were well used, but would no doubt hold up for quite a few years to come filled the room. Modern–day appliances were so well disguised in the counters that I almost missed them. I ran my hand along the counter and there were divots and gouges in it. I half wondered if those daggers they carried were what put them there.

The living room was comfortable and open, with windows straight from a castle that stretched high to the vaulted ceilings. It was a huge expansive room, which had all the comforts of a cottage room. Our shoes clicked across the hardwood floors, but I noticed the room was much larger than the outside proportions would have allowed. It was almost as if we walked into a different house.

"Naggle, please take a seat while I get Megan and CJ settled in a room?" Jean asked. "I will be just a few minutes."

There were doors upon doors down the bright hallway. The outside had definitely been warped to show something that could not contain this much of a house. Jean turned an old fashioned handle and ushered us into a room that was centered around a light grey sleigh bed. I walked to the left side of the room and ran my fingers across a smooth matching vanity dresser. CJ stood near a corner where a matching desk with an intricate etched design that resembled the same markings on the blade that Clarice had showed us earlier. What did she call it?

"There is a bathroom there to your left. Help yourself to any of the clothes that are in the closet. Get a good night's sleep, and we will talk more in the morning." Then she turned sharply on her heels and shut the door a little harder than was necessary.

I just stood there staring at the closed door. CJ slowly walked around the bed hardly making a sound on the plush carpeting. Once his hand touched mine, I threw my arms around his waist and held him tight.

"I am so sorry Ceej." I muttered against his chest.

"Everything will be okay." He said against the top of my head.

His reassurances, despite his own concerns, undid me. I started crying and I couldn't bring myself to stop. I wasn't mad. I wasn't angry or even sad. Just augh. He just held me and kept reassuring me that everything would be ok.

"Are you sure you want to stay?" He asked after my breathing calmed.

It took a few moments for me to formulate an answer. I mean it wasn't like we could just get in the car and leave. Someone would have to take us back. Was there really any way to go home? There were answers I wanted. Like how did they know who I was and what were Sangra? Mom and Dad were always very sketchy about my family history. Maybe they could fill some of that information in.

Then there was Grandma. What did they know about her? If this was her house, then how did they come into possession of it? Did they buy it from the Estate? Why didn't Mom and Dad move into it and raise us here?

Finally, I said, "Yes. What about—"

"Then we stay." He said before I could say anything else.

"What about you though?" I said again, not able to meet his eyes.

His finger slid under my chin, forcing me to look at him. His lips met mine soft as a gentle breeze. Despite everything that simple gesture made my toes curl.

He leaned his forehead against mine. "I love you Megs. That hasn't changed in the last couple of hours. The only thing that has changed is that I get to tell you that I love you now. You are mine, and if you want to stay, we stay."

"But –" I tried to say, but he cut me off again.

"We stay. Now, let's get some sleep and we can talk more in the morning. We both have a lot to think about." He said with a heavy sigh and ran his hand through his hair.

I just nodded and headed to the bathroom to wash my face and get ready to bed. I tried not to think about what he meant by *both* of us having a lot to think about. He said we would stay, but how long would it stay we? Would he be thinking about whether he would stay with me now? They had claimed that I wasn't even human. Would he want to stay with me if that is true? Add that to the fact we were not even in our own dimension anymore, but in an alternate dimension. That alone would make anyone's head spin.

Grey wood and glass met me through the bathroom door. Hexagon white, light grey and, dark grey tiles flowed through the space to a full walk-in glass shower and hidden toilet behind a half wall. The vanity was made from a rough grey wood with a glass waterfall faucet that flowed water before I could touch a thing. I sighed letting some of the tension flow out of my shoulders and took one of the light grey washcloths. The towel itself felt like feathers. I don't think I had ever felt towels so soft at home. I have to find out what kind of fabric softener they use. I stopped and giggled. Of all the things that I could think of, and I was thinking about what kind of fabric softener they use?

I opened the cabinet looking for any type of soap to find it was completely stocked with a whole beauty store assortment of products. There were no less than 20 different face creams and washes, 30 different shampoos and conditioners, all in little sample bottles, and on the top shelf, there were 8 different brushes to choose from. I sifted through, found a face wash, and randomly pulled a brush down from the top shelf.

The faucet turned on and the water was instantly warm and soothing. I pulled my long blonde hair out from my ponytail and washed the make-up from my face. Gods, I looked like death warmed over. There were already dark circles under my blue-green eyes. I finished washing up quickly.

I peeled the tight blue dress that I had put on for CJ and I's date off, and wondered how it was only a few hours ago that I had gotten dressed for that date?

I put my palms flat on the counter and leaned in looking at myself in the mirror. Not human. I looked human. I felt human. I mean, sure I've always had comments on how beautiful and big my eyes always were, but I thought I had just gotten my father's eyes. Though, maybe that is exactly what I did get. If I wasn't human, then maybe that was a feature of his ... race. What race did she say they were? Sangra? Did she even mention what the other part of me was? I sighed, turned from the mirror, wrapped myself in a towel, and went to the bedroom.

There was a closet in the short corridor that connected the bathroom and bedroom where I found some night clothes and other change of clothes for us in the morning. I thumbed through them and they were miraculously all our sizes. How did they know? How could they? We only showed up, what? Not an hour ago? Tomorrow. I would worry about that tomorrow. I threw one of the night shirts on and hung the towel up.

Coming out of the bathroom, I looked to CJ who had also changed out of his clothes. He laid there bare-chested with the blankets at his waist. I blinked. I just stood there and blinked. He caught me staring at him and just opened his arms in silent request for me to come to bed.

"What, not asking for a separate bed this time?" I said with a smirk.

"Oh, shut up and come to bed." He said jerking his head to the side.

I climbed in and he pulled me close, kissed the top of my head, and said, "I love you Megs."

Then in what couldn't have been more than 30 seconds, he was passed out cold. I smiled. That man could sleep anywhere. I, however, laid there unable to sleep.

"Who is this girl from the Manusia?" I heard faintly from the other room.

"She is Arimas's granddaughter. She doesn't know anything other than it was a Tulainar that killed her." There was a tone in her voice that confirmed Jean was keeping a lot more information from me. How did she even know who I am?

"But that would mean... (silence) ... ummm yes, this was wise of you to have us speak alone. The Council and more importantly Julian, will be interested in knowing this. Though it poses a question, was she trained? And by who, certainly not Symatha. Does she know that her daughter is here?"

Naggle was from a Council? No. They said, "The Council". That sounded like a formal governmental body. What would that mean to me though? Nothing.

Wait.... Symatha? How did they know Mom's real name?

"I don't think Ansel or Symatha trained her at all. I watched her eyes carefully as I started to explain where she is, but there was not a single flicker of recollection in her eyes. None. Nothing. Not even at the mention of Nalrin. She is untrained and completely unknowing of our world. She was totally petrified when she arrived." Jean's voice was almost angry as she explained, but there was a touch of astonishment to it also.

Another female voice then said, "She must have large amounts of inner power since she was to be able to bring both of them here. I mean considering the age limitations."

"But she would have to have known the incantation. How did she know what to say? Then to just *happen* to come to her grandmother's garden in another dimension?" Naggle said.

"Great power indeed." Someone else said.

Naggle continued as if they hadn't said anything, "I would have been instantly informed of the inter–dimensional transportation, when she arrived, but ... nothing. She came through without a trace. If she had arrived anywhere else, no one would have known she arrived at all. I will have to inform Julian immediately."

"As for how she knew the incantation, I'm not sure. Though it's possible Symatha may have told her of the garden as part of some kind bedtime story as a child. It always was Symatha's favorite place as a kid." Jean knew my mom! How?

The questions flew through my mind and I made a mental list of them to ask tomorrow. The exhaustion was fighting against my will to listen to their conversation and finally won out.

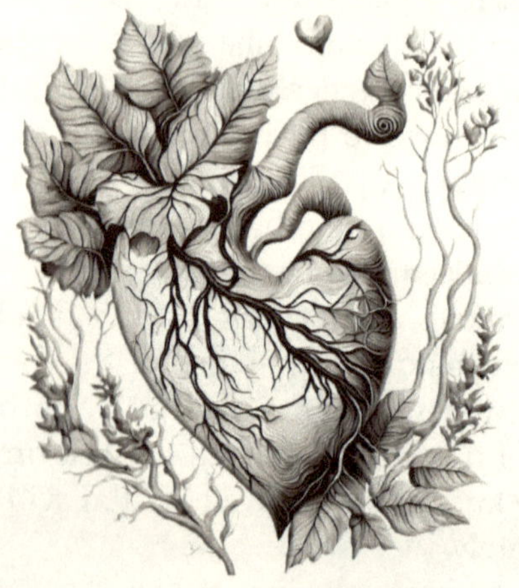

CHAPTER 6

I WOKE IN CJ's arms, in a soft warm bed. He was already awake and when I rolled over, he kissed me gently on the forehead. "Good morning beautiful".

His smile lit up his face. He had one hand draped over my stomach, and the other propping his head up.

"Hey" I said. "How'd you sleep?"

"Fine." He said half shrugging as his hand drew lazy circles on my stomach. I felt myself tightened deep, and I had to take a deep breath to not just roll him over right there. That thought stopped me in my tracks.

I was laying here... with CJ. How had things changed so quickly? Had it been even two full days since he landed in Monterey? This all had to be a fever dream. It had to be a fever dream.

I looked up to his face not believing the loving look he was giving me. After all the years, I was laying here, like this, with CJ. I smiled.

He had said he loved me last night. CJ had actually told me that he loved *me*. That he had for a long while now. How had it taken so long for us to get here? This felt so natural. There was nothing awkward about us laying here, half-clothed, snuggling.

My eyes lowered to his lips, then trailed down his neck, his chest ... He took a deep shuddering breath as I lifted a hand and pressed it against his chest, and ran one finger down the center of his torso. When I reached his belly button I paused and quickly looked back up to his face. My hands flattened on his stomach and snaked around to rest on his side. Gods, he was always so sexy in the morning, but then I remembered where we were, and my heart fell.

The garden. The blue smoke. Jean. The little five-foot man.

Not human.

Not. Human.

It wasn't a dream. I was really hoping that had all been a dream.

"What are you thinking?" I asked softly, focusing on the hollow of his throat.

"What do you mean?"

"What are you thinking about right now?"

"Everything! How beautiful you are. How lucky I am to *finally* have you." I eyed him. He knew exactly what I meant. He sighed. "and how this is ... just a lot to take in. I mean I always knew there was something special and wonderful about you."

"You're biased." I said frowning. "and not the point of this conversation."

He just looked at me and smiled. It so felt good to be normal for a second.

"This is just all so surreal. I feel like I should be waking up from a dream. Everything about this place just seems like it should be right out of a book or a fairy tale. I mean, how in the world does the house look exactly like the picture you have drawn since we were kids, Megs?" he said. I met his eyes, unable to answer that one. "Not to mention magical powers, alternative dimensions. It's straight out of a movie."

"But your still here." I said lowering my eyes. "I thought for sure you would want to go home. In fact, I was shocked when you said we would stay. I even had a passing thought you would have snuck out in the night."

"Never. When have I ever snuck out in the middle of the night when I was with you?" He interrupted.

"Sophomore year. March. You went to meet up with Jackie out in the back yard when Matt and I stayed at your house because Mom and Dad went to a funeral in Wyoming." I said smirking at him.

"Wait. That isn't fair. You are the one who talked me into doing it in the first place. Matt was even the one who helped me with the window." He said sternly as he kept drawing those damn lazy circles on my stomach. Some lower, some higher, and everywhere in between. I subconsciously squeezed my legs together. He smirked noticing the motion.

I laughed. "Regardless. You left me for another woman!"

"Megs. That hardly counts and is completely unrelated to what we are talking about here."

"Still, you left me for another woman." But I saw the look on his face and sighed. "I did think you might have asked them last night to send you home so you could get away from all of this."

I started to feel panic rise deep inside my chest. Truth be told, his mere presence is probably the only thing keeping me from completely losing it. He's always been there for me. Always. It's just... I mean he isn't just my friend anymore. He's here as my better half. How did this happen? We hadn't even had a chance to revel in that happiness before whatever is messed up in my life took over. Couldn't I have had even just a few days of a silver lining before it all went to crap? Why does everything in my life have strings attached!? Don't the Fates have something better to do than mess with me? Seriously, is it not enough that I have to deal with my visions? The loss of my brother and parents?

He placed his hand on my cheek and made me meet his gaze. I took a deep breath to calm down and instantly leaned into his touch.

"I will not leave you. I will be here for you through whatever this is, just as I have for everything else in your life. After everything we have been through together, you should know I'll always be there for you. Granted this is way beyond crazy, and I'm still trying to figure out if I'm just dreaming, or if the plane crashed and I'm dead." He let out a little laugh and I leaned into him a bit more.

"Now that your mine, really *mine*, there is nothing that will tear me away from your side. All those years..." he hesitated, closed his eyes, then after a moment he opened them and looked at me with new determination.

"I will never leave your side Megan, unless you ask me too. Even then, good luck. Whenever you want to leave just say the word and we will be out of here. Start our new life together back home." Then he pulled me close and just held me until my breathing calmed and my heart stopped racing. He said it all with such determination as if we had been on holy ground. What would a declaration of that kind mean? I was speechless. This really was something out of a romance novel. My life is in chaos and I STILL get to keep the prince?

A dream. This is all a dream. None of this happens in real life. I do not want to wake up.

"Now let's get cleaned up and go talk to Jean. Find out all those answers you have running through your head." He said.

"What? How?" I stammered.

"Please," he said rolling his eyes "you were talking in your sleep again last night. I heard all sorts of questions pouring out of you."

I smiled and kissed him, and everything around us seemed to slip away. It was just the two of us. Lips against lips. Body against body. It was so easy with him, going from friendship to relationship. It seemed so effortless, so easy.

When I pulled away a mischievous grin crossed his face as I felt him harden against me. His grip tightened on me slightly and I felt the restraint in it. His eyes stared into me, and then he said with a voice that melted me to the core, "Now do you want to stay in bed or get up and go and talk to Jean?"

I sighed, threw my pillow on his face, and climbed out of bed. *That* was just going to have to wait a little bit.

CHAPTER 7

WE HEADED TO THE kitchen to see if there was even anything edible. My stomach growled as I opened the cupboards and found nothing but dishes. I jumped when I heard CJ giggling behind me. I turned to see him shaking a box of cereal in one hand and a gallon of milk in the other. "Well, at least they have real food here."

"I asked Lindy if she would go and get a few things from the Mansuia so you would have something to eat." Jean said walking into the kitchen. "You don't have the same taste as we do. She spent some time there a few years back, so she knows the food better than any of the rest of us, though I did ask her to pick up some noodles and sauce, which are in the cupboard to make spaghetti."

"How do you know about spaghetti if you've never been in our world?" CJ asked like it was the most normal conversation to be having. I had to give the boy points, he knew how to control himself.

"It was Megan's grandma's favorite. She used to make it with ... cheesy garlic bread." she said as I poured the cereal with just a splash of milk.

I sat at the table and played with my cereal. CJ looked at me and jerked his eyes to Jean in silent command to start with the questions. I just couldn't figure out where to start. She was leaning against the counter obviously deep in thought. I just watched her to see if she would say anything, but when she didn't, I started with the obvious.

"You knew my grandmother."

"Hum, what was that?" Jean said.

"I was just saying that you knew my grandmother." I said looking back down to the bowl in front of me.

"Yes." There was a hardness in her voice that grated against my nerves.

"Was this her house? I mean if that is her garden we landed in, then I would assume that this was her house." I said with a touch more bite than was probably needed. She was being short with me, so I'm not going to feel bad about being short with her. I am the one in this totally foreign environment and I wanted answers, not walls thrown in my face.

"Yes, it was." Quick short answers. She was not volunteering any information here. "You also know my mother." I said a little more curtly than I expected.

"And how do you assume that?" she practically spat the words at me.

Now I was getting testy.

"Well, no one knew that my mother's real name was Symatha. She always went by Bethany at home." I paused, took a deep breath, and continued. "Her real name was Symatha Bethany Keller. She kept it a secret even from me for most of my childhood. I only found out because Dad called her Symatha once when they didn't think I was home from school yet. And you and that guy from ... the council called her Symatha, not Beth or Bethany like everyone else did."

Every muscle in her body was tightening. I could literally see the muscles in her arms flex under her shirt. Why didn't she like me asking about my family? It was my family. I looked to CJ and he was giving me a look that clearly meant to warn me to be careful. It was hard to take him seriously when he had a mouth full of cereal that made him look like he was a chipmunk. I took a deep breath and turned away from him.

"So how do you know her? How did you come to live in my grandmother's home?" I fired at her. I sat back, pushed my cereal away and crossed my arms.

For a long time, we just stared at each other. She was tight as a drum. She didn't even let up when Lindy came into the kitchen and stood at the doorway. I didn't break her stare. She wanted to fight on this. Then let's fight. CJ however, just continued to eat and tried not to call attention to himself. Brat.

Eventually, she let out a huff. She walked over to the refrigerator, poured herself a glass of a milky but yet still clear liquid, then she came to sit down at the table with us. She looked to Lindy who I saw give the smallest of nods, and then she let out a really long breath.

Note to self: Do not ask questions when you're not prepared to hear the answers to said questions.

"When Arimas Tudor, your grandmother, died I inherited the house and the property around it. Since your mother is in the Manusia, she has no rights to inheritance, under Nalrin law. My full name is Rysil Jean Tudor. Arimas was my mother and Symatha is my sister. My mother and father had Symatha when they were very young and me quite a few years later. Your mother and I have never gotten along. In fact, there is so much bad blood, we haven't really spoken to each other since she married your father. My father died when I was only eight and all I really had was my mother. After your parents moved to the Manusia, Mom went with them for a while. It didn't help your mother and I's relationship by any means. When your grandmother returned, she told me that I had a niece. Megan."

"You are my Aunt?" I said, looking to CJ who had completely frozen, spoon halfway to mouth, shock written all over his face.

She simply nodded.

Wow. I sat back and let what she said wash over me. She was my family.

"But if you never met me, how did you know who I was when I showed up in the garden?" I asked.

"You look so much like your mother. Your eyes are your fathers." She said then smiled. "You can thank your grandmother for the high cheekbones. "

I realized she kept referring to my parents in the present tense. She didn't know my parents were dead. She talked about my mom like she was still alive.

"You don't know then?" I asked quietly.

"Know what?" Lindy said from the door jam.

I took a deep breath as Owen and Clarice walked into the kitchen.

"My mother and father are dead."

"That's impossible." Clarice whispered in horror. Her entire 5'8" solid frame was dressed much more casual than yesterday. Today was just a simple pair of jeans and white t-shirt, which looked harsh against her dark skin. Even though she had her black curly hair up in ponytail through a hat, it still ran most of the way down her back. Her hazel eyes were wide with shock.

"Symatha and Ansel can't be dead. They have protection." Owen said arrogantly.

Jean, Lindy, Owen, and Clarice started to mumble to each other. I caught pieces. Stopped using. Council. Worn off. Syth.

Then Jean turned to me and squared her shoulders. "How? How did they die? Explain it to me. Now."

"Excuse me?" I said with so much attitude that CJ shooshed me.

I looked to CJ. I raised an eyebrow at him and finally, I rolled my eyes. He was right. I should be nice. At least for now. I wasn't sure I could tell them though. I'd have to tell them everything, wouldn't I?

"You're gonna have to tell them from the start you know." CJ encouraged.

"They're going to think I'm crazy, not to mention I still feel incredibly guilty." I told him.

"He wouldn't have stopped driving for goodness sakes." He rolled his eyes and then looked at me seriously. "Tell them. They have a right to know. If they really are family, they won't think you are crazy." He promised as he put his hand in mine.

"Mom and Dad did." I said quietly. "and they were family."

"Why did they think you were crazy?" Lindy asked from across the kitchen.

With a hefty sigh I started to retell the last few years of my life. "I can *see* things. I dream them. Mom told me it was just an overactive imagination growing up and Dad wouldn't comment on it." I saw Clarice and Jean eye each other. Yup! They thought I was nuts. A one-way trip to the dimensional loony bin. Here we go. "Anyways, I saw Matt die in my dreams for months before he died a couple of years ago."

I paused to try to keep my emotions in check when Jean gave me a peculiar look. "Who's Matt?"

I looked back at her. What did she mean whose Matt?

"Matthew Thomas Keller." I was left with blank stares from everyone. "My little brother..." Still nothing. "You didn't know I had a brother?"

"No. No, I didn't." She said looking off in the distance.

"He was only about a year and a half younger than me." I said slowly. CJ gave me a reassuring look and I continued. "He died in a car crash that involved a drunk driver, who hit Matt straight on when he was on his way home from work. When Matt died it destroyed my father. He became vengeful, thought it was the work of evil powers or something that had really killed Matt. He started mumbling to himself all the time. Saying how they had found them and if they found him there, where could they go that would be safe? I tried to tell him that he was being ridiculous because we all knew it was just a drunk ass driver." My voice caught and CJ got up from the table and rested his hands on my shoulder. I reached up and grabbed one of his hands, taking comfort in his touch.

I looked up to Jean and she had tears running down her cheek but had a very strange look on her face. It was then I noticed Owen was standing next to her. He was about CJ's height, thin, brown eyes, and brown hair that was messy. He looked a lot like an older version of Matt, and I felt a pain in my heart that he would never grow up to look like that.

Lindy and Clarice looked at me expectantly and I realized they were waiting patiently for me to continue. I sighed, closed my eyes, and saw the whole thing over again.

"It was a little over a year ago. I was over at their house in Seaside helping Mom with some cleaning and such. Mom was singing to herself when Dad got up and started screaming at her. Yelling about curses she was putting on him, and how he couldn't trust her anymore. She started crying and screaming at him in a language I had never heard them speak before. There was a bright light, a loud bang ... I flew backwards as the house exploded." I closed my eyes to hold back the tears.

"The first responders found me 30 feet from where I had been standing just next to my mother and under a bunch of burning debris. The neighbors told them to look for me because my car was there, so I must be as well. I was told it took them hours to get the debris away enough for them to pull me out.

"I woke up in the hospital 16 days later with CJ sleeping next to me. I had been in a coma, but other than that, just a broken leg from where a beam had landed. The doctors were shocked at the lack of burns or injuries. I had them, but they thought I should have had more considering the state of the house."

I turned to look at CJ, he squeezed my shoulder, as I remembered how he never left my side, he picked up the story and said, "The doctors said the coma was strange. There was no reason for her to even be in one and they couldn't figure out why she wasn't able to wake up. There had been no swelling in the brain and that her brain activity was off the charts.

"When CJ woke up, he told me briefly what had happened. I knew my parents were dead, even though the rescue workers couldn't find either of their bodies. Later, when the police came to see me in the hospital, they told me they thought there was a gas explosion and their bodies had likely been destroyed in the explosion. They asked me what I remembered, which obviously wasn't much." I said.

"The only piece of evidence that was left was Mom's melted and warped charm she wore. CJ said he went back to the house when I was in surgery for my leg and found it near the center of the blast where they believe Mom had been standing. He put it in my hand one day hoping that it would give me some connection to come back. I woke up the next day. I was able to leave only a few days later. The doctors said it was one of the fastest releases after a patient woke from a coma they had had. Since there was no physical reason for the coma in the first place, they couldn't come up with any reason to keep me. They set up physical therapy for the broken leg and let me go home with CJ. He stayed with me for two months while my leg healed. I later had a loop put on Mom's charm so I could wear it as a necklace. I always wear it, just as she had." I reached up and started playing with it between my fingers as CJ wiped a tear from my cheek.

"It used to be shaped like a heart and filled in a swirling pattern. It always amazed me how the metal never met anywhere. I tried to have it reshaped into a star, but no jeweler could manipulate the shape. No matter how hot they got the metal, or what method they used, they couldn't reshape it. I always feel stronger when wearing it. Like my mother is there to protect me from harm." I said letting out a shuddering breath and looked back up to them.

Lindy stared at the pendant in my hand for a moment before walking up to me and taking a closer look at the bent and twisted metal around my neck. I felt a pulse of heat when she touched the charm and then she said, "May I see that for 5 minutes, please? I promise to have it back to you within that time."

I eyed her carefully. "Umm, ok." Finally deciding, that I probably couldn't fight her off if she really wanted it. I took it off and handed it to her. I felt oddly weaker, just like every night when I removed it for bed.

Everyone was dead silent as Lindy disappeared into the other room. No one said I was crazy. No one tried to convince me that the years since high school had all been a dream. They kept looking at each other, silent questions on their faces like they were trying to put all the pieces of a puzzle together.

A few minutes later, Lindy came back into the room and carefully placed the necklace into the palm of my hand. CJ took it from my hand, re-clasped it around my neck, and kissed the top of my head.

Everyone looked at Lindy. Their face was filled with awe and wonder. It was almost as if they knew what she was looking for.

"First of all, that is a horrible turn of events for you." Lindy said sadly. I almost felt like there was extra meaning there, but she continued, "I'm really sorry you have had to endure all of that."

"Lindy?" Owen said drawing out her name and being very impatient.

"You don't get to gloss over those horrible events that she has to go through because you want to know more Owen. Have a little bit of kindness." Lindy berated.

Owen had the good sense to look sheepish and actually turned to me and mouthed, "Sorry."

"As for the necklace, it is the real thing. Where she got it? Angels only know." Lindy said with a snide smile on her face to the others, then turned back toward me, "That is not just some ordinary piece of jewelry you have there sweetie."

"What is it?" I asked confused.

Lindy stood up straighter and said beaming, "That is the Golden Medallion of Sa Ra."

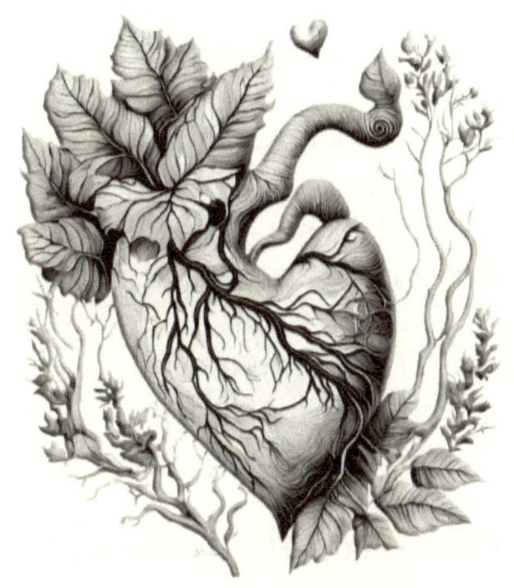

CHAPTER 8

The Golden Medallion of Sa Ra according to lore, belongs to the Angel of Healing. It is supposed to have the power to keep people safe, hidden, healthy, and of course, the ability to increase healing incantations. The person wearing it would always feel stronger when wearing it, but I have no idea how Symatha came into possession of it." Lindy had continued after she noted CJ's and my confused face.

"Have you ever broken a bone, gotten ill, or so much as stubbed your toe since you started wearing it, Megan?" Owen had asked me. "I saw how you hunched down just the littlest bit when it was taken off and how you straightened right back up once you had it back on. Don't you feel stronger when you're wearing it?"

I couldn't think of any illness in the last year since I had started wearing it. I was always good for a good cold or flu during the winter, but I had gotten off lucky this year, that's all. Figured my flu shot actually worked.

The only problem was that Lindy said it was supposed to be indestructible. They were so convinced that this was the melted remains of the Golden Medallion of Sa Ra, but that only extremely magnified powers should have been able to manipulate the charm.

"You speak of it with such reverence. What is the deal?" CJ asked. "We are missing a piece of the puzzle here."

Clarice answered first. "The Golden Medallion of Sa Ra is one of the pieces needed for the creation of the weapon of the Five Angels."

"The Five Angels?" I interrupted and when I looked around the room I was met with blank stares.

"OH! You really don't know *any* of your history, do you?" Clarice said.

I just shrugged, trying not to feel too much like an idiot, as she continued.

"The Five Angels are our protectors. The Angel of Healing, Remembrance, Beauty, Death, and Love. Each represents a very special part of how we live." She said.

"Legend says," Lindy said taking over for Clarice. "that the Five Angels would create a weapon that was unbeatable for the wielder. The weapon would level all those who would stand in the wielder's way. No man nor beast could ever defeat it. See the weapon that is built, is not a specific thing. It is specific to the wielder, depending on the meaning of the pieces that one uses to call it to him. One piece has to be used from each Angel.

"The Angel of Healing said that only the Golden Medallion of Sa Ra, which she crafted from the purest of gold in Nalsar would be used to mold together the item. The Angel of Remembrance requires a crystal from the clearest reflection. There is a mirror in Nalrin that when you look into it, you relive your worst memories, fears, and the darkest parts of yourself. If you survive, he rewards you with the crystal. The Angel of Beauty requires the rarest flower that only blooms on the third Friday the 13th of a year. Since the flower must be plucked at the time it blooms and this occurs so rarely, it is very difficult to obtain. The Angel of Death requires a book said to be locked up in Noctulanar. It holds the incantation needed to summon the Angels. This would be the last piece you would get as the ritual is also performed within Noctulanar Castle. Finally, the Angel of Love. This is simple, but possibly the most painful. The Angel of Love requires the heart of a loved one."

"But couldn't you just manipulate the loved one to sacrifice themselves?" I asked.

"It's not that simple. See in our world, when you marry or fall in love with someone you have given your heart to that person. So, for instance, Jean's heart is within Owen and vis versa. In this case, for example only," she met the glare from Jean, "if your grandmother wanted to wield this item, she would need Owen and not Jean, for he carries her heart."

"There's a common theme here. Hatred and Pain. Soooo, doesn't sound like Angels you should be worshiping if you know what I mean." I said rolling my eyes.

"This is a weapon of destruction, so the fact that what you need to create it requires hatred and pain, well that's pretty much what it's all about right?"

"Yea I guess so. I just can't imagine hurting someone that much." I said.

"This is only one part of the Angels story. The point of their existence is really to guide you to love, understanding and non-violence." Lindy said.

It was then I realized that Jean and Clarice were talking to each other with such intensity it brought everyone in the room to attention.

"Ummm would you guys like to fill us in on what's going on?" Lindy said.

"It's just that I hadn't thought about it until I heard you retell the story again. Add in Naggle's visit last night and what he told us. Then *she* shows up?" Clarice's eyes flickered to me. "Not to mention her father's history with the council, her mother had the Sa Ra, their death, which there were no bodies found and now there was the break into Nalrin Library, near where the mirror is stored. It sounds like Ansel and Symatha are trying to get to the pieces needed to create the weapon."

"You are suggesting that Ansel and Symatha are trying to actually build it?" Owen said.

The room was silent as they thought over that possibility. I looked to CJ who seemed to be seriously thinking it all over. Could he really be buying this?

"Wait!" This wasn't possible. I looked at them like they were crazy. "You're kidding, right? You can't be serious!"

"Yes I am." Clarice said. "I'm very serious."

I just continued to look at her like she was crazy. Didn't I just get done telling them that my parents were dead? These guys had to be about as sharp as a bowling ball to forget that little detail.

"Let's look at this. Let's just say, I have the Sa Ra, which I'm not completely convinced of yet. I'm the only *loved one* my mother and father have left, save Jean. You've already said you've had no contact with her since she married my father and there is likely no love lost between the two of you." I said pointedly looking at Jean. She didn't bother to meet my eye.

"Oh wait, there is one thing that I'm forgetting. What was it?" I said thick with sarcasm. "Oh yea, that's it... Let us not forget that my parents are DEAD!"

There was a long silence in the room. I looked to each of them, none of them looking at me.

"I don't think they are Megs." CJ whispered a moment later. I whirled around to him. I couldn't believe that he could be the one saying this. "Don't kill me for this but think about it. According to these guys they had some kind of protection, your father was worried about curses, he was blaming evil for Matt's death, you miraculously survive their house being blown to shreds and your mom had this medallion thing that was supposed to protect her. The most important part is that the police never found an ounce of either of their bodies. That's a lot of co-inqu-e-dinks."

"CJ. They were blown apart in the explosion." I said my voice thick with emotion.

"But you lived, with only a few scratches and a broken leg. Yet they were incinerated? That does not line up. If what they are saying is true, then it is possible they survived the explosion, and just covered their tracks. Megs. Don't get mad at me, but people have been known to fake their deaths before. What is to say your parents didn't do the same thing to come back here?"

I looked at him and there was resignation on his face. He thought that this was plausible. When I could speak again, I whispered. "Ceej you can't possibly think."

He nodded his head, but his eyes were full of sorrow.

"You think my parents faked their death? Why would they do that to me?" I said almost under my breath. Why would my parents want to go after this place? I don't understand. They never told me anything about Nalrin or that I have an Aunt either though. Were they really the people I thought they were?

"Clarice, what did you mean considering my dad's history with the council? What happened?" I said quietly.

Clarice looked to Jean as if asking for permission. Jean nodded her head. "She has a right to know I guess."

"Growing up Ansel was always fascinated with knowledge. He wanted to know everything. The more forbidden, the more he wanted to know. The weapon of the Five Angels, well it's about as forbidden as you get, especially for council members, and yes, he was a council member. Everyone knows the basic principles, like Lindy just told you, okay, a little less on the details, but no one knows the exact process. It was the council's hope that in a few generations, even that common knowledge would die out. Just the basic knowledge of the story is usually a deterrent for us to pursue it any further. Theoretically, it's written in the Nalrin's library in detail though, except for the incantation, that is in the Book." Clarice said.

I saw her eyes flicker to Lindy who had her head hung low and chewed on her thumb but then continued, "Your father was caught in there reading up on the process. Regardless, when the council confronted him, he denied it, but there are ways among our kind to determine liars in front of the Council. He was lying, and they banished him."

"Your father was furious, and it turned into one hell of a battle." Owen said as he rubbed circles on Jean's back. "He ended up killing two members of the council. When he was finally stopped, they told him his punishment would be the loss of one of his loved ones. He instantly thought of your mother, which may be why she had the Sa Ra. They had you in the Manusia, so there is no official record of you, or your brother's, birth in our world. There had been rumor that your father had continued to gain access to the library numerous times since they were banished, though obviously he was never caught. Now he may have finally gotten all the information together to create the weapon. "

"That is what Naggle was telling us last night. Someone broke into the library and got into the Angels archives. With everything you have told us, it is possible their punishment may be the death of your brother, and not of your mother." Jean said trailing off lost in thought.

"No. Matt died in a car crash. I had to identify his body. I saw him die time and time again in my dreams." I was shaking my head back and forth crying freely now as CJ pulled me closer. This was so overwhelming. I was basically being told that my whole life, everything my parents had told me over the years, was a lie. How am I supposed to deal with that? Overwhelmed didn't even come close to explaining how I was feeling.

After a few moments, Owen said, "Megan, you have to understand the council members are our most powerful beings in this realm. They could have made his death look like anything they wanted. I have to agree with Clarice. This is pointing toward your parents. There are way too many coincidences for this to be overlooked."

I tried to find holes in their logic but couldn't find any. My whole world had just taken a 180, then flipped on its lid, in the span of 24 hours. And yet ... I wanted to believe it, even though I didn't want to believe it.

"If my parents are doing this ... they need what?" I asked very hesitantly as I looked up at CJ, already starting to piece it together. His eyes met mine, and I could see that he was already thinking the same thing.

Lindy spoke first, "Healing. You have the Golden Medallion of Sa Ra, so they will need to find you. You should stay here where we can protect you. Maybe we can even see about training you some so you can protect yourself if for some reason we aren't around."

I nodded. What was I going to do? Say no? Right now, I would probably agree to an elephant and bunny rabbit being my guards.

"Remembrance is something that your parents are going to have to do, but we will just have to keep them from getting to the mirror in Nalrin." Clarice said quietly, but very much deep in thought.

"Beauty. The Flower. We will have to find out more for Death, I've heard rumors of where it is in Noctulanar Castle, but that's all. Rumor." Owen explained.

"Love." I whispered and turned ice cold as the realization snapped into me and I could feel CJ's muscles tighten at the thought as well. With absolutely no emotion in my voice, I said to him "They will be coming for me, since I have the Sa Ra. And that also means they will be coming for you."

His face went completely still. He knew exactly what I was saying.

"Why would they come for CJ?" Jean asked.

"Angel of Love." Lindy said barely above a whisper, her mind doing quick work on what CJ and I had already figured out.

Clarice, Owen, and Jean still didn't understand. Didn't I just get done telling them?! CJ looked deep into my eyes and cupped my cheek in his hand.

"Because in your world, I have her heart." he finished for me, at the same time Lindy whispered in awe and understanding, "You are mates."

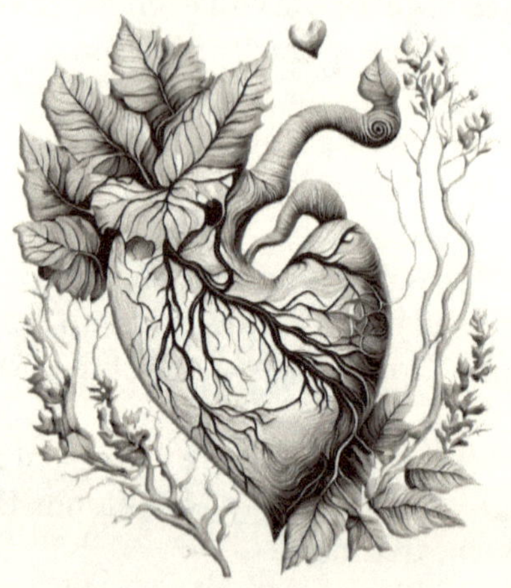

CHAPTER 9

"CONCENTRATE MEGAN." OWEN SCOLDED, "You have to just let it flow through you. Like water. Don't force it. Try thinking and feeling the incantations instead of saying them or just whispering them."

"I'm trying for fuck's sake!" I said panting, sweat dripping down my back.

In the days that followed our arrival, there had been much discussion regarding strategy and it was ultimately decided that if my parents were going to need both me and CJ that we could either be locked up in a cell for our protection, or we could help. Obviously, CJ and I were not too keen on becoming prisoners.

Once the decision had been made that CJ and I would help, there was the question of whether I would, or even could be trained. Over the next few weeks, they had me go over all the beginner material and then started testing me to see if I could even do anything. Much to Clarice and Lindy's excitement, I was able to do most of the beginner incantations with little to no trouble. I remember sitting on the floor a few weeks ago, in the living room with a bowl of water in front of me, sweating profusely in concentration because I couldn't slide the bowl toward Lindy.

"This is what I mean. If she had been trained like she should have, then this wouldn't be a problem." Jean had complained.

"Well, I wasn't, was I. So, you can either be helpful and supportive or you can fuck off, Jean." I said through gritted teeth.

"We will find another way for you to protect yourself. Hand -to hand combat. You will just have to be more careful. There are plenty of Sangra who haven't been born with the ability to master their power. We will treat you as one of them." She said starting to reach for the bowl of water on the ground.

My eyes flicked to her as I felt my power surge at that very moment and wrap around her wrist, just before touching the bowl. The water sloshed, but half a thought had it settling. Jean eyed me carefully and then looked at her wrist. You could see the imprint of where my power was wrapped tightly around her wrist and even Lindy's eyes went wide.

"Don't you fucking touch it." I said. She nodded and I let her wrist go.

Taking a deep breath to shake off the anger I realized that burst was enough to unlock my power from whatever was holding me back. I could feel it keenly as it spread through my body, as I looked at the bowl. I pictured hands, the same hands that had grabbed Jean's wrist, lift the bowel and hand it to Lindy.

The bowl lifted and was carried on an invisible string and hovered in front of Lindy.

"Take it." I told Lindy who was just staring at me. She looked down quickly at the bowl, back at me, and then at the bowl. Her hands raised, I slowly placed it in her hands.

"What. The. Actual. Fuck." CJ said from the kitchen doorway. I didn't even know he was there. No one else said anything. "I felt something plow through me, and when I got to the door, you ..." his voice trailed off.

"You felt something?" Lindy said to CJ turning and spilling some of the water.

"Yea. Didn't you." CJ said.

Lindy just shook her head and said, "I need to talk to Clarice. Megan, go work on your stretches to get ready for sparing practice."

With that she was off, leaving me, CJ, and Jean all looking at her in question. Fortunately, Jean didn't complain about my training anymore.

Clarice and Lindy were training me in defensive maneuvers, which always made CJ antsy. He kept trying to intervene, and it got to the point that Owen would occupy CJ's time while I was training. I think Owen was secretly hoping to help Clarice with the hand-to-hand combat training, but he just made me promise to spar with him one day. It was an easy request to agree to.

Now, I was able to use simple powers without much thought. I breezed through many of the beginning levels and even some of the intermediate levels. Moving objects, putting up a wall, and small jabs of pain were a cinch for me now.

Today, I was supposed to be able to throw a large burst of my power at an opponent to throw them backwards, but it just wasn't working. Well, I had been able to tip over a jar, but anything bigger than that just wasn't there. It frustrated me to my core. How was I was going to be able to protect CJ if I couldn't do this? On the surface, it seemed so easy.

CJ was off to the side with Lindy working on some hand-to-hand combat skills. He was progressing much better than I was in that department. He was able to best her more and more often, where Lindy was still able to beat me more often than I her. While I appreciated the help he was getting, but I still felt it was my responsibility to protect him.

"Megan, will you please focus on what we are doing, instead of undressing CJ?" Owen said with his hands on his hips.

I glared at him then repositioned myself. That sassy shit. I tried to resettle my mind and concentrated on the need to protect

CJ. I took a deep breath and gently moved my hand across my body and out, thought "*lintal magmo*".

Owen flew back a few feet and almost fell on his butt when his feet landed on the ground.

"Well," Owen said. "That was an improvement."

"I just had to realize what I have to protect." I whispered to him so no one else could hear. Clarice was staring at me dumbfounded. It was a marked improvement over my earlier attempts today. They had felt a jolt earlier, but I wasn't able to make anyone fall back or anything.

Jean strode over, put her hand on my shoulder, and said softly, "Good Job Megan. I want to test something. Let's see just how powerful you are." She eyed Owen and sighed.

"I am going to tell you an incantation. I just want you to visualize what it does. Do not move your body in any way. If you can do this, well... let's worry about that later." I just nodded my head. She leaned down and whispered in my ear the incantation and the meaning, then stepped back.

"CJ, come over here and hold her hand." Jean said.

When I had CJ's hand in mine, I closed my eyes, willed myself to be still and relax. I let the words fill me and a warmth swam throughout my body. I cracked open an eye and could barely see a faint golden shimmer over my body. CJ smiled brightly and squeezed my hand. I wanted him to feel it.

As if it knew what I wanted it slowly spread up his arm, and covered his body. He closed his eyes and I knew he could feel it too. "Wooo." I heard him say, only his lips didn't move, and I jumped back losing my concentration. The glow was gone.

"How? What?" I turned to Jean. "I *heard* him, but his lips didn't move. You didn't tell me that was what the spell did. You told me it was a protection incantation."

"It is. The warmth and glow you felt is the protection, but we can't see it. That is why that incantation is so powerful." Jean said and stopped, looked at the others, then continued. "As for hearing him, well that isn't normal. I have been trying to do that with Owen for years. There is only one other person in recent history that I know of who that has been able to hear the other persons thoughts when using that incantation."

Everyone looked at each other but avoided looking at me.

Sighing I stated the obvious, "Mom."

"Your mother. Your grandmother couldn't and neither could your father." Clarice whispered.

Owen quickly changing the subject. "I believe you are ready for your trials. Just need to cram a little more into your head and you'll be fine. After you pass, you'll receive your Maltal and I'll have your syth prepared."

"No. I'm not ready yet." I was shocked he would even suggest it. "I still have too much to learn. I'm only at like a 10- or 12-year-old level. My follow though isn't anywhere near consistent enough. Not to mention all the book study I still have to do. I haven't even touched on Midlife History of Cinder. The Fairies history is so intense and ... long. What if I have to write an essay on how they won the war against the Farlaree? Not to mention hand-to-hand combat. Clarice is doing a great job training me, but she still whips my butt every time."

"Clarice whips everyone's butt. It's part of who she is. Megan, you're ready. You have been working your ass off. You are in the training ring and studying more hours than you are sleeping. When was the last time you got more than four hours sleep?" Lindy said.

"The night we arrived." CJ said when I pursed my lips.

Putting his hand on my shoulder, Owen said. "Besides, it will take them time to prepare a quorum of Council members to perform the trials and to schedule it. You still have time to study ... and practice. I know today was the first day you were able to stun and knockback, but it just goes to show how much you've been working on it. You don't have to get perfect scores. You can struggle on portions of it and still pass your tests."

"I still don't think I'm ready. I don't think I have the time." I said under my breath.

"Come on sweetie, let's go and get some rest. You've had a hard few of months." CJ said.

"MONTHS?! Has it really been that long? What about your job? Don't you need to head back to get a leave of absence or something?" I said as we were walking back to the house. I did a quick calculation. We had been here for two and a half Nalrin months and if I had done my math right, which converted to about ... four months in the Manusia? We missed all summer.

CJ just looked at me and laughed. "Megs. Don't worry about it. I'll find another job if we go back."

"What do you mean if we –" My head suddenly felt light and my knees buckled. I tried to shake it clear, but the fuzziness wouldn't shake off. I was staring straight at CJ's face, but not really seeing it. His arms tightened around me, holding me up.

Another picture was forming in front of my eyes. A man and a woman. They were arguing in an ancient gothic styled castle, I hadn't seen before. The windows were dark black and it reminded me of a church, but there were no pews, no religious symbols that I could recognize, but there was a huge pipe organ in the background, with black pipes reaching to a three–story roof. The whole thing was hazy to me, like a dream.

My breath caught as I realized that the couple... they were my parents. My mother was dressed in a purple corset dress, but her haystack–colored hair was shorter. Much shorter. It had always hung to her tailbone, but here it was cut above her shoulders. She looked paler and gaunter than I remembered, but she was yelling at my father in a language that sounded like the one she had spoken just before they had died. They did die right?

"Focus Megan!" I told myself.

My father, leaner than I had last seen him, had a piece of paper in his hand that he shook into Mom's chest.

"It has to be her! Your sister will not work! You don't love Jean. It has to be her in order for it to work Symatha, besides the flower comes first. We only have a few weeks until it blooms, and we still have to find the garden."

I focused on the piece of paper, which was a list of names that he had in his hand. I could just make out a list, with "Love" with my name next to it in my Father's handwriting before the world faded away.

I blinked as I leaned against CJ on the ground. Everyone stood around me. "My parents were fighting in a castle." I crooked out.

"You just had one of your visions?" CJ said just above a whisper, trying very hard to hide the fear in his voice. If I didn't know CJ so well, I could have missed it completely.

"But I wasn't sleeping." I whispered to him my chest tightening and snuggled up closer to him. "I have only ever *seen* while sleeping? I don't understand."

Clarice chimed in. "You've honed your powers and your abilities are stronger here. Megan, you are possibly one of the most powerful Sangra I have seen this untrained."

"Please stop saying that I'm so young, or this untrained at this age. It's driving me nuts." I said through my teeth.

"Plus, with your ability to see the future, well, once you get your Maltal we will take it from there." Clarice said ignoring my retort.

"Never mind that right now Clarice." Jean said with a harshness that clearly ended that conversation. She sounded just like Mom when she was putting an end to a fight between Matt and I. "Megan, what did you see? We need to know."

I retold the vision to them as I had seen it. When I explained how I focused in on the piece of paper in my father's hand Owen asked, "You were able to focus in on a specific item during the vision? Have you ever been able to do that before?"

"No, like I said this was the first time I was awake. They have always been in my sleep, somewhere between a dream and reality for me. I could still sort of see CJ's face, but only faded off way in the background."

"But you are sure about what it said?" Owen asked again.

"Pretty sure." I hesitated. There was something not right about the words though. "Wait! It said Love with MY NAME! Not CJ's they don't know that I'm in love with CJ!" my face filled with hope. When I looked at CJ his eyes were filled with fear. He didn't see this the same way I did.

"How could they not know that you're in love with him?" Jean questioned. "We knew from the moment you arrived there was something between you."

"I didn't ever really tell my parents. CJ and I have been best friends for so long, that I didn't realize I was in love with him until ..." My eyes flickered to CJ, "well, and I didn't tell anyone. Remember after my brother died that was all my father and mother were consumed with until they faked their death. They wouldn't even know who I was anymore. I've changed so much since then. Not to mention the fact CJ and I didn't declare our feelings to each other till much more recently. It's not like we are married." I explained to them.

"Yet" interrupted CJ. I shot him a puzzled look and was about to say something when Clarice interrupted him.

"Hey that's it!" Clarice shouted. Everyone just looked at her. "That's why CJ has the sight and was able to come here with Megan. It's because they are mates!" When everyone looked at her like she was crazy she continued, nodding her head, and smiling, "Love is very powerful."

"Wait. This is not the first time you guys called us mates. Lindy mentioned it before too." I said letting CJ help me off the ground. "Why mates? Not boyfriend and girlfriend or husband and wife?"

"Being mates, being soul bonded, with someone you love, is a much more powerful bond than just falling in love with someone. You can be madly in love with someone, live your entire lives, raise a family, but not be mates. Being mates is something more ... how do I explain it? When two people are mates, there is not another love in the world that can keep you from finding each other. They are extremely rare." Clarice said.

I looked at Jean and Owen. "Are you?"

"No." Jean said taking Owen's hand in hers. "But that doesn't stop the fact that I love Owen and would do anything to protect him."

I looked to Lindy and Clarice, "What about you two? Were you ever mates with someone?"

"I haven't found mine." Lindy said sadly and when I looked to Clarice, she simply looked away.

"You may be on to something there Clarice. I'll check on it next time I'm in Nalrin. Doesn't matter though. He's here and not going anywhere." Jean said as she tried to cover for Clarice.

"Ok you two love birds, you two need your rest. Both of you worked hard today." Owen ordered as he headed for the door to the house. My word he's pushy. "I'll get the council here as soon as possible to get you your trial completed."

"Are you sure I'm ready? I mean there is so much I still need to learn." I said.

"You are a quick learner dear." Jean said to comfort me.

"Really. You are. Now let's get some rest" Lindy answered me.

"I'm actually hungry. Do you have a barbeque?" I asked as CJ smiled and shook his head. He knew exactly what I wanted.

"No, but we can get one from the Mansuia if you want." Jean told me with a questioning look.

"I'm just really craving a cheeseburger! I haven't had one in what feels like AGES! Barbequed. Not fried in a pan. Barbequed. I have a BBQ at my place. Someone want to go with me to pick it up? I'd like to pick up some clothes and things from there anyways. It shouldn't take long. We could be back in 30 minutes if we hurry."

"You are not going alone." Jean demanded.

"I figured, hence why I asked if someone wanted to go with." I said rolling my eyes. "I also haven't mastered the teleportation spell, and don't want us to end up in the ocean or something."

I remembered trying just to go from one side of the room to the other, because we weren't supposed to teleport within a dimension, but we could within the property for training purposes. I kept ending up half in a chair, which was very painful, or too close to a wall, or a tree. One time I scared the crap out of Owen who was tending to the horses, when I just popped into the stables when I was really trying to get to the tree line.

"Clarice and I will go with you. CJ, I want you to stay here." Jean said.

"But I need some new clothes too. All my stuff is at the apartment. And what about Betsy? She's probably been towed by now." He complained and I froze. His eyes went wide. He knew what Betsy meant to me. "Babe..."

"Betsy?" Lindy asked.

"My car. And don't you get silly over me naming my car. Betsy is a Ford GT350 Shelby. She's a fucking badass. If she's sitting in an impound yard right now ... oh GODS ... what if someone picked her over!" I started to hyperventilate. "She needs to get back to the apartment."

"Don't worry. Betsy ..." Owen said trying to hide a smile. "I left her sitting in the driveway. After you and CJ arrived, I went and took care of a few things in the Manusia, while Lindy got some food, to assure that Ansel and Symatha didn't suspect you were here for any reason. They would see that there was movement and activity back at the house, even though there wasn't."

"Megan, you did call in "sick" to work for an extended time period though. They hope you get better soon." Jean said turning to me. "You won't have any problems there for a while. We also sent text messages to your most current contacts that you were going to be unreachable for a bit, but you would contact them when you felt better. We will grab your things from the house for you CJ. We can't take a chance if something were to happen at the house." Jean told him.

He looked at me with a determined look on his face. I knew he didn't want to leave my side for anything now. I don't know if it was more that he finally had me, heart, body, mind, and soul, or if it was because of the threat my parents posed right now.

I walked up to him, wrapped my arms around his waist, and said, "Honey, you'll be safer here. I'll have Jean and Clarice with me. Give me your phone and I'll call Mom to let her know you are okay, but we are not reachable for a bit. I'll be fine. 30 minutes from start to finish. Deal?" He looked at me carefully for a long time. He searched for any trace of me lying and I put my brave face on. Finally, after what seemed like an eternity, he exhaled, "Just bring the duffle bag. It has the most important stuff in it." He gave me an impish smile that I couldn't decipher, but before I could say anything, he said, "I unpacked the suitcase. Mom is probably freaking out. Call her. Don't text her, please. She's probably called in the National Guard by now." I nodded and he looked over to Jean and said, "30 minutes. Please keep her safe."

"Of course, I will. She's my newly found niece. I'm going to do everything within my power to keep her safe." She said.

"Newly found being the key word there, *Aunt* Jean." I saw her grimace at the word. Granted CJ put a lot of emphasis on it, however, there was obviously some really bad blood between her and my mother. I really need to ask her about that later.

"Don't CJ. I know you just want to protect me, but DON'T." I told him sternly.

"I know. You know how I can get. Hurry back." Then before I could respond he kissed me hard. When he pulled back, I was breathing hard, but looked at him firmly, "30 minutes I promise." I ran to the bedroom to grab my keys and our phones before meeting the others outside.

I felt guilty, but really it was only 30 minutes, and I was just running home to get a few things. They were about 50 feet from the house and as I approached, Clarice grabbed Jean and I's hand and we were floating in that blue smoky mist all over again.

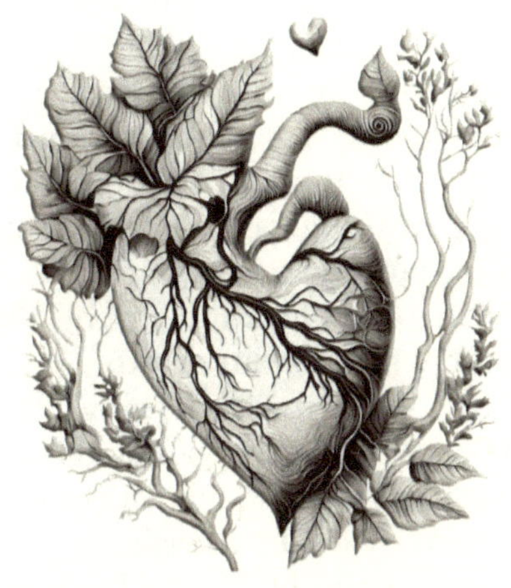

Chapter 10

When we landed, it was midday and the sun was trying to come out through the fog. Typical Monterey Bay weather. Jean was immediately off to put Betsy in the garage under the apartment, and Clarice ran off into the backyard. Pulling out our phones, I saw the group message that they had sent to our friends after turning them back on, I cringed and waited for the phone to reconnect to the tower. When the phones did, they both went crazy with texts that had come in while the phone was off. Sighing, I sent another one to them.

"Hey, guys. I know you are probably worried sick about CJ and me. We are good. We are together, but you won't be able to reach us for a while. I know it is total bullshit to do this all over text without talking to you in person, but we are dealing with some major shit for my parents' estate and there isn't any cell service. I will explain what I can when I can. CJ and I just wanted to tell you we love you all. Stay safe."

I stared at it for a long minute before I hit send. I could re-word that for months, and never get it right.

Once it went through, I turned my phone back off because they would be blowing it up immediately once they saw it. Gods, if Amber didn't show up here at the house while we were here after getting that I would be surprised. I turned around and sat on the stairs to call Annie from CJ's phone. I took a deep breath for the screaming that would occur and pushed the contact on his phone. She picked up on the second ring.

"Cory James Mathewson. Are you alright? I've been worried sick!" She screamed when she answered.

"Hi, Annie. It's Megan." I said grimacing a little bit.

"Megan. Is CJ okay?" The sheer panic in her voice broke my heart. How had we not thought to contact her sooner? Of course, she would be a total wreck. CJ was right.

"He is fine. Great actually. He said you can call off the National Guard." I said smiling a little bit.

"Let me talk to him." She said relieved, but I could hear the ass chewing he was going to get.

"He isn't with me at the moment. It's sort of why I'm calling."
"Where is he?"

"He is safe. I can't really explain everything. I really wish I could, but let me just say what I need to say okay?"

"Okay." I could hear the hesitation in her voice. I heard the deep breaths she was taking to calm down. She *really* was trying.

"He showed up. We talked. Strange shit happened, and now we are going to be out of cell service for a long while okay? I promise we are good. You just won't be able to reach us for a few months, but I promise that once we can make contact we will."

"Megan. What sort of corrupted bullshit did you get into?" She said fear coating every word of her voice, "You know George and I will help with whatever it is that we can. We have money. We can help."

"It isn't like that. It has to do with my mom and dad's estate okay." There. Let her make of that what she will.

"So, you weren't taken by the mafia or anything?"

"Gods NO, Annie." No wonder she was freaking out. "I'm literally dealing with my mom and dad's shit right now, and CJ is helping me. Things happened so fast we didn't have a chance to call you before we had to leave." Truth. A resemblance of it anyways.

"Thank Fucking God." She said letting out a huge relieving sigh. "We thought you..."

"No more worrying okay Annie?" I said trying to sound lighter. There was a long pause where my phone buzzed. I looked at it and there were now 10, no 11, no 12 text messages coming in from our friends.

"Okay, Megan." She said bringing my focus back to her. "When you said you and CJ talked... He went out there to... well *talk*."

I smiled. Annie was trying to be so delicate in case CJ chickened out. "Yes, Annie. CJ and I talked. He didn't chicken out if that is what you are thinking. Yes. He told me he loves me. I love him too. We are trying, okay?"

"FINALLY?!" She screamed and I heard George in the background wonder what was going on and when she screamed that CJ and I were dating, George and who I assumed was his brother Logan screamed, "Well it's about time."

I rolled my eyes. "Subtle."

"Well! What did you expect Megan? You've already been a part of this family forever. We have never made it a secret that we thought you two should be together. Forever. Now, for the hundred-thousandth time, stop calling me Annie."

I chuckled.

"Look, Mom. I gotta go. We love you, and punch Logan in the balls for me okay?" I said laughing. I wasn't even going to go there with her on the forever part. They hadn't made that unknown. At least if we do get married, I know that the in-laws like me.

"I'll leave that for you to do when you get back okay? Any idea when that might be?"

"We will see if we can get back in time for Christmas, okay?"

"Fine. You must be really far in the sticks." She said with a tone that was begging for more information.

"We are. Love you guys."

"Love you too, and stay safe." Annie said before hanging up.

That went better than I could have expected. I hated not being able to tell them everything, but it was as much as I could tell them right now. I opened the banking app and set the bill pay to auto issue my rent, car, and a few other essential payments for the next six months out of my savings then turned to the door and unlocked the apartment. When I walked in, I noticed a peculiar smell and froze.

"JEAN! CLARICE!" I yelled. I never scented my house. I tried to place the fragrance. Something super floral. I stepped back outside. They were there in moments.

"Someone's been in my house. I don't scent my house. CJ is the only one with a key, no entry notices from management so it wasn't them, but if the smell is still here then it's been within 24 hours."

Clarice had syths in her hands and went room to room with the efficiency of a Navy Seal. As Clarice rounded the corner to the bedroom and bathroom, Jean unsheathed hers and backed me into a corner until Clarice came back.

"It's clear. No one is here, but sweetie your room is a mess. You really should clean it more often." She said winking at me when she returned carrying CJ's duffle bag. "Hurry. Get your things and we need be out of here at once."

I went to my room and found it turned upside down. "By the way Clarice, I do keep my room clean. Someone really wanted to find something and obviously thought it was going to be here since the rest of the house is just as I left it." What could they possibly have wanted?

I grabbed what I could. A few pairs of jeans, clean undergarments, and a few shirts. I even threw in some of CJ's other clothes that he had indeed unpacked into my dresser. Sneaky little shit.

I went into the kitchen cleaned out the fridge and freezer and took it out to the garbage. Then I grabbed the key to my house safe in the back of the freezer. Winking at Clarice's dumbfounded face as I went and opened the safe that's in my video closet. I grabbed what cash was there, my passport, Matt's graduation ring, and the few pictures of my family from years past that I had left. Quickly, I grabbed a few papers off my desk, along with my dream journal, pictures of CJ and I's friends, and my good jacket off the hook by the door. I stuffed it all into my own duffle and headed out to meet back up with Jean and Clarice.

Jean and Clarice were standing in the dining room, staring at the drawing of the house framed up on the wall. Clarice smiled and Jean just kept looking at it, then at me, then back at it. I walked up to her and tried to explain.

"Since I was a kid, I always saw the house. So, I started drawing it. It started out as a rough stick figure place, with really bad trees in the background. Mom and Dad used to laugh at me when I would babble about the different parts of it that I couldn't figure out how to draw. They never once told me it was a real place or questioned how I got it so right." I said looking back at it. "Over time it became clearer, and my drawing got better. This version won me an accommodation at the Art & Wine Festival in Capitola, which is across the bay a few years back. Mom and Dad were proud of the accomplishment. They never let on... CJ and Amber insisted I just hang it up. They always loved it."

"It even has the purple smoke, and the archway to the garden." Jean said, a couple of tears escaping and slowly rolling down her cheeks before she looked back at me. "Those never changed?"

"The smoke was always purple." I said shrugging.

Jean simply walked over to the drawing, gently lifted it off the hook, and ran her hand over the frame. More tears caught in her eyes before she blinked them away then said softly, "This is coming with us."

I couldn't do anything but smile and nod in agreement. I didn't know the next time I would be back here, if ever. I pulled CJ's phone out, emailed the property manager to allow Amber access to the apartment, and then texted her asking her to please clean out the cupboard so if we did come back, it wouldn't be to rank in here. The text messages were coming in hot from our friends wanting more information, and I felt a lump in my throat as I replied, "We love you." hit send, and powered down the phone.

We headed back outside where the barbeque was all ready to go. She had even grabbed the coals and chimney to start the fire. When Clarice had ahold of my hand, we turned on the spot stepping into the blue smoke. It took longer this time and there were hints of dust and wet cement in the air just before we landed at the cottage.

I turned to Jean who looked back down at the picture and then at the house. Clarice handed me CJ's duffle back and headed toward the backyard with the barbeque.

"Jean?" I asked, not sure exactly what I was going to ask. Was she okay? Was it wrong I had drawn it? Should I have taken someone else so they wouldn't have seen it?

"Can we hang this in the house?" she said jerking her head up to me.

"Um, sure. I don't see why not?"

Jean just curtly nodded her head, wrapped her arms around the picture, and walked toward the house.

CJ must have been watching from the window because he met me just outside a few feet from the door. His eyes roved over me assessing, making sure that I was fine.

"I'm fine Ceej." I said with a sigh.

"What's going on? Is Jean okay? What happened?" He asked.

Someone broke into the apartment, but I can't figure out what they were looking for and I'm not even sure what they took. The only room they tore apart was the bedroom. Everything else was fine.

"Give me your bag, let's get unpacked." He said.

When we got to the bedroom, I told him about the conversation with his mom, and that I told her we were together. He smiled at that, kissed me then asked, "and what happened with Jean? She was clutching something and wouldn't say anything when she got back to the house, just headed back to her room."

"While I was packing, Clarice and Jean saw the picture hanging in the dining room."

"Ahh." He giggled. "I bet that was weird."

"Yea I'm sure it was, but Clarice just smiled. I think... I think it hit Jean differently." I said quietly.

We finished unpacking our things and headed back out to the main room. Clarice had filled in the others on what had happened at the house. Owen however, kept looking toward the bedroom.

"Don't worry. She'll be fine." I told him hoping I was right.

"What was that she brought back?" He asked. "She didn't say anything or show anyone when she came in. Just went straight to the bedroom and locked the door."

"A picture I drew." I said.

Owen's eyebrows raised in question, but I ignored him and turned to CJ, batting my eyelashes and in my sweetest voice, I cooed, "I'm starved, honey. Can you start the coals please?"

He laughed. "Oh, you are definitely one powerful being!"

I turned on my heels smiling and trotted off to the kitchen to start prepping the hamburgers.

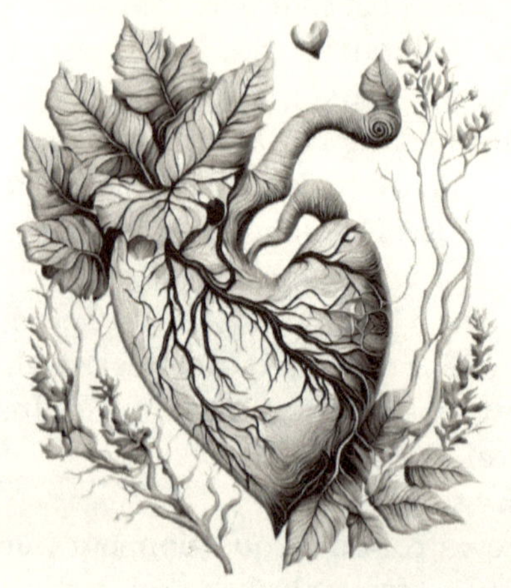

CHAPTER 11

OWEN HAD INDEED SENT word to the council that I was ready to complete the trial. To make it worse, the jerk asked for them to rush the request. Whatever pull they have with the Council apparently worked because it was granted. The whole idea of having to take a competency test for something I didn't know existed six months ago was ludicrous. Sure, I had taken other big and important tests before, but it still didn't make sense to me. They had told me over and over again I was ready, and that I would likely pass with flying colors. I didn't believe a damn word of it.

So, I crammed. When I say I crammed, I mean I studied every book I could get my hands on and spent every ounce of time I could out in the garden with Owen and Clarice as my training dummies. I wore them out to the point of pure exhaustion every day.

They would head off to bed, and I'd be back with my head in a book. I thought my head was literally going to explode. Thank the Angels for a simi-photographic memory, caffeine, and the 38-hour days here. I went to bed and passed out within seconds each night, but still only got a couple of hours of sleep a night and had the bags under my eyes to prove it. I didn't know how I was going to be able to retain all this. It was if I was going to school overseas and having to prep for the SATs in that country's native tongue, not knowing a single word of it before showing up for the test. Every night I went to bed wondering if I would just die from a brain aneurysm from all the information we were cramming in it.

CJ just sat there and tried to help me study all the books. He quizzed me, tested me, and even helped with flash cards, much to the entertainment of Lindy and Jean. He was supportive, but I knew he was worried too.

I was also working out more complicated incantations centered on protection and offense. Clarice had made it a personal priority to get me as well-rounded with a syth as possible. She had snagged a couple of Jean's spares and had been ruthless with me. I had been diced and sliced so much that if it were not for the Sa Ra around my neck, I would look like a cheese grater. The wounds healed quickly though and by the time we sat down for dinner at night they had almost healed completely. I'm not sure where they were getting a supply, but every week a new batch of clothes would arrive. Everything was just shredded by weeks end.

My trials were in a week and I still had so much to go through. The session with Jean and Owen today on incantations was unproductive, to say the least. Only because I had a hard time concentrating because Lindy was working with CJ in hand-to-hand combat. Each time he would take a swing, or work on defensive maneuvers, the rippling of his muscles would distract me to devastating levels. Owen on many occasions had just stood there poking me as I watched him. I couldn't help it, the sweat that ran down his temple, down his arms. The way it ran down his stomach when he lifted his shirt to wipe the sweat from his face... I was mesmerized.

"Sorry, Owen." I had said for the hundredth time.

"It's fine. I was young once too." He said and I glared at him. "Let's call it a day. You know all of this. It's just repetitive at this point. You should rest."

While CJ went and got cleaned up. I had tried so hard to stay awake. As he came out of the bathroom drying his hair, he took one look at me and told me I should be asleep. He crawled up into bed and laid down next to me, resting his hand on my hip.

"But I don't want to sleep." I said trying to pull him closer, but my arm muscles didn't have the strength they should.

"Megs. You can't even pull me to you right now." He said softly. He brought his head down to mine and kissed me softly. I wrapped a leg around him and used it to help pull him closer.

"I can muster the strength." I said against his lips, but then I froze at a thought, "unless you don't want to?"

"What? Megs." He said pulling back to look at me evenly. "Do you really think I don't want to have sex with you?"

I couldn't look at him. I kept my head down and he lifted my head to make me look at him, to meet his eyes. "Trust me when I say I do. Gods, every morning I see you head out to work with Clarice, it is so hard to let you walk out and not keep you captive for a few hours."

"Then why?" I said feeling very, very small.

"First of all because you need to rest. You have bags under the eyes that look like Clarice punched you. You need to get as much sleep as you can so the next day of studying and training will be productive. This is important, and I don't want to get in the way of it." He said firmly.

"Sex helps with stress." I said smiling as I ran my hands over his chest and down the side of his stomach.

His eyes shuddered and there was a small annoyed moaned at that, and then he let out a long, long ... long breath.

"You do not make it easy. That is for sure." He said heat in his eyes, as I ran my fingers along the waistline of his pants, "but the *other* reason I have been trying, so very ... very hard to wait, is because when we do cross that line Megs. When I do finally make love to you for the first time, I don't want the others to hear you scream in pleasure. I want you to myself, and I do not, under any circumstances want an audience."

"Scream in pleasure?" I said coyly. "I don't believe I'm a screamer."

"You will be by the time I'm done with you." He said nibbling on my ear. Everything in my gut tightened and a small whimper escaped.

Then that bastard, that wonderful, ever-loving bastard, rolled over, and said, "Good night, Megan."

I had laid there for a good 30 seconds just staring at his back before I pinched his ass and he rolled over and pulled me close.

"We have all the time in the world love. Get some sleep." He said tucking the blankets around me tight. I had been asleep within moments.

The council arrived exactly twenty days after Owen made the request. We were dressed in what was considered standard dress-casual wear for Sangra; blue jeans, a royal blue shirt with a black fitted coat that stopped mid-thigh, which I had to admit was very comfortable. When I saw CJ walk out of the bedroom in it, my jaw dropped. He strode out into the hall buttoning his belt as I made the turn around the corner and froze. I hadn't meant to stare, but for all that was love and holy.

"What?" He said genuinely perplexed.

"Um." I stammered while I slowly looked him up and down. "Um."

A slow sly smile crossed his lips. "Megan you are drooling."

"I am not!" I said hastily wiping my mouth because frankly, I could have been.

"You were and thank you." He said redness filling his cheeks.

It took everything I could do not to pull him back into that bedroom and have my way with him. We had teased each other each night since that night a week ago, but we still hadn't crossed that final line.

CJ just took my hand and led me out to the examinations. The thought of CJ and I tangled up in bed together was making me smile like a schoolgirl, and it wasn't until Owen jabbed me in the ribs that I realized I hadn't been paying attention to the proctor.

"Megan, please take a seat and we will get your examinations completed." A woman in a short royal blue wraparound dress said. The Nalrin proctor they had told me, but she refused to give me her name.

My eyes flickered to CJ as I headed for the desk and he gave me a reassuring smile and mouthed, "You got this."

I sat down and saw the examination tablet in front of me. The woman picked it up, entered my information, pressed her pointer finger and pinky to the screen, and then asked me to do the same. I did, and the first section of the exam showed on the screen. Language Skills. I knew there were a lot of basics included in the written portion of the test. Things like language skills, mathematics, Nalsar history, Nalrin history and science.

I passed the written part of the trial but missed questions in regard to some of the ancient history and science, but Owen told me that was to be expected considering I have only known of Nalsar's existence for less than a year. There was no way I could know of Nalsar's history and scientific advances to the extent that someone who had lived here their whole life had.

My physical trials were scheduled for the afternoon, and I was allowed to have lunch, under the proctor's supervision in the living room. I wasn't allowed to talk to my family or study anymore during that time period. I either knew it or I didn't at that point.

After eating, I had my incantation practical, which I passed without too much trouble. I just had to show I knew how to cast specific incantations, verbally and non-verbally. Piece of cake.

By mid-afternoon, I was ready for my physical combat practical which included a syth usage examination with another proctor, whose name again, wasn't given to me. She was a woman who looked to be about my age, and when she took her jacket off my stomach dropped. She was completely ripped. Our syths were enchanted to leave bright yellow or green marks on the other's body to show where we would have made a connection instead of slicing each other up. I had just had the thought of killing Clarice for not doing that during training when the proctor said, "You may start."

The woman lunged for me, and I saw her just in time to duck and swing my leg out to knock her over, which she had the grace to miss. I crouched a moment longer and then swung up to hit her in the ribs, but she blocked it with her forearm, moving in a way to keep me off balance as I fell to the ground. On my way down she sliced my arm and there was a bright green slice from my elbow to my wrist. SHIT.

Without thinking I went for a good old fashion punch that connected with her jaw, and as the momentum of the swing followed through, my syth left a gash of yellow on her cheek. I brought my knee up to her chin as she bent over, kicked her legs out from under her, and flipped her onto her back. When she landed, I had my knee on her chest and my syth at her throat.

"DEAD!" The proctor yelled.

I looked up in shock. It hadn't been five minutes, but the woman under me took advantage of my distraction and swung me around and onto my back, locked my arms, and put her syth just under my ribs angled for my heart. In an Irish like accent, she whispered in my ear, "Even if you think your ahpponent dead, dahn't 'esitate to ensure it, fahr if ya 'hadn't, you would now be the dead one."

"Also, dead." the proctor said with a small smile.

The woman I was sparring with smiled and helped me up. "Pass 'er." She said with a wicked smile.

The proctor looked at her and then to me, then back to her. "but you pinned her after. There are also supposed to be three fights. Syth, staff, and longsword."

My stomach dropped. I had practiced many times with a staff, but longsword? I had no idea how to use one. My eyes flicked to Clarice and narrowed on her. She had a small smirk on her lips and was trying not laugh.

"Yes, but she mahved quick and doesn't 'esitate. Clarice training 'er. Aye? I know dat style anywhere." She said grinning to Clarice, who just gave an imperceptible nod. "Plus, she 'ad me dead, before I 'ad 'er. We can do the other mediums, but I still recommend pass."

A nod from the proctor and she said, "Go into the garden to await all results."

I reached out my hand to CJ, who shook his head. The proctor saw the motion, and said, "You are to wait alone. You are to reflect upon your teachings, and we will meet you shortly."

I sat there on the ground in the corner hidden behind a fern. It blocked some of the light, and I just sat there, knees to my chest, head on my knees and wrapping my arms around my legs. It's an electronic test, they already told me I passed. The physical trial was supposed to be a pass, but why not move forward with the other two weapons? I turned my head and saw a lot of bright green marks on my arms and a couple of them down my leg. How many did I really get on my opponent? Are they re-evaluating them?

CHAPTER 12

TWENTY MINUTES LATER, A thin man who was no more than 5 feet tall, with bright electric blue eyes was talking to Jean and Owen as they came through the archway of the garden. It took me a minute to recognize him as Julian the Head of Nalsar. I had seen a lot of pictures of him, and those made him look older. His pitch-black hair was shaved on both sides, the top French braided and wrapped in white leather at the various intervals that went halfway down his back, but there was one small section that was in a dread with silver accents. His beard, which was braided in 6 strands down his chest, was black as night and he wore a white fitted coat, white pants, and a dark red shirt, instead of the blue ones, like the others. The coats were tailored so that no matter how tall a council member was, it always stopped about mid-thigh.

They turned to me and I stood up without thinking.

"I am Julian. Head of Nalrin." He said as I bowed formally.

"Nice to meet you sir." I said trying to keep my voice from shaking.

"I would like to congratulate you on completing your trials. You have passed and now it is time to perform the Maltal ceremony."

"I'm sorry? Now?" I said completely blindsided and standing up straight. Why had no one told me? Was this normal? Did it usually happen immediately after your trials?

"Who will stand with her and perform the application of the Maltal?" Julian said as the rest of my family walked in behind Julian.

"Owen and I will as her relatives, Julian." Jean said with a short bow of her own. Owen bowed beside her and looked at me with respect and reverence.

"Hope you don't care for that shirt too much." Jean said smiling at me as she and Owen came to stand in front of me and set a hand on my shoulder.

Julian placed a stone tablet that looked to be about 8 inches by 8 inches and a thick odd pen looking instrument just in front of me on the ground. He started humming a tune as he drew green vertical ovals in the air with both hands around Owen, Jean and me.

When he had finished drawing the green ovals, which ended up looking like an intricate green band around us, Julian looked at me, clapped his hands together, and then said in a booming voice that made me want to cover my ears, "*Qualium testalin Maltal soolimar binaltar.*"

The green band bent and stretched until it extended to meet above us like a closed flower bud. I looked to Jean and Owen, not knowing what to do next.

"Pick up the instrument and draw your Maltal on the stone. It will be transferred onto your back between your shoulder blades." Owen instructed me in a whisper.

We knelt to the ground, I picked up the instrument and turned to Jean still not completely knowing how to do this. "Why didn't you warn me about this? I could have practiced. How do I even know what to draw?"

I was starting to panic. There were all these people here to watch this happen, and I just knelt here like an idiot. My hands were shaking, and I was sweating profusely.

She leaned in to whisper into my ear, "Don't think, just let it move across the stone. You know what to draw, you just have to let it flow out of you."

When I just stared at the stone, Owen whispered, "It can be anything. Anything you want. It can be as small as an ant, or as large as your shoulders. The only requirement is that the center must sit in-between your shoulder blades. So, pick a small flower, a phoenix, an arrow, a wolf, or your own design that encompasses everything you love in your life. It is yours, and uniquely yours. "

I closed my eyes and took a deep breath. Anything. It can be one thing or many things. I closed my eyes and let my power guide me as I searched through memories. CJ was always present. There was the beach back at home, the warm sun in the fall, all of it within my box of memories.

I felt my hand moving across the stone, first a circle to contain it all, a warm sun that flowed into the waves of the ocean, the beach, a tree to represent the roots of CJ's love. Those roots became the circle to encompass it all.

There was more though. More that I hadn't thought of. There was the warmth of a new family I had found here. Jean, Owen, Clarice, and Lindy had to have representation. This was part of my life now too. I let their warmth and acceptance decorate the outer edges of my circle as sporadic daisies and leaves. Representations of me growing as a person and as a Sangra.

When I opened my eyes and looked down upon the tablet, it was PERFECT. It glowed the same deep shade of green as the ovals around us. Jean and Owen looked as if they were going to cry as they looked at me.

"Finished" I whispered not knowing how long I had been kneeling there working on it. It showed everything and everyone I cared about in ways I hadn't thought possible. Owen and Jean stood up, left a hand on my shoulders, and took each other's hand.

"*Qualium testalin Maltal soolimar binaltar.*" They whispered together. The outer green ovals sparkled and slowly pulled in from the bottom to the top point of the flower bud that completely surrounded us. When it reached the top, it morphed into the shapes I had drawn on the stone. Owen and Jean's hands slid down my arms and held onto my hands.

I was weightless as I was lifted from the ground to the symbol. No, to my Maltal. It circled me for a minute, then positioned itself behind me. I felt heat against my back and a moment later there was a burning sensation where my Maltal was now pressing on my back, burning through my shirt just between my shoulder blades. I gritted my teeth. It didn't hurt per se, but it singed and pulled at my bones. There was a sharp jolt that burst through my veins and I twitched just once. It felt like I had put my finger in a light socket and the electricity was binding to me. It was the binding that continued to pull on my core as electricity flooded through me, as it filled every crevice of my body. I could hear it crackle and hum in my ears and as I felt the burning sensation on my back retreat, bright green light with thin small streaks of blue burst from my chest.

Moments later, I slowly felt myself being lowered to the ground. When my feet touched again, I looked up to my family, to the Council members, and to Julian. Their eyes were wide ... in shock? CJ stood there beaming at me, his eyes lined with tears he sniffed back. Slowly the Council and my family looked to Julian who gave a quick shake of his head as if he were trying to clear something and smiled. Julian, the Council, and my family bowed in unison. When they rose, my family stared at me for a long moment, awed but confused looks on their face.

Julian walked forward and said, "Congratulations Ms. Megan. Your Maltal will continue to set in over the next few weeks and will center your power. However, you will need to be careful with your powers as they will continue to grow more powerful as your Maltal settles. You have a solid family base here to help you control and learn how to use them more effectively."

Julian looked at each and every one of my family with a look to convey a message that I did not understand. His eyes had sat on Clarice a little longer than any of my other family. She had even lowered her head to break the eye contact. Julian simply smiled at CJ before turning on his heels and walked to where the stone I drew my Maltal on, now sat blank. It lifted from the ground and into Julian's hands along with the writing instrument.

"Farewell all, the Council will leave you now." Julian said, and everyone, including CJ and I, bowed to them in respect.

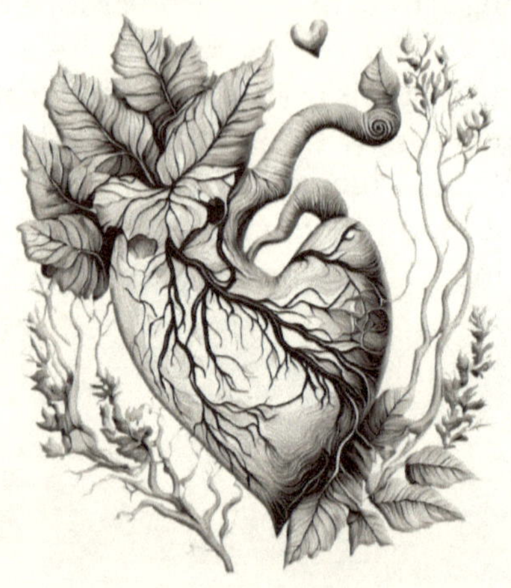

CHAPTER 13

IT HAD BEEN A long emotional day. We came back into the house, and after everyone ate dinner, I told them I just wanted to head to bed. My Maltal was still warm against my back, and energy was crawling throughout my body, but I was mentally exhausted.

I shed my clothes and let them lay in the corner as I took a quick hot shower. I grabbed a short light-weight pink sleeping gown with lace trim and thin straps from the closet. I had thought that this probably wasn't made for actual sleeping, but I was too tired to care. It slipped on easily, and it was long enough to cover my ass.

I pushed the blankets back and proceed to lay there for over an hour, tossing and turning. The feeling of the power coursing through my veins made it very difficult to sleep. It felt as though I had put a 9V battery to my tongue, but through my entire body. My leg muscles were twitching so bad that I gave up sleeping entirely and started pacing the bedroom. It was another hour before it calmed enough that I was able to at least sit somewhat still.

I climbed up on the bed, sat cross-legged, closed my eyes, and just tried to take long deep breaths. I focused on grounding the electricity firing through me and coiling it up at my naval.

Breathe in. Breathe out.

I pulled at the energy and coiled it up into a ball.

Breathe in. Breathe out and coil.

Breathe in. Breathe out and coil.

Click.

I twitched and some of the electricity bolted to my fingertips. I could almost feel them sparking before I gritted my teeth and started in again.

Breathe in. Breathe out and coil.

Breathe in. Breathe out and coil.

Over and over again until I didn't feel like my power was going to make a run for it. I slowly opened my eyes and found CJ sitting on the other end of the bed reading a book.

I cocked my head to the side. When did he come in?

I just stared at him. He had even showered and changed for bed without my notice.

My stomach tightened at the sight of him sitting there in a pair of lightweight sleep pants, hair wet, disheveled, and reading. I bit my lower lip as my power responded as well, and I had to take a real deep breath and coil it back in again, or there were going to be real live sparks flying in this room tonight.

"Are you going to say anything or are you just going to look at me like I'm a midnight snack?" he said not taking his eyes off the book he was reading.

I bit my lip a little harder. I could eat him up. The thought of that had electric heat burst through me and settle between my thighs pulsing. Think of something else Megan. Something else. Anything else. Grandma's teeth in a jar, the smell of sewer overflowing in the street...

"Thought I'd find you conked out." He said quietly. He slid a bookmark in and put the book on the nightstand.

"I feel like my skin is electrified." I said as he moved to come sit next to me.

"When I came in you were in your own little world." He said tucking a hair behind my ear and smiled.

"What?" I said.

"Your eyes. They seem ... brighter." He whispered. "Come on let's try to get some sleep. It's late."

I didn't think I could sleep yet, so I just laid there watching him. He didn't sleep either, but instead slowly and lightly ran his hand up and down my arm. It took a bit of concentration not to let my power uncoil, but there was something just so intimate about laying there with him.

My mind started to wander, and then a question came to mind.

"Yet?" I asked quietly. While I tried to say it with a whisper, it still sounded too loud for the room.

"Hum?" He was obviously in deep thought.

"You said *yet* when I was explaining to everyone that we hadn't made anything official." I could feel the blood rushing to my cheeks. "In terms of our relationship I mean."

He was smiling that same smile he knew I couldn't resist. "Yes *yet*. I don't care if we get married here or at home, but I do want to make it official."

"Cory James if that is a proposal, you seriously have to work on your delivery." I sat up and chuckled. He laughed nervously and I knew he was waiting for my response.

"Of course, I'll marry you, but..." I paused and I felt his whole body twitch. "I would like it to be after all this is done with. Is that okay?"

"Perfectly fine. I'm not going anywhere and well you couldn't get rid of me if you tried. Yes, even with all that power you have." He said relaxing and letting a sly smile cross his face again.

"What?" I said when his face dropped.

"It's something I've been thinking about for a while, and I have to ask. Will you want someone to give you away? I'm sure Owen or even my dad would be more than willing. It's always been every woman's dream to have her father give her away. You had yours, lost him, and now we believe he may be alive, but..." he trailed off.

I knew what he meant. He didn't want to say he didn't want my father there, and I honestly at this point, wasn't sure myself.

"I don't know babe. I mean if my father really is building the weapon of the Five Angels. I don't want anyone in my life who can be that mean and cruel. Let's not forget the fact that you have my heart and he's gonna need that in order to create this damn thing..." my voice caught on the verge of tears. I couldn't and wouldn't think of that as even being a possibility. "I will use every ounce of myself to protect you."

"I know." He said and then looked me up and down, raised eyebrow and all. "I like the nighty."

"It's surprisingly comfortable." I said heat rising to my cheeks.

"Then we will have to get more." he said as he pulled me on top of him. I straddled him and felt him hard against me. I wiggled a bit and the sound that came out of him was between a whimper and a yip.

"You foul beast." He said through his teeth.

I bent down to kiss him softly and his hands roamed under the hemline and squeezed my ass. I ground into him more.

"Megs." He said against my lips.

"Hum?" I said grinding against him some more.

He ran his hand up my side and ran his thumb back and forth across my stomach, just under my breasts, and kissed me again. He pulled back slightly, his eyes full of heat, and whispered, "At this point, I don't care if the entire dimension hears you scream."

He ripped the nightgown off in one swift motion and had my left breast between his lips half a second later. His tongue flicked the nipple and my back arched, my breasts tightening.

I felt him smile and move to the right breast, biting down on it causing a wave of pleasure to wash over me. I ground against him more and he moved his hands around to my ass again, his lips never leaving my breasts.

CJ rolled me over onto my back, nipple still between his teeth. The motion caused it to stretch and for him to bite down harder where I let out a whimper. His eyes met mine and there was question there. As in answer, I pulled his pants off.

As I looked down at his considerable length, my mouth watered. I reached down and took him in my hand and stroked him gently. His lips found mine and I swallowed a moan from him. He released the kiss and slowly kissed his way down my neck and bit down hard on the left breast before he kissed his way down my stomach, hips, and then my thighs. His eyes never once left mine.

"I am not done feasting on you yet." He said with a raspy voice. "I have had years to think of how to pleasure you."

Throwing my legs wide, he kissed each side of that spot between my legs, before taking one long sensuous lick down the center. When he reached my nub, he sucked down on it at the same time he slid two fingers inside me.

"OH, FUCK CEEJ." I said unable to help myself and grabbing onto the sheets. He just kept licking and sucking as those fingers curled in and out of me. It didn't take much before I was riding his face. He didn't miss a step. His tongue met me stroke for stroke as his fingers fucked me.

I felt myself getting closer and closer. I reached down and moved his hair out of the way, gripping it tight. He moaned as he took another long lick up my middle, nipped my nub, and sucked it just as my thighs pressed against him and I came. I could swear the room got brighter and dimmed as he slowed, but only slightly, taking his time to drink it all in.

Taking one last nibble at my clit, making my whole-body spasm, he brushed slow kisses on my stomach, each breast, then I was tasting myself on his lips, sending another wave of pleasure through me.

He leaned back a bit and brushed a hair off my face. "Gods I've wanted to do that for so long. You tasted better than I dreamed." He whispered before he kissed me again.

"Now that you've had your taste, it's my turn." I said wryly, as I reached down and ran one nail along his length. With the other hand I pushed him onto his back and kissed down his stomach. When I reached the full length of him, my mouth watered again in anticipation. I stroked him a few more times and held his balls in my hand as I heard him moan.

Just to be a tease, I slowly let my tongue circle around the head of him and his hips rose ever so slightly. I ran the tip of my tongue down the underside of him and around each of his balls, to the base of his shaft twice, before as he started wiggling against me. I pushed down on his hips with both hands to keep him from moving as I slowly, very slowly ran my tongue up to the head.

"You tease." He said throwing his head back and grabbing onto the headboard.

"You have no idea." I said and repeated the motion three more times. He was hard as a rock, and I couldn't wait anymore.

I slide the tip of him into my mouth, sucking gently and releasing him with a pop. I slowly took him back into my mouth and all the way down my throat. He moaned a curse under his breath and writhed under me. I slowly sucked and licked his length up and down a few times, before taking him fully again. I marveled at the silkiness of him as he slid in and out of my mouth.

When he was fully down my throat, I moaned at the taste of him. The vibration from my moan caused a real hiss and a loud curse to echo through our room. I repeated the motion over and over again, as I felt him tightening under me and I did not stop. I moved faster, ensuring he went deep down my throat each time.

He placed his hand on my head and in a few deep thrusts, spewed cum straight down the back of my throat. He moaned loudly as I swallowed each and every delicious drop. The feel of him releasing to me was so satisfying that I could feel myself getting wet all over again. I slowly, very slowly licked him clean.

When I looked up, he put both hands on my cheeks, pulled me up to kiss me hard. I grabbed onto his bottom lip, biting it gently as I wrapped my leg around his hip.

"I ... I" CJ said through panted breaths. "I've imagined what having your lips around me would be like, but *fuck* Megs. I have no words." His hand circled around behind me to play with my ass, but noticing how wet I was, slowly slid a finger into me while pressing another against my ass.

"Ceej." I breathed reaching down to stroke him.

"I knew you were an ass girl." He said smirking, but I just ground against him in answer.

He laid onto his back and allowed me to straddle him. He was hardening quickly against me again, and I moved my hips in small precise movements. When he was good and hard again, I leaned forward to kiss him, but he took advantage of me being distracted to plunge deep into me.

"For the Angels, Megan." He said when he was fully in me as I let out a moan of pleasure.

I looked down at him and we just sat there frozen for that one moment. After years of envisioning this, of wishing I could have CJ in this way. He was mine. Heart, body, and soul. He really was mine. And damn he felt good. So damn good.

When I looked down at him again, a small mischievous smile crossed his lips. There was a flash of wicked need in his eyes, as he slowly retreated to the very head of him and thrust back in. He repeated the motion a couple of times before I slammed back into him as he took my breasts in his hand and bit down on my right nipple. I saw stars as the mix of pleasure and pain made me orgasm again.

I met him thrust for thrust. I was moaning and hissing at the pleasure that went through me. His teeth scraped against my neck as he slapped my ass hard.

"Fuck yeah." I said through gritted teeth. I sat up straight and rode him harder. At every deep thrust, he slapped my ass hard. I dug my nails into his shoulders and was getting closer and closer to that final release.

We were drenched in sweat as he sat up and I wrapped my legs around him. I moved my hips against him as he kissed me with my name on his lips. I could feel him twitching inside me as I moved against him again and again. He held me close as I rode him faster and faster.

"Please, Megs." CJ said as he held me by the ass and laid me on my back.

He kissed me hard then pounded into me hard and fast.

"Yes." I moaned loudly, as I felt my tension mounting. I raised my hips to meet each one of his deep pounding thrusts.

He grabbed my hands and pinned them above my head, kissed me, and in a few more deep strokes, released himself deep within me. He continued pounding into me and reached down to flick my left nipple with his tongue and then bit down sending me over the edge.

My release was hard and fast as I indeed, roared his name for the world to hear.

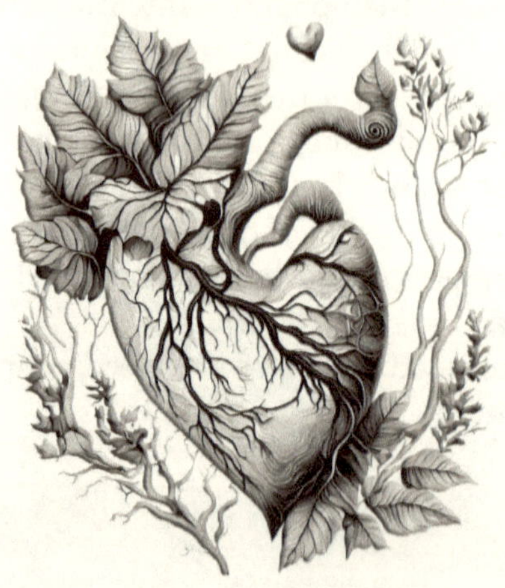

CHAPTER 14

AFTER BREAKFAST THE NEXT morning we sat in the main room discussing all the different aspects of the Five Angels and what my parents would need for their weapon. I kept getting side smiles from Lindy and finally growled at her, "Say it Lindy."

"Enjoy your night?" She said smiling.

I sighed and debated what to say.

"I don't know Lindy. CJ was quieter than she was. Not sure—" Owen said as CJ threw a pillow at him.

"Shut it!" I said to them all. They just looked at me with huge smiles on their faces. I just quipped the stupidest thing I could think of, "You're just jealous that you didn't get any last night."

Owen went to open his mouth, but Jean threw a book at him, narrowly missing his ear.

"I'll teach you the incantation to keep sounds within a room." Jean said.

"WHY DID YOU GUYS NOT TEACH THAT TO ME EARLIER!" I retorted.

"We thought maybe you two were just quiet when having sex." Lindy said smirking then shrugged, "We were wrong."

Heat flooded my face and I looked to CJ who just stood there smiling. I could almost hear him say, *See I told you I would have you screaming.*

Clarice came to my rescue though and said, "Don't worry, once we heard the first moans from the bedroom, we went out to give you guys privacy. We didn't hear everything."

I sighed and went to get some water. CJ muttered something under his breath that didn't sound so kind as I stepped into the kitchen. Owen just gave him a thumbs up and bellowed a laugh.

I reached into the fridge to get a bottle of water and thought over the story Lindy had told me the second day I was here. I walked back into the other room and they had brought the subject back around to the matter at hand. I went to plop back onto the couch and vaguely heard Lindy chatter, "...one thing that has been bothering me about that. Something that she saw in her vision... Megan. ... Megan." she said pulling my attention back to her.

"Hmmm, what was that?" I said.

"After you had your vision, you told us that your father said that the flower came first and that they only had few weeks. But this year doesn't have a third Friday the 13th. In fact, there isn't one for another 46 years, I think. Can you really see things that far in the future?"

"Well, I saw CJ flying to see me often. I've seen people calling before they do. Not to mention that I saw Matt die for months before it happened. I'm only 24. I don't remember at what point my visions started coming true. I knew I had them at least from 8 years old and on, and they came true, but I don't know the accuracy over a longer length of time." I told her somewhat preoccupied.

Something wasn't right about what she said about Friday the 13th. There was a third Friday the 13th before that right? I got up and went into the bedroom. Didn't I read something off of a website not too long ago about it? I dug through some of the paperwork I had grabbed from the house, and there it was. An article off the National Geographic website back in March. So, I wasn't crazy! Okay, maybe I was, but that wasn't the point.

As I walked into the main room all eyes were on me. "You were saying there wasn't another third Friday the 13th occurring for another forty some odd years. Right?"

"That is correct." She eyed me curiously.

"See, back in March there was an article by National Geographic that explained the Friday the 13th phenomena. They were saying how every 11 years it falls in consecutive months, as it did this year, but that this year it also falls on three Fridays: March 13; April 13; and again on November 13. So, there is another Friday the 13th coming soon, just not here. It is back at in the Manusia. My guess is that they will be plucking that flower from my dimension, not yours." The room was so quite you could hear a pin drop.

I studied everyone's faces. I had to be right. "If that is true, we should check other dimensions to as well to see if there are any falling this year. If the Manusia is the only one that has one, then we have a little less than a month till the next Friday the 13th? Question is, does anyone know what and where the rarest flower in Manusia is?" asked Jean.

"Actually, I do. I did my Botanical Biology paper on it in college." CJ said. "It's the Desumo Nitor, or Electric Brilliance. It's a pure snow white flower that has 13 wide pointed petals with bright blue tips. It hangs upside down from a vine. What makes it so rare is that the Desumo Nitor only stays in bloom when attached to the vine from midnight to dawn, and blooming only on Friday the 13th. From what I read the flower will stay in an open bloom for up to six months if it is cut from the vine when it blooms. Botanists who have studied it say that as it hangs from the vine, it breathes.

"The only known location for where the flower grows in the wild is in São Tomé. It is said there is a meadow filled with them, but it is so hard to find, that botanists only study the captive grown ones." He paused, thinking for a moment before explaining, "In fact I think there is usually a huge viewing scheduled in San Francisco of some that are privately grown."

"I'm sorry where does it grow? Sow what?" I asked him. The place rang a bell, but I couldn't place the location.

"São Tomé. As in São Tomé and Principe. It's off the African coast right on the equator."

"Isn't the question, whether they are going to go to the wild in São Tomé or steal one from the viewing?" Jean asked looking at both of us.

"From the wild I'm willing to bet. They don't want to be discovered. Something like stealing one of the rarest flowers from in front of thousands wouldn't fit into keeping everything on the down low would it? I mean it would be a red flag to the Council." Lindy said as she paced. "Remember that lore says that you have to pluck it when it is in bloom. They will go to the meadow and pluck one of the flowers in the wild and keep it to give them time. I'm sure of it. The room for the ceremony in Noctulanar is far too difficult to find to rush it."

"But if it's so hard to find, would they take that chance?" Jean asked.

"It all makes sense now." I said.

"I'm sorry what makes sense?" CJ asked.

"Well, São Tomé is an island off Africa? Tropical? Rainforest or Jungle?" He nodded and I continued, "I've been having dreams of us walking along a river in a jungle rainforest area. We were looking for a meadow. I really thought those were just dreams, but it makes sense now."

I watched Lindy pace the whole room. No one said much of anything for a long time, but everyone watched her. Clarice sat down next to me on the couch and I leaned over asking her, "Why does she happen to know so much about the Five Angels? You and Owen always turn to her for answers to them."

"She was on the council," then she hesitated a minute, "just as your father was banished ... and the battle. As a council member, you know more than your average Sangra, and she knows more of The Five Angels than any other council member. Probably ever. That is all I will tell you." Her voice had a finality to it, that I just nodded and leaned back.

After several more minutes the room got fuzzy and I wasn't looking at the main room of the house anymore. I forced myself to sit still and appear as though I was still staring at the vaulted ceiling, even though what I was really looking at was could only be described as a castle entryway. There were books everywhere. A library maybe? No that isn't quite right, but there were a lot of scrolls, books ... archives? Ancient archives maybe?

I saw myself being held midair, a black misty rope pinning my arms to my sides, Jean in a heap on the floor, Owen standing straight as a stick like he was bound and gagged by an invisible force, staring horrified at Jean. Lindy was off to the side fighting off a creature that had the head of a bobcat, the body of a cheetah, and claws like a raptor. She jumped onto the being's back, and she used her short sword to decapitate it. Before her feet hit the floor, she had turned to my father glaring.

"Don't do this Ansel." She said.

"Angel of Love. I need my daughter's heart." Ansel said turning to face me and with a voice, I would have never expected to hear from my father he spat the words, "Apparently your mother and I were not the only ones keeping secrets all these years, were we Megan. You will pay for Matt's death."

The look on my face was horrifying, as I struggled to break free. "I will pay for Matt's death? Matt was killed in a car crash, you idiot! How could that possibly be MY fault!? I was at work when it happened."

My vision shimmered and I was looking into CJ's eyes. Then there was nothing but blue smoke. My mother had disappeared as well.

"NOOOOOOOOOOOO!" I screamed as my eyes refocused.

Owen was the first to speak. "What did you see?"

"Nothing. I need to get some fresh air." Then I was at a dead run to the garden.

I sat among the vines and flowers for an hour or more before CJ came out. He found me sitting with my knees to my chest, chin resting on my knees, and my arms tightly wrapped around them. For minutes or hours, he sat in front of me as we just looked at each other.

"You're not going to tell us what you saw are you?" he finally said reaching over and taking my hand.

"No. I'm not." I told him breaking eye contact. I expected him to put up a fight. Tell me that we can't try to prevent it or prepare for it unless we know what to prevent or prepare for, but he didn't.

"Ok, well let's go inside. Get some lunch." He sighed. He pulled me up and half carried me back to the house. Halfway back, I held on to his waist as tight as I could. He stopped and looked at me.

"Ceej. I will keep you safe. I promise you that." I swore to him.

"I know." He said bringing his forehead to meet mine. "And know that I would die to keep you safe. I would do anything to keep you safe."

"I know." I breathed and felt a zapping pulse flow between the two of us.

He heard the sadness and truth in my voice.

He stopped and met my stare again. There was realization and a touch of fear in that gaze. He opened his mouth as to say something, but instead reached up, cupping my cheek, and kissed me softly.

He knew what I had seen had to do with him getting hurt or killed and he wasn't going to make me relive it by giving him the details. Yet.

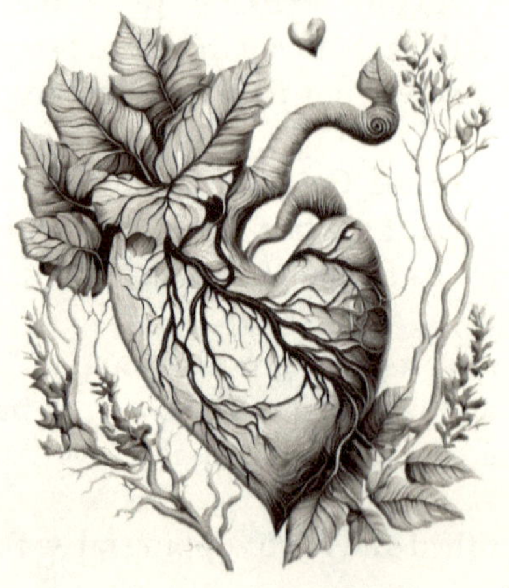

CHAPTER 15

I WAS GETTING BETTER at hiding my visions when I was awake, but the ones at night were harder to hide. I would dream of us fighting creatures made of pure black in an old stone room with a giant black pool, or of skeletons circling my waist. Worst of all, I still saw the vision in the hall where CJ is taken by my father just about every night. I would wake up screaming or thrashing and CJ would just comfort me and tell me they were just dreams. The rational part of us both knew better, but it calmed me. A solid night's sleep just wasn't something I had since my Maltal ceremony.

I would of course have some that didn't wake CJ. Those usually consisted of a power I was able to perfect, or a conversation with the family, or of us standing in a courtyard with fountains surrounded by some sort of army. One that was perplexing was one where I was sitting in an old abandoned overgrown church or castle, unwrapping a black crystal. Just as my fingers would touch it, I would be surrounded by a bright white light, and wake up.

Others, however, showed glimpses of us in São Tomé. I had actually laughed out loud at one I had while Jean and I were standing in the kitchen making lunch one day. Owen had just reached out, grabbed a snake that was hanging from a tree, and launching it 100 yards from where he was before, then he just kept calmly walking along the path as nothing had happened.

"Yea that sounds like him." Jean had told me with a laugh. "He doesn't like snakes at all. Unless they are in a soup."

In a little over a week, we were heading home. Home. Wasn't this home now? Would CJ want to live in this world or in Manusia? What would I do if he wanted to go home and I wanted to stay here? Could he even live in this world? Would he even be allowed to live here? Would life really ever be normal again? I was still learning so much about this life I had never known and wanted to know more.

I sat on the edge of the bed in the bedroom twirling a shirt in my hands, that I was supposed to be folding and putting away. I stood up and threw it on the bed. My heart was racing, and I felt my power rise and make my skin crawl. They kept telling me how powerful I was, how I was able to do things with little or no instruction, and how rare a gift that is. They all trusted my visions so truly, and I couldn't.

What if my visions were leading us down a road that leads to disaster?

What if I get someone killed because of them?

I was pacing in the bedroom when CJ walked in. I threw myself into his arms and starting crying.

"I don't know if I can do this!" I sobbed.

"It's okay, baby. Calm down. Don't know if you can do what?" he said.

"This! I mean, this whole saving the world of Nalsar thing. I know that no one has worded it that way, but that's what it is. Isn't it?" I mumbled into his shoulder.

He pulled me back and looked me straight in the eye.

"I'm not a hero CJ. I'm just Megan. What if everyone gets hurt? What if we go to one place because of a vision, but we needed to be somewhere else? I can't handle losing another family member! I've lost my parents and my brother. Worst, what if someone else dies? What if I lose you?!" I looked at him wide-eyed pleading with him to understand.

"Well, you haven't really lost your parents." He tried to comfort me, but I shot him an evil look. He was avoiding the last part of that obviously.

"It feels as though I have. I lost them in the house explosion, and now ... JUST KIDDING! THEY ARE ALIVE! Great, now I have to lose them twice?!" I got up again and started pacing.

"Oh, wait there's more. Yea, that's right, not only are they alive and well, but guess what, you have phenomenal cosmic powers! Even though I hadn't been using them for 24 years, but now that you are here, guess what, CRASH COURSE!" CJ just looked at me, cocked an eyebrow, and crossed his arms across the chest.

"Oh, what that isn't enough crazy shit for you? Did I forget to mention that not only are they alive, but because of them, some great council may be to blame for killing your brother, and now your parents are on this journey to destroy a world you have family in? And you guessed it; Now it's all up to you to make it right. Go against your parents to save the new family you have found and SAVE THE NALSAR WORLD MEGAN!" I shouted at him as I threw my hands up and crumpled to the floor. Angry, frustrated, red hot tears were now freely flowing down my cheeks.

He started to chuckle. "Ok first of all. It sounds ridiculous when you put it that way."

I shot him another look as I said, "It is ridiculous. But here we are."

"Megs, look at it this way. Even if it weren't your parents, even if they were just some other crazy people doing this, would you still want to help?"

"Of course, I would. You know that." Sounding very small.

"I do, that's why you just have to trust in yourself. They are trusting you. You also have to trust in them to help you. They will. I overhear them talking all the time. They truly believe in you. That includes your visions. Trust in me to help keep you safe."

"But what if they or even worst you get killed? I can't handle that. I can't control these visions. I can only focus on so much jungle. Not to mention I'm getting visions of us in a library or maybe it's an ancient castle, and it's all starting to look the same. I've never had this many in a week, and it's getting to the point, I can't tell the difference anymore. I don't know what they all mean." I got up and plopped on the bed.

"It's all just becoming a big jumbled mess. Then I have to get used to having all this power running through me. Not to mention how much everything has changed in so little time. Ceej, five years ago things were so much different. Hell, just three years ago. It's all so unbelievably frustrating."

CJ sat on the bed and just watched me. He knew I just needed to rant it out at this point. He knew me better than anyone. Sometimes, I didn't need him to fix it. I just needed to bitch. He also knew he couldn't fix it, which I think really frustrated him.

"SHIT!" I cursed. "Just stop already." I banged the heels of my hand on the side of my head as my head got fuzzy again. I was in a big room with castle like décor and archives everywhere. Someone was crying. I followed the sound around the stacks and I could feel CJ squeeze my hands just to let me know he was there and that it wasn't real.

I rounded a corner and saw my mother hunched over my father crying with his eyes wide open in front of a mirror. The mirror was just a simple wood framed mirror with no decoration. There was no reflection to it. Just an ominous mist beyond the glass.

"Ansel don't, I'll do it." My mother said but he just waved her off.

"MATTHEW!!!! ... Why? ... It's my fault! .... No, it was her. Your sister! She's the one who did this to you. If she hadn't seen this, it wouldn't have happened!" My mother jumped back; shock clear across her face.

What? Was he really blaming me for Matt dying?

My father started mumbling again "No. I don't want to kill you, but you will not take Symatha's life." He was quiet again.

"Sorry, my brother." My brother?

"No, you can't take my Symatha." He paused only for a moment then continued. "Yes, I will. All of them shall be avenged."

Then the whole vision shimmered again, and my father and mother were standing in front of the same mirror holding a crystal that glowed. Then the whole thing faded away.

I blinked and CJ was in front of me.

"How often are your visions coming?" CJ asked my face in his hands as my vision blurred.

"Like I said, I have never had this many in a week, a month, or even on the daily. The one I saw of you coming to Monterey the last time was the only one that I saw multiple times in the last year. Before Mom, Dad and Matt that is. Now? All the time. They vary, but all the time. I don't mind the little ones. These though ... I hate it Ceej." I said my voice trembling. He didn't say anything, just sat there watching me. He wiped away the tears.

I sighed and leaned into his touch. It gave me so much strength. I looked at him and said, "This one though, I hadn't seen this one."

CJ's hands left my face, and he sat back a bit on the bed. "What was it?"

"My father will survive the mirror. He will get a glowing crystal, but he's also blaming me for Matt's death. He said something about if I hadn't seen it, then it wouldn't have happened." I said quietly. There was a long silence before I continued, "We need to tell the others."

I slid out of the bed and headed for the main room.

"Wait. The other one of your mom and dad..." He hesitated and I froze with my hand on the handle of the door. "Taking me, hurting me. Which was it?"

I felt a tight band constrict around my lungs. I just looked at him.

"I know that's what you saw the other day when you ran out to the garden. The others suspect that's what you're seeing too ya'know." CJ said without an ounce of judgment.

I met his eyes, "Now you listen to me. They will not take you Cory James. Do you understand me?"

Then there was a soft knock on the door.

"Come in." I said without backing away from CJ.

Owen and Jean walked in holding an elegantly wrapped package. They must have completely missed the look CJ and I were giving each other because there was no reaction as they handed the box to me.

"Jean and I have missed so many of your birthdays, we wanted to get you your first" Jean jabbed him in the ribs and he gave her a quick glance. "... well open it." Owen said.

I opened the box and gaped. I felt my mouth drop open as I saw two shiny golden syths lying within form-fitting green satin. I flicked my eyes up to them, then back down. I ran my fingers over the perfectly smooth engravings and felt my eyes swell with tears. The engravings were a replica of my Maltal. The roots and leaves ran the length of the 7-inch blade like they were floating over the ocean waves closer to the hilt. The hilt was a representation of the tree with a smooth handle. I slowly lifted one of them out of the box and twirled it in my hands. Perfectly balanced.

"It's absolutely beautiful. I'll need practice with it though. I've gotten so used to Jean's, and this one feels ... different." I said smiling.

"Which is why I had them patterned after mine. It's slightly shorter, you had mentioned how 8 inches was a bit too long for you."

CJ coughed. I turned to him glaring and felt my face flood with embarrassment. When Jean and Owen burst into laughter, I let a small smile cross my lips.

CJ finally looked at me meaningfully and I sighed remembering the vision. Right. Mom and Dad. I groaned.

"What's wrong?" Jean asked noticing the change in my demeanor.

"We need to get everyone together. I had another vision. Just before you came in, I mean." I said quickly. "I saw my father get the crystal for Remembrance."

Their eyes widened and Owen let out a hissed, "Shit."

We got up and walked into the main room. Lindy and Clarice were in their favorite chairs. Clarice's foot tapping on the floor as she quickly snapped each page to the next made me wonder if she was actually reading the book in front of her. Lindy was studying a book on Noctulanar Castle and there were a lot of confused noises coming out of her. They both looked up as we neared and when they noticed the look on Owen and Jean's face, Clarice turned to me and said, "What did you see Megan?"

How do they know? Their ability to read each other was unnerving sometimes.

"Mom and Dad." I said hesitating. "I saw Dad on the floor, Mom behind him. Dad was curled up in a ball in front of a simple framed mirror that had smoke where a picture would lay. He was crying, screaming, and making a bunch of allegations ... when it was over, they had the crystal of Remembrance."

Lindy started pacing the room again, and I was surprised she hadn't worn a track pattern in the flooring from all the pacing she did.

"What allegations?" Lindy demanded.

"He blamed me for Matt's death, but he also kept apologizing for killing his brother. Which I didn't know he had." I said the last bit with a bit more bite than I anticipated, and I saw Lindy flinch and ball her hand up into a fist.

"Jean..." I started but had a hard time finishing. I took another deep breath then said quickly, "Why didn't you tell me my father had a brother. Maybe we can find him, and he can help us too."

"No. He can't." she said softly watching Lindy as she walked out the door.

"Why the hell not? Aren't family supposed to stick together? Help each other out? Stop each other from doing shit like this?!" I started screaming, but she interrupted me.

"Yes, they do sweety, but he can't because," she turned to Owen. He encouraged her along. "He died a long time ago. He was one of the council members that were killed in the battle with your father."

My heart dropped. *I'm sorry my brother.* That's what he said when he killed him. How many more family members did I have to lose, whether I knew them or not.

I really knew nothing about my parents. I knew that my life had been a lie, but to keep having it thrown in my face was… well, pathetic. Why hadn't I seen the signs? Was I really just some pathetic child?

"Easy." CJ said in a calming voice.

I looked at him and he was looking at my fingers. There were faint streaks of electricity passing between each fingertip. I jumped up in alarm and the sparks grew brighter. He turned me to face him, my face in his hands.

"Remember what you did the other night?" I gave him a questioning look as he lowered his hands from my face and slowly slid them down my arms to firmly grasp my hands. He flinched like it hurt but held tight. "The night of your Maltal ceremony. When I came in, you didn't register I was there. When I closed the door, you flinched. I froze because you had sparks just like this at your fingertips. You reeled it back in, so I let you be. You need to do that again."

I thought back. That night I had felt as if electricity was firing throughout my body. I took a deep breath in and concentrated on reeling my power back in just as I had that night.

"What do you mean she had sparks at her fingertips?" Clarice said in a voice more demanding that I had heard her before. "Don't you think that is something we should have known. Elec—"

"NOT NOW CLARICE." CJ and I said interrupting her. My power snapped back out like a rubber band, and CJ flinched, gripping harder on my hands. I heard a humming in my ears and I shook my head to make it stop.

"Everyone out." CJ commanded, then softer he said, "You got this Megs."

I vaguely heard footsteps and then CJ stepped closer to me. I could feel his breath on my face as he brought his forehead to mine.

"Focus." He said barely above a whisper. There was a cringe to his voice that made me open my eyes. I looked at him, and his face was tight but his eyes burned into mine. I looked down and there was electricity flowing brightly over both of our hands.

I bounced backward and CJ met me step for step until we were a few steps from the wall. He looked at it, then picked me up and forced me against it. I saw the electricity flow up his arms, and I started to panic. The threads of electricity glowing brighter.

There was a physical spark in his eyes, like the whisper of lightning in them, a cringe and then he said sternly, "Focus."

I felt the complete demand in it and closed my eyes again. I took a deep breath in, and out. I focused on coiling the power from his arms, his hands, up my arms, and into my naval, just as I had that night. Over and over again, I focused on it.

CJ's grip loosed slightly, as he whispered, "That's my girl."

In.

Out.

Coil.

In.

Out.

Coil.

Several minutes went by where I repeated the exercise and when I felt calm again, I waited for a heartbeat before I opened my eyes.

"We good?" He questioned sternly.

I took a deep breath and looked down at his hands. He released them and hid them behind his back. I saw a touch of red on the edges, but said, "Yea. I'm good."

He gripped his hand into a ball.

I narrowed my eyes at him and grabbed it. He let me take it, and I saw red burn marks that looked like lightning strikes across his hands and forearms.

"Ceej. I'm so sorry." I breathed not knowing what else to say. I felt an ounce of panic at how I had hurt him, but I took another deep breath to calm myself.

"I'm fine." He said just shaking out his hand.

"Why didn't you let go. I hurt you." I said panic rising again.

"I'm fine." He said again more sternly.

"Ceej." I said worry on my face.

"Megs. You needed grounding." He said firmly and I looked at him. There was that whisper of lightning again in his eye that was his mark of pure determination. Before I could say anything else, he said "I will do everything I can to help you. Getting a few burns on my hands. No big deal. It will heal. The burn lines look kind of cool anyway."

I rolled my eyes and said, "Give me your hands macho boy."

He did, and I pulled at one thread of that power in me and said, "*Qillis Chatu Bylind*". There was a faint blue glow that surrounded his forearms and hands and when it faded, he was back to normal.

"That could be useful." CJ said flexing his hand. "When did you learn that?"

"I didn't. Saw it in a vision a few weeks ago. Hadn't had the chance to try it on anything." I said shrugging, but the look on his face was a cross between astonishment and amazement. "Well, I wasn't about to go just slicing my arm to try it." I said with a laugh.

"I would have stopped you." He smirked

"I don't think it will fix anything major, but for minor things like this..." I trailed off and looked up at him. "I'm so sorry Ceej."

"Like I said. No big deal, and before you say anything, I will do it again, if you need to be grounded." He said taking my hand.

There was no fighting him on it, so I turned and made my way outside. "Come on. Let's go outside. I want to do some physical training. Take the edge off."

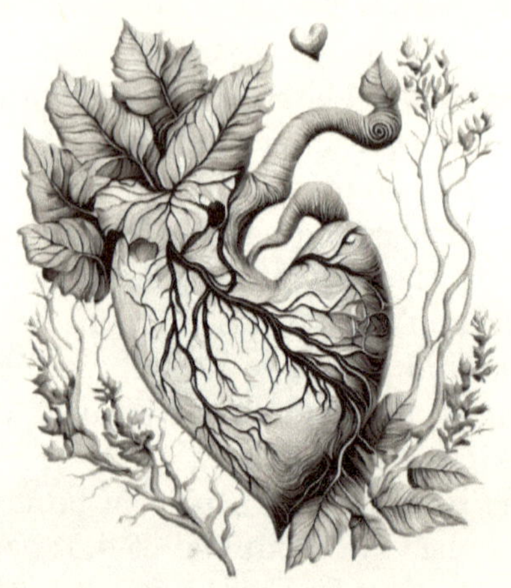

CHAPTER 16

WE WALKED OUT THE back door only to be met with Clarice standing there, wide stance, arms crossed, eyes narrowed. The Sangra version of a leather-clad brick wall. Today she was wearing a leather tank top, matching booties, with leather pants that were laced from ankle to hip. "Mind tell me why you didn't tell me you had electric powers?"

"I don't even know what that means Clarice." I said rolling my shoulders and neck.

"E–lec–tric–ity" she said slowly. I just rolled my eyes at her and looked at Lindy, Jean, and Owen who were working very hard to stay out of Clarice's way.

"Mind sparing with me. I need to work off the edge." I said blatantly ignoring her and rolling my shoulders as a I felt a thread of my power wind around me.

Narrowing her eyes again at me, there was barely a twitch of a muscle before she lunged with me with both syths out. I'm not sure if I shoved CJ out of the way or if he had grabbed me, but

110

my syths were out in the next heartbeat and we were moving. As she passed by us, I threw a leg out, tripping her sending her through the air. I lashed out with my syth and sliced through the laces on her thigh. As she moved, they released the rest of the way down leaving her pants flapping.

CJ and I hit the ground hard, and he let out a big humph before rolling on top of me, pinning me. I glared at him, and he let me loose.

"What the fuck Clarice. I said spar with ME." I said bouncing up and trying to keep my power from uncoiling. "CJ is not to be part of this."

"He did just fine. Did exactly what I've trained him to do." She said with an evil smirk. "You think that attack was for you? That was to see if he would do exactly what I've been training him to do."

CJ slowly backed away, noting the look on my face, and headed to stand next to Lindy, Jean, and Owen. All of which were also backing away, knowing that this was going to be all-out. No one would be holding back this time.

I flipped my syths in my hands and glared. "I thought Lindy was training him."

"I've been giving a few tips here and there." She said her eyes flicking to CJ and Lindy. "Now, are you going to just stand there, or did you not ask to have your ass beat for not telling me you had Angels be damned electric based powers."

Half a step was all I managed before she was at my side kicking a knee out from under me. I jabbed my elbow up and hit her jaw. I swung around as she spat blood on the ground.

We went after each other again and again. By the time we were done, we were both panting, bloody, and clothes shredded. I may have a broken nose, and her pinky was sitting at an odd angle.

"Are you done?" She said, ready to defend if I wasn't. She quickly reset her pinky with a mild flinch and grabbed her syth from the ground.

My arm was bleeding, and my tank top didn't leave much to the imagination, since she had sliced through one of the shoulder straps. There were so many holes in it that it was holding onto a thread. One side was really all that was holding it up. I looked at her and released a giggle.

"Only if you don't kill me because I destroyed your pants." I smiled and stood up straight. There was a long gash down the right side. She could have saved them with just new leather laces if it had been just those that I had destroyed.

"For the Angels. These were my favorite." She said stomping her foot. The swaying leather slapped against her calf as she stomped her feet over and over again heading toward the house to change.

She shouted over her shoulder, "Owen you are going to be a guinea pig again."

"Will it hurt?" He said as he looked to Jean who smiled at him and shook her head in disbelief.

"Does it matter?" Clarice quipped.

Owen stood and came to stand behind me. He looked at me and raised an eyebrow. "Seriously though, are you okay?"

I nodded.

Jean walked over and said, "Let's just work on some defensive incantations. Close your eyes and concentrate. Use whatever comes to mind. Don't hold back. Let your power run *freely* through you." I looked over to Lindy who was whispering fiercely with CJ. There was a bit of shock in his face and was whispering back. Finally, he just nodded his head and started working on his hand-to-hand lessons.

"Ok, Owen give me your worst." I said as I closed my eyes. He was hiding in the garden somewhere.

I listened for him, but I couldn't hear him anywhere. Just when I started to think I was going to be standing here all day, I realized I could *feel* him. He was about 40 ft away to the left of me behind the tulips, watching. I could *feel* everyone else in the garden too.

It was if they were embers of a campfire. I could differentiate between the each of them. A smirk crossed my face before I turned on my heel to face Owen and blasted him 15 feet back up and over the stone wall that surrounded the garden. When I opened my eyes, Owen was just standing up.

"How did you know where I was? Jean placed a silence incantation on me to make it harder. I could have played the dramdils in front of you and you would not have been able to hear me."

"Dramdils?" I asked.

"An instrument that looks like the bagpipes but plays music that ... well sound like a trumpet and flute? Sort of." Lindy said.

"One day you are going to have to explain to me how you are able to explain things in ways we understand." I said smiling.

"Oh, that's easy. I spent some time in Cairo deciphering ancient Egyptian text a few years back." She smiled brightly. "I traveled all over the Manusia and loved every minute there. "

Owen shook his head. "No avoiding the subject. Now how did you know where I was?"

I wasn't sure if I wanted to explain it, so I let the smirk stay on my face and lace my voice with temptation, "Care to try again? Maybe I just got lucky."

He eyed me carefully, not sure what to make of my tone.

"Ok. Jean honey put it on again please." He said carefully as my eyes narrowed at Jean.

This time everyone was paying closer attention. I turned to face CJ, closed my eyes, and let Jean turn me in circles a few times for me to lose my orientation. Once I let my power settle, I pulled at just one tiny thread and I could feel them all again. I smiled.

I sent a short hot shock to Owen, who was standing directly behind me, keeping my eyes shut and perfectly relaxed. I knew it had hit him. I could tell in the variation of his ember, and I just smirked.

When Jean went to walk over to him, I threw a wall up and whispered "I don't think so Jean. This is payback. He has wiped the floor with me time and time again." She froze, noticing I still hadn't opened my eyes.

I could hear CJ trying hard not to burst into laughter, but it escaped in small sputters. Meanwhile, Owen started circling the garden.

"UGGG!" My whole torso felt like someone had twisted it in half. "FOR THE LOVE OF ALL THAT IS HOLY!" I squealed.

I fought against the pain and tried to relax. My power burst for a second, and I coiled it back in me. I could feel the sparks at my fingertips for a split second before I pulled it back in. I think Owen had seen my hesitation and twisted my insides again.

"FUCK!" I hissed through my teeth, the pain came from my twisted insides and the zapping electricity throughout my body. I concentrated on building a barrier around that coil of electricity. It fought me, zapping me over and over again, but I pushed back using its own energy to conceal itself. When I had it in place and holding firm, the twisting of my gut stopped. I felt my power pulse against the barrier I had created, but it held. I no longer felt that 9-volt battery throughout my body.

Everything inside of me was... quiet.

Pure Silence.

For the first time since my Maltal ceremony. Pure silence.

I looked down to my naval and smiled, then threw a string of shocks toward Owen in quick succession. He conceded step upon step until he was against a row of large tulip like flowers.

With a couple of flicks of my wrist, I lifted Owen from the ground and turned him upside down. I turned around and slowly opened my eyes as everyone around us became dead silent. I smiled and proceeded to bounce my fingers up and down, which caused him to bounce on his head through the flowers.

Boisterous laughter spewed from him as the silence incantation wore off because Owen was sneezing through his laughter.

"OK! OK! You win this round, just put me down!" He said. I flicked my wrist, which put him right side up, and set him down next to Jean, Clarice, and Lindy who were holding their sides they were laughing so hard.

"How in the name of the Angels did you do that?!" he said.

"It's difficult to explain." I thought carefully. How was I going to describe it? "When I closed my eyes to concentrate, I couldn't hear you."

I glared at Jean, and she had a smug smile on her face. "Which by the way, I will be paying you back for missy."

"Well, I umm... well... umm.... OK! Just don't dunk me in the flowers, ok?" she giggled as she looked at Owen still covered in pollen of every color in the rainbow.

"Anyways, when I closed my eyes and really concentrated, I could *feel* you. Like glowing embers from a fire. I couldn't feel your warmth, but I could tell the difference between which of your embers." I looked to Jean.

Owen rubbed his side. "That shock hurt like hell!"

"GOOD!" I said smiling.

Clarice looked at me carefully, "And how did you reel in the electricity?"

"I... umm... I coiled it back up around my naval. That's how I make it subside when it wants to burst from me. I coil it up at my naval." I looked down at my stomach again and could feel it sitting there, calm and happy.

"Okay, but you..." Clarice started, but she trailed off thinking.

"It's contained. I've figured it out." I said quietly. "I have it cocooned. I built a barrier around it."

"You what?" Clarice said incredulously at the same time Jean said, "You can still access it though, clearly.".

I nodded in answer to Jean and ignored Clarice, as CJ reached my side and I wrapped an arm around his waist, just to have him touching me.

"In all my years, I've never heard of anyone being able to do what you just described Megan." Lindy said thoughtfully. She froze, her eyes widened as she looked up at me and then she bolted for the house.

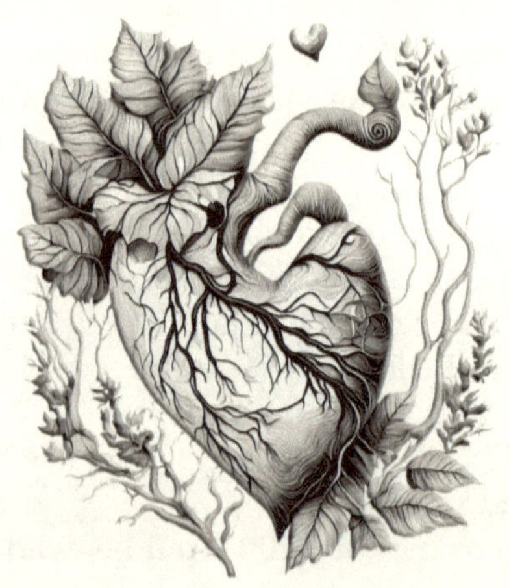

CHAPTER 17

"MAY I GET SOME time alone with Megan? Just for a few. We will just be in the woods, and I have reason to believe that CJ will know immediately if there is trouble." Lindy asked when she returned. Then she looked at me straight in the eye and said, "CJ, before you go into the house can you hold on a minute, I need to talk to you as well."

He ran his fingers along the bare skin at my waist making my toes curl. While Clarice had had a chance to change, I had not. I leaned against him and tried very hard not to let my mind wander in that direction.

Lindy turned to CJ and handed him a small flat grey oval stone. "When you hear Megan, I want you to tap on this three times."

"What is it?" he asked flipping over what looked like a flat jade colored rock.

"It's a Calling Stone. You'll be able to respond to her, by tapping on the stone. It will then reverberate to the sister stone here."

She said handing me a second one. "It's not quite a two-way conversation piece, but you can sort out a code for how to respond to her if this works."

"I'll be able to hear her?" he asked his eyes alight with awe.

"She'll be pushing a message to you. Go back inside and when you hear her, just tap it three times." He nodded, kissed me quickly, and went into the house.

I looked at her skeptically.

"We are doing an experiment." She said proudly as we headed for the tree line. "Your powers are different. We just need to make sure that no one outside our family knows about."

When we got into the forest edge behind the cottage, I turned to look at her. "Why does that scare you? All of you can do the same incantations I can."

"It scares me because you are not only able to do everything we can, but you can also feel others presence, you can see the future, you are showing *electric* abilities. Do you have any idea how incredibly rare that is?"

"Lindy, how would I know that?" I kept my voice low and head down as she continued to rant.

"Let's not even mention that when you use your power, they go off much stronger than any of us with very minimal effort Megan. Underworld being! The electric tendencies you are showing are a sign from the texts of the Five Angels of being Angel *BLESSED* Megan."

She paused and paced a few steps back and forth before continuing, "Not to mention you're still so new to using your power and you don't even have to be told half the time how or what to do. You can just use your powers however you deem fit, with or without an incantation. Building a wall or cocoon to hold your power in check? Megan, I've *never* heard of such a thing."

"But..." I started to say before she cut me off.

"You want another example? That stunt with Owen, while hilarious, is you welding your powers to do what *you* want. There is no incantation I know of that would allow you to manipulate anyone the way you did. There have always been rules and restrictions for the usage of power. You did it with such control and ease. You certainly didn't appear to be struggling or forcing your powers to do that. Your face had a huge smile on it, and you looked totally relaxed. Pure power can corrupt Megan. We have to make sure you can control it, and it doesn't control you. I don't envy you for having it. Having a limit on power is a good thing. It frankly scares me to the depths of the Underworld and back, that you have an inner power so pure."

"Oh." was all I could say. "But do you think that I could manipulate them so easy because it wasn't a person in my mind that I was manipulating? It was the embers?"

"See Megan that's just it!" she said through gritted teeth, trying not to scream, "I don't know. I've never heard of someone seeing people as embers before. Again, creating a barrier for your power to sit? Never. Heard. Of. That."

"Clarice said that you were part of the council at one time." Her head shot up and she glared at me. "Is that why it bothers you so much that you can't explain what I can do?"

"Clarice told you I was a council member?" Shame coated her face.

"Yes, back when we were discussing the flower and CJ had told us that we need to go home to get it."

She sat down on a nearby rock and sighed. "Did she tell you why I'm not anymore?"

I shook my head and after she took a really deep breath, she continued, "I was young and had an ability to read ancient text without ever actually learning the language and to see the unfiltered meaning behind them. After I returned from the Manusia, I started out in the Halls of Nalrin studying ancient readings for the council." There was such reverence in her voice, "When they realized how much I could read and do, I started working closely with one of the other council members. We grew very close, and eventually, we fell in love and got married. We, well I, was assigned to translate some of the later writings from the Five Angels. No one else had ever been able to translate so much of it before, and with such accuracy. Obviously, the original writings of the weapon of the Five Angels had been translated long before I had ever seen it. The original Sangra who translated them was so overcome by the hatred and hurt required that he ended up killing himself.

"Because of my work, I was able to earn a position on the Nalrin council." She eyed me carefully and her voice changed. "Then *it* happened. When your father was accused of reading on the weapon of the Five Angels. As you know a few died that day. One of them was the man I loved. I have blamed your father for his death for a very long time. I stepped down from the council after being a member for only 6 months. I just couldn't do it anymore."

"Lindy." I was putting it all together in my head. The vision. "*I don't want to kill you.*" and "*I'm sorry my brother.*" One of the few who died that day was Lindy's husband. I looked at her. The pieces. The pieces were slowly falling into place, "You were married to my father's brother weren't you."

She nodded her head and I noticed that her eyes had filled with tears.

"That also means that you were one of the council members to order the death of a loved one of his. Your own brother-in-law, knowing full well that it could be your sister-in-law or even your niece or nephew." I said shock thick in my voice and as I thought of Matt, I felt that lump in my throat build painfully.

"Yes. I have felt the guilt of that decision ever since I voiced my vote. I'm sorry Matt was the one to die." She sighed and looked at me with pleading eyes. "You have to understand the state of how things were. Put it all in context. He had killed council members. His personal death would have been nothing to him. The council wanted to hurt him as he had hurt them. ... As he had hurt me." She added with a sadness that was so genuine, it hurt my heart.

I looked back toward the house. Yes, I could understand, but I had the unique perspective of being one of the possible innocent loved ones to die by the hands of the council.

"I don't pretend to agree with the decision the council made. I understand how it ripped the council apart, how it was betrayed by one of its own. I know I would feel the same way if I were to be betrayed by someone I trusted." I looked at her very seriously, hoping to get my point across. "But to have an innocent person killed basically as an act of revenge. I don't know if I could agree to that."

The look on her face was mixed with pain and guilt. She opened her mouth to say something, but I continued, "I can't say I wouldn't. If anything happened to CJ, ... well, it hurts just to think about it." I said quietly once again focusing on the house.

We continued to sit in silence for a few more minutes before Lindy stood up and sighed. "Well let's get a couple of these tests underway. I don't want CJ to get anxious. Let's start with contacting him."

"You want me to what?" I said head jerking up.

"I want you to look at me and concentrate. I don't need to know what you tell CJ. The stone will glow and mimic his taps if he hears and responds."

"How? I mean, I don't know how. We've only used the golden protection incantation to talk to each other." I told her.

"Talk to each other? As in he can hear you?" She said.

"No, he can't hear me, but remember I can hear him." My cheeks warmed at the thought.

She nodded at me with a smile and said, "Now, imagine he is standing in front of you, and you want to tell him something, but just don't use your voice. Imagine pushing the words to him."

I took a deep breath and felt my power almost laugh at me. I glared at it and defiantly thought, "*Hey Ceej. Lindy says you should be able to hear me. Tap away if you can.*"

I looked down at the stone. Nothing.

I tried and tried again. Sweat formed on my brow and my power was dancing the jig in that new cocoon I held it in. It really was laughing at me.

"Maybe you have to center yourself better." She said pointedly.

I took another deep breath, willing the calm, and created a small little window for one thread of my power to feed through and thought Lindy must be off her meds.

"I'm not on any meds to be off of Megan. Just focus." She said rolling her eyes. I looked at her a little shocked. I hadn't said anything.

"Umm, Lindy..." I said looking at her in astonishment.

"Well! I believe you can do it." She interrupted. "Just concentrate damn it."

"Lindy. Stop." I said grabbing her hand to make her listen. She looked at me questioningly.

"I hadn't said anything ... out loud." Then realization hit her, and she smiled.

"I can't believe it worked." I shouted. After calming down, I tried CJ again, not knowing exactly how I did it before.

"Hey umm, Ceej. Ya there?" I pushed the thought toward his ember at the house.

The calling stone glowed and twitched in Lindy's hand as if someone were tapping it. Lindy was smiling brightly and handing it to me.

"You heard me?" I pushed toward CJ crunching my eyes in concentration.

Then I saw the stone glow again. It twitched once, then paused, twitched four times, paused again, and twitched three times. I giggled and pushed, *"I love you too."*

Lindy looked at me with questions and concern written on her face.

"1 - 4 - 3. The number of letters in the phrase *I love you.*" I told her smiling.

"Such raw power." She mumbled and started pacing again. "There is much I need to find out first, but there are so many coincidences."

"Question. Can you feel me here? I mean if you just let your power run can you feel me here like you did Owen earlier, but this time without closing your eyes."

I thought about that for a minute. I wanted to tell her no, but the truth was that I could. It was strange, I wasn't even trying. Something happened today that changed how I was seeing things. It wasn't like I could just feel her presence because I knew she was there. I could feel her ember... like ... "Yes. I can.

It's more like that ember is your power. I can feel the *presence* of your power, not just your physical being. That doesn't explain why I can feel CJ's though."

She turned to walk away from me, but after a few feet turned lunged towards me. Bouncing off an invisible wall laughing she said, "That's what I thought. Sorry. I just wanted to see if you could protect yourself instinctively. Rarely, can even a 16-year-old who has had 10 years of intense training do that. Now, can you feel the others in the house?"

I turned my back on where the house was and felt out, making sure to keep my eyes open, not that I could actually see them. "Owen is pacing in the main room, Clarice is sitting in her favorite chair, Jean in the kitchen cooking, and CJ in the bedroom lying on bed. Then ..." I turned to Lindy.

"There are more embers to the west. At least three." Her face lit up for a moment till what I was telling her sunk in.

"Send CJ a warning. Let's hurry." She said almost in a panic.

"*On the way back, three people coming from the west. Warn the others.*" I felt the stone move three times.

CHAPTER 18

"Who are they?" Clarice asked as we walked in and threw me a new shirt to put on.

"I don't know. I don't know the ember pattern. I'm new at this. I can tell your patterns apart because of the slight variations in coloring to them. They match your personalities. Their embers look the same, but different from yours, darker somehow. I've been able to see embers for all of what two hours?" I told them slightly panicked. I threw my shredded shirt into the hallway and put the new one on.

My eyes flicked to CJ. I let the golden warmth spread through me and I grabbed his hand, his fingers intertwining with mine, to let it pass through him.

In silent conversation I told him *"Don't let go of my hand. Always touch me."*

"Don't be scared. I won't let them harm you. No one gets to you." Hearing him through the golden glow.

"Everyone else seems to be on edge."

He pulled me close and kissed me. I could feel the glow grow stronger.

There was a soft knock on the door.

"*Time of truth.*" I told Jean silently. She looked at me in shock.

"How did you..." then looked to Lindy.

"It is what we were working on in the woods." Lindy explained, but there was a slight edginess to her voice that I couldn't place.

"You know this is starting to freak me out. Just how much you are able to do just what you will with your powers." Jean shook her head and sighed. "Lindy, you and I need to talk when this is all done."

Just as she was turning the handle a wave of power that had a cold edge to it, knocked her back to where we were standing halfway across the room. On instinct, I had a wall thrown up. Owen's meeting mine. A short, pudgy, sweat covered man with jet black hair and black eyes bounced off the wall and rubbed at his nose which looked a bit flat at the end. I half wondered if it was the wall or if he had already had a pig snout.

A tall thin bleach-blond haired man with vibrant blue eyes snarled at us from beside his friend. The third sauntered up next to the others and I was able to get a better look at him. He was wearing a suit, with his hands in his pockets as he smiled brightly toward Clarice. He was about the same height as the other two, medium build, short brown hair, and his eyes were a deep brown. No, they were dark red, almost making them appear brown.

"Hello there, dear princess." He said bowing deep at the waist toward her. The leader of the group then.

Clarice strode up just behind the wall then said through her teeth, "Don't call me that. What in the hell do you think you are doing here? What do you want?"

"You, my princess. It's time for you to come back and take your rightful place among us." Said the leader cocking his head.

"I'm not going. You know that. I've told Benedict that many times. I won't go back."

What was she talking about? What did she mean go back?

"Don't you miss the times we had as a kid? The walks along the Gendril beaches and watching the sun set along the water?" His words were smooth as honey. I saw Clarice's face grow hard and her ember pulsed to life.

Owen's eyes flicked to mine in command as he let his wall fall. He casually reached for his syths, and I pushed mine to cover the space his had left. I let a little more of my power escape that cocoon I created. I only hoped that they didn't notice. The short stubby one kept poking at it and I let a little bit of electricity flow into it.

Jean gave me a bit of a side eye as a light crackling hum entered the room.

"AHHH how cute. You're trying to persuade me by taking me down a childhood memory lane." She said mockingly. He didn't like that at all. "I've made my choice. I will *not* go back."

The leader turned to me, cocked his head to the side. "You've got a couple of new friends there. Are they a new project? New pets perhaps?"

"No. You barge in here and think you're going to persuade me by hurting them?" She huffed him off.

"Awfully brave behind a wall, aren't you? Maybe I'll take one of the females for a consort. Maybe the blonde over there." He said gesturing toward me. I felt CJ's muscles tighten under me.

She glared at me, "Remove it. I'll rip his throat out."

"No Clarice." Then silently told her. *"Get rid of them."*

She narrowed her eyes at me and I levelled a stare back at her. I wasn't sure how long I could hold the electricity to the barrier, but the pudgy one touched one of the outer edges and jumped back.

"Megs. Don't give yourself away." I heard CJ say through the glow. I mentally sighed and coiled the electricity back up into its cocoon.

"Look boys. I'm not going. If he has a problem with that then tell him to come here and I'll tell me so myself." She sighed.

I felt miscellaneous shocks hit the wall. Anger flooded through me, and I could feel that internal coil pulse against the cocoon and beg to be released. I wouldn't let my family get hurt.

I closed my eyes as I inhaled, and on the exhale, pushed the wall to bump against them trying to corral them out the door.

The short one looked to me. "You've got some guts in that power of yours don't you little girl."

"Wanna test it? Bet I could wipe you with my hands tied behind my back. What do you say?" I told him, my power lending me confidence and strength I didn't exactly feel.

Silence filled the room. I could feel CJ's stare on me, but his mind was blank with shock.

"Megan." Clarice said, "You don't know what you're saying. If you bet them, they get what they want and that's me."

"Or you as a sex slave to the ugly dude." CJ said through his teeth.

"And if I win, then they never step foot in the Nalrin province again." I told her as my power sparked to life and filled each corner of me. The room was still and quiet. I looked him up and down, a red–orange haze at the edges of my vision, then shrugged.

"I can handle him" I said like it was nothing.

"I'm not sure you can. Your power is still erratic. Even you said that you are still new to all of this." Clarice said.

I shrugged as my power pulsed again. I looked her in the eyes and silently told her, *"Remember what I did to Owen? Blink once for no and twice for yes."*

She blinked twice and I raised my eyebrows, *"I just have to concentrate. Will you please let me do this? Let me test myself. Real experience Clarice. I need real experience before going against my parents."* She stared at me for a long time and finally blinked twice again sighing.

I turned to our short little visitor. "Outside... just out of the forest."

"What do you think you are doing Megs?" CJ finally asked, but the question was written on everyone's faces.

After we got outside, I was careful to keep my wall up between us. Quietly, I whispered, "Guys I can do this! Don't worry."

"What makes you so sure of that Megs?" CJ whispered. His eyes flickered to them and back to me.

"Owen." I said with confidence raising my eyebrows. One by one understanding crossed their faces, except for Lindy, who looked like she would love to say something but kept her mouth shut. Ignoring her, I said, "Jean, Clarice, and Owen can you guys take over wall duty while I take care of this punk?"

I walked over to the tree line. "Okay, you little shit. Give me what you got?"

"Didn't you say you were going do this with your hands tied behind your back?" he said.

"Of course, if you think that's the only way you're going to beat me. Fine by me." I shrugged. I pulled my hair down out of my ponytail and put my hands behind my back and tied a knot. "All set. Bring it on."

"Just how I like my females. Bound. I'll give you everything I have." He said hungrily as he looked me up and down and grabbed his crotch. CJ took all but a step before Clarice had him by the upper arms, mumbling something in his ear.

"Sorry. I don't play with limp dicks." I said closing my eyes and saw his ember not 25 feet from me.

I felt the heat of a fireball he threw at me but caught it mid-air. A thought of cooling water had the ball evaporating to steam. I opened my eyes and through a red-orange haze saw the shock across his face. Closing my eyes again, I started twitching my fingers throwing shock aftershock at him till he was a heap on the floor.

He stood up and threw a blanket of darkness over me. I smirked and a laugh that sounded very evil burst from me.

He charged and he threw a punch, which I dodged, and moved to stand behind him. He turned around just in time for me to kick him in the jaw. Thank the Angels, and Clarice, for my flexibility. The darkness he had placed vanished to him spitting blood as I took a few steps back.

"Ahhhhh, what's wrong hun?" I taunted him. His friend tossed him a long sword.

I concentrated on his ember and how it moved as he swung it around him. Rough and wild. He lunged for me over and over again as I ducked, dodged, and moved gracefully out of the way of his swings.

"Her eyes are closed! How does she know where Jobe is coming from?" I heard the leader say. I closed my fist and mentally picked Jobe up and threw him against a tree. I heard him hit with such a force I couldn't tell if the crack I heard was him or the tree breaking. I hope I didn't damage the tree. I kept my eyes closed but knew he was about 10 feet from me on the ground.

"You bitch!" Jobe spat as I opened my eyes to look at him. That red - orange haze made his ember look almost non-burning.

"You really should watch your language. Didn't your mother teach you any manners in regard to women? Besides just what are you going to do? Ready to call it yet?" I said. I had to admit I was having fun.

"Fat chance. I'm going to slice you up and feed you to my pets!" He said as I raised him back up against the tree with a couple twitches of my fingers.

"Oh, I don't think you will. See, you have to get down from there first." I said with a sly smile.

I could feel his friends coming up from behind me. I picked them up and threw them into the trees right next to their little friend. They fell to the ground, the look of shock on their face was just priceless. I let Jobe down and get to his feet.

"You two are so worried I am going to win against your little friend you decided to sneak up on me? That's not very sportsmanship like. You want to have the numbers? Fine. Bring it on. I'll take all three of you." I said in a hiss as my power pulsed and that haze grew brighter. Then they swung their swords in front of them and charged.

Everything and everyone moved as if I was in slow motion. I moved, ducked, and slid away from each of their swings. I felt a running gash spread across my upper arm just below the shoulder. I swung my leg around and kicked one of them in the jaw, blood splattering the leader's face.

There was a double punch to my side and a knee to my spine, but it was the swords I was worried about. I saw the leader swing his sword just for my head as I ducked and knocked his feet out from under him, stomping on his knee. He didn't get up.

I opened my eyes and cackled. Through all the wild swipes at me, they had cut each other's clothes to shreds. When they realized they were each standing in front of us virtually naked they took off limping as fast as they could into the forest.

Just out of spite, I sent a shock of my electricity to their asses. The yelp from them even made Owen and Lindy laugh out loud.

I strode back to my family, coiling that power back up into its cocoon, and took a deep breath. When I turned back to them, I motioned for CJ to untie my hands. He came up next to me, and licked my ear before purring, "I kind of liked the sight of you with your hands tied behind your back."

Heat flooded my cheeks as he pushed down my hands. The force of it pulled me back into him, and my chest up toward his face. I felt a very powerful spark of my power dive between my legs, but once his lips touched mine, there was this wave of calm that flowed and fizzled out my power. It calmed the wildness of my power within me, and I winked at him.

"Well then, guess you will just have to try to tie me up then huh." His eyes filled with a lustful heat that made my core melt.

"Promises, promises." He said putting his arm around my waist, but not before he gave me a good smack on the ass. The sting of it made me close my eyes and take a deep breath as the pain turned to pleasure.

"See Clarice, it's just in how you handle them." I said turning to her with a huge smile, but when I saw the look on her face I cringed.

"You were toying with them! Your powers are still settling in. You are hardly trained. You let your power control you. WORSE! You let the electric power control you. CONTROL YOU, MEGAN." She screamed at me, finger in the air, and hand on her hip. It was a little comical if she wasn't so pissed. Then she growled at me, "If I ever see you do that again I will personally report your ass to the council. You were reckless, arrogant, pig-headed, and a showoff! How did you know they couldn't handle themselves as well as they appeared?"

I cringed. I knew she was going to let me have it, but I didn't realize she would be this mad. CJ was snickering and trying very, very hard not to laugh his ass off. I knew I deserved it, because looking back, I had let the power influence me. That was exactly what Lindy was talking about in the forest. I let the power influence my better judgment and I put everyone at risk. I took a deep breath and coiled it back up tighter inside its cocoon.

"First off. Yes, you are right I was toying with them ... and okay, showing off. I was having fun! I'm sorry, but you have to admit that was funny! Besides as stubborn as those boys are, I'm sure that they won't tell anyone that they got beat up and had their clothes torn to smithereens by a girl. They will probably say it was Chalakbear or something." I couldn't help the smile that pulled at the corner of my lips.

Jean started laughing so hard, she was crying. "Did you see the look on those boys' faces when you pulled them from behind you up against the tree! That was priceless."

"I took a gamble that they were not as trained as they appeared. Firstly, because of the way they walked. They slouched and walked rough and jagged. People who have trained tend to walk with more confidence. Second, their embers. Remember how I said their embers were darker, not as bright as all of yours? Well, one possibility is that their powers are not refined and as well trained. The other is well," I looked to Clarice, "because they come from a much darker family society. The leader had mentioned Gendril, and I knew from the studying of maps for the trial that is on the Obsecuritan continent."

"Which we have been studying at great length because of the Five Angels." Lindy said smiling at me with pride.

I nodded my head. "It was a gamble on whether the darker embers were because of them coming from a darker area or because their powers were not as refined. It could be a combination of the two, but I won't know that for sure until we head off to Noctulanar."

Clarice looked at me and smiled. "You used your brain and observed. I commend you for that."

"But?" I asked carefully.

Her face went very serious again. "But, if you ever pull anything like that again, I will report you to the council immediately. You can't afford to lose control Megan."

I bit my lip and nodded. "Yes, Ma'am."

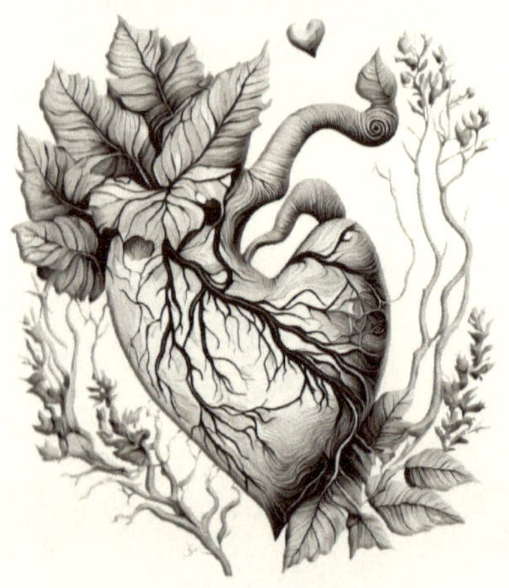

CHAPTER 19

IT HAD BEEN TWO weeks since that encounter with the males from Noctulanar, and we were packed and ready for São Tomé. The deadline was in 2 days, and we have studied all we could about the area. The meadow wasn't supposed to be easy to find, and we were hoping two days will help give us a little extra time. I had a lot of visions that they were hoping would help us, but I see what is going to happen. Not what will happen IF we are on the right track.

There were visions of Owen and a snake, Clarice painting her toe nails along a creek, Owen jumping across some logs in a river bed with tall trees and ferns along both sides, Owen and Jean talking about how we had hiked from a coastal village, which was possibly the most helpful in this case along with numerous other visions of us that I hoped would be helpful in convincing me if we were on the right track.

Then there was CJ proposing in a place that wouldn't fully form. That was quite frustrating for a couple of reasons. The first of course because I couldn't see WHERE he was going to "*officially*" propose, and the next because I knew he was going to. That was a downside to the whole seeing the future thing.

I confronted him with what I saw when we were packing the last of our things in our backpacks, but he laughed nervously and said, "Maybe you couldn't see where because I haven't decided where and how I'm going to ask you yet."

"First of all, you know decisions have nothing to do with the who, what, when, where, and how's, of what I see in my visions. Second, we've already talked about getting married. I will marry you after all this settles down." I sighed. "There is no reason for you to ask me again."

He just gave me a meaningful look, walked across the room, and whispered, "but you had said that I needed to work on my proposal skills." I rolled my eyes as he winked at me, he kissed me softly and ran a single finger up the middle of me.

"That doesn't mean that you have to propose again." I said as I shuttered and maneuvered out of his grip. I walked over to the door as he gave me a look that made me think he would devour me right then and there, so I slowly shut the door, throwing a silencing incantation on the room.

"Don't look at me that way." I said as I sauntered over to him, exaggerating each swish of my hips.

"Did you just?" CJ said his eyes filling with desire. I smirked at him. CJ pulled me closer almost grinding his hips against me, "Silence?"

"Make me scream and find out." I said grinding back against him. "We don't have long. They will be waiting for us. I give you 15 minutes max before they come to check on us."

"You foul evil creature. That is nowhere near long enough." He said, a wicked gleam in his eye.

I backed away from him then. Slowly I removed my pants, unbuttoned a couple of the buttons of my shirt, and with exaggerated slowness, moved my bra to the side to release one of my breasts. I fondled them a moment before I took one breast to my lips and licked a nipple. CJ's eyes glazed over and there was an audible shudder that went through him.

I looked down and saw that he was indeed having the same thoughts I was. Another flick to my nipple and I said, "Better get started then."

CJ growled as he pushed me up against the wall. I felt him grab my ass and my back chaffed against the wall as he lifted me up. I yipped when he bit at my neck. I reached down and removed his belt. A few quick movements of my hands and he bounced free.

I scrapped my nail down him as I brought my hands up and around his shoulders. I swung my leg up and around his hip, urging him to give me what we both wanted. His teeth were against my neck as he teased me by sliding his length up and down my slit and flicked my nub.

"CEEJ." I pleaded. My hips moved of their own accord trying to get him inside me.

"What do you want Megs?" He whispered against my ear still teasing me. "Do you want me inside you? Do you want me to pound you hard enough to take the pictures off the wall?"

I whimpered and bit my lower lip.

There was a husky giggle in my ear, and in one thrust he was deep inside me. He didn't even give me a chance to adjust to him before he plowed into me over and over again. I dragged my nails down his back as another whimper passed from my lips.

CJ slowed and pulled back enough that he met my eye. He looked straight into my soul as he slowly pulled almost all the way out, a sly smile crossing his lips before he slammed into me again. An orgasm ripping through me as he did it a few more times, before he breathed, "Fuck Megs."

He looked at the clock and let out a frustrated groan. "For the record, quickies are not my favorite." He said before he slammed into me again. "I do not get to worship you the way you deserve."

"Ceej. Just –" I was cut off by him thrusting into me again and kissing me hard. I grabbed his bottom lip and trapped it between my teeth.

"No playing dirty. Two can play at that game" His voice rumbled against me as he thrust in again, sticking his finger against my ass at the same time.

I screamed as pleasure ripped through me like a hurricane. "YES!"

I writhed against the wall, feeling that orgasm building. He brought me just to the edge of it as I tried to move against him, but he separated from me and moaned, "Please..."

He threw my other leg around his hip and carried me to the bed where he laid me on my stomach.

"Don't move." He breathed in my ear as he slid back into me. He took one hand to grab my hips and slid a thumb back up my ass.

"FUCK!" I grunted into the blankets.

"What as that?" He said, a smile clearly on his face.

"FUCK ME Ceej. Please. Fuck me." I said. I was panting. I felt my core tighten and knew I would be moments from a second orgasm.

His finger wiggled with each slapping connection of us. I was writhing. Moments later we released together. I felt myself almost disconnect from my body. There was nothing but pleasure and CJ.

We laid there for a moment sweaty and a mess. He slowly slid out of me, rolling me over to give me a soft kiss before he carried me to the shower.

"Let's get cleaned up. The others will be waiting on us." He said ever the responsible one. I would have been content to lay there with him for another few hours. Okay, so there would be another round, or two, but the world did not wait for us.

It was so hard to put together a coherent thought to push to Lindy, but finally, I pushed, *"Be ... few ... minutes. Shower."*

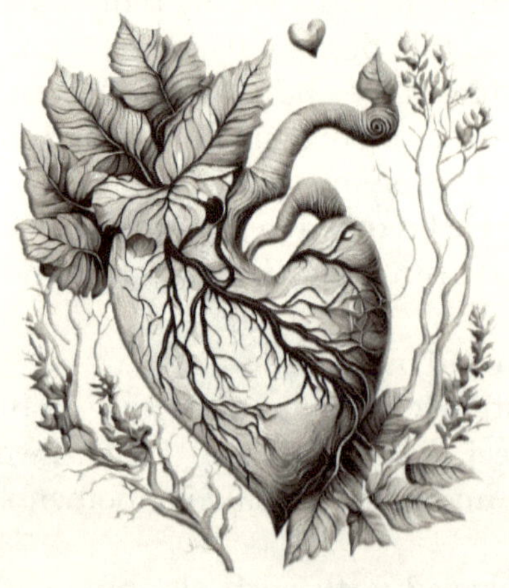

CHAPTER 20

"OK SO ARE WE ready?" I asked.

Lindy gave me a little wink as she saw us walk up. Our clothes still clung to us where we were not fully dry, and I had just thrown my hair up in a quick braid. CJ's hair, however, did not want to tame down, so was still a bit unruly.

"If CJ and Megan are done making everyone else wait." Owen said trying to sound annoyed, but it came off more amused than anything.

"Give them a break hon." Jean said giving him an eye full. "Don't make me remind you how many times we've made Clarice and Lindy wait."

"Alright. Everyone ready?" He said red as a tomato. He reached his hands out to everyone. I took CJ and Clarice's hand as everyone nodded. Then we were gone in swirling blue smoke.

We were standing in the middle of a dirt road surrounded by adobe looking buildings, with pig pens between them. I sighed heavily at the smell of fresh baked bread in the air.

I saw a gentleman walking down the road in a worn t-shirt and shorts whose skin was black as night and asked him, "Você diz o inglês Senhor?"

"Não sinto." He eyed the packs on our back.

"O meu português não está bem." He nodded and then I asked him where we could find the river that joins with the ocean. He gave me very simple instructions with hand jesters and a lot of pointing. His tone insinuated I was crazy for even asking such a question, which I'm sure did. Any visitor here would have known exactly where the river was no matter where they were on the island.

"Obrigado Senhor." I said to him as he continued on his way. "This way." I told the rest of them.

CJ looked at me with amazement. "I didn't know you spoke Portuguese. When did you learn? Was I in Chicago longer than I thought?"

"I don't. I studied some before we left. I did some research on São Tomé after you told us that this was where the flower was and found out that this is a Portuguese speaking country. We needed some way to communicate with people while in the towns. If he had given me anything more than what was directly asked for, then I would have been toast!" I said laughing.

"Amazing." He said taking my hand and kissing the back of it as we walked.

It had to be over 80 degrees here, and it was so damn muggy. When I looked out beyond the town, I saw what could have been rain clouds. They were dark and heavy, and I sighed. Just what we need, rain to make the trek that much more interesting.

We got a lot of strange looks as we made our way down to the main road, and I giggled. Of course, we would. We were all pretty much dressed the same. I had my hair back in a braid with a leather string, wore a royal blue tank top, form fitting jeans, which CJ had already reminded me numerous times that my ass looked wonderful in, and the standard Sangra formfitting jacket that stopped about halfway down my thigh.

I had never understood the need for the extra length, but it made sense to me now as I had my syths strapped to the outside of my thighs for easy access. Before we left, I had a couple more syths made up for the trip and had them tucked on a weapons belt within easy reach. Not to mention the switchblade I had tucked on the inside of my knee-high boots. Before we left, Jean told me I looked just like my grandmother had in her warrior days.

We stopped inside one of the hotels and exchanged some of the cash I had for local Dobra. Since apparently, I was the only one who had done any language studies, I was negotiating in my broken more than pathetic Portuguese at the market to obtain some "real food" as CJ called it. He really just wanted some Manusian fruit and sweets.

"Are you sure that we are going to the right part of the isle?" Jean said.

"I'm pretty sure this is the right island. I had a vision where you and Owen were talking about how we had hiked from Priaia Melão, and another one of us wandering down a river, so this is as good a place as any." I kept the part about how I felt that it might have been a self-fulfilling prophecy to myself. I knew that if I saw them there, we would go, but we would go because I saw us there. I huffed out my nose and took off down the street.

"Besides," I called out over my shoulder, "CJ said it only grows on São Tomé. It's not that big of an island, right? Well. Welcome to São Tomé. Now let's get moving."

I hadn't realized how much I missed the smell of the ocean until I looked out at the large expanse and took in the sounds and smells of the beach. It was hot and humid just like I remembered when we went to Hawaii as a child. I had sweat running down my spine and the air was heavy to breathe.

"If I wanted to drink my water I would have said so" CJ said at one point. "It's like being back in Louisiana in the dead of summer."

I laughed and Lindy smiled. She knew what he meant, but the others hadn't spent as much time in the Manusia as she had. As the road started to pull away from the beach, I sighed, took another deep breath to savor the smells and feel of the ocean spray.

CJ took my hand and said, "You'll see the ocean again." Damn that man for knowing me so well.

Owen had pulled the snake down and threw it and Clarice had painted her toenails when we stopped for something to eat, just as I had seen in my visions.

"How ya doing?" I asked CJ trying to distract myself. We had been hiking at a pretty steady pace all day.

"Don't worry about me babe." I could swear that his eyes flickered to Clarice as he smirked. I just narrowed my eyes at him, and he smiled.

"Clarice, what did you do?" I shouted over my shoulder.

"I don't know what you're talking about." Her voice was thick with sarcasm. I turned around, crossed my arms over my chest, and glared at her.

"Oh, all right, geesh. Don't get your underthings holed up. I simply cast the Patientiam incarnation on him. It comes quite in handy sometimes." She let out a wicked smile cross her face. "Isn't that right Owen?"

I didn't see the rock Owen threw, but I certainly saw it hit Clarice's head as she laughed hysterically. I had to admit it was kind of a low blow.

"My *stamina* is perfectly fine, thank you very much!" Owen growled at her.

"Clarice! Can we not make comments about my sex life? Or... if you really want to talk about sex lives, we can talk about yours. Ya'know, if you really want to." Jean told her, letting the same wicked smile that Clarice had on her face a moment ago spread across her own.

"So… the Patientiam incantation is like a stamina buff I take it?" I said.

"Patientiam is Latin for Endurance. So yes. Essentially." Clarice said.

"Latin? Why Latin?" I said a little surprised a Manusian language was used for naming a spell.

"The one who created the incantation lived in the Manusia and loved it so much that when he returned to Nalsar, he pursued his love of creating incantations and named many of the ones he created in that language." Jean said.

"You can *create* incantations?" CJ asked in shock.

"Yes. Like that one where Megan dumped Owen in the flowers upside down," She said as I looked to Owen who was blushing, "If you could come up with an incantation and body movement for it, then it could be recorded in the Hall of Incantational Studies and others could use it."

How hadn't I realized there were incantations that could increase his stamina for this trip. I turned to CJ and narrowed my eyes assessing him.

"What?" he said.

"Is that why you had some extra spunk in you before we left?" I asked quietly.

A wicked smiled crossed his lips as his eyes, oh so slowly, went up and down along my body. Oh, if there hadn't been other people around right now, I would put that stamina buff to really good use.

"No Megs." He said lifting my chin to look him eye to eye. We were standing so close I could feel his breath on my face as he said, his voice low and gravely in a way that made my insides liquify. His thumb ran across my lips as he said, "You drive me crazy. You have for longer than I can say. You drive me wild each and every day. It takes every ounce of self-control to allow you out of the room before noon each day. I just wish we had had more time this morning."

He kissed me and I just stood there after he walked away. For what felt like my whole life, I had waited for him to say such things to me, and here I was, once again, dumbfounded and speechless just like that day in Russo's.

I blinked to clear my head and reminded myself we need to press forward. "Let's keep moving. We only have a day and a half before the Desumo Nitor bloom, and I would like to get there before my parents."

My parents. Now that was going to be an interesting confrontation. *Hey Mom. Hey Dad. I thought ya'll were dead. Then a year later, somehow, I ported CJ and I here to where Grandma used to live. Oh, and I found out I have an aunt, a whole life you kept from Matt and me, and that it is all your fault Matt died. I seem to be forgetting something, RIGHT! You're alive and trying to destroy a whole world I have grown to love since I arrived.*

I really didn't know how I was going to confront them about all of this. I froze. Could I? CJ came to stand in front of me and forced me to look up at him.

"It's going to be okay, Megs. We will stop them." He said trying to comfort me. His skin sizzled against mine as the electricity I had allowed to stay flowing through me hit his skin. He didn't even flinch.

"But Ceej, what if we don't?" I whispered as my eyes shifting quickly to each of our family. "What if everything I've seen does come true? What if you or someone else gets hurt?"

"We will be fine. Come on." He wrapped his arm around me, and we continued on. I coiled more of that power back into its cocoon. I didn't dare look to see if I burned him again.

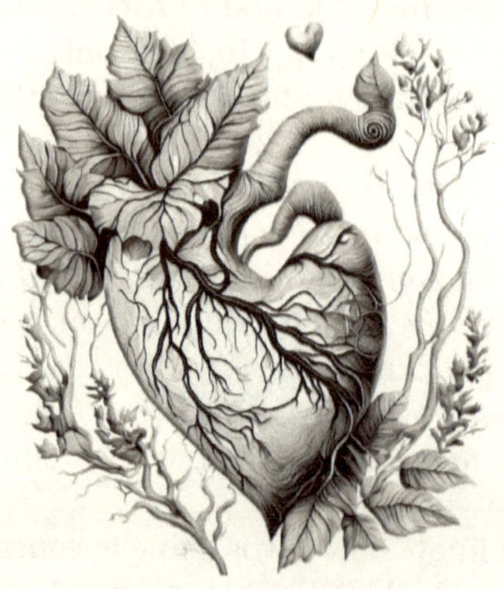

CHAPTER 21

I HAD TO ADMIT, it wasn't the vacation I would have booked for us, but at least the scenery was nice to look at. I saw all kinds of plants and wildlife that I had only seen in science books. There were a few different types of primates, a plethora of birds, and an endless supply of the bug of your choice. I swear I even saw an elephant, but maybe it was just my eyes playing tricks on me.

Lindy had been unusually quiet during the entire trip. Clarice was trying to engage her in conversation, but she just nodded her head yes or no.

"Ceej..." I whispered as I started to get an all too familiar feeling again. I reached out for his hand, and he wrapped his arm around my waist. He guided me to sit down on a rock and let me concentrate.

I put my head in my hands and saw a waterfall.

I saw myself slip and fall into the pool below it, but just before I broke the surface everything shimmered, and I was surrounded by rock. A cave?

The vision shimmered again.

Blue. Just an ocean of blue.

Shimmer.

Bright light.

Shimmer. I shook my head. Why was this jumping so much? I can't catch anything.

Tall stone walls.

Shimmer.

"DAMN IT!" I spewed, just before things went into crystal clear focus. CJ and I were bent over Owen, who was bleeding and moaning in pain. Jean, Clarice, and Lindy were chanting and when I turned around to look behind me, my mother was standing so close I actually jumped back.

I felt my chest hollow out and a rock hit the pit of my stomach. My Mothers eyes were not the beautiful green I had seen when growing up. They were almost black with a hint of red, not to mention she looked pale and like she hadn't slept in months.

"Hello Megan". She said looking straight at me, not the Megan bent over Owen, but me. I jumped back, and then I was back in the middle of the rain forest with everyone else, where I had fallen from the log CJ had originally sat me on. I gasped for air and after a few gulps looked to CJ, then Owen. I looked him over and he was okay.

Breathe in.

Breathe Out.

Owen was okay.

Breathe in.

Breathe Out.

I took one more deep breath and forced myself to calm.

Everyone had the same questioning look on their face. CJ helped me sit up and made me take a sip of water from the canteen as I tried to sort through what had just happened.

"How is that possible?" I whispered, staring at the ground. How could she possibly?

"How was what possible?" Owen asked.

"What did you see?" Lindy pressed.

"I saw us in ... I don't know where, it kept jumping around. There was a large expanse of blue, tall stone walls, but ... my mother ... she..." I looked up at them, my eyes wide. I was shaking. Even after verifying Owen was okay, I was still shaking. "She saw me. Not like in my other visions where she saw me as I was in the vision. She saw me watching the vision. Only she ..."

I shook my head, pausing again. I didn't want to see her eyes like that. My heart raced. They were not right.

Not right. Not right. Not right.

"She what?" Lindy said with a hardness I hadn't heard from her before, coming to move closer.

"Her eyes looked like the one from Gendril that we dealt with back at the house. They were tinted deep red. They were not her eyes." I said.

A look of shock crossed Clarice's face, then a look of worry came through on Lindy's before she asked, "Megan, did she look paler than she usually does? This is extremely important."

"Yea. How did you know? She looked like she hadn't slept in months actually." I said staring at the ground.

She paced up along the path for about a minute before she stopped, looked at Clarice who gave her a small nod, then turned to me and lunged at me with her syth in hand. CJ jumped in front of her and was holding her back when she growled over his shoulder, "What did I tell you in the forest before the visitors from Gendril showed up?"

"Lindy!" Owen and Jean said.

I looked at her, questioning her insanity, but silently pushed to her, *"You told me you had married my father's brother. He was one of the ones my father had killed while you both were on the council."*

She relaxed, put her syths away, and backed away from CJ.

"What the fuck was that about Lindy?" CJ said through gritted teeth.

Lindy nodded to Clarice who turned to me. "You said that your mother's eyes looked like the one boy from Gendril right?"

I nodded my head trying to push the memory from my mind.

"Well, Eldrin, he's not Sangra. He's a Proteus. A demon of sorts. Nalrin made a treaty with his kind thousands of years ago, but there were ... conditions. They couldn't *feed* on Sangra, they had to be, as you would say, humanoid in appearance, and they could only perform their rituals within Obsecuritan."

"What do you mean ... feed?" CJ asked.

"They feed on the blood of beings, which is why Eldrin has a red tint to his eyes. The blood they obtain here would be red... well mostly. If they feed off of other demons they could have a green tint, blue tint, or even purple or yellow. It is dependent upon the blood color of the being they feed on."

"So, vampires are real!" CJ said excitedly.

"Honey, you have watched too many movies." I said patting his arm and rubbing the bridge of my nose.

"Megan. They are real, but no Eldrin isn't a vampire. Yes, his kind survives on the blood of others, but only because of the iron that is in blood. They survive on liquefied iron. Only most do not like the synthetic that we have created here for them. They prefer it in a more natural state. And no, they aren't like vampires because they usually feed only on animals within the forest of Obsecuritan or go to other dimensions to feed. They can also come out in sunlight. They live just like anyone else, and no CJ, holy water, or anything of that sort does not kill them. Well, none of that works on what you call a vampire either, but that's an entirely different subject. In fact, Proteus live just like we do. They age, get sick, die, everything. However, they are manipulative, evil creatures. "

She took a deep breath before continuing. "They also have the ability to shape shift and even possess other beings, which is one of the reasons why in the treaty they had to agree to stay in humanoid form. However, if what you described is true, it is possible that your mother may be possessed by one of these creatures, and it would heighten her abilities, even awaken dormant ones. What I don't understand is how she was able to recognize you, separately from you in the vision."

"Yea, you and me both." I said as I stood up and headed back down the path. The sum of what I don't know in the way of the dimensions was staggering and was going to death of me. "Let's keep moving guys."

"You didn't tell us what else you saw in your vision, Megs." CJ asked.

"It kept bouncing around. Like I said I got glimpses of things." I said as nonchalantly as I could, but it stopped them from asking any further questions.

CHAPTER 22

THE NEXT MORNING, I woke before the sun and quietly got my things repacked. There was space by the river, so I went and sat down where self-doubt reared its ugly head. I looked at the electricity weaving between my fingers and I had confidence in it, I just didn't believe in myself. Everything was just so crazy. How could I believe any of this so thoroughly? Maybe it was all a fevered dream and I'd wake in the hospital, no parents, no CJ, no nurses, nothing.

"Megan?" I heard Owen say quietly.

"Ya, Owen."

"Can't sleep?" He said in a low voice.

"Slept most of the night, but just thinking." I said. We sat there for a long while before I sighed heavily and said, "When will I wake up Owen? This is all a dream, right? I mean, I don't want to give you and the others up, but... this whole thing feels like I'm in a movie. This sort of thing doesn't happen in real life."

"It's going be ok. We will stop them. It's two against six. They don't have a chance." "But they know what they're doing. We don't. We are guessing and making decisions off what I know of my parents, and I don't know shit about them. Everything I knew about Mom and Dad was a lie." I said picking up a rock and chucking it into the river.

"It wasn't a lie. It was your childhood reality." He said trying to comfort me. "They just didn't tell you about their life, or anything related to before you and your brother were born."

"How are we sure we are even making the right decisions though. I can't make any judgments off of what I think they would do. You are trusting my visions to lead us but what if they are wrong? What if one of you get hurt? What if I fail?"

"I won't lie Megan. The truth is you are right. Those are all reasons to be concerned. We are all trusting your visions. That includes trusting you." He said trying to be reassuring.

"But I don't want to trust and believe in them. I've lost loved ones in my visions." I sighed heavily while keeping my eyes firmly on the ground. "I don't know if I can handle losing anyone else."

"It's all or nothing." Owen said a sly smile crossing his face.

We sat there for a long time waiting for the sun to rise.

"What was Matt like?" Jean said about twenty minutes later. She walked up quietly and sat down next to Owen who put an arm around her, pulled her close, and put a quick kiss to her temple.

"I'm sorry?" I asked a little distracted by his outward show of affection. Owen was usually pretty reserved.

"What was your brother Matt like? I've never asked you about him before. Technically he was my nephew and I'd like to know a little about him." She said quietly.

"Well, he was born on November 20th, and he hated it." I laughed at the memory of him complaining how it just got mixed in with Thanksgiving. "He was like any other normal little brother I suppose. Annoying, pain in the butt, and always blamed everything on me. Well, I certainly blamed my share of things on him too. It really was just like any other brother - sister relationship. We fought, but we loved each other immensely." I trailed off at the end. My vision blurred as tears filled in my eyes and starting to run down my cheeks.

"He was happy. He was an average kid for the most part. He and his girlfriend, Melissa, were living with each other when he died. It devastated her when we told her what had happened. I think they would have gotten married if he were still alive. She moved back to Andorra with her parents where they run a ski resort."

"Andorra?" Owen asked.

"Yea it's this itty-bitty country between Spain and France in the mountains of Europe."

"What did he look like?" Jean asked hesitantly, shifting her weight uncomfortably.

"Well surprisingly, a lot like Owen. He was about 6 foot 2, big blue green eyes with a dark rim around the outside. He was always told how stunning they were. He had blonde brown hair that was just slightly too long and always a little messy. The little brat was always on the skinnier side too, which made me mad. It didn't matter what he ate, his body just absorbed it without ever making him fat, where I have to work off every bite of cake." I started to laugh.

Jean started to laugh a little too. Then she got a very contemplative look on her face.

"Go ahead. You can ask me anything about him. You didn't get to meet him." I said when she didn't say anything else.

"Well ... I was just wondering. ... Did he have visions too?"

I sighed.

"No. He didn't have visions. He..." I looked out across the river to the thick ferns and trees on the other side. They waited patiently.

"He had an ability though, didn't he?" Owen said breaking me out of my hesitation.

"Yeah. ... He could sense other people's feelings. It took him a long time to be able to handle it. High school was really hard for him. With all the raging hormones and other changes teenagers go through, it was just really difficult. Basically, he didn't just have to deal with his own but all 1300 of the kids in our high school. It came in handy at times though because he could tell what kind of mood Mom and Dad were in before they even walked in the door. And before you ask, no, he never told Mom and Dad about it. He saw how they treated me with my visions and trust me it wasn't kind. Told me I was just seeing things from an overactive imagination."

"They were very, very wrong." Owen said trying to comfort me.

"I know." I said looking over the river. "Doesn't make it any better. When your own parents don't believe you. It's hard. She just tried to medicate me to make them go away. There is some file somewhere where she actually got me diagnosed with schizophrenia just to make sure she could get medication for me. I quickly learned to not tell them about anything that came true from my dreams. At 14, I just started throwing them down the toilet, and at 16, she was convinced they had stopped and agreed I didn't need the meds anymore."

I saw Owen and Jean look at each other, but they didn't say anything else. We just sat there quiet until the sun started to lighten the sky.

"We should wake the others and start heading out. We still have a lot of island to cover before tonight." I said heading back to camp.

It was early evening when we reached near the top of the mountain and Owen bounced in front of me and across a creek using the logs as stepping stones. I smiled. Another vision down, I thought to myself.

"Wait, can you feel that?" I asked holding my breath. I don't know why but I felt like I was being pulled down an off-shooting creek.

Please tell me someone else feels it.
Please tell me someone else feels it.
Please tell me someone else feels it.
"Yea, I can. This way down the creek." Clarice said.
Thank the Angels!
"It's a pull, isn't it?" Jean asked heading down the creek.
"I don't know what one is supposed to feel like." I stopped for a minute. I heard what sounded like rushing water. It wasn't coming from the main river, but further down the creek. "Can you hear that?"

"A waterfall?" Owen asked looking at the creek. "There isn't enough water running down the creek for a waterfall. Well, one that sounds like that anyways."

I took off running down the creek, soaking my boots and laces half way up my shin. Sure enough, there was a waterfall about a quarter mile down. I looked down about a hundred-foot drop. Owen was right about one thing, there wasn't enough water running through the creek to justify a large amount of water running off the edge.

When CJ caught up with me, he looked back up the creek and back over the edge. "How can so much be running off? Where is all the extra water coming from?"

"Could this be?" Lindy said with a look of utter amazement on her face. "There were things that alluded to it in the texts, your power, but..."

"How could what be Lindy?" Jean asked.

"It's said that the Five Angels created a place in an alternative dimension. It's very similar to the local lore here that CJ mentioned now that I think about it. Julian was so sure of its existence that he had me looking for *The Garden of the Five Angels* in the ancient text. I never found anything specifying a location in all of my translation of the Five Angels documents. It's said that the one who finds it would have been touched by the Angels themselves ..." She turned to look at me curiously.

"You don't think Megan." Jean said in disbelief as she looked from Lindy to me.

"Don't think I wha—" I said shifting my on a rock, but my foot slipped and then there was nothing but air around me.

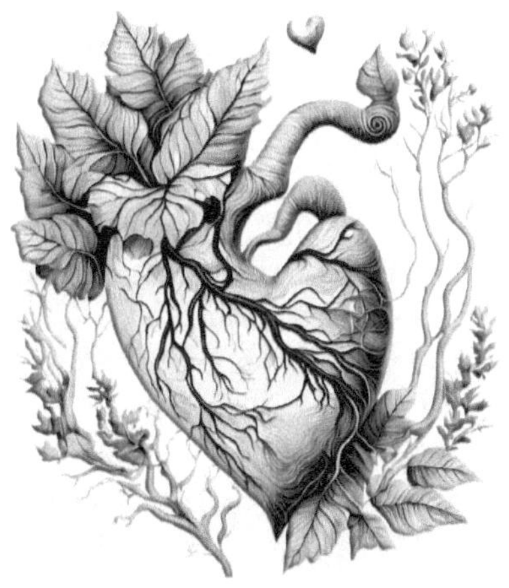

CHAPTER 23

I CRUNCHED MYSELF UP into a ball and when I hit the water it was warm. I was so used to the cold water back in Monterey the warmth surprised me. As the water soaked into my clothes, I could feel my pack pulling me under like a lead weight. I got to the surface just in time to see the others splash into the pool beside me at the base of the waterfall. I pulled my pack off and dragged it behind me as I swam to get to the shore. I threw my water-logged pack a few yards away and looked around.

"It's the waterfall from my vision." I said trying to catch my breath and heading toward the base of the waterfall.

"What?" CJ asked chasing after me. "Megs!"

"Grab my pack." I looked around. There had to be a cave here somewhere.

There, just behind the waterfall was a cave entrance.

"Come on scaredy cats." I could see the uneasiness on their faces. I grabbed CJ's hand and walked firmly into the darkness. I spread the golden glow around him and he instantly relaxed.

It was pitch black in the tunnel, and I could hear the footsteps of the others as they walked behind me. We rounded a corner and saw a blue glow around another corner about 10 feet ahead of us. We walked up to the corner, and there was the sea of blue I had glimpsed. Only, it wasn't a sea of blue, but a huge blue sparkly wall.

"This is it. This is how we get into the garden." I whispered. I waited for them all to get right behind me. I couldn't see past the blue wall, but the blue sparkles created a thick barrier that curved around another bend of the cave.

I let go of CJ's hand and reached out to touch it. It was hard against my hand, but gave just a little, like plexiglass.

"Through there?" CJ asked hesitantly.

"Yup. It will lead us straight into the meadow with the Desumo Nitor." I said smiling at them. Granted, it isn't that I had seen it. I just knew.

I took a deep breath, grabbed CJ's hand tight and touched the wall again. This time my hand pushed through and as I took a step in, we were lifted up from the ground and floated through. CJ and I floated through blue sparkles that swirled around us.

When we reached the other side, I turned to smile at the others to encourage them through, but when I looked behind us, I couldn't see them. A moment later, Owen and Jean came through, hand in hand, and right behind them Clarice and Lindy were next facing each other touching fingertip to fingertip.

No one spoke. Not a single word. I turned and walked down the hall, which was smooth to an archway with bright sunlight shining through. The archway had small versions of each of the Five Angels carved into the stone. I ran my fingers along the carvings marveling at the detail and how smooth they were. The carvings were so precise that it appeared that each were wearing sheer clothing. More than that, you could see the fine lines in each individual face, full and thin lips, each bump on a nipple, each ripple of skin in the stomach, each hair in the pelvis, and each toe perfectly.

"Megs." CJ said breaking my study. "You did it. You found it."

I turned toward him, took a deep breath, and took a step through the archway. I was glad I had taken that breath because the sight before me it took it right away again.

At the north end of the meadow, there was a statue of one of the Angels, that was just as detailed. Beauty I assumed, but the most fascinating sight were the Desumo Nitor. It was just as CJ had described. Vines branched out from a tall stone wall with stems that hung heavy with buds only hours from blooming. There was no breeze but the flower buds, and the buds alone, moved as if they were breathing, just like the ones in grandma's garden.

The realization hit me like a ton of bricks.

"Lindy." I said just above a whisper. She didn't hear me. "Lindy!" I said louder.

"Humm?" she was so engrossed in the view that laid before us she hadn't heard me.

"You said that the Five Angels had created a place in an alternative dimension. Right?" I said.

"Yea." Lindy said, still half listening to me.

"Look at this place. There are statues of the Five Angels around the gateway we just came through, and a larger one over there on the north end of the meadow. Notice how the flowers are moving just like the ones at home. You wouldn't think twice about how the flowers moved, because all flowers in Nalsar move like this. Flowers don't move like this in the Manusia. They are stationary unless moved by an outside force, like the wind. Well except for carnivorous ones, but that's a whole different kettle of fish." I shook my head to keep myself on track. "Is it possible that these are not the rarest flowers in your world, but the flower themselves are from yours and put here? That would make them extremely rare here in the Manusia."

She just nodded as she continued to take in the view laid before us.

"What time is it?" CJ interrupted. "They only bloom between midnight and sunrise."

I turned to him my power pulsing against that cocoon again. Anger boiling to the surface, "WHAT? Don't you think that is something we should have known earlier? What if we didn't get here till sunrise? We would have missed the whole thing. My parents could have come and gone."

"Assuming they even find this place." Owen said quietly behind me.

"Honey. Calm down. First of all, I didn't want to worry you about making sure you were here before midnight. Besides, you had always planned on being here before that, so it's a moot point." He continued to look at me until I finally relaxed. He raised his eyebrow and asked again, "So what time is it?"

"It's only 9:oo pm local time." I told him "You should get some sleep hun."

"I'm not tired." He said nervously and not making eye contact with me.

I sighed and turned to Clarice. "Clarice what else did you do to him?" Jean and Owen were staring at her in disbelief.

"We placed complete travel protection on him okay!" She said cringing. Jean and Owen just laughed and shook their head.

"It's a series of incantations that help you travel for long periods of time without the experience of fatigue, clumsiness, prolonged hunger, or sleepiness. He should be good for another week before he loses any of that." She smiled brightly at me. "And for the record Megan. He came to me. He was worried that being human may slow everyone down. I tried to tell him that it wasn't an issue and that we could just leave a day earlier to give us the extra time for him to rest. Then the little shit said that he was reading through some of your books and had seen the travel protection line of incantations. He worked me for a couple of days before he talked me into it."

"Megs." He started to say but hesitated when he saw look on my face. Then his voice got very serious. "I want to help as much as I can. I do not want to slow ya'll down. So, I went to Clarice and begged her. I think she did it just to shut me up because I know I would have. I was really starting to whine like a baby. If she had refused, I would have gone to Lindy, then Jean, and then Owen, until I got what I wanted."

I was still mad but couldn't help but smirk. I could see how Clarice didn't stand a chance when CJ got like that. He whines so well.

"But you slept last night?"

"Just dozed in and out."

"Well, let's get something to eat then. I'm starved." I said as I rolled my eyes. There was no use in fighting over it. What is done, is done.

We started the fire and cooked up some hamburgers. I sat in silence as the others chattered about this and that. Unfortunately, my mind went back into self-doubt. When it came down to it, I knew I was more than just a little scared. After the incident with the guys from Gendril I knew I could fight. But what if I wasn't able to protect the ones I love. I heard the others discussing the Five Angels, but I wasn't paying much attention when something that Lindy had said earlier, started burning in my mind.

"Lindy?" I interrupted them.

"Yes?" She said jumping a little.

"Just before I fell down the waterfall you said that there was a story about the garden?" I asked her keeping my voice low.

"I'm sorry sweety." Everyone was now paying full attention. Owen stuffed another big bite of his hamburger in his mouth, and I tried to keep the smile off my face. He really loved them.

"I found vague references to it in the translations of the Five Angels documents. Trust me, when I say that I translated a LOT of them and Julian is persistent, to say the least. The story says that they built a place for them to commune in a peaceful location far away. *The Garden of the Five Angels.* Only Sangra touched by them would be able to find it. That Sangra would have inner power greater than any other Sangra in our history. When that Sangra found the garden, they would be able to call to the Angels, who would then appear and give that Sangra their heart's desire, in exchange for a favor for the Angels."

"But what could the Angels want with a Sangra, even one touched by them. Couldn't they just send them on that course without having to find this place and if they wanted something done, couldn't they just do it themselves? I mean they are the Angels." I asked.

"I don't know. Maybe they have a flair for the dramatics. I'm guessing that it would be something that would try the Sangra into determining their worth. A way of proving themselves to the Angels. I think."

"The Five Angels really do know how to leave things vague, don't they? I mean it's not like they say that this will happen and that will happen. The weapon is specific to the wielder, the favor asked isn't specified. The Five Angels are so confusing! I just wish I knew what my parents would want to build to destroy Nalrin."

It was Jean this time who said, "It is confusing at times. You have to remember though it's free will and dependent on what the welder wants to destroy. You wouldn't defeat a Bakta with a sword, you would defeat them by somehow depriving them of any and all happiness. Sangra are like humans, there are many ways we could die."

"But do they want to destroy all Sangra, or just the Council? That would make a big difference in what type of weapon they would need, a sword, pathogens, a spoken incantation for destruction? I know the components that are needed, but how do we prevent it?" I asked.

Everyone was quiet for a long time. Obviously, this had been a question that had been on everyone's mind. "I guess preventing them from getting the flower is the first act and if that fails, we move on from there." I said quietly.

They nodded in agreement.

CHAPTER 24

EVERYONE, INCLUDING CJ, STARTED fidgeting and getting uneasy the closer it got to midnight. However, I couldn't help but feel at totally at peace here. There was something about this place. I kept looking through the vines and other plants, but this place was huge. I had stared through them so much that I was starting to think I saw things moving through the fauna, but when I focused on it, I wouldn't see anything there. My power's electricity was strangely smooth and flowing. Not edgy and jumpy.

When I heard CJ's watch beep at midnight, I jumped a little. He laughed at me, and I smiled as I tried to focus. I closed my eyes and felt out watching for any hint of my parents. I couldn't feel anything beyond the gateway. Usually, the embers of living things faded into the distance, but there was a harsh wall of black beyond the stone walls and gateway. There was just nothing beyond the archway to the garden.

159

I felt each of my family, their embers bright and glowing, but the place itself... I don't know how I didn't notice it before. The flora and fauna were also emitting an ember brighter than we were. I tried to separate out the different levels of embers I saw, to separate the people from the soundings, but it was hard. I had sweat slipping down my back, but after a few minutes, but I found my balance. My parents had to be here, but I couldn't see anyone other than my family.

The garden was taking on a life of its own. The Desumo Nitor hung upside down from the vines and slowly, 13 pure snow white wide pointed petals and bright blue tips started to unfurl. The electric blue rims sparkled and lit up the garden with a brilliant blue glow.

We just stared for minutes on minutes. CJ came to stand next to me and slowly took my hand, I held it tight. A moment later, he turned me to face him and knelt down on one knee. I felt every ounce of air leave my lungs. He brought out a small black box with his other hand and looked up at me.

His eyes rimmed with silver as he said, "Megan Isabel Keller. You've been there for me through everything. Every memory I have that is worth remembering has you by my side. I want that to continue for the rest of our lives. I love you more than any man could love a woman. I promise to love and protect you for the rest of this life and any life that I am blessed with afterward. Will you marry me?" His voice broke at the end, and it made the tears in my eyes fall over the rim.

He opened the box and inside was the most beautiful ring I had ever seen. Sitting in dark blue satin, was a crystal-clear diamond with slightly smaller sapphires on either side centered on a simple platinum band.

"Yes." I tried to whisper but nothing came out. When I found my voice again, I said. "YES! YES! YES!"

He took the ring out of its satin confines and with a shaky hand he slid it onto my ring finger on my left hand. He stood up, put his palms on my cheeks, and whispered, "Thank Fuck!" and kissed me hard.

I would have probably fallen to the ground if he were not holding me up. I felt as if I was flying. I kissed him back and let everything else float away into the ether. CJ was mine. He would be mine forever.

When the kiss broke and I opened my eyes, we were floating 20 feet above the ground surrounded by the same blue sparkles that came from the Desumo Nitor when they bloomed. CJ held his eyes to mine.

"Can you feel that?" he whispered to me. He looked at his hands and there was an electrical current between us. It bound our hands. No stings of pain, but it bound us together.

I felt into my power, to coil it back in, but it slumbered quietly in its cocoon. I could feel that electricity between us, but it wasn't mine.

"It's not mine." I whispered.

Slowly, the blue sparkles that were holding us pulled into the space between CJ and I and we were lowered to the ground. When our feet touched, a bright blue light shot out and surrounded us, retracted back between us, and flowed into our chests. It was the strangest sensation. It was warm and tingly, but then there was an electrical snap that I felt deep in my chest. CJ and my eyes met, and I swear I could see true lightning crackle in his eyes.

When the light vanished from between us, I saw it.

There in the vines. Right next to the entrance to the garden.

My parents.

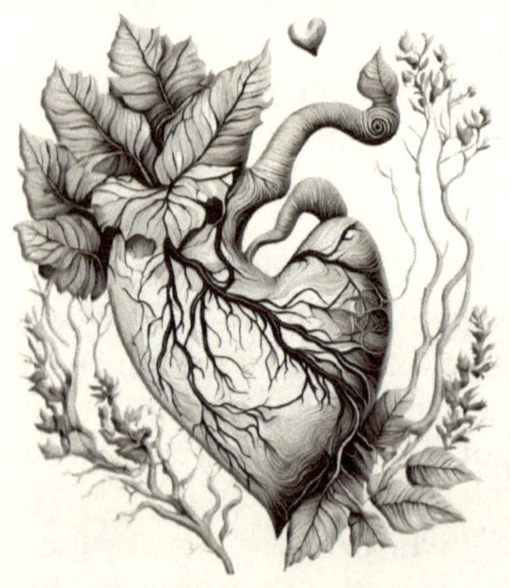

CHAPTER 25

"Mom! Dad!" I said once I had found my voice, pulling CJ behind me. "You can come out from the vines now."

Instantly, the others were behind me crouched and ready to fight. Lindy had both of her syths in her hands, as did Owen and Jean. Clarice, of course, had her whips, her preferred way of fighting. I had asked her once about it, and she just said she felt she had more control.

My mother walked out with her hands up in surrender, but my father walked out, syths in hand, eyes glaring at Lindy as she moved in front of the others.

My father turned to me and smiled my favorite daddy smile. "Megan, you're alive!"

"Oh, stop with the bullshit, dad." I said unable to keep the venom out of my tone, but something settled in me that I couldn't place. The sight of them, alive, when I had had to mourn their death. Hell, I had still been dealing with much of the estate in the Manusia when I came to Nalsar.

"I'm just so pleased you lived through the explosion." He said in what used to be his daddy voice.

"Daddy." I said a lump settling in my throat. I tried to get words out, but I couldn't make my lips move. I looked to CJ. We had only talked about it briefly. I wanted to try and talk them out of this. I wanted to try to stop it before it went too far.

"*CJ. I can't ...*" I pushed to him.

"Mr. Keller." CJ said, my dad's eyes snapping to him. "Please. For Megan's sake. Please don't do this. You've already lost Matt. Don't lose Megan too."

My dad just glared at him and said between his teeth, "You two don't know what you are talking about. You have no idea what has happened."

"That's because you lied to me. How could you never tell Matt and I about any of this?" I said sounding like I was a six-year-old again.

"We had our reasons, Megan." It was my mother. When I looked at her, she wasn't even looking at me but at Jean.

CJ grabbed my hand and said, "Matt and Megan were children. They asked you hundreds of times about any extended family. She saw our friends have grandparents, aunts, uncles, cousins over all the time, and they just wanted to understand what having an extended family felt like."

"They—" My dad started to say, but I interrupted him.

"Daddy, please." I said with a small breath.

They looked at me. Looked to my new family behind me.

My Dad looked to me, then to Lindy.

"You are nothing but a child. You are pathetic and broken. We tried to fix you, but you can't be fixed." He said then cocked his head to the side, "Unless you join us and make it all right. Kill Jean and Lindy where they stand and maybe you can be fixed."

Then my mother said, "If you stand with them. Then you stand against us. They killed your brother. You stand with them, and you are no daughter of ours."

"You fucking bitch." I heard CJ and Jean say in unison.

"Watch your attitude boy." My mother scowled.

"Or what? You'll put me over your knee and spank me?" CJ said rolling his eyes.

I felt that piece, that small piece, break loose from my heart and float off into a dark pit. That small shred of hope that I had been holding onto that this wouldn't go down this path. The hope that this was all some huge misunderstanding. I felt a part of my past slip away inside me and that cocoon snatch it up. The electricity, still safely wrapped up in its cocoon, flared. Strands burst through my tiny window, and I clamped down on it.

CJ squeezed my hand again tightly and I looked down, there were rings of current weaving between my fingers. I could feel them now. Bright and daring. They flowed over my fingers like water and one side of my lip twitched up as I looked to CJ.

"You know it's Lindy's fault that Matt died right?" My father said loathingly bringing me out from inside myself.

"Yes. I do, but only to an extent, Dad." I paused as he looked at me questioning how much I really knew. "It was in response to you killing council members. One of which was your own brother, my uncle, and Lindy's husband. I know all about it. How you were a council member yourself and started looking into the weapons of the Five Angels. They were doing their job and you murdered them for that."

I saw my mother moving toward the flowers. "Mom, I wouldn't move any closer if I were you."

My father gave me questioning look. "Why are you here?"

"Stop with the bullshit. You know damn well why. You will not get the components needed to make the weapon of the Five Angels." My mother made another move to the flowers and I threw my hand up, a wall going up blocking my mother from the flowers. She bounced back and growled at me.

"I told you not to move any closer, Mother." She looked to my father, confusion clear on her face, as I continued. "You had no clue I had developed my Sangra power, did you?"

Then my father did the one thing I had hoped he wouldn't do, he turned to me, anger flashing in his large eyes as he twirled his syths in my direction, and said, "You may have Sangra power girl, but you don't know how to work that power. You were never trained. Do not stand in our way child." I felt like I had been kicked in the gut.

Anger, sadness, and pain flowed through me. He had always told me that calling an adult daughter or son, "child" was the biggest insult of all. It hurt to admit but I couldn't claim him as my father. Not anymore. I stepped toward my father as I pushed my thoughts to Lindy. *"Protect CJ. That's all I ask."*

"There is no love left in your soul is there, father?" I said, whirling my syths around effortlessly in my fingers to make my point. I circled him to be between my parents and the wall of flowers. "You have no idea how powerful I really am Ansel."

"And who has trained you? Jean? Owen?" he laughed, "They couldn't protect a squirrel!"

"Oh, they can do much more than that."

"How dare you." He said snarling, showing way too many teeth and moving closer and closer to me. Electricity crackled in my ears and all I saw was his dark ember. I felt out feeling everyone's ember glowing brightly, then stopped short when I saw CJs. It seemed brighter somehow, even brighter than Jean's.

"Oh please! If you think I'm nothing of consequence, then push me aside and take your flower." I said concentrating on my father again. I had to keep their attention on me.

I hardly got the phrase from my lips before he lunged at me. I moved to the right, but that movement cost me the wall between my mother and the flowers. It dropped and Jean ran after her toward the vines.

A sharp pain ripped into my stomach, dropping me to my knees. It ran slowly up through my rib cage and stopped at my heart. It wrapped and squeezed around it. My entire being froze. I looked down but there was nothing there.

An illusion.

I took a deep breath, pulled more of that thread of power to encircle me. A shield. It flickered under the pressure of my father's power but held.

I forced myself to my feet and I mentally picked my father up and threw him against the stone wall near the gateway. That gave me a moment to turn toward CJ and make sure he was ok. Lindy and Clarice were in a protective crouch in front of him, and Owen and Jean circled my mother doing their best to keep her from grabbing one of the Desumo Nitor. I felt my father behind me and when I whirled around to face him he stopped in shock.

"How?" he growled at me.

"I told you I was more powerful than you know. Now would you like to leave or do you want more." I snarled.

"I don't want to hurt you, Megan." He said, "But I will kill you to get that flower. They must pay for what they have done to my family."

"I won't allow you to create this weapon. It won't change anything. It won't bring Matt back!" I told him as we circled around each other, my heart breaking with each word.

"Didn't you love your brother at all? Don't you want to punish those who caused his death?" He snarled each word at me.

"Revenge? That's your reasoning? By that reasoning, it is you that should be punished for his death. If it were not for you then we --" I never saw him pounce. One second he was there, the next I was screaming in pain as his syth tore through the muscle in my shoulder.

"MEGAN!" I heard CJ scream as he rushed toward me.

Ansel yanked out the blade and as he moved back, I sliced through his right side feeling it grate against something hard as it sliced through flesh and muscle. He stumbled back as I swung for him again. I still didn't have use of my left arm but was still able to dodge his attacks.

I saw CJ try to move towards me, but Lindy reached out to pull him back. CJ dodged her, but Clarice had him with a crack of her whip by the wrist and pulled him back. He fought her, but between Clarice and Lindy, he couldn't dislodge them.

"CJ. She's fine." I heard her say. I nodded to him not daring to take my eyes off my father. I heard the sounds of syths clashing between my mother and Jean, but worst of all, I saw Owen lying motionless on the ground out of the corner of my eye. His ember was fluctuating, and he was hurt bad.

Anger. Frustration. Perseverance. I pulled it all from inside of me, gripped my syths tight, and took slow meaningful steps toward him. Crackling electricity flowed down my syths. My power numbing the pain in my shoulder. The hum of electricity in my ears. I felt the strands of my hair rise above me. The hair on my arms even rose with the power that was flowing through me.

"You. Will. Not. Hurt. Anymore. Of. My. Family." I said with each step. I was solely focused on him. Just as I was about to throw my syth, I had another thought. I took a deep breath, willing my power to calm silently. Half a thought and I pulled at the vines. His attention had been on me and hadn't expected them. I cocked my head to the side, willing them to wrap around him tightly, a strand of electricity flowed from my hand I had stretched out to the vines, trapping him in electrified vines. I shook him up and down, and then with a few flicks of my fingers flung him up against the stone archway with a large crack. He did not get up. The vines that had held my power, crumbling to dust.

I walked up to him. Kicked his syths from his hands and I heard my mother screaming at Jean, "It's your fault! If you hadn't let Dad die--"

"Symatha, leave Jean alone." I said with a chilling calm as I threw my hand out and held her in electric ropes, where she was mid-jump. She turned her head to me with wide eyes.

"Don't act so surprised." Her eyes traveled past me and looked at my father.

"What have you done?!" she spat with fire in her eyes.

"Don't worry the asshole's not dead." I told her.

"Don't you speak about your father that way." She scolded.

"I'm sorry what? I mean, are you seriously going to try to teach manners today?"

"Well, we are still your parents Megan."

"Bullshit." CJ said, and I tried hard to suppress a smile.

"Biological parents, yes. But see, you abandoned me a year ago. What kind of parent does that to their child?" I didn't realize I had started to scream at her. "Seriously, Mom. What parent has their daughter come over for lunch, housecleaning, and family time, then blows the house to smithereens, making it look like a gas explosion? Oh, yea, and then allowing that daughter to believe that her parents had been incinerated in the explosion of the house."

In my anger and frustration, my hold on her was stronger than I realized. She was moaning and twitching in pain. I loosened the grip I had on her just slightly. She gave me an evil grin and threw her power at us.

It felt like someone had taken a brick to my chest. I fell back and struggled to keep her in place. She slithered out of the hold I had on her and fell to the ground. As she ran to my father I threw a wall up, and she bounced against it laughed loudly as her whole demeanor shifted.

"You think you can stop me with a simple wall little girl?" She was standing up straight, almost growing taller as her eyes turned that eerie muddy red color. "You have no idea the dark powers I have come to possess."

My entire body went ice cold, as I saw the exact expression she had in my vision. She placed a hand on my wall and it crumbled. I hardly saw it. One moment she was standing there laughing at me, the next she had grabbed my father and bolted through the barrier, a Desumo Nitor in her hand.

I had failed.

CHAPTER 26

THEY HAD BEEN PLAYING with us. With what she just did, she could have stopped the fight at any point. She had been playing with us.

I took in everything in slow motion. Owen was breathing erratically, and his ember was fading. If we didn't do something soon, it was going to go out completely. He had a deep jagged wound from his right shoulder that cut straight across his chest down to his left hip. Blood was flowing from the wound but down the center was a yellow creamy substance that just sat there. Festering. Angels it smelled horrid.

Jean was in hysterics as her mouth just repeated, "No. No. No. No. No."

Owen screamed in pain. Clarice and Lindy were leaning over Owen chanting.

Through the gaps of space and time
We ask the Angel of Healing to bind
The wound of Owen Kayl Tudor

I felt panic rise in my chest. What good is it to be above average power when you can't fix your family?

The flowers continued to sparkle throughout the garden, just as they had when CJ had asked me to marry him. I looked down at the ring on my finger and it was coated in blood. Blood still flowed down my arm and I still couldn't move it. I looked to my shoulder and I could see electricity along the edges of the wound trying to knit it back together. My eyes knitted together at it, but at Owen's next scream I turned back to him.

Shimmering flickers of light floated down and around Owen circling him and raising him about 4 feet off the ground. The wound continued to bleed and ooze. He screamed in pain at the movement and Jean grabbed his hand.

"Megan." She pleaded, and I looked away. I had no idea what to do. For how powerful I felt only moments ago, I now felt so powerless.

Now that he was raised higher, I could see just how deep the wound was. No longer supported by the ground, the weight of his body allowed it to open wider. His ribs.

Oh Angels. Those were his ribs. They stuck out on the left side, but no matter how Owen moved the yellow creamy substance stayed and spread within the open wound. The sight of it made bile rise up in my stomach and I cupped my hand at the base of my neck.

Owen howled in pain again as the blue sparkles moved to the edges of the wound that started to glow and sizzle. Clarice and Jean cringed. I jumped back even further at the sound of his scream, but when I removed my hand from my neck, the healing stopped.

What the-?

I stood there stunned for a minute, my mind racing through what had just happened. Lindy looked at me. No, she was looking at the pendant around my neck. Was I touching it ... Why ... Owen? My mind was spinning so fast I couldn't even track it when understanding crashed over me.

The Golden Amulet of Sa Ra. It should be able to heal Owen. Very slowly I moved my hand back up to the pendant. Once my fingers touched the pendant my shoulder spasmed as Owen screamed in pain again, but the wound had started to mend as the sparkles lit up brighter.

I removed my hand from the pendant again. Immediately, Owen stopped screaming and the wound stopped mending.

Jean looked at me again, angry questions in her eyes. CJ took my blood covered hand and his presence grounded me.

I closed my eyes, to block out his screaming before I gripped onto the pendant. Only this time Owen didn't scream. My eyes flung open as I saw the wound mend just as before, but Owen just laid there, calm, and serene. I let go of CJ's hand and immediately Owen started screaming and twitching again and I jumped letting go of the pendant.

I looked to CJ questioningly, shrugged and put his hand out again for me. I tried to move my arm, but pain lanced my shoulder and I winced. He reached over and carefully took my hand in his as I firmly grasped the pendant. Not only did the wound start healing but the blue sparkles slowly lifted the yellow creamy substance from the gash across his body and evaporated into the air.

I held CJ's hand tight and thought,
Through the gaps of space and time
We ask the Angel of Healing to bind
The wound of Owen Kayl Tudor
Lindy and Clarice hadn't stopped their chanting,
Through the gaps of space and time
We ask the Angel of Healing to bind
The wound of Owen Kayl Tudor
Never once did Owen even so much as wince in pain.
Through the gaps of space and time
We ask the Angel of Healing to bind
The wound of Owen Kayl Tudor
When the yellow substance within the gash was gone, the blue sparkles covered the area and pulled themselves into the scar that was forming in its place. Owen was lowered back to the ground and when the last sparkle had disappeared from his wound, he took a deep shuttering, wet breath and passed out.

"OWEN?" Jean whispered fear coating that word so deeply I felt the stab in my own heart.

"Jean, he's breathing. It's okay." Lindy said trying to comfort her.

No one spoke for the next half hour. We just sat there either pacing or watching him, waiting for him to wake up.

When he did open his eyes, he tried to slowly sit up on his elbows.

"Stay laying down honey." Jean said, putting her hand on his forehead.

"Button, next time you're mad at me, can you just give me the silent treatment instead of setting your sister on me?" He said with a raspy giggle, which he cut short wincing.

"Well, at least you didn't lose your sense of humor." Jean said as she ran her fingers over the now thick light pink scar that had formed across his chest. "Owen, I thought I had lost you. I only lost sight of her for a second. I'm so, so sorry."

It all came out in such a rush, that it sounded like one long word.

"I'm fine." He said as he tried to get to his feet, but he was still too weak to move much. "Okay. Not fine, but alive."

"Just relax a little bit. That was one wicked wound." Lindy said.

"What caused that kind of infection?" Jean asked. "What was that yellow...goo?"

"I've only seen that kind of infection in books." Lindy said.

"It's a demon–based poison. It's meant to cause great pain when one attempts to heal it. The more you try to clean it out the more it spreads. It slows the bleeding as well, to maximize the pain the victim receives. By the time anyone could fix it, the one who is wounded would likely bleed out instead of having the wound tended to. It's used a lot in Gendril." Clarice said.

"I saw Symatha do it, but ... how could she have access to that?" Jean asked.

"The Protus." I said with a whisper, surprising even myself. Everyone's head turned to me with blank stares. "She must be possessed by one. Remember when I told you how in my vision her eyes..." I waited till they all caught up with me. One by one they all came to the same conclusion.

"Just before she left, the last thing she said to me was '*You have no idea the dark powers I have come to possess.*' Her face, her body language, and most of all her eyes looked exactly like they had in my vision." I said barely whispering the words.

"Okay. So now we have that to contend with." Lindy said sadly, then turned back to Owen. "One thing I don't understand though. How did you heal him?"

"My necklace." I said. "The Golden Amulet of Sa Ra. When I touched it, his wound started to heal, but that was when he was screaming in pain. When I took my hand off the pendant it stopped. Then..." I turned to CJ.

"That doesn't explain why he stopped hurting when you and I were holding hands." CJ said thinking along the same path as I was.

"When you held my hand though, I felt ... calm, but you always calm me down." I shook my head not understanding.

"I just wished he couldn't feel the pain. Just like I wanted to make the pain in your shoulder go away." He said as he fingered the fabric where my shoulder had been stabbed. His eyes crunched together, "Um ... Megs."

I looked down at my shoulder and it wasn't bleeding anymore, hell it wasn't even injured. There was just a light pink line in the same exact spot where my father had stabbed me with his syth. I moved my arm, and it was stiff, but it didn't hurt.

I looked around at everyone else. No one else seemed to be hurt. Sure, there was dried blood where wounds had been, but I couldn't help myself in asking, "Was anyone else hurt during the fight?"

Lindy checked her leg through the hole in her pants and was rubbing her thigh. Jean was looking at her arm in amazement. Clarice was rubbing her forehead, but only wiping away dried blood. It seemed that all of their injuries had also been healed.

We were all quiet for a long moment before Lindy said, "Local lore and legend said anyone who stands in the meadow at the time of blooming would receive powers. CJ was the only human to be standing in the meadow when the flowers were blooming. We wouldn't receive anything because we already have an inner power."

I looked at CJ who was looking at me a silent question written across his face. "Your ember. It's brighter."

I turned around to face away from the others and sat down on the grass a few feet away, putting my head in my hands. I needed to think. Could that really be it?

CJ. I sighed heavily and fell back into the grass, staring up at the star filled sky.

Why was all of this happening to me? Why CJ? What had he done but love me? I looked at my hand where my ring sat, and I sighed again. I don't want him to have to deal with this. I should just lock him up in a castle somewhere until all this is over. I let out a giggle at the ridiculousness of that thought and rubbed my hands over my face.

I wish I knew what the Angels wanted of me. There must be a reason why I was granted more power than my family has seen before if there is a shred of truth to what Lindy is saying.

Doesn't really matter. Power. No Power. Super–power. I had to help stop my parents. There was no question about that.

If only there was a way to really know what to do. I laid there just watching the stars shimmer in the clear night sky. Now, what do I do?

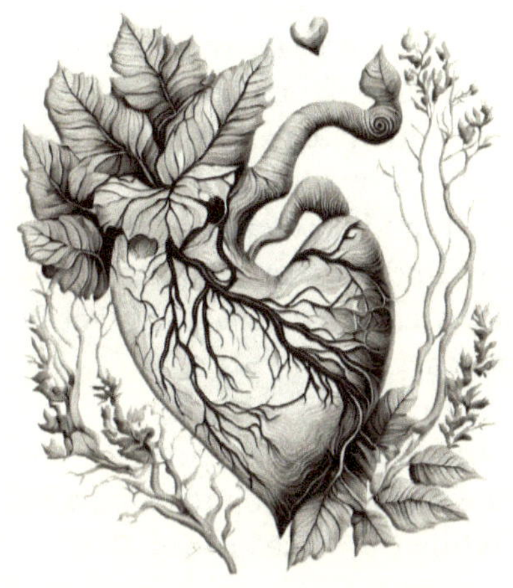

CHAPTER 27

"MEGAN! LOOK!"

I rolled over to see everyone pointing to the back edge of the garden. There a ghostly figure walked toward the statue at the north end. I had seen the statue when we came in but hadn't thought too much of it. I was so engrossed in the flowers of the garden that I had just glanced over it. I got up and slowly walked closer toward it.

As I got closer, I realized just how perfect it was. It didn't have the look of an ancient statue that had been out in the elements for a millennium. It was smooth, precise, and very life like. Exactly like the ones back at the archway.

"Angel of Beauty." Lindy said and then turned to me with a smile. "And no. No wings."

I glared at her and she just smiled back nudging my arm.

The Angel of Beauty faced upwards, her arms outstretched as if to give everyone a hug.

Owen attempted to stand, but his legs were still too weak to hold his weight. He moved to sit on his knees and as the ghostly figure reached the statue, it came alive. Slowly she stepped down from her perch and when she was standing in front of us, she folded her hands, shook out her snow-white long hair, and looked down at us with warm eyes. My power snapped and sizzled under my skin in response to her gaze, but just as quickly as it had occurred it dyed down to nothingness.

"Faithful Sangra and dearest ... Human. I welcome you to the Garden of the Five Angels. I am the Angel of Beauty." Her voice was soft and smooth.

We bowed in greeting.

"Please, please my children, rise, and let's discuss things. Ms. Megan, what is the reason for you to call upon The Five?"

Everyone, including CJ, looked at me with a shocked look on their faces. I looked up at the Angel. "I'm sorry?"

"Were you not just wondering what The Five wanted?"

"Well yes. That was only because everyone seems so sure that I have so much more power within me than everyone else." I said meekly.

"But you do child. Don't you see, and it's something more than just your power. Didn't you just stand up to your parents for what was right?"

"What does that matter? What they are doing is wrong. They made mistakes when they were younger and they have to live with the consequences. Ironically, they taught my brother and me that. To live with the consequences of our own actions and decisions." I said quietly, then stood up straight, "Two wrongs don't make a right. That goes for what the Council did to my brother, and what my parents are trying to do to the council and Nalsar."

"Very intuitive to recognize, and brave to voice, the faults of the council. However, your Ansel and Symatha have been seething in their despair for so long that darkness has taken over. I'm sure you noticed that in the color of their power. While you could show them love and compassion, they are beyond being able to accept it. It is up to you to stop their darkness."

"I want to, but I have already failed. They got the Desumo Nitor. I saw it in my mother's hand as they passed through the gateway."

"That is only one piece of the puzzle my dear, and frankly the easiest." The Angel of Beauty said with a chuckle. Then she looked at each of us, and said, "You will have to make some horrific choices in this path Ms. Megan, but it is a path you must take."

Sadly, even though my family looked at me, I knew exactly what she meant.

Then Lindy interrupted my thoughts. "Angel of Beauty, it is such an honor to meet you. I have studied the Angels writings and translated many of them. I have read and studied much on the weapon of The Five Angels, but so much of it is subjective that we don't know how to proceed. Is there any help that you could give us?

"Ms. Lindy, you are most talented, and have done well with the power of knowledge, but know that books cannot answer everything. Forgiveness, my dear, is something that you must learn. There is nothing I can tell you that Ms. Megan doesn't already know, or you and this family will be able to tell her about this journey. She will need all of this family to help her. Trust in her choices and in her gifts. She has been touched by The Five. This one journey, Ms. Megan, is what The Five have asked of you."

"The story of the Garden of the Five Angels is true then?" Lindy said a bit more excited than I was.

The Angel of Beauty simply nodded.

"That would mean since Megan found this place, she is the Sangra with an inner power greater than any other Sangra in our history." Lindy said in awe.

I stood there stunned for a moment as they looked at me. No one looked at me like I was crazy, a freak, or anything of that sort, they just looked at me. But being touched by the Angels?

"No not me! I'm just Megan." I said barely above a whisper.

The Angel of Beauty giggled. It was a light childlike sound that almost made me smile.

"Just Megan. My dear, you have never been just Megan." The Angel of Beauty said with a sweet smile.

"What great power would I have obtained? Honestly, I'm going to need all the help I can get to stop my parents." I said a bit stunned.

"That's an interesting thing to be said from you, Ms. Megan. Pure Power. You have a unique freedom with your power that others do not have. You see it manifest in electricity do you not?"

I nodded but kept my head down twiddling my fingers.

"This is not what we had originally envisioned. It is true that the one who could find our garden would have been blessed with a great power, and in return, they would prove their worth and completing a journey. Yet, it hasn't occurred exactly the way The Five thought it would when that legend was born." Beauty looked up and glared at something we could not see as if even she had just realized something. "Now, here there is love in its purest forms."

She looked to CJ who reached out and took my hand. Everyone else looked at each other for answers and I was glad to see that everyone else was just as clueless as I was.

Clarice's face slowly changed to understanding. When she spoke it was with wonder, "CJ and Megan. Something happened when CJ asked Megan to marry him. The flowers sparkled and raised them off the ground."

"There was also the bright light that shown from them when they landed back down." Jean said in awe.

I looked at CJ as his smoldering eyes grabbed mine, a whisper of light flashed there. He grabbed my hand and looked at the ring on my finger. "I asked her to marry me in this garden because I couldn't imagine any place more perfect and beautiful than here."

"Yes. CJ and Megan. You proclaimed your love to each other in one of the most powerful places in any realm. It was that dedication of true love that has cemented your paths."

"I ... I don't understand." I said.

"Your dedication to each other changed the ... mechanics, if you will, of what happened. Neither of you thought solely for yourselves. You were and always have had more concern about others. It was not just a pure heart that found this place." She turned to CJ and in a tone that commanded attention, "Mr. Cory James. You have been blessed with the affinity of soothing. Together, with Megan as the new rightful custodian of the Golden Amulet of Sa Ra, you will be able to heal anyone without causing pain to them. Be careful with this however, sometimes pain is needed to strengthen the mind."

"I'm only human though, not Sangra." CJ said.

"Only? Are you only a human?" She said with a smirk. "What is wrong with being human? Humans are amazing creatures."

"I'm not Sangra like everyone else here. I have no inner power. I can't move things, I can't fight, I can't even protect Megan. I'm a liability. I'm only human." CJ said sadly and my heart sank, but before I could say anything the Angel of Beauty spoke.

"Again, what is wrong with being human? You call yourself one, but is that what you truly are?"

The cocoon of my power pulsed twice quickly when she looked to me and then back to CJ.

"Cory James Mathewson, you will be able to protect her in ways that you can't even imagine. Your love has only strengthened that."

He looked at me and even though I could see his love for me in his eyes, I could also see fear and sadness. It broke my heart.

"Now I must return to my brothers and sisters. It is wearing on us to take upon physical forms in the realms. I leave you all with the Blessing of the Five. Love will mend all." Then with incredible softness said, "Remember your heart Megan, it will not lead you astray. Love will mend all." As her image faded, her statue slowly returned to its original state, leaving us staring in awe.

I'm not sure how long they let me lay on the grass thinking. The Angel of Beauty had given me so much to think about my mind hadn't stopped spinning since the Angel returned to her realm. Sure, I had questions for her, but she really only created more than she answered.

Will have to make horrific choices. No shit. It scared me to the point I didn't want to think about. Am I going to have to choose who of my new family dies and who lives? Would I have to make life or death decisions for others? Or is it just so straightforward that by the time my parents are defeated, not everyone will still be here?

Remember my heart. Remember my heart? I trusted CJ if that what she meant. Why wouldn't I trust him? He's the one I would trust over anyone else in this whole damned dimension. Any dimension.

There was also the comment about how I noticed the difference in color of their power. Wonder if that has any connection to the differences in the embers with the Gendril boys? We had established that Symatha was likely possessed by a Protus.

I put my hands on my forehead feeling the dried blood crust and flake off my arm. Every inch of me felt dirty, grimy, and itchy. I could not wait to get back and take a nice long hot shower. Then a hot bath. Then maybe a shower again.

CJ came over, sat down and I put my head in his lap. He silently stroked my hair, and just looked at me.

"Ceej. What do we do now?" I sighed.

"I don't know. I'm still trying to figure out what she was saying about me. Just one more thing to sort out."

"You still want to stay?" I said, daring myself not to overthink the question.

"I'd like to get back to the house and take a shower soon if possible. I feel gross." He said sniffing himself and making a show of smelling his own stink. I tried not to laugh at it.

"Ceej. I mean," I hesitated this time, "Are you sure you want to stay with me? Knowing just what kind of shit show this is going to turn into."

His eyes furrowed. "What?"

"I wouldn't blame you. If you want to go back to the Manusia and forget about all of this. Find someone to settle down with, raise–" I rambled, but he cut me off.

"Megan Isabel." He said admonishingly, "If I wanted to get out of all of this, I would have run tail when we first arrived at the house. I am not leaving you."

"But things have gone way more to shit than just that first night." I said a lump forming in my throat at the thought of him leaving, but I had to give him the opportunity.

His hand ran down my arm to the ring on my finger, he lifted it and kissed it. "I would not have given this to you if I weren't in this for the long haul. Today should have proven that to you."

I just looked at him, tears welling in my eyes. I blinked and one escaped down the side of my face. CJ's other hand rubbed it away, smearing blood and dirt down my cheek.

"I meant what I said. I will love you and protect you for the rest of our lives, and into the next. Whatever that may be." He said it softly but fiercely.

I pulled him down to me and kissed him. When he broke the kiss, he just curled up with me and we sat in silence for a long while before he looked down and said, "She gave you a lot to think about?"

"Yeah."

"Don't worry. I'll keep your ego in check so you don't get all high and mighty. With all this awesome power you have, we don't want to have to deal with an ego too." He had the sexiest smirk on his face as he said that.

"Seriously? You're worried about my ego?" I said not believing a word of it.

"Absolutely! You're not all that powerful missy. Just because you're the most beautiful creature in either Nalsar or the Manusia doesn't mean that you don't have your flaws." CJ said smirking.

I sat up and raised my eyebrows at him. How dare he say I have flaws. "Oh really? Like what flaws?"

"Well ... there's that whole sarcasm thing you have going on. That's a bit annoying. Oh, and you snore." He said smiling.

"I do not snore!" I lightly slapped his chest.

"Shall I tape you at night?"

"Oh, if you want to get into that conversation, then let's just jump into that earthquake maker!" I was trying so hard not to burst into laughter, that when he returned my stare, I burst into a fit of giggles. He always knew how to lighten the mood for me.

"I love you babe." He said between laughs. He moved his hand to rest on my cheek.

"Love you more." I replied with a smile and leaned in to kiss him. We fell back onto the grass, and that's when Clarice came over and suggested we head home.

Home. That sounded nice. I looked to CJ and in unison, we said, "Dibs on the shower."

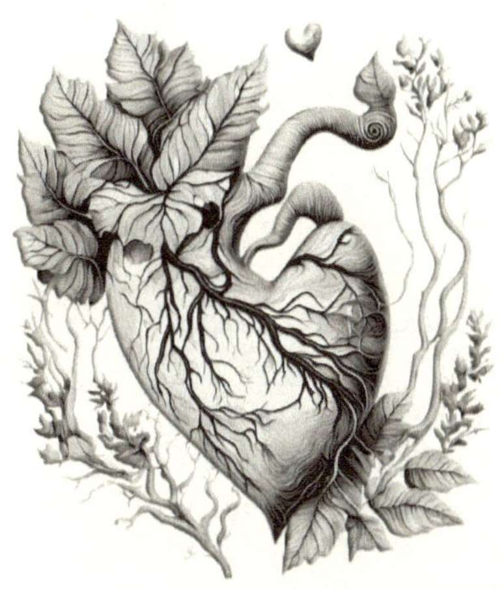

CHAPTER 28

It's cold, wet and I'm alone.

I'm disoriented. It's like I'd been twirled around repeatedly. I looked around and took a few unsteady steps. My feet sloshed on the muddy ground covered in black clover. Trees sagged under the weight of water in the air. Everything is wet. No wildlife.

None. Nothing.

A place like this should be full of crocodiles, frogs, or at the very least, this should be mosquito heaven, but not one.

I was soaked to the bone. How can it be so wet and not raining? Not even drizzling from the fog.

"Megan! Megan!" I hear in a distant voice.

"CJ?" I shout back my heart racing.

"Megan! Megan where are you! Come to me!"

"Where are you?"

"You'll never find him. He's mine now." I turned around but no one was there.

"I now have your heart my girl. The ritual is almost complete." I turn around again and nothing.

"It's just a dream. It's just a dream." I tell myself, willing myself to wake up.

Please. Just wake up Megan.

Wake up!

"He's MINE." I heard again. I grasped both sides of my head as my father's laughter rings through my head.

Silence.

The silence was deafening. I didn't hear anything. Not one single sound.

Was it getting harder to breathe?

I gasped for air, but nothing. I couldn't get enough air.

A hand reached out of nowhere and pulled me forward. Everything around me blurred and I couldn't move my feet. Then everything just stopped.

I blinked.

I blinked again, trying to make sense of what was laid before me, my heart racing the more and more I took in.

CJ was tied down on a round stone table in the very center of the room. I tried to run to him, but my feet were nailed to the floor.

"Megan." I heard him shouting through a broken hoarse voice.

"CJ!" I screamed. He didn't so much as flinch.

"CJ! Can you hear me?! CEEJ!" I screamed again, feeling my vocal cords break at the force of it. He just laid there.

I was standing next to a pillar in a circular courtyard with 12 massive stone pillars circling the room. The walls were tall and dark, with covered walkways around the inside area. The pillar I was standing next to had the number 6, the month of June from the Gregorian calendar, the Astrological sign of Virgo, the Greek Olympian God Ares, and the Roman God Mars. However, there were five other symbols on the pillars that I could not identify. Each pillar was adorned the same: a number, a month from the Gregorian calendar, an Astrological sign, an Olympian God, and a Roman God. All symbols from the Mansuia.

I looked to the pillar with the number 1 on it, it had ... no it couldn't be... a depiction of Jesus Christ? What the hell? The more I looked at each of the pillars the more I was confused. All twelve pillars had a line in the stone floor from the base to the center table. Then I noticed as CJ writhed on that table, a number 13 was etched in the center underneath him. Around the table were the Five Angels carved around the column holding the stone table. Why the 12 pillars with a central 13?

CJ was whispering through gritted teeth. "Megs, I'm so sorry. I love you so much."

"CJ!" I screamed feeling my voice crack as I tried to move toward him. Why wouldn't my feet move? He couldn't see me. He couldn't hear me. He didn't know I was here. My breathing became fast and labored.

Ansel, my father, had a sharpened dagger in his hand and my mother was standing next to CJ with a box, an evil pleased smile on her lips.

"It's ok CJ. It will be all over soon." She told him.

"Megs, I love you. In every lifetime." He continued to whisper over and over again.

Ansel stood over him and with both hands on the hilt of the dagger he raised it up, "With the heart of a loved one, I offer this to you Angel of Love" and then swiftly thrust the dagger down toward CJ's chest.

"No!" I sat straight up in bed, my hair sticking to my face where sweat poured down. The sheets stuck to me anywhere my skin touched, and my nightdress was drenched.

I reached over to where CJ should have been, but he wasn't there.

Cold sheets. Blank empty space.

"No." I whispered in horror. I got up and started running through the house checking every room I passed for him.

When I got to the main room, he was sitting in the chair talking to Lindy. I felt a wave of relief flow through me so fierce I collapsed to the ground. CJ was at my side a moment later and held my head in his hands. I shook him off and frantically checked him from head to toe to make sure he was ok.

No marks, no scars, nothing.
He's ok.
He's ok.
I sighed again in relief.
It was only a dream.
Only a dream. It was only a fucking dream. I thought pressing my eyes tight.

"Angels, what's wrong babe?" he said while brushing my wet hair away from my face. I pulled him close and every time he tried to pull away, I held onto him tighter.

"Megs. What did you see?" He asked for what was probably the hundredth time, but I just gave him a short small grunt. I couldn't voice that vision. Maybe if I didn't voice it, it wouldn't come true.

Lindy was standing next to us and put her hand on my back. With an uneasy soft voice, she asked, "What did you see?"

I ignored her.

"Tell us what you saw Megan." She said a little stronger.

"What are you two doing up?" I asked looking at them, momentarily distracted.

"We were just talking about living arrangements. You know after we are married. I wanted to find out more about how we could get our own place and the lifestyle here. But that's not what is important right now. What did you dream that got you this upset? I haven't seen you like this since you first told me how you saw Ma–" His eyes grew bigger and his voice trailed off.

He stared at me for a long agonizing minute. He was searching for something, anything that would go against what he was thinking. When he saw the confirmation in my face, he tried to avoid my eyes. There was a quick, almost indistinguishable nod from him as he pulled me closer in full understanding.

I couldn't bring myself to even nod in confirmation. I crawled up pressing my chest to his and wrapped my legs around him pulling him closer. He wrapped his arms tighter around me without saying another word, leaning against the wall. I could feel his heartbeat faster against my chest. He knew more than anyone the weight my dreams had.

His whisper so light in my ear, that only I could hear it. "Oh, babe."

"What did you see Megan?" Lindy was begging. I couldn't speak. I didn't know if I could speak. I was feeling colder and it was seeping into my core. My muscles twitched.

I felt CJ take a deep shuddering breath. He turned his head to face her and said with next to no emotion in his voice, "She saw my death."

Lindy was quiet for a moment before saying, "I'll be right back."

She ran from the room, but when she came back, she was with Clarice, Jean, and Owen. They were all still in their nightwear and sleepy-eyed, but when they saw my face, they woke up like they had just jumped into the Arctic Ocean. Owen asked, "What happened?"

I was so cold. I tried to reach for the electricity in that cocoon to call it forth to warm me, but it was dark. It was as if someone had cut the power cord and the lights had gone out completely. Even my power ran from the thought of losing CJ.

"She saw CJ's death." She told them. I didn't turn to look at them. There was nothing but silence from everyone.

No one tried to tell me it would be okay.

No one even tried to say that it was only a dream.

I only felt CJ hold on to me a little tighter.

I sat and sipped on a few cups of hot chocolate while they continued to discuss it all. I had blocked them out and just sat in CJs lap. At some point, someone had suggested that I sit on the couch under a blanket. Apparently, there was a growl that came from me that even made CJ hold on to me tighter.

Luckily, they didn't dwell on the final few seconds and wanted to know more about the room. What still baffled me was the use of symbolism from the Manusia and the use of 12 pillars with a central 13.

"Across most dimensions, numerologists consider 12 a complete number. Here, however, the number 13 is." Lindy explained.

"There were so many symbols though; 12 months in the Gregorian calendar, the 12 Astrological signs, 12 Olympian Gods and 12 Roman Gods. I get those, but there were 5 other symbols I couldn't identify. One looked like it could be a carving of Jesus Christ, and there were other symbols too." I told her.

"I would venture to guess that they were the 12 labors of Hercules, the 12 tribes of Israel, the one for Jesus Christ, if you're sure, it could symbolize the 12 apostles. Those are the ones from the Manusia that I can think of. The others are probably from other dimensions. One most likely is the 12 beings of Losinar; The Royal Fay court. Another, well could either be the 12 symbols of Sintal, but there is a huge debate over if there are 12 or if there are only 10, or it could be the 12 Herbs of Hendril."

"Wow. There really is a huge coincidence for the number 12." I sipped my hot chocolate thinking. Even though my mind was racing, I could feel my body warm a little, and my muscles didn't feel as tight. I wouldn't put it past any of them, CJ included, to put something in it to help settle me down.

"Focus, Megan. The courtyard. Is there anything else you can tell me? I know that would be in Noctulanar Castle, but do you know how to get there?" Lindy asked.

"No. I was ported, pulled there, but not in our way. It was weird. Like someone grabbed me and hit the fast forward. So, I didn't get anything from the swamp to the courtyard. Don't you know where it would be though? If that is the courtyard for performing the ritual, wouldn't you know where that is since you were on the council? Didn't you tell me that the ritual had to be performed inside of Noctulanar's castle?"

Clarice answered, but her voice was low and had some emotion in it that I couldn't understand. "Yes, it's common knowledge that it would be performed there, however, if you have ever seen Noctulanar Castle in person, you would understand. The place is huge."

"Yeah, that's an understatement, one could walk in the doors and walk around for 3 years and never see the same place twice." Lindy told us. "There are levels upon levels that dive deep underground. There are even theories that the walls change on some levels so you literally can get lost in there."

"Look guys," I interrupted, sleep heavy in my voice. Yeah, they had definitely put something in that drink. "I don't know how to get there. The courtyard would have been beautiful and majestic if my father were not ..."

CJ poked me, reminding me to be nice.

I sighed and gave him a side eye, which he ignored like nothing happened. I knew being vicious with them wasn't going to help anyone. "Look, I'm really tired. I'm going back to bed. In the morning we need to go over what to do next. Now that my parents have the Desumo Nitor, time is not on our side."

I got up, put my cup in the sink, and headed back to bed.

I laid there slipping in and out of consciousness. CJ had stayed in the main room with the others, which a part of me was actually grateful for. He needs to sort out his feelings too.

As much as I wanted to, and as heavy as my eyes were from whatever they put in that drink, I couldn't sleep. I just laid there dozing in and out. I vaguely heard Jean and Owen head back off to bed and Clarice in the shower, but I had no idea how much time had truly passed.

I was giving up on the whole sleeping thing and was halfway out of the bed when my vision became unfocused again.

OH, no, no, no, no, no, no, no. I can't handle another one right now. I tried with everything I had to shake it off, but of course, it didn't work. Leaning back and staring at the ceiling I was transported to a forested area where I was standing in a crowd of people. Me. I wasn't watching someone else do things. I was me in this vision. Everyone was dressed in suits and elegant dresses; flowers and decorations were everywhere. People I knew from the Manusia, and others that were clearly not human mingled about in a circular seating area with an elegant archway covered in flowers in the center.

"Attention! Attention!" Everyone turned to look at the man who was near the center. I knew this man. It's the man from the council who performed my Maltal ceremony. Julian. The Head of Nalrin. Angels. The Head of all the Nalsar dimension. His voice carried far without much effort at all as he said, "Will you all please take your places. It is time to begin."

As people stood and went to their respective seats, I saw CJ's parents, Amber, Owen, Jean, and Clarice. Off to the side Julian stood talking to CJ, and ... his brother Logan? What in the Underworld's darkness is going on here?

CJ wore a uniform of sorts that was black with silver embroidery and an emblem over the heart, but I couldn't quite make out what it was. A dark cape hung over his right shoulder secured by a silver cord that matched the trim. My vision hung on CJ for a moment as I looked him up and down and appreciated the view. Whatever uniform it was, I had to admit, CJ looked marvelous.

Damn it! Focus Megan. What is going on? What am I supposed to see? I looked around and there were lots of people standing around the perimeter in a similar uniform to what CJ was wearing. Then everyone turned to where I was standing. I looked down at my hands. I was holding a bouquet of red tulips and the most absolute perfect wedding dress I had ever seen. The white A-line strapless satin dress had a gathered wrap from under the right bust line to a smaller gather at the left waist, above the wrap was an intricately beaded pattern that looked similar to the pebbles and sand on the beach. The skirt was beak-front with some of the same beaded accents in the under side, with a long train and red lace-up ribbon closure to accent my waist.

I felt my eyes fill with tears as I looked back up to CJ, who stood at the end of the isle smiling brightly at me as it all faded away.

I laid there staring at the ceiling grasping ahold of the happiness of what I had just seen. Why had I just seen CJ and I's wedding when I literally had just seen my father kill him for the ritual earlier. Not to mention, where was Lindy? I didn't see her anywhere!

I jumped out of bed, got in the shower, and let the hot water try to relax me. It took a while, but after a while, I felt the muscles in my shoulders loosen and my head clear.

When I was done, I stood there staring at my closet. How could I have had two visions that clearly could not co-exist? How could CJ and I get married if Ansel was going to kill him in the ritual? We didn't have time to go through a wedding of any kind now that they had the Desmo Nitor. Not one of that size and magnitude. There were so many people there.

Sighing and giving up for now, I got dressed in my practice gear, grabbed two of my syths, tied my hair back and strode out to the main room. CJ was sitting there reading a book, but when he saw me, he smiled appreciatively and waggled his eyebrows a bit. Anxiety lined his face, but he was doing his best to hide it, so I did my best to ignore it.

"You know how awesome you look in that?" He said. I smiled and shook my head as I walked over and gave him a quick kiss on the cheek.

"Thanks. Where is Clarice?" I asked.

"Kitchen. I think. Where do you think you are going?" He said grabbing me by the waist and pulling me into the chair with him. His arm reached around to cup my ass and gave it a firm meaningful squeeze.

"Maybe it is time we go back to bed." He said kissing my neck. I may have clinched my legs together and bit because he smiled and looked at me. There was a searing heat in that gaze that made my insides swim.

"Ceej." I said half in protest.

He sighed dramatically, and said, "So why all dressed up if not for me?"

I gave him a quick kiss and disentangled myself from his grip. "Just wanted to get some sparing practice in. Can't really sleep so might as well train. I can't rely solely on my powers. I need to make sure I can hold my own in hand to hand." I could tell by the look on his face that he didn't like me talking like that. It probably didn't help to alleviate any of his worrying.

"But it's only five in the morning." He said whining. Five huh. I guess I got some sleep then.

"You need some sleep, so go to bed." I ordered. He leveled a look at me that clearly meant that he knew I was explicitly not saying something. I shook my head and sat down on the ottoman across from him. Deliberately not sitting on his lap again, because my resolve may have faltered at that point and we may have just ravished him here in the living room for all to see.

"Clarice is up, and you know how much she enjoys beating the crap out of me." I said smirking at him, but then my face fell. I knew what he was thinking. "Look this isn't just about that vision. It's about being able to protect you, Clarice, Jean, Owen and Lindy too."

"And what about you? Who's gonna protect you?" He said his face suddenly inches from me, running his finger along my cheek.

"Well, that's why I need the practice. So, I can hold my own, and no one else has to worry about me. I know as long as I can use my power, I'll be ok, but what if something happens and I can't?" I said putting my hand on his.

"Do you think something will happen that you won't?" he raised an eyebrow.

"That's not what I'm saying. I... I just want to play it safe Ceej. So, if you aren't going to sleep, do you want to come and watch or do you wanna read?" My eyes flicked to the book he had tucked between the cushion and the arm. The title was hidden, so I asked, "What are you reading anyway?"

"Ahh, nothing. Go practice with Clarice. I'll be fine here." He put his hand protectively over it, and I glared at him.

"Ok." I leaned over to kiss him and just before our lips met, I grabbed the book from his hand and jumped back.

"Hey, no fair you tease!" He said laughing.

"Oh hush! Like your one to talk." I said giving him a very pointed looked.

"Ohh that's it!" Then he tackled me before I could see the cover of the book. We crashed to the floor fighting for the book when Clarice walked in and had to jump out of the way to keep from being tripped by flaying arms and legs. I had my legs firmly wrapped around his waist and he was trying to pry them off, without much success. He even went so far as to grind against me, but I held fast.

He somehow knocked the book from my hand and was able to grab it just before it hit the floor. He pushed his forearm against my chest and held the book high out of reach. Angels, I wish I could at least see the title. I could just make out a sword and a small vine behind his hand on the spine.

CJ moved the book high in the air just at the tips of my fingers, when Clarice grabbed it, freeing CJ's hands to pin me down. He sat on my hips and pinned my hands next to my head.

"I told you, no." He said with a huge smile on his face.

I placed the biggest pouty face I could manage on my face and batted my eyelashes. "But you never tell me no baby. Pllleeeassseee tell me what your reading?"

He laughed so loud I thought he would wake Jean and Owen. "Oh no, sorry. My secret!"

After staring him down for a minute and said, "Fine. Let me up."

"Nope. I like you like this." Then he leaned down and kissed me hard. I softened up instantly. I couldn't help myself. Curses! When he pulled back, he asked. "Promise to behave? I'm not telling you what I'm reading."

"OH, not on your life." I said smiling.

"Megs. I know you don't tell me everything." He said still pinning me down. When I went to retort he just said, "I get it.

I'm not mad. There are things you see in visions you don't want me to know. This is one of those for me okay. I need to do this. I promise I will tell you ... just .... later."

I sighed in defeat. "Fine, I promise. Geesh. If you weren't such a good kisser. I'd kick your ass right now."

"Promises. Promises." He said with a wink and helped me get up.

I turned to Clarice who was eating a bowl of cereal. "Any of that left? I need something to eat."

"Yup. Going to need to send Owen back for more. These are really good. Didn't realize that Manusia food was so tasty." She said mouth full.

"He's really taken to hamburgers too. Say, after I eat, I need your help. I need some hand-to-hand practice. You up for it?"

"Oh yea! You're fun to kick around!" She said her eyes lighting up with way too much enthusiasm as she handed the book back to CJ. Unfortunately, she also gave it to him in a way that hid the title, but I did see some sort of crest or insignia on it. It tickled at the back of my mind, but since I couldn't get a good look at it...

"Study it." She commanded CJ interrupting my thoughts. "And No. You aren't going to miss anything outside. I'll beat you up later."

"Clarice." I said slowly. "What are you guys doing?"

"None of your business for now." She said. "10 minutes. Be out there."

For as many times as Lindy backed me up in every little thing, Clarice seemed to have CJ's back just as much as Lindy had mine.

"Be careful with her Clarice. Or you'll deal with me." CJ warned but with a giggle in his voice.

"Ohhh I'm shaking in my boots!" she said putting her hands up shaking them mockingly.

Angels I love my family. So much sarcasm everywhere!

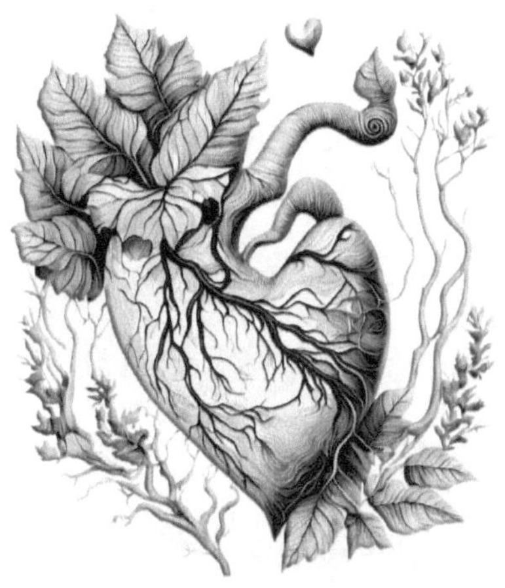

CHAPTER 29

I GRABBED A BOWL of cereal and had been moving it around for a few minutes when Clarice walked into the kitchen.

"Hey. You know I'm always up for sparing with you, but why at 5 in the morning?" I just continued to stare into my bowl. I didn't know how to explain it to her. This is just something I have to do. Whether it's to keep my mind busy or just to wear me out so much physically I could sleep without nightmares. I didn't know.

"Well, like I told CJ, I need to be able to hold my own in hand to hand in case there is a situation I can't use my power." I said. There truth. Excluding more truth, but truth.

"Do you think there will be a time you won't be able to use your power?" DAMN, same question as CJ.

"No, not that I can think of, but gotta be ready for anything. I asked Lindy when we got back from Manusia last week if anyone else had been through this before. If the weapon had ever been attempted at this caliber in history. She said she hadn't heard of any other serious attempts like this one, but it isn't like it's something that is going to be advertised. So, we need to be prepared for anything and everything. That includes the possibility of not being able to use any of our powers. Besides if you're going against someone and your power abilities are matched up, what's going to make the difference?" I forced myself to take a big spoon full of cereal.

"Hand to Hand." She said in a low voice. "You're right. I'll go outside and set up some obstacles. I know I said 10 minutes, but give me 15 okay?"

I nodded and shrugged at her. At least she understood it.

"Oh and go talk to Lindy before you come outside. She needs to speak to you for a few." She said over her shoulder.

"What about?"

"Not sure." She said laughing and headed out the door to set up. Liar. Little liar.

I ate quickly, washed my dishes, and then went and knocked on Lindy's door. "Come in."

When I opened the door, CJ was sitting on the bed looking very sheepish. "Ahh, what is going on?" I asked as my heart started to pick up speed.

"Lindy. She has to come with me. I won't go without her." He told her crossing his arms attempting a mini hissy fit. What was he two? I tried to keep the smile off my face.

"No. She doesn't. She's going to stay here." Lindy replied firmly.

"Then I'm not going." He said in a huff and pouting. He looked so cute.

"Um...Ya remember me? Girlfriend here." I said pointing to myself, "Someone want to tell me what you are talking about?"

"I'm taking CJ to Nalrin to get him registered for residency so that he can stay here permanently. It's like a Visa in the Manusia, well sort of. He seems to think that he needs to have you with him." She said, but I didn't miss the flick of her eyes back to him.

"So ... why can't I?" I asked still confused. "Besides don't I need to get registered also?"

"No. Only those who don't have Sangra blood have to register. We just had to send word and tell them that you were back in this dimension when you got here. And you can't go with us on this trip because there is a lot of long and boring paperwork to fill out. Plus, reasons." Lindy said bouncing up and smiling.

"Why do I have a feeling this has something to do with our wedding?" I said sitting down next to CJ and resting my head on his shoulder as he put an arm around me.

"Because it does, and it doesn't." She said cocking her head from side to side.

"Is this the sort of thing that is going to make my heart stop?" I said glaring at her before continuing, "And are you forgetting the vision I had earlier this evening?"

"Nope." She said with a pop.

"I'm not." CJ said in a whisper. "Which is exactly why I want her to go with. If my days are numbered, then I want to spend every moment I possibly can with the girl I love." I flinched. I hated hearing him talk like that.

"No, she's not going." Only it wasn't Lindy who was answering. It was Jean and Owen standing in the doorway.

I sighed turning to CJ. "Something tells me the whole house is against us on this one. Promise me you'll be careful."

"I promise baby." Then he kissed me. His hand trailed my face, brushing any stray hairs away, and then down to my shoulder and ran down the length of my bare arm, giving me shivers all the way down to my fingertips where he entwined his fingers with mine. I pressed myself into him, wanting more. Our kiss was soft and loving, but there was a fire simmering under it that made lava coil in my gut. Against my lips, he whispered with a smile, "If this were our bedroom, I would kick everyone out."

"Okay, you two. Your dead cute together, but this is MY bedroom. Not yours!" Lindy said, and I could just hear the eye roll in her voice.

"Which is why I said, IF this were our bedroom." CJ said with a glare.

"So, there is no way I get to go?" I said as I stood up off the bed.

"Nope, none. Sorry. We leave in an hour." Lindy said and then raised her eyebrows, "Don't you have a sparing practice with Clarice to get to?"

"Yeah. Yeah. If anything happens to him, I'll hold you personally responsible." I told her then turned back to CJ and kissed him quickly. "Be safe. I'll see you before dinner tomorrow. I love you."

"Love you more." He said with a smirk. Then I headed out for my beating with Clarice. I may have let my hips sway a little extra on the way to the door. There was an audible grown and I heard something hit the mattress as I shut the door behind me.

After four solid hours of training, I was sore, but much more relaxed. I had gotten some great hits in on her and I'm sure she would be sore as well. We went over blocks, stuns, and more disarming techniques, which she said I was improving on even without using my power. Clarice also taught me some new ways of centering myself physically, which reminded me a lot of the drills taught in an older karate movie.

"Backbends, and more yoga." She had told me when I said my back didn't bend that direction. I'm flexible and can do the splits no problem, even kick my leg up high enough to kick someone in the face if need be, but my back and arms are apparently too tight for what she was trying to show me.

"You've got the strength, but you need to be able to move a bit more. Your shoulders and back are way too rigid." She said.

"What do you mean too rigid?" I asked.

"That sandbag that got you in the rib. If you were more flexible, you could have bent back farther and missed it entirely." She suggested.

"Or I just need to be faster." I said under my breath.

"Megan, you already move faster than most because of your power. What would you do if you couldn't move faster, or you were in a tight space?" Then she proceeded to bend over in a backbend that brought her hands almost to her feet and then gracefully swung her feet back up and over her. She stood there with her hair blowing in the breeze, her hands on her hips, and a smirk on her face.

"Stretches. Got it." I said with a sheepish grin.

"Let's get you cleaned up and make up some lunch. You look exhausted and we need to put some ice on that hand. I don't think you broke it, but it's going to be a little tender." She said assessing my hand.

"It's only mid-morning. Too early to sleep and actually, not tired. Besides nothing but an empty bed awaits me." I eyed her and shook out my hand. She's right it would be sore, but I have the Sa Ra on, and it will be fine in a matter of hours.

Clarice smiled at me and shook her head. "Nope, sorry not going to tell you what's going on. CJ needs to find his place here. Let him work it all out okay."

Her voice left no room for discussion. I just wish I knew what they were talking about. Wish he would tell me. I headed inside a bit defeated. She was right of course, but that really wasn't the point.

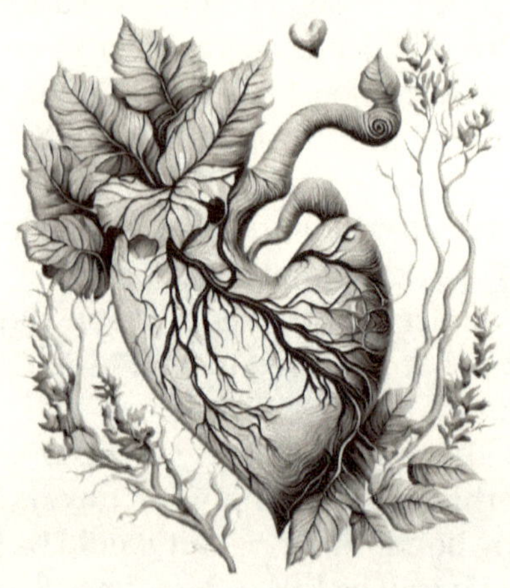

CHAPTER 30

WHY DON'T WE JUST not go to Nalrin, Megan? You've already seen Ansel get the crystal and he can't get CJ if we don't go. I'll send a message and have him return home now. Change the schedule. Make it so there isn't a chance of him getting taken from Nalrin." Owen asked after we received a message from Nalrin that there had been rumors and possible sightings of Ansel and Symatha around the city.

"I'm sorry what?" I looked at him a little surprised. When I looked at the others, they were looking at him with the same expression. Even though I wanted to get raging mad at him for even asking, I couldn't. That's just how he is. Good. Bad. Loony. Didn't much matter. He just spoke what was on his mind.

"I know it's not a popular idea because it would guarantee one more piece they have, but it would save CJ." Owen said.

"No. It's not an option. We will have to face him sooner or later regardless. The only sure-fire way is to just let my parents create the weapon. I can't allow that. I'll stop my father and

200

I'll make sure CJ is safe." I stood up and walked out the door. I couldn't entertain that idea. If I stopped, they won. I wouldn't let them destroy a world.

When I got to the garden, I looked to the tree line and took off running. I didn't think. I just ran. I concentrated on the feel of the air flowing in and out of my lungs, my feet hitting the ground, and the strength of my muscles pushing me along. Slowly everything left my thoughts and I felt the tension in my body release. All I concentrated on was the air and my muscles pushing me along. When I reached the river 10 minutes later, I slowed to a walk.

The river was such a serene place that I stopped and hopped on the row of rocks until I was on a large rock in the center of the river. I sat there and listened to the sound of the water rushing over the rocks, the birds chirping in the trees, the frog like sounds that were more guttural than those back in the Manusia, and the occasional sound of wild animals roaring and howling in the distance. I took a deep breath as the clean smell of the forest engulfed me, then let it all out in a long breath. I watched the water gently flow over the rocks and I thought I saw movement just around the bend. Without thinking it through, I headed for it.

When I turned the corner, where the river swung off to the left, about 100 yards away were five Nandi. I froze where I stood. Nandi were a lot like a dog or hyena with shoulders higher than their haunches and big bulging muscles to cover their legs. Carnivorous pack animals that were not very picky about what they ate, their backs had to have been as high as my shoulders.

I made sure I stood tall and proud, checked the coil of electricity in my cocoon and willed myself to stay calm and slow my heart rate. Not easy when one of the pups looked my way. All I could think at that moment is that animals could smell fear and weakness.

"Don't look weak, but don't look like a threat either." I whispered to myself. I hadn't run across wild animals here in Nalsar, and I really rather not have my first encounter so far out in the forest alone where no one could hear my screams. My mind went into overdrive picturing my body in ribbons and my entrails laid out for a mile.

The largest of the Nandi stood up tall and sniffed the air in my direction. I heard the hum of my power in my ears, and I knew if I looked down, I would see it coiling around my fingers. Deep slow breaths.

Deep. Slow. Breaths. The humming decreased, but it was still there.

A faint sharp bark was on the wind as the largest of them turned and headed up the hill. The other four looked back at me, took one more drink of water, and trotted up after the largest. Only when I saw them crest the top did I release the breath I hadn't realized I had been holding again.

I carefully headed back up to the waterfall and climbed around the edge to stand on the large rock at the base. Water flowed over the top of my head and down my back, instantly cooling me down. It felt like ice in comparison to my hot skin. I rinsed the sweat off my body in the falls, coiling any extra of my power up, all the while keeping an eye out for the Nandi in case they reconsidered my threat to them.

When I was done, I went and sat back in the center of the river to just clear my head.

When I got back about four hours later, they were still sitting there reading over ancient texts on Nalrin when I returned. The last thing I wanted to do was to sit there and read more books on history, so I went to the kitchen and started cleaning up lunch.

Maybe it was the Nandi, or the absence of CJ, but I wanted something warm to eat. Good old fashion comfort food. I guess the stress of all this was getting to me.

Absentmindedly, I pulled ingredients out of the cupboard and got to work on cutting potatoes, carrots, and celery. About 20 minutes later, Owen came into the kitchen and leaned on the refrigerator, studying my mood.

"You know I didn't mean to give up right?" I stopped my work on the carrots.

"I know Owen."

"Then why ..."

"Why did I walk out at a simple suggestion? Then go run to clear my head?" I turned to him.

He nodded his head and raised an eyebrow. "You've never done that. I know that you want to save CJ, and it is an option."

I set the knife down and leaned against the counter. "First, because CJ isn't going to allow us to just put him in solitary confinement to keep him safe. As much as it temps me sometimes" I said gritting my teeth. Then I looked at Owen whose eyes were wide for a minute then he huffed a small laugh and shook his head.

"Yeah. He wouldn't allow that. He would break out repeatedly."

"Second, I just can't accept that option. It feels like losing or giving up either way. Yes, staying here might delay or even prevent my father from getting CJ, but I've seen it. So many times, Owen. I don't know that would prevent it. I don't accept it, but it just feels inevitable. I know that doesn't make a whole lot of sense." I was gripping the knife tightly, and I noticed that Owen's eyes kept flicking to it, so I set it down and turned to face him.

"If we stay here, it feels like I would be giving my mother and father permission to do all of this ... I haven't given up, I just think we should fight, regardless of what my visions say. I know ya'll believe in them 100%, but I want to believe they can change. Even after everything." I picked the knife back up and went back to work on the carrots.

He was quiet for a moment, then asked, "So, what's for dinner tonight?"

"Stew." I said, smiling at the memory. "Mom used to make it on cold days. After school when Matt and I would come home we would smell it cooking in the croc-pot, we knew it was going to be a family night. At dinner time, we would snuggle up on the couch with a warm blanket and watch movies together as a family. Usually, Star Wars or some nature or science show would end up on the television."

I let out a big sigh. "That was a long time ago. Before I knew what my dreams were, before Matt died, and before I knew my parents twisted story. Before my life changed, for better or for worse."

"Well, if it's anything like those hamburgers, then I'm all for it. I never knew Manusia food could be so good." He said smiling.

"It's not like hamburgers. It's a thick soup of sorts, but you have good food here too. I really enjoy Clarice's Tolkis and binesk with the mushroom sauce. The way she cooks the Tolkis meat is amazing. It just melts in your mouth. Plus, nothing beats fresh veggies. It's a good thing she can grow the binesk here at the house. It's a lot like cauliflower back in the Manusia. Well in taste anyways. The texture is more ... bready. Like cauliflower pizza crust."

"Hum. We will have to pick some up next time we go to get groceries from there. The cauliflower. Not cauliflower pizza. No. That just sounds wrong." He said appalled.

"I'd like to go too. Get some miscellaneous things from the store that I can't get here."

"It's really not a good idea for you to dimension travel right now Megan." He said lowering his head, but his voice was firm.

"Owen, you can't be serious. The Manusia is my world. I'm safer there than here. Same with CJ. Besides if we go to Monterey or Chicago, we are ahead of the game. That's home. I know it in and out." I said taking the knife and stabbing it into the cutting board. He just stared me down. I knew it was probably worthless to fight him on this, but since when has that ever stopped me?

"Sorry Megan we have ALL discussed this and you and CJ stay here." He stayed firm.

"All of you? Was CJ in on this?" I wined.

He must have known his cover was blown. "Be right there, Jean!" with a swift evil smirk on his face he turned out of the room. Oldest trick in the book. I don't think so.

"Conversation isn't over. And yes, CJ will be in a heap of trouble when he gets home." I called after him and then opened the refrigerator to grab the stew meat.

"You guys are being ridiculous about this." I said rolling my eyes. "It's just a shopping trip. I need to do something NORMAL. All I've done since I got here is study and fight. Not that I'm complaining because it's what I need to do. Would it kill you to let me do something normal, like grocery shopping?" I said after we cleaned up dinner.

"Megan this is about your safety. We don't know if they have help to stop us along the way, or where they are hiding." Jean told me.

"I feel like a kid asking to have my curfew extended. This is so far past ridiculous that it is just about ludicrous. I can't believe we are even having this discussion." I said throwing my hands in the air.

"CJ..." Clarice cut off when she saw the look on my face.

"Yes. About that." I eyed Owen. He was staying very quiet in this whole conversation. "You discussed this with CJ, didn't you? Why is everyone discussing this with everyone else, but failing to mention it or even discuss it with me? Oh right, because you know I'm right and don't want me to point it out to you."

It wasn't a question. I knew I was right. "Am I the only one who thinks this is silly! I mean we are going for groceries and supplies. There are personal items I need more of."

"Then give me a list. We will get it. For the record, you're not the only one who thinks that this is being overprotective. Lindy thinks we are going too far also. She seems to think you can hold your own there." Jean told me.

"And CJ?", bringing the conversation back around. I really wish he were here. He's so going to get an ass chewing when he gets home.

"Thinks that even though you can use your power in the Manusia that it's much stronger here. You are safer here." She said.

"Which is true, but I lived for 24 years in the Manusia. I was able to use my power just fine when we went to Sao Tome. Not to mention the hand-to-hand combat I've learned thanks to Lindy and Clarice's sessions." There. They couldn't refute that.

"The answer is still no. We still don't know what your father and mother are doing and we can't take any chances." Owen said quietly.

"So, I can't go with you to the Manusia, but you'll just leave me here with no one while you run off. Love your logic." I knew the conversation was over by the look on everyone's faces. They weren't going to budge, which was really frustrating even after I put all kinds of holes in it.

Stubborn people. Boy isn't that the pot calling the kettle black. I laughed to myself as I picked up a book on the Nalrin library and sat down in my favorite chair, but I couldn't focus on it. So, got up and just headed to bed. Sitting down in the chair had really allowed the exhaustion to catch up with me. It had been a long day after all. A little over 23 hours ago I woke up from the vision of CJ and my parents. My body was used to the longer days here, but it had been a rough emotional and physical day for me.

Emotional nothing! I needed the training to wear my body out enough to sleep. I climbed into bed and grabbed his pillow. I inhaled deeply, cherishing CJ's scent and letting it wrap around me like a blanket. Five minutes later I was dead asleep.

CHAPTER 31

I WOKE UP REACHING for CJ and was greeted with cold empty sheets. Groaning at the reminder, I looked at the clock and was shocked to see it was already 8:30 in the morning. I slept... 14 hours. I hadn't slept that much since I arrived. Angels, the last time I slept that much had to be ... high school maybe? The sun was bright through the window and I had half a mind to just throw the blankets over my head regardless of what time it was. While the option was nice, I knew I wouldn't be able to rest.

Sighing, I threw the blankets back and put my robe on. The house was indeed quiet. Too quiet. Eerily quiet. I felt out to see where everyone was, but there was no one around. It was strange to be alone in the house. Back in Monterey, I would have relished the quiet, but here, it just didn't feel right. Someone else was always here. Even if they were outside chopping wood, or tending to the garden, someone else was always ... here. I really enjoyed the feeling of a house full of family. Sure, it could make sexy time with CJ difficult, but this place felt like ... home. I hadn't had that feeling in a very long time.

When I got to the kitchen, I grabbed the last of the cereal and headed to the table to sit down. Maybe I could run home and do some grocery shopping without them knowing until I got back. Maybe I'd even stop by Russo's for some pizza. My stomach growled in response. Boy that sounded good.

I wonder if Amber is working today. I could stop by and see her. Catch up. See how things are going. What day was it in the Manusia? I tried to do the calculations, but it just made my head spin. Then I saw the note sitting on the table.

Megan:

We ran to the Manusia to restock your favorite foods. You know cereal, mint chip ice cream, burgers. Okay, so Owen wants more hamburger supplies. It's entirely your fault he's addicted to those things. I also made a list of toiletries that you were running low on.

Don't be too mad at us for leaving you behind. We have some technicalities to take care of here that you would have been bored to death over anyways. We will stop by your apartment as well and take your messages.

See ya soon.

O–J–C

"Jerks." I said as I stuck my tongue out at the note. Rudely, my tummy reminded me I needed to actually eat the bowl of cereal in front of me to get nourishment. My mind started thinking about some of the technicalities that I needed to take care of back home. I needed to officially quit my job, move out of my apartment, get a PO Box for any bills that would be coming in and sell Betsy. I really didn't want to sell Betsy though.

I sighed. I'd also really needed to talk to Amber. It had been months since I last talked to her. She was probably in total freak out mode since I sent that vague pathetic text message to everyone. They all probably hated CJ and I both right now.

What about CJ, didn't he have some of the same things to take care of? At least I had talked to Annie about CJ and I and she knew we weren't dead in a ditch somewhere, but CJ would need to quit his job, work out his bills situation, etc.

I giggled. Quit our jobs. Hell, we would be lucky if we both just had letters stating we no call, no showed, so we are assuming you abandoned your position. Here is your final paycheck. Have a nice life. There really was so much that needed to get done, and they wouldn't let me go with them to the Manusia to do any of it.

I blinked. I was actually seriously considering severing my ties with the Manusian world in a very permanent way. Somewhere along the line, I had unknowingly decided, this was home. This is where I wanted to live my life. I looked down at the ring on my finger.

It seemed CJ had started down that path as well. We hadn't talked about it. Never even discussed it. We talked in vague terms for the short term, but not in a more, forever way. I looked at what was left of my cereal and sighed again. I forced myself to finish, put the bowl in the sink, and headed into the living room.

I randomly grabbed a book off the bookshelf in the main room, plopped down in my favorite chair, and rubbed my hand over the cover. The cover was made from thick leather and was closed with a cord around a small elaborate knot on the front. The front also had a symbol embossed in a deep shade of red with intertwined branches that formed a circle. The letter "O".

I opened the book, and a single sheet of paper fell out onto my lap.

The paper was thin and fragile, almost like tissue paper. The writing was slightly faded and not in black ink like everything else but in brown. I held it into the light and along the top was written Darkness, Lord Byron, July 1816. It looked like a poem, and the title sounded familiar ... I started reading and an ice-cold shudder went through me as I got to the end of the page. There had to be more though. When I looked inside the book there was nothing. What is a poem from Manusia doing in an ancient book in Nalsar? I wish Clarice were here so I could ask her about it.

As I started reading through the book, it had a lot of the same information I already knew from my studies for the trials and from some other books, but this particular one had some maps that I didn't recognize. They vaguely looked like maps of the Obsecuritan area but different. The boundary lines and areas within the continent were in different places. I looked back at when the book had been written, and I was astonished to see that it was written over 1300 Nalrin years ago.

I skimmed over the table of contents and almost half the book was on Noctulanar Castle itself. Most importantly, there were maps of the castle. The maps were fading, but ...

How could we not have read through this already? I sat up and laid the book down on the ottoman in front of me as I thumbed through looking for anything that may help us in locating the courtyard.

I got more and more confused the more I studied the maps. When I tried to piece together the floors, some of the floors didn't connect to others. No matter how much I tried. There were floors and floors of maps. Nothing connected to each other after going three levels down. Lindy and Clarice were right about one thing, you could walk for weeks in this place and never find your way out or see the same thing twice.

I continued to sift through map upon map, following different entryways but they either lead to larger rooms or to stairwells to different floors, or nowhere. This was so frustrating. "Anyone say Winchester Mystery House?" I mumbled. I'd been there once as a kid on a middle school field trip, but this place was worse.

I was still studying the maps and was once again thankful for my simi-photographic memory when Jean, Clarice, and Owen walked in the door, arms full of bags.

"Well, look who decided to wake up this morning." Clarice said with a giggle.

"Yeah. I kinda needed the sleep and it wasn't like you were going to let me go to the Manusia or anything." My voice was way too snarky for civilized conversation, but I continued anyway. "Clarice, when you can fit time out of your busy schedule, can you come here and look at these?"

"Someone put moody juice in your breakfast this morning." She said, but my attention was on the map in front of me. The map said it was on a below ground level, with the only two access points from a level above. There was only one room on the entire floor. The room depicted was square on the outside, but the interior was circular. On the map where there should have been the detailing of the center area there was just a note. *Non Carnotense.*

"Latin?" I whispered.

"No, it's a really old language from Noctulanar. My father still speaks it. Only no one uses it as a common tongue anymore." Clarice was standing over me looking down at the map. "What are you looking at? I don't remember seeing this with the other maps we've been studying?"

"It isn't." I bookmarked the page and showed her the cover and her eyes froze.

"Where did you get this?" She said with a shadow of horror in her voice.

"Ah bookcase, you know the place we keep books." I said pointing to the empty slot on the shelf. She didn't say anything. I looked at her questioningly, but I couldn't make out her facial expression.

"Clarice, what is it? I'm sorry if I shouldn't have taken this book down, I didn't know what I was grabbing. For all, I knew I would pull down a book of pictures, or history, or fables or even poems." When I mentioned poems, she turned around.

"Poems." She took a deep breath. "Did you read the sheet of paper in the front of the book?"

"Yea. It's very dark. Destructive. It's missing the ending though. The poem is cut off."

"Cut off? What do you mean?"

I flipped the book open and pulled it out. *"And, terrified, did flutter on the ground, And flap their useless wings; the wildest brutes".* It sounds like it's cut off. Like there should be another page, but I couldn't find it." I told her with a questioning look. "Clarice, again. What is it?"

"This book has been handed down in my family for generations. I didn't know it was one that came with me." Her voice was very flat… distant even. "That poem is from the Manusia, written by Lord Byron in 1816 when many believed the world was ending. There had been a volcano that erupted at some part in Manusian history, and a large part of the Manusia was covered in ash. My relatives had said that it may have been written to signify that event, but … it described Obsecuritan in so many ways."

"Oh." I didn't know what else to say. She never talked about her family. I tried to talk to her about it after the three boys from Obsecuritan had come to visit but she blew me off, just said the past was the past and that I needed to get back to studying.

After a moment of silence from her, I focused back on the maps and rubbed my head. Great. Just what I needed a headache. "Clarice, I think these maps may be able to help us. I haven't seen such detailed maps of the castle before. Look at this one though, I'm almost sure that it's the area of the courtyard."

The room went deathly quiet.

"You found the courtyard?" Owen asked barely above a whisper.

"No. I think this could be where it is. This area is drawn in, but it is perfectly circular."

As they looked down at the page, no one spoke. Then finally Clarice whispered, "Megan, there are so many rooms and levels to the castle. This room could be anywhere."

"I know that. But I haven't found another room in all these maps that look remotely circular, let alone one that appears to be *perfectly circular*. Feel free to look through them yourself. Every room, except for the entryway, in the castle, is rectangle or square."

My world faded away to the library in Nalrin. I slowly sat myself back in the chair and just let the vision come.

Lindy was jumping off the dead remains of a creature she had just beheaded, and she turned to ... my father... oh no not this one again.

"Don't do this Ansel." He laughed at her again, but then it shimmered. I instantly started to pay more attention. I had never skipped over this before. I always relived the conversation between my father, mother, CJ, and me. What's changed? When nothing materialized, I thought maybe I had pushed the vision out of my mind, but instead, I was looking at my mother sitting on a throne in a field of black tulips. I looked around and didn't see anyone else.

"It's about time you showed up. I've been trying to find you since we got back from the Mansuia." She said.

I looked around still wondering who she was talking to. I looked at her and she seemed to be talking directly to me, but when I looked around again, it was only the two of us in the field.

"Megan. You have indeed become more powerful since you found your way to Nalrin." Symatha said as she looked me up and down. Studying me. Like I was her prey.

What the actual fuck. She really was talking to me. ME! The real me? "Excuse me?"

"You can talk. Good. I wasn't sure this would work both ways." She said clapping her hands down on the arms of the throne. "That will make this so much easier."

"What in the hell is going on here?" I asked. Distantly I could hear everyone back at home asking what was going on and trying to answer my questions. I must be talking out loud.

"It's one of the benefit's to being back in Nalrin, and fine tuning your power. I had a feeling you inherited Cognitis. I had thought you might when we still lived in the Manusia, but you never did respond to me. Figured I would try now that you are here."

"What are you talking about? Cognitis?" I asked carefully.

"It is how you can communicate with others with just thought. It is how I was able to initiate a vision with you and how we are having this conversation." She said waving her hand like it was everyday knowledge.

"Why? I don't want to talk to you."

Distantly I could hear Jean telling me that I was sitting in the living room, having a vision, and to try to describe it. "Hold on Jean."

"Jean? HA! That woman is pathetic. No matter. She will be done with soon enough."

"Over my dead body."

She stood up and glided over to me. "That's where you are wrong."

She would have looked like an angel and for a minute even looked like the mother I knew and loved growing up. For the briefest of moments, she was the one who would comfort me, hold me when I fell and scraped my knee, or the one who told me everything would be ok when I broke up with my first boyfriend.

"You know it's strange. I thought I may be able to read your mind now that you have had some training. I never could when you were a child either." She said cocking her head to the side.

"So, you knew? You knew I was having visions of the future and you let me believe that I was crazy? You shoved pills down my throat. Why?"

"Yes, we knew. And before you ask, yes, the demons outside your window as a child were real too. Well, not all of them were demons, some were just associates of ours. Helping us out." She added nonchalantly.

"I know they are real." I said grinding my teeth. "What did you think you were protecting me from? In school, I realized I was seeing the future and when I told you, you just blew me off! Again, you shoved the pills down my throat to try to get them to stop. Only they didn't. Why?"

"We thought the Council would find us through your visions." She shrugged like it was no big deal.

"But I thought that when Matt died, you would have finally believed me." I said faking being small. I was so over this bullshit. I wasn't going to tell her what I knew, better to let her slip and tell us what she knows.

"*Ahh, yes Matt. About that. Let me give you some insight as to how your visions work. See what you see, whatever you see, is what will happen. It's because you see it that it will.*" When she saw the fear I plastered on my face, she giggled and continued in a small, petty voice, "*You're nothing more than regular, plain, boring, run of the mill, seer. Nothing more, nothing less.*"

"*You can't blame me for Matt's death. It wasn't my fault! It was because of your actions that Matt is dead. Because you went against the council, you brought that down on us. Dad even killed his own brother.*" I said trying to sound like an angry child who isn't getting her way.

"*He did because he was part of the problem! The council punished us for researching the Five Angels weapon. He was just trying to learn. Gain knowledge! But they didn't so much as lift a finger when my father died. It tore my mother up. She blamed me. Jean was always her favorite, and so I was outcasted.*" She said her face starting to contort.

"*You killed him?*" I said in a whisper.

"*Of course not! He was a cold-hearted snake that didn't love your grandmother any more than the books that line the bookcases in that house. I may not have been the favorite, but I didn't want him dead. Talk to your perfect little Aunt. Ask her what happened.*" She spat.

"*Jean may not be perfect but at least she isn't out to destroy all of Nalrin.*"

She shrugged nonchalantly and ran her finger up and down the arm of the throne. "*And what are you going to do? Stop us? We have the flower, the mirror is within our grasps, and we will have your heart very, very soon Megan.*"

"*And what about the Sa Ra? What of that? Don't you need it? And the book for Death?*"

"*I see you have been well versed in what is needed. I have the Sa Ra,*" she said as she fiddled with something around her neck, "*and we will get the Book of Death too.*"

"*Do you even know where to begin? I don't think you do. And,*" I said growling the words, "*You will never have my heart.*" I said growling the words.

"Oh, but I will. All we have to do is get CJ and harvest." She said with a quip and a slicing motion of her hand.

"And see that's where your plan will fail. Let alone do you even know where the ceremony has to be done?" I said.

"The ceremony can be done anywhere." She said with a lazy slur.

"No, it can't. Actually. ... Don't believe me? I know exactly where it will be done. If you are even able to get The Book of Death, you will see. Though, good luck getting in there." Her eyes were bright red and her face was slowly twisted into something unrecognizable. "Now I'm done talking to you."

"You won't be able to stop this." She growled in a deep otherworldly voice. "Each and every one of you will die."

"Goodbye, Mother." Then with as much strength as I could find, I pushed her from my mind.

It was like waking from a sound slumber. Like dreaming that your alarm is going off, but not realizing that your alarm is going off. I forced my eyes open and slowly my family came back onto focus, but I didn't have much strength and my head was pounding. I struggled to sit up but gave up and slumped back down.

I turned to Jean and said, "Jean you were wrong about my mother's power."

Pound.

Pound.

Pound.

As the pounding in my head echoed, everything went black.

CHAPTER 32

BLACK TULIPS AND A throne flashed before me, and I sat straight up. Head spinning, I slowly looked around the room. Clarice was sitting back on her knees holding a wet cloth. Jean and Owen stood a few feet back, Jean with her finger in Owen's face looking like I just interrupted a very important conversation.

"What's going on?" I said, rubbing my head.

Jean came and sat down next to my feet on the couch. "We were kind of hoping that you would be able to tell us. What was your vision? We have never heard you talk through one before. You've shouted a few things, but never full conversations. And why were you talking to your mother?"

"That wasn't a vision. Well, it started as one, but it was just a way for Symatha to talk to me. I can't explain it. How did you know that I was talking to my mother? Anyone got aspirin? My head is pounding." I massaged my temples as Owen disappeared into the kitchen.

"You were talking throughout the whole thing. What do you mean a way for her to talk to you? I don't understand." Jean asked. "Not to mention just before it was over... you well." She looked to Clarice.

"I what?" Owen handed me an aspirin and a glass of water.

"Well, ... you said something like '*I'm done talking to you.*' Then you, you glowed, well your Maltal glowed enough we could see it through your robe. There was a sharp electrical crack." She said shaking her head. "Then you looked at me and said I was wrong about Symatha's power. That's when you passed out."

"My mother's power." I said and sighed.

Jean raised her eyebrows at me in silent command to keep talking.

"You said she didn't have mental capabilities like I did. You're wrong. She can send messages just like I can to other people, or some version of that since this just happened." I rubbed my temples. "She called it being Congnitis or something like that."

"It's the ability to speak to others through thoughts. Like telepathy, but slightly different. How was she able to do it through your vision though? Congniti need to be within a certain range. Do you think that she's close enough? Around the house?"

"I don't know." I said as Owen got up and headed toward the door, syths in hand. I pushed my power out looking for any embers on the horizon but didn't see anything.

"Maybe you both were using your mental abilities at the time? But then how did she know you were having a vision? Was she somehow able to feel it? Maybe because of the Proteus living inside her?" Clarice was just spewing questions but stopped and took a really deep breath letting it out in a long breath to try to calm her brain. She put her head in her hands before continuing, "We can't underestimate her. The Proteus will continue to make her not only more powerful, but also more unpredictable."

"I don't plan on underestimating her." I pulled my knees to my chest and wrapped my arms around myself.

For over an hour I listened to them discuss my mother. During that brief encounter with Symatha we had learned a lot. Symatha and Ansel were not completely prepared for what they were doing, and that they were definitely not as informed about the things that had to happen as we thought. I took it as a small victory. Clarice and Jean did not. They claimed it made them more desperate. More unpredictable since there was a time limit on the flower.

Looking out the window to the garden that my grandmother had built, I tried not to focus on the fact that Symatha could put images directly into my head. I tried to picture my grandmother standing out in the garden and I could almost see her smelling the various flowers, on her hands and knees working the ground and even reading a book on the bench.

A bird circling the garden caught my eye and I admired at how it could just ride the air currents. Not a care in the world, but for basic survival instincts. Fly. Eat. Breed. Fly. Eat. It circled the garden one more time before it made a hard turn against the wind and flew directly toward me and landed on the windowsill. Its song was light and musical and it lightened the weight on my shoulders just that little bit.

It looked a little bit like a skylark, but this bird was about a foot long and a foot and a half high. It had a brilliant golden chest that matched its beak, a white band around the neck, and an upward crest on the top of its head. Not to mention beautiful red markings in the wing and tail. What surprised me most was the way its blue green eyes burned into mine, like it was trying to tell me something. I inched closer to the window and moved slowly enough not to scare the bird off.

Owen eyed me and the bird. It stared at me, ignoring everyone else and continued its lilting song. I inched closer and Owen whispered, "Megan, it's a Lark Messenger. It has a message for you from Nalrin."

"How do you know it's for me?" I asked as I continued to stare at the bird.

"Because it only sings for the person the message is for. We cannot hear its song."

I was standing right next to the window now, face only a foot from the bird's beak. "So how do I get the message. There is no note attached to its leg and it isn't carrying anything."

The bird placed its foot on my hand, and I heard CJ's voice as clear as if he were standing next to me.

Megan:

Lindy is meeting with the council.

Has something to do with your parents.

I think they are here from the way the message came through.

Anyways, Julian said it was extremely important.

He has requested your immediate presence.

The meeting is late tonight at 14.

The council is holding a special session to allow you travel time.

Nalrin is a beautiful city.

Stay safe.

See you soon.

Love Always, CJ

P.S. Tell the bird thank you and he will return to Nalrin.

I blinked. How did this bird just tell me that, in CJ's voice? It just kept staring at me with those eyes. It lifted its clawed foot and pressed it again to my hand and CJ's voice rang through my head again.

"Thank you. You may return home." I stammered as it finished the second time. The bird removed his foot from my hand, brought its beak to the stone windowsill, in what was easily a bowing motion, and took off into the sky.

"What was so important from the council that they sent a Lark Messenger?" Jean asked as she put her hand on my shoulder and watched as the bird flew off out of sight, my mind racing.

"It was a message from CJ. Lindy is meeting with Julian." I paused for a moment replaying the words in my head. There was a loud click deep in my consciousness, and my stomach dropped. "We have to meet the Council at 14 tonight."

"14 tonight?" Clarice said, "Why so late? Why not just wait till morning?"

"How long will it take us to get to Nalrin?" I asked my voice more earnest than I expected.

"It's going to take us the rest of the day to get there. We will probably arrive just before dark if we leave soon. Though once we get to Nalrin, with the tram ride, we will get to the center just in time for the meeting, but we have to leave soon." Owen said.

"Well, let's go." I snipped as I headed off to the bedroom to shower and change.

"What's the meeting about?" Owen asked.

"Megan, what else did CJ say?" Clarice asked.

"Megan!" I heard Jean yell as I turned the corner ignoring them and slammed the door to my bedroom.

I didn't trust myself to answer them. I knew where this would lead. My heart threatened to stop beating as I pictured it all in my head again.

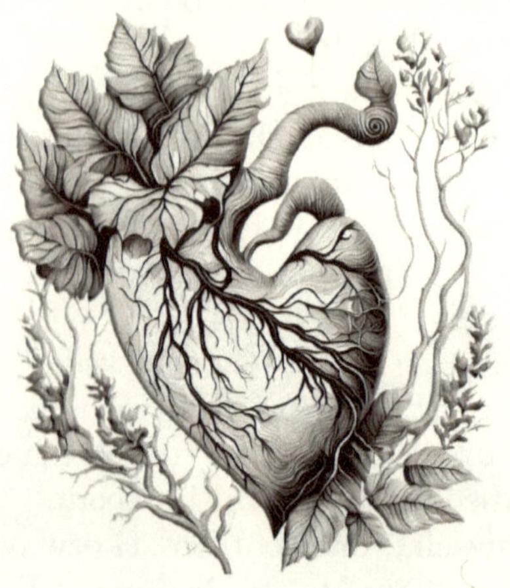

CHAPTER 33

I HAD ALREADY PUT my syths in the sheaths at my thighs, strapped one in my boot, a switchblade in the other, two additional syths were attached to my belt on my waist, and I secured two short swords crossed across my back at my shoulders. I grabbed a couple of changes of clothes, threw them in a small bag, and as I reached for the doorknob, I saw it sitting on the dresser. The Calling Stone. I stared at it for a long, long moment. Sighing, I grabbed it, put it in my back pocket, shutting the door behind me.

In the living room, Owen, Jean, and Clarice were dressed for a casual meeting with the council, as if there is such a thing as a casual meeting. When they noticed how I was dressed, Jean asked "Expecting a fight?"

"Actually yes, and I don't believe we will be back here any time soon either. So, you can travel in that if you'd like, but I'm just taking what I know I will need, and you should too." Of course, I was expecting a fight.

"Um ok." She said looking to Owen and Clarice who mirrored her shock, "Give us 10 minutes and we'll be ready to go."

I went out to the stable and retrieved the tack. After I got the bridle on, I led her out and waited for the others. Unable to hold still, I double checked the strap, tightening it a bit more now that the mare had let some of the air out of her belly, and fiddled with the bridle.

When there was nothing else to do, I played with the electricity between my fingers. I had been working on letting more and more out of the cocoon so I would eventually not need it anymore. I estimated that I was able to let about half of it out at once, but any more than that, and I would get really antsy.

As I watched it though, I realized it wasn't really fair to give them any attitude. It wasn't like I gave them any inclination to what I know, but HELLO! They knew that we have to fight my parents in the Nalrin library soon, and now the council wants a personal meeting with us ... tonight. What's left? Like five weeks at best before the flower wilts?

I started pacing. If CJ's information is correct, Ansel and Symatha are not going to risk cutting it that close. They still have so much to do and after my vision with Symatha, well they were going to get more desperate the closer to the deadline we got.

I smiled. They don't have a Lindy, though. *The* walking Five Angels encyclopedia. They don't know where the ritual has to take place. Not that we know exactly where it is to take place either.

What are they going to do when they realize they didn't have the true Golden Medallion of Sa Ra? How and when were they going to come after me?

If they have CJ, they know I'll go to them.

No. They won't get CJ. I can change my visions. I just have to try hard enough. That coil of electricity lit up in the cocoon, and I felt it crawl up my back. I stopped pacing, took a deep breath, rolled my neck, and coiled some of it back up.

Clarice came out first dressed much like I was, including the additional short swords across her shoulders. She didn't have much in the way of extras, either. In fact, she almost completely mirrored me except for her whips instead of syths, at her hips. It was another 10 minutes before Owen and Jean came back out.

"Sorry, Owen couldn't find where to put his back up syths." Jean said rolling her eyes. "The bedroom is a mess. Going to have to clean it up when we get back."

When everyone's packs were secured to the horses, we turned, and with a quick chirp, the horses were galloping through the forest.

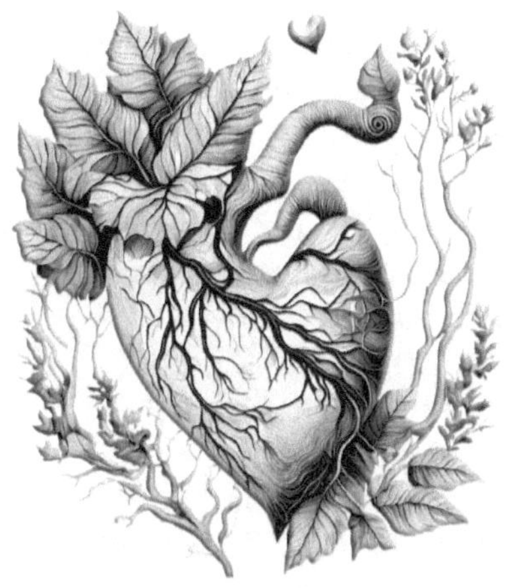

CHAPTER 34

BY THE TIME WE were approaching the Nalsar River, it had started to rain. Everything changed when it rained here. Not just in the scientific way that it did back in the Manusia, but you could see in real time how the trees moved and stretched their limbs as if they were arms trying to catch as many of the droplets of water as they could. The ferns stretched and curled, and the flowers opened their buds to catch whatever they could. I watched a patch of cup shaped purple flowers spread their petals just slightly and start to fill with water. I smiled and shook my head. Would I ever get used to how the trees and plants moved here?

As we got closer to the river, the port lined the bank with a makeshift farmer's market and a loading dock right in the middle. This was the main hub for the people who live far away from any main city. On the surface, the place looked run down, but each shopkeeper's area was clean. Sure, it was muddy, but everything was wet from the rain.

We lodged the horses at the stable and grabbed our packs. When Owen went to get us tickets for the ferry it gave me a chance to wander the market. There were dozens of different kinds of fish, fruits, meat, and crafted goods that were just, well stunning. Their craftsmanship rivaled those great artisans in the Manusian world.

There was one dark olive-skinned lady, who I swear looked to be 180 years old, selling elaborately carved bowls and plates that made me wonder if anyone would ever really eat out of them. When I asked her about them, she said that her family had been crafting them for thousands of years. I was looking at one in particular in such detail that when Jean tapped me on the shoulder, I almost dropped it. She giggled and turned to the old woman and smiled.

"Balincha, Madam Winters" Jean said putting her hands to her forehead and extending it out to the woman.

"Balincha Ms. Jean. Heading to the Nalrin City to meet up with Ms. Lindy and Mr. Cory, are we?" Madam Winters answered giving me a coy smile. Her accent was thick, throaty and the r's were long and rolling like she got stuck on it.

"Yes ma'am." Jean said.

"Do take care. I sense much turmoil and pain in your future." She said.

Great, just what we need another person telling me about *turmoil and pain.* Don't I predict that enough? I tried very hard not to roll my eyes at her. Besides, what did she know about my future.

"Of course, Madam Winters. We will be careful." Jean turned to me, "Megan the ferry will be ready to leave shortly, we should head out."

I made to put the bowl down, but when the bowl touched the table Madam Winters grabbed my hand and I felt the coldest sensation rip through my whole body like I had been turned to ice. I looked up at her in horror. My power became exceptionally still. I had never felt anything like it in my life.

Madam Winters looked at me and said, "I know that Ms. Jean does not believe in my warnings, but you must child. You will lose one of your loved ones. You won't be able to stop it."

"How... do..." I stammered.

"Shush child! I don't have much time before she comes back looking for you. You must remember. Look to the dark and you may find what you're looking for, but if you stay in the light, it will lead to their success." She said.

"What are you talking about? What do you mean look to the dark?" I said.

"You will know what it means when the time is right. Now GO!" She said.

She released my hand and warmth crashed back into my body. I looked at her carefully again then took off running toward the pier.

When I caught sight of the others waiting for me, I slowed to a walk and rubbed my hand. How could she turn me to ice like that? Does she know what is going on? How could she know what was going on? She couldn't, right? Or could she? To my knowledge the council was doing everything in its power to keep this under wraps. *Look to the dark you may find what you're looking for, but stay in the light, it will lead to their success?* What could that possibly mean?

I looked back the way I came, and Madam Winters was standing in the middle of the road. After staring at her for a moment, I realized her ember ... didn't look right.

"Jean?"

She was busy talking with Owen and Clarice.

"Jean." I said louder.

"What is it, Megan?"

"Madam Winters." I said as I pointed to her.

"Why is she staring at you like that?" she asked with question and concern in her voice.

"Her ember, it's fluctuating." I finally said cocking my head to the side and drawing out each word slowly. It seemed to flicker around the limbs of her body and move inward to where her Maltal would have been. Then it just went out. Like someone had flipped the light switch off. Madam Winters collapsed in the arms of the woman standing next to her, who I hadn't noticed before, as I ran toward her.

I turned to the woman who was now holding Madam Winters' body. "What's wrong?"

"She's exhausted. She just needs to rest. She's way too old to be selling family nick-nacks anymore. She insisted on coming this time. Stupid woman!" her accent was clearer than the woman she was holding. She turned to me, "I'm her granddaughter Ariel Winters, and you are?"

"Megan Keller." I shook her hand and got that same ice feeling all over again, but not to the point that Madam Winters had earlier.

"Ahhh." Ariel Winters said, "So you're the reason she was so stubborn about coming. I hope you listen to what she told you."

"How ... wait, what?" I said. Who are these people?

"The women in my family have abilities that are beyond that of typical Sangria. Usually my sister Colletta comes, but she was birthing a calf today. I see you too have sight. Heed what my grandmother told you. She is never wrong." She said with calm understanding.

"Megan!" I heard Jean calling for me.

"Go. Looks like the ferry is ready. Grandma will be fine. She just needs to rest. GO!"

I got up and slowly walked to the ferry contemplating their words. I jumped on the ferry just as they announced last call.

The ferry had a huge open back area and almost pitch-black deck. The ferry's hull was a dark purple that transitioned about 10 feet above the river to the same black wood as the deck for the siding and large open windows. Not to mention the hay-colored thatch roof that started about a quarter of the way back from the front, with openings to let in sunlight. The thatch roof was laid out and curved around in such a way that it reminded me of an older Dutch house. Inside they had benches along the walls so you could easily watch out over the river and across the countryside. At the back of the ferry, near the base of the stairs, there was a fully stocked bar and pastry counter.

I slouched down on the bench and tried to relax. I concentrated on the sound of the waves crashing against the ferry, the birds singing, and the sound of the breeze as it passed through the ferry and the roof. It was almost musical.

It didn't seem long, though I may have fallen asleep before Owen nudged me. "We are about to enter the Nalrin Bay. You have to see this." He said pointing off to the right.

As the ferry opened to Nalrin Bay, the City of Nalrin literally shone into view. The sunlight reflected off the buildings in the city center shone so brightly it was like a beacon. The city was built upon the mountain, with the inner walls gradually getting smaller to the center of the city. Below the outermost wall was a large nature preserve that stretched all the way down to the water. The City was literally built on an island in the center of the bay.

The nature preserve had been established over a Nalrin millennia ago to preserve the wildlife of the area. It was against the laws to either build or hunt in the acres that surrounded the city. The penalties for being caught there were brutally harsh.

The bay was crystal blue. Even though you knew the ferry had to disturb the water as it moved through, it stayed smooth as glass and crystal clear once we entered it. You could see the multitude of fish, in all kinds of bright colors swimming around in the bay. As we got a little closer to the city, dolphin like creatures that were bright blue and purple with black markings on their tail fins started swimming and playing in the non-existent wake of the ferry. I was mesmerized. It was like they could feel the water disbursement even if we couldn't see it.

"I never would have imagined such bright colored dolphins." I hadn't realized I had said anything out loud, when Owen who had been standing next to me said, "Well that's because they aren't dolphins." I jumped.

"Don't sneak up on me like that!" I said smacking his arm.

He just giggled and continued. "They are Bluchree. They are said to have been put here by the Angel of Beauty herself."

"I don't doubt that, but they look a lot like dolphins. I mean they are a LOT larger, and the head is broader. Not to mention dolphins are not this brightly colored."

"Yeah and get this ... they lay eggs." He said his mouth twitching to the side.

"Really?!" I said.

He looked down at them and nodded. "Yup. The eggs are buried in a sacred place that's very well protected and stay there for over 4 years before they hatch." He said nudging me.

"Wow, that is different. Guess the long incubation time, makes them all that much more special." I couldn't take my eyes off of them, they were stunning. I thought about Becca back in the Manusia who would have gone crazy for them. She loved dolphins. After about 10 minutes, they retreated from the ferry and when I looked up, I saw why.

We were pulling up to an enormous stone building to dock. It reminded me of Grand Central Station in New York. I had studied pictures of it and had just marveled at the details in the building. Nalrin Dock had huge sculptures of the Five Angels strategically placed over pathways and phrases carved in stone.

"Amazing, isn't it?" Clarice said sighing as she came up next to me.

"It really is." I whispered. Was everything in Nalrin supposed to take your breath away? Hell, if this is just the dock, I can't wait to see the city and council buildings in person. I had seen them in my studies, but I doubt they did them justice.

"You have the exact same look of awe on your face that I did the first time I came to Nalrin." She sighed then continued. "I knew I had made the right choice by leaving home when I arrived here."

"Why did you leave Obsecuritan?" I asked before I really thought about it.

"My father is a very dark and evil man. I couldn't live with it anymore." She said softly.

"Oh. I'm sorry." I said.

"Don't be. When the boys came from Obsecuritan, you remember when you were a little cocky and beat the shit out of them?" Clarice said smiling brightly.

I laughed. "Yeah. I remember."

"I had actually been expecting them to come. They had been sending me letters trying to get me to come home because my father is dying. Technically, I'm supposed to take over his position. Birth right and all, but I have no interest in it. I don't want to live in the dark. I want to live in the light. So, when I left, I told him I wouldn't be back, and I came here. It's where I met Jean and Owen. They took me in, and I haven't looked back." She said it so matter of a fact that I just stared at her.

I thought about what she said. It made sense. In some ways what she did is what I'm doing. Granted a lot more action based, but emotionally, she was still trying to find herself. I looked up at the grandeur of the dock again and tried to lose myself in its beauty. *I don't want to live in the dark. I want to live in the light.* I sighed heavily.

"Come on, let's head to the trams. I know you could look at this for hours." Clarice said as she put her arm around my shoulders and led me away. "I did the first time I was here. Sat right over there for almost the whole day just taking it all in."

As we walked, I kept admiring the architecture and if it weren't for Clarice guiding me, I would have walked into someone or stopped all together. We stopped in the waiting area for the tram, and it was just as exquisitely decorated as the rest of the station.

When the tram pulled up, I had expected some kind of a subway train. You know, metal, windows, the stereotypical subway train. Nope. This tram was completely made of stone but the seats inside were like a brown crystal. The tram hovered just slightly over rails, but I heard breaks as it came to a stop in front of me. It was completely modernized, but with the look and feel of something ancient. I looked around and each line had a tram was a different stone colored tram. It was utterly fascinated.

"Sit down Megan, it's gonna take a while to just get to the outer wall." Jean told me.

As the tram moved on and out of the station, it took us through a vast open plain, that was full of lush greenery and animals that ran wild. There were Camaboo, an antelope hippo looking thing, playing in the pools of water below, a herd of six-legged horse running across the plain, and birds flying in color combinations I had never thought possible. I felt like I was 6 years old, experiencing the world for the first time.

All my worries and fears seemed to melt away as we rode through, which luckily was no short trip. It took us about an hour and a half just to get to the outer wall of the city, and it was starting to get dark. Owen had said the trip would put us in the inner city just before the meeting, and when I looked at the time, it appeared he would be right.

We passed through the outer wall and into a very poor area, I remembered from my studies they had the inner walls built for two reasons: erosion control and strategic protection. The inner walls were built deep into the ground to help keep the mountain from eroding away underneath, and if the city were ever attacked, they would've created multiple layers of defense to protect the council chambers.

Unfortunately, it allowed for an economical status barrier as well. The tram we were on didn't stop in this area, as it was bound for the upper levels of the city, but I couldn't help but feel sad for those people. The smell alone emitting from this area suggested that the availability of working toilets and baths were a luxury this section of the city could not afford. The streets were filled with people, trash piled along the side of homes that were built out of concrete, blocks, siding or whatever else they could find. Some of the more permanent structures had no windows or only sheets as curtains.

I hadn't really seen this level of poverty in my time here in this dimension. Even at the river's edge, it wasn't "dirty" per se. Sure there was dirt and mud everywhere, but that was just because there were no paved streets. The buildings and stalls were in fairly good shape. The people were clean and hygienic. I know I had been preoccupied since I got here, but I don't know why it seemed to shock me that there were places that had people actually living like this.

Through the next wall, the streets were cleaner. The homes had yards, some maintained, some not so much, and young children playing. I even saw a school with children playing in the courtyard.

When we entered through the third wall about ten minutes later, this section was clearly designated for the middle class. The lawns were kept up, the schools looked nicer, which had a baseball-like field and a football field. When I asked Clarice if that really was a football field, she told me that kids here loved football. It had caught on a while back after some Sangra came back from working in Europe in the Manusia. They had changed the goal system though. I smiled. Soccer, not American Football like I was so used to watching on Sundays.

Beyond the fourth wall, which was designated for your politicians and higher classed citizens, the houses were larger and the nicest homes available. I knew that from my studies, but the difference was astounding. Huge homes that looked like they could have been plucked right out of the richest communities in the Manusia and placed here. You could see the homes getting bigger and more elaborate as we got closer to the city center. I could not help but be amazed at the harsh lines in economic status that were drawn in this city.

It took us thirty minutes to get from the fourth wall to the thickest wall of them all. The fifth held the center of the city. Even as fast as the train was going it took longer to go through Nalrin's center-most wall. The center was where all the city and providence buildings were. The only people allowed to live here were the Council members themselves, or other foreign dignitaries.

The train came to a stop and guards were posted at each door. As people got off the train, they checked identification and asked the reason for coming to the center.

When I got to the check point, I froze. The only identification I had was my California Driver's License, and that was back at the house. What would I need that for here in Nalsar? Even if I did have it with me, I hardly thought that they would accept that as a proper form of ID. Owen and Jean were in front of me and flashed some sort of card that had the guard nodding them through.

"ID, ma'am?" Said a man in a red leather jacket just like the black one I had on.

"Um, well I don't have Nalrin identification." I said as I looked to Clarice for help.

"She's with us sir, we are meeting with the Council." She handed him her card over my shoulder and as he took it, he caught the swords at my back and the syths attached to my thighs. Clarice was just as armed as I was, and she didn't even need them to kill someone.

He reached out and grabbed me by the upper arm and pulled me off to the side. On instinct, I broke his grip, twisting myself inward so that he couldn't keep ahold of me. I started to grab for his head to knock him out, but Clarice called me off. By some silent signal, his partner had closed off the doors behind us and instructed everyone who was left in that car to go to the next to exit. Jean, Owen, and Clarice were right on my heels, trying to explain what was going on to the officer, silenced them.

When we got to the wall, he turned to face me and asked, "Why are you caring enough of an arsenal to wipe out a small army, if all your doing is going to speak with the Nalrin Council?"

I was totally speechless. I concentrated on not letting the electricity come to my defense as I could hear it starting to hum in my ears. How do I explain something to a guard who is only doing his job, that he really needs to slack off this time to let me through? I looked to the others for help.

"It's a bit complicated." Clarice told him meeting his eyes. "If you could contact your supervisor and have them ask Head Julian directly, it would sort everything."

In a stroke of luck, or horrible timing, two additional guards, dressed in a different uniform with a symbol at the left shoulder, which looked familiar, made their way to us.

"Please release Ms. Megan, Ranquel." The taller of the two instructed the guard.

"Sir, she is caring short swords and syths, and a lot of them at that." he said as he snapped to attention. "You know they are not allowed within the center walls by those without proper identification."

"That I do Ranquel, however, she is a special guest of the council today, and is allowed to do and carry what she wishes. I will ensure that she obtains the proper identification so this doesn't happen again."

Ranquel hesitated, eyeing the guard, but finally said, "Yes sir." with resentment and hesitation thick in his voice. He turned on his heel and went back to unloading the train.

"Thank you." I said eyeing the symbol on his left collarbone; Three vertically alternating swords with a laurel around it. Where had I seen that symbol before?

"You're welcome, Ms. Megan. I apologize for the confusion. We were running a bit late." He said as he bowed. Did he actually bow to me? "I am Vernadali Nathanial, and this is Vernadali Colin. We will escort you to the chamber hall immediately. Do you have any bags you need to get from the tram?"

"No, we only brought what was on us." Jean told him.

"I can see." He said as he scanned me from head to toe. It was a methodical and professional scan, but I still buttoned up my jacket despite the almost 85-degree weather. "You did bring a small arsenal. No wonder Ranquel was so persistent with you. I will make a note of commitment on his record."

"You aren't Nalrin Guard?" I asked.

"No ma'am. Colin and I are Vernadali." One of them said.

"I'm sorry, what?" I asked.

"Vernadali. We inherit the trait through our families' bloodlines." Vernadali Nathanial said.

"Like a different species?" I said genuinely interested. The different beings in this world fascinated me.

"No. We are Sangra, but there is a trait in our blood that allows us to be Vernadali. Basically, we are super bodyguards." He said smiling. Vernadali Colin stood straighter as Vernadali Nathanial said that.

"There is a lot of additional training that we go through that is separate from the Nalrin Guard, and we usually start at a much younger age. Usually around the same time that we would start our usual Sangra studies."

I nodded and thought about that for a moment, "So are you assigned to the dignitaries only then?"

"Any high-ranking official really. Could be anyone. Could be a dignitary, a dignitary's family members, someone from another dimension. It can be changed for short-term assignments, but often we are assigned to one person for life."

"How—" I started to ask, but he cut me off.

"Ma'am. There is only so much I can tell you. I'm sorry." He said giving me an apologetic look.

We continued in silence, but as we walked toward the council chamber, I marveled at the intricate stonework on all the buildings. They were not like the old stone buildings we have in the Manusia. Those are so dark and rustic, not that I don't like that style, but these were clean, pristine, more how I imagined the Greek temple buildings must have looked when they were first constructed.

We must have walked about a mile, but when we turned the corner, and I stopped in my tracks.

CHAPTER 35

THE NALRIN COUNCIL BUILDINGS were spectacular! Three large white stone buildings sat in the center of three reflecting pools. There was one bridge that crossed over the largest of the reflecting pools to an enormous smooth cobblestone courtyard. As I stared at the reflecting pools, water started dancing around in a spectacular water display.

There were a few smaller reflecting pools around the smaller buildings on this side of the bridge, which were scaled down versions of the one in front of the main buildings. Even so, it wasn't any less breathtaking of a sight. From my studies, I knew that the smaller buildings contained the Council member and Dignitary residences, the Nalrin Library, and many of the other territory and city offices.

I stood there staring completely mesmerized. When the guards realized I had stopped, they started to say something, but Jean and Owen shook their heads and they waited patiently. I had seen pictures of the Nalrin Council buildings of course, which were different than the other buildings in the center as I studied for the trials, but they didn't do them any justice. They were just something you had to see in person.

During my studies, I had realized there was something very familiar about the architecture itself, but I had never been able to place why they felt so familiar. I knew I hadn't seen it in a vision or anything like that, but then it hit me.

"The Taj Mahal. The building itself looks so much like the Taj Mahal, except the roofs are more English Tudor without being so exaggerated at the point. The way the grey and white stonework… it's so intricate!" I said, not fully making coherent sentences.

"A lot of the architecture from your dimension and ours are a lot alike." Owen said with a gleam of satisfaction. He had been letting me puzzle it out instead of just giving me the answer. Jerk. I went to punch him in the arm when I saw a figure just across the bridge to the courtyard.

"CJ!" I breathed running straight for him. He stood there in Sangra dress and FUCK he looked good! He just stood there smiling with his arms ready as I jumped up, wrapped my legs around his waist, and kissed him. "I've missed you so much." I said into his neck as I continued to hold him tight. He put me down and giggled.

"I was only gone for a couple of days. Maybe I need to go away more often?"

"HA! Over my dead body!"

"I prefer not." He said smiling, but then noticed the arsenal I was wearing. "Expecting a fight?"

I just looked at him. Nothing.

"Actually. Yes." He looked at me a bit weird. "Ceej, Julian wants to see us?"

Nothing.

"My freak out vision?"

Finally, the realization hit him, about the time Owen spoke up behind me. "So that's why you were so mad at us when we weren't prepared back at the house."

"Yeah. I kinda assumed. I'm sorry I didn't explain it to you all then. It's just that you know, I've had the visions, and the pieces were all there. Better safe than sorry, right?" I explained.

CJ just took my hand, kissed the ring I wore, and said, "Well it's almost time to meet with the council. Let's go."

"So, what have you been doing here?" I asked CJ as we made our way through the courtyard. I saw Nathanial eye him and give him a shake of his head so small I almost missed it.

"Oh, just taking some aptitude tests?" CJ said like it no big deal, but Nathanial's muscle twitched in his shoulder.

"Aptitude tests? Why?" I asked.

"Well after we are married, I'm going to need to get a job to provide for you in a manner of which you will become greatly accustomed." He smiled brightly then continued. "Seriously babe. It's no big deal. I don't have Sangra blood, so they couldn't do the usual testing to see where I might fit in best. I'm ... different."

He said it in a way that wasn't necessarily a bad thing. He said different almost with pride, but with a twitch of fear laced in. Before I could ask him about it though, Nathanial stopped before the main doors.

"Once we enter the hall, it is highly suggested that your voice be kept low and soft." Nathanial said as Colin opened the large triple wide doors and stepped inside.

They lead us through the main building and down hall upon hall. Finally, we made it to the large double doors that separated us from Julian. I'd be lying if I didn't say I was more than just a little nervous. I was about to stand before the head of Nalrin. I huffed out as much nervous energy as I could, but then realized, that I wasn't meeting just the head of Nalrin, but the head of all of Nalsar. Our whole dimension. He was the leader and ruler of everything here. If he didn't like me or got one negative thought about me, I'm toast.

No pressure.

No pressure at all to make a good impression.

Sure, he proceeded over my Maltal ceremony, but it wasn't like we had sat down for a chat or anything. He was in and out. Off to whatever was next on the list. I coiled my power back up into that cocoon, just in case. Wouldn't make a good impression if I knocked everyone out with it.

No. That would not be good.

The Council chamber doors opened, and CJ held my hand tight as we walked through the doorway. It felt more like what I expected it may have been like to walk onto the floor of the Coliseum in Rome during its heyday.

When we walked in and saw who was standing before us, I instantly felt small and meaningless. My power coiled faster in its cocoon, asking to be let out. It seemed to be screaming, DANGER. DANGER. I gritted my teeth against it. Even's CJ's hand tightened in mine.

My entire family looked at each other with looks of shock written over each of our faces. It wasn't just Julian and the Nalrin council members that stood before us.

No. We had been called by the entire Nalsar Dimensional Council.

EVERY nation and territory, big or small, of this dimension, was represented by both their Heads of State *and* Take Overs. I recognized many from my studies and yet, there were still many, many more that I didn't. Ones that were not here personally were here by LightCall, a video conferencing orb that hung over their seats to hear and see everything that was occurring in the chamber.

Julian was here along with his takeover to represent Nalrin. The Gurglins, frog like with oversized feet and hands, had come up from the Seltic Marsh. The Fairies of Cinder, whose wings were individual to each fairy, had even made the very long trip from the western continent, which was so rare that many in the council were gawking at them.

Even the Ralvins from the most southern and darkest parts of Noctulanar were here. Their bat like wings, which were riddled with holes and looked shredded, seemed to pulse, even though they weren't moving, they still gave me a chill to the bone.

Then there were the Chandils from Obsecuritan, who looked at Clarice with an intensity that even I wouldn't make eye contact. I could see Clarice shift her weight uncomfortably, which put me on guard. Nothing. Nothing makes Clarice uncomfortable. It was a little strange and disconcerting actually. She relaxed a bit when Lindy and Jean took her hands and squeezed them.

There were many, many more, but I leaned toward Lindy and whispered, "Has the entire Council ever been called to session before?"

"Not for over 70 years. The fact the Cinder Fairies, Ralvins, and Gurglins are here, means this is *really* important. They almost NEVER leave their territories. They usually appear to vote via LightCall." She said with reverence, then quietly added, "But why us? What are we doing before everyone?"

Julian called the Council to session and proceeded to introduce us to each of the dignitaries, to whom we bowed in respect. Julian turned to the dignitary of Gendril, and said, "and as you know, this is Benedict, Take Over for your father Clarice."

We all bowed, well except for Clarice. She just stood there, straight backed. He... actually ... bowed to her.

"Your father was saddened that he could not be here today ... Ms. Clarice." Benedict said. Clarice narrowed her eyes slightly, but there was respect in her posture, "He wanted me to relay a message."

He snapped his fingers and one of the runners came up and handed her a scroll which was sealed with wax. "Please read it when you are on your way to Obsecuritan. We know you will need to be entering Noctulanar, and he wishes to see you."

"For what in return?" She said with grace.

"I do not know the contents of the scroll Ms. Clarice." He lowered his head and in a sad, longing voice continued, "I was only asked to relay the message and to deliver you the scroll."

Clarice muttered something in a language I didn't understand. The man named Benedict replied to her, and she bit back some sort of retort.

"Ms. Clarice. He is gravely ill. He speaks of you fondly and ... he just wants to see you." Benedict said softly before bowing to her again and taking his seat.

"Now on to business, shall we." Julian said turning his back to the Council to face us. I suddenly felt as if I was on a stage that stood before the whole world and gripped CJ's hand tighter.

"Ms. Megan. The Council knows of your mission, and you have our deepest respect for this. We have received notification that Ansel and Symatha have been seen in the inner walls of Nalrin. I believe they are attempting to gain access to the Mirror of Remembrance using secret underground tunnels that had been previously sealed off. Obviously, they are receiving help from someone within the city to get access." The whole room erupted in mummers.

Well, the council hadn't known everything.

After the murmuring had quieted down, Julian continued. "Penelope Hephaestus, Head of Nalrin Relics, will meet with you to go over the layout, dangers and securities of the Nalrin Library."

I nodded acknowledging him but wondered why we had to appear before the whole council for this information. Why not meet privately? Why put everything out in the open? That would only breed fear and mistrust through all of the territories.

CJ elbowed me and nodded toward Penelope Hephaestus. CJ leaned over and whispered "She looks exactly like..." I shooshed him, but I knew who he meant. I rolled my eyes at him smiling. CJ's celebrity crush. Though, even I had to admit the resemblance was uncanny. Julian asked us to take a seat and continued on with other matters of concern.

Most of those issues on the agenda were the same issues we dealt with back in the Manusia. Things like water allocation, immigration between territories, and even inter-racial and gender rights. I frowned when that subject came up. No matter where you go, the right of true equality was always going to be a fight. CJ took my hand, squeezed it, and nodded toward Clarice. Clarice was rolling the scroll Benedict had given to her over and over in her hands. What happened between them that it created so much animosity?

After Julian closed session and the last dignitary had left, Julian came down from the stands and formally introduced us to Penelope Hephaestus, who quickly corrected him and asked us to call her Penny. CJ was right. She was a dead ringer for the actress; the fiery red hair, green eyes, light skin, even the way she stood and carried herself.

"Hephaestus... Greek God of Fire..." CJ asked. That's why the last name sounded so familiar.

"It's not just a resemblance. There is a lineage that actually connects us." She created a small fire ball in the palm of her hand. "I'm not Sangra, and not an elemental either. I'm Tellgin."

"A Tellgin? I thought they had died out over 300 years ago?" I asked as we walked to a private room. The racial history portion of my studies had a whole section on the Tellgin. They were a fascinating race. Hephaestus was visiting the Manusia when the Greeks saw him, and he was instantly escalated to god status believing he was a son of Zeus.

"Nearly we have. There are only 50 of us left. My brother and I are the only ones left from my family. My parents died about 75 years ago."

"75 years ago?" CJ said astonished.

"Yes. Once Tellgin reach their 30's we don't age physically." She said. "I'm 164 years old."

We were quiet the rest of the way as she led us back through the main hall, and into an adjoining building to her office.

"Why was the entire Council called to address us?" Lindy asked Penny.

"Why to show the importance of the situation, of course." Penny said, though her words may have implied she was being condescending, it didn't come across that way. Penny spoke in such an ancient way, and with such sweetness, that the words didn't matter, it was all in the delivery.

"But my parents want to destroy Nalrin, not the entire dimension." I said.

"That isn't how the Council sees it. Nalrin is just one piece of the puzzle. Once they destroy Nalrin, who isn't to say they won't go after the Curtails of the North, or Fairies of Cinder, or the Gurglins in the Seltic Marsh. Angels, or even the Ralvins."

"I hardly think anyone would go after those Ralvins. They make me cold to the bone." CJ said with a shudder.

"Aye, they do have that effect, but what your parents are doing is affecting the whole realm. If word were to get out that they could combine 'de Angels weapon, then others will try to follow, or ask assistance in destroying other territories." Penny explained.

I hadn't really thought about that. How could I have been so short sighted to not think about all these other cultures that could be affected. I heard Penny talking to the others, and I knew I should be paying attention, but I just couldn't concentrate. My head was getting fuzzy, and I shook my head to clear it as a headache started to form as I heard a woman's laugh ring loud.

My heart stopped.

My mother's laugh.

I rushed down the hall with my syths suddenly in my hands.

"You think you can stop me?" Her voice seemed to whisper right in my ears. My vision shimmered and I leaned against the wall and saw my mother standing in front of me. Defiant and tall. Nothing but blackness behind her.

"Do you think you can stop us little girl?" She took a single step toward me. "The entire Council is here and they still hide in their cages." Her eyes glowed that deep red, and it made me step back."

"You're such a child. Do you think two kids can do anything against us?" She hissed.

I forced all my fear down and made myself stand as tall as I could. It felt as if there was this huge weight on me, and I struggled to just stay on my feet and leaned against the wall.

She threw her head back and laughed at me. I felt like the pathetic child she thought I was. I could feel someone's arms, trying to hold me up, but I couldn't tell who it was. "Don't worry Megan, it will all be over soon."

She disappeared with a crack.

As soon as the crack dissipated, my legs gave out under me. I forced myself to sit up and rested my arms on my knees. My head flopped forward as I concentrated on breathing.

"Megan, what did you see?" Jean was crouching before me with her hands on my shoulders trying to get me to focus.

"Symatha, she's...." I tried to say, but my mouth was bone dry. I can't explain it. Out of the corner of my eye, I saw Penny eye me a little more carefully when I mentioned my mother's name.

"See? What do you mean, she sees?" Penny asked.

"She has visions. But lately, they are more than visions, she actually..." Owen stopped mid-sentence and turned to me. "Symatha contacted you again, didn't she?"

I could only nod my head. This vision communication thing was so much different than the others.

"What do you mean—" CJ started to say before Clarice shooshed him and gave me a small cup of water. I downed it one quick gulp.

"At least I didn't pass out this time." I smiled at the thought and looked at CJ, and my fingers sparked with electricity as I felt that fear and protection rush back.

I have to save CJ.

I can change what I see.

I can change what I see.

First things first. I made myself stand up tall, and act normal again, even though I was not feeling it right now, and I wanted a nap. I turned and faced Penny. "If they are here, then they are heading toward the Mirror of Remembrance. Penny, please give us directions to the mirror, and what can you tell us that will make our journey through your security systems easier?"

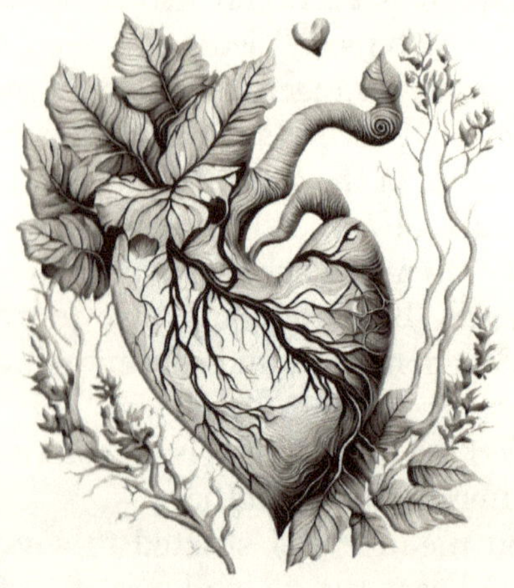

CHAPTER 36

IT WASN'T JUST TECHNOLOGY and Sangra power that protects the most sacred parts of the Nalrin Relics' storage. There were puzzles, tests, and the creatures. Those creatures were bred to protect and kill anyone who gets close. Unfortunately, Penny wasn't able to tell us how to get past those creatures. She simply claimed not to know, which I called total bullshit on. She did give us a map of the underground storage that would help us get to where we needed to be while avoiding as many of the creatures we could. However, the closer we got to the Five Angels relics, the more vicious the creatures we were going to come across. As if that wasn't enough to think about, there was also the fact that my parents already had a head start on us.

Penny lead us down hall after hall, Lindy rolling her eyes the entire way day. When Penny was ahead of us a bit she muttered, "The Head of Nalrin Relics would have the highest clearance there was. She has to be able to get down to the Angels level."

"Maybe there was a specialized clearance system? Surely those who were charged with protecting the most dangerous and important items in all of Nalrin had clearance to those sections?" CJ said.

"I could have led us this far just from my time years ago." Lindy said.

When we got to as far as Penny claimed she could take us, she closed and locked the door behind us, a faint smirk crossed her face. I rushed for the door but there was no way to reopen it from this side. "That fucking bitch!" I said turning around to look at the others.

"She was delaying us?" Owen said.

"I think so. The smirk she had on her face certainly makes me think so." I took a deep breath, "Well Megan. Time to go save the world."

We passed through room upon room of relics that I would have loved to stop and look at. It was the museum of all museums, only without the crowds. The knowledge here was indescribable. The history and information in just one of these massive hallways would keep me busy for years.

We turned the corner and entered a huge room with what appeared to be a huge stone sphinx in the back of the room. Halfway across the room it slowly sat up and shook off the dust, stopping us dead in our tracks. It resembled a sphinx, but while the face resembled that of a human's, its head was bald. There was no mane, no headpiece, no hair, nothing except for a bright orange stone that sat evenly between its feline ears near the top of its head. It sat there studying us, just the same way we were studying it.

I sighed and said, "So this is the first obstacle." I took one step before it spoke.

One Human and Five Sangra
But what do they seek?
The treasures of Nalrin
They wish to hold?

It seemed to wait for our response. But none of us knew what to say.

One Human and Five Sangra
But what do they seek?
The treasures of Nalrin
They wish to hold?

"We do not wish to hold the treasures of Nalrin." Lindy said. I just looked at her. How could she find her voice to talk? I felt like a blubbering idiot.

What do they wish to hold?

"We wish to proceed on down, to stop two who do. They wish to reach the Mirror of Remembrance, obtain the crystal and build the weapon of the Angels."

The Mirror others seek?
Much deeper it is.
To reach you must have wit, strength, and courage.

No sooner were the words out of its mouth before it stood and roared loudly. I clasped my hands over my ears. When the roaring stopped, we all looked at each other. None of us had moved so much as an inch. No one had drawn a syth, sword or whip.

"Man, that thing has a voice!" CJ said. I giggled. CJ could always break the tension somehow.

Courage you do have.
What about wit?
Answer these four and they shall pass,
To prove their strength,
they will, to reach the Mirror.
Think your answers carefully,
For if the answer is wrong,
Sunlight you may not see.

Immediately Lindy formally bowed in respect. In response, the creature sat back down and looked to study us.

One Human, Five Sangra
The answers you must decide.
First....
I give and I make things green...
I go away and make things brown...
If I push hard, I cause destruction....

If I lap I can be calm....
I can be found on land or in the air...
Yet you need me to survive.
What am I?

"Riddles? How cliché! But ok." CJ giggled. Owen gave him a look that clearly meant for him to leave his snarky comments back home.

"... give something to make it green, but when it doesn't get it, it turns brown." Clarice mumbled.

"It causes destruction, but can calm?" Owen said out loud confused.

"And found on land or air..." Jean said.

"But you need it to survive. What do you need to survive? Air, Water, Food ..." CJ said.

My mind was racing through it. It sounded familiar. I was sure I had heard this one before. Then it hit me. I turned to the creature, bowed respectfully, "Water. Water makes things green, without it, things die. Water surges cause destruction all the time in hurricanes. The sound of waves crashing can calm, and water is found on land and air. Then, of course, we need it to live."

That is true little Sangra.
Second....
I am an insect & the first half of my name reveals another insect. Some famous musicians in the human world had a name similar to mine. What am I?

"OH! I know that one. Dad used to tell it to me all the time." CJ shouted. Then he turned and bowed. "A Beetle. First half Bee, then to complete, you have Beetle. Well, and of course there was the British Invasion of The Beatles."

Again, true little human.
Third....
I can be large or I can be small.....
I can run, but I cannot walk...
I have a mouth but cannot speak....
I have a head, but never weep....
I have a bed...but cannot sleep,

I knew this one before he finished, I could see the others mulling it over when I turned and bowed again to the creature, who was surprised at my quick response. "A River."

True.

Now your last, answer correctly and

Thy shall pass, to prove your mental strength.

...

Pronounced as one letter, And written with three, Two letters there are, And only two in me. I'm double, I'm single, I'm black, blue, and gray, I'm read from both ends, And the same either way. What am I?

This one I was clueless. I looked at everyone else, and they just looked at me and CJ. We had the other answers, why not this one. "Sorry guys. I knew the others because I'd heard them before." I told them.

"Ok, so think it through. Sounds like one letter but spelled as three. you, are, aye ... two only in me? Double? Single? Black, blue, and gray?" Owen recited and thought out loud.

Then Clarice picked the rest up, "Red both ends..."

"No not red, Like the color, ... read like a book? And the same either way. The word is a palindrome?" Jean said.

"It's an eye!" Owen said. He turned to bow to the creature. "It's an eye sir."

That it is...

And you will need all of yours on the way down.

The creature moved to the side, and a door opened just behind where he was standing. As each of us passed, we bowed respectfully and proceeded through the door.

When the door closed behind us, lights flickered down the massive hall. It had to be 20 feet across, with bookshelves lining the walls all the way down. I really wanted to stop and look at what kind of books needed this kind of protection and secrecy, but we didn't have the time and continued on. Maybe I could be a Nalsar historian and able to look upon these treasures if I survived.

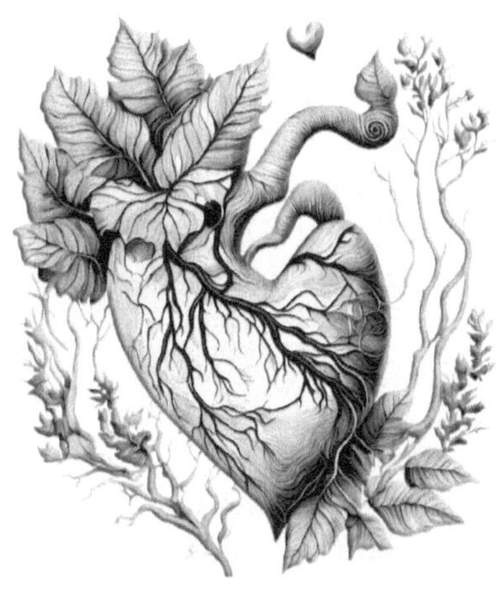

CHAPTER 37

AFTER ABOUT FOUR HOURS we still continued to make our way down. So far, the obstacles on our way were pretty easy. There was the invisible bridge, that I thought was right out of a movie, the potion that had to be crafted, just right, so that it would dissolve the wall, thank the Angels for Clarice on that one, among others. I don't know why, but I had this feeling we had to be to be getting close.

While walking down a hall with jars of "things", which made my stomach flip if I just glanced at them, I had to stop and lean up against the wall. I saw my parents in Noctulanar Castle. My mother reaching for a book off a pedestal that looked like an old tree, with finger like branches that held the book in place. The book looked brand new. It was made of black leather, and it had a symbol on it made up of vines in a Celtic type pattern, in deep blood red that was etched on the leather. When my mother opened the book, the pages were made out of a paper that didn't look like anything I had ever seen. I had the very real sense that

251

the paper was screaming in pain. The writing on the pages in a language that used symbols and a flowing swirling text that I didn't recognize.

When the vision shimmered, we were back in the circular room with my vision locked onto CJ sprawled on that Angel's be damned table. I hated this. I once again watched CJ on that table, at the brink of death. Here, in the real world, his arms were tight around me. I clinched his sleeve tight in my fingers until the knife swung down.

I blinked at CJ and held him tight. He murmured in my ear how much he loved me, that everything was going to be okay, and I was safe. Generic words of comfort regardless of whatever I saw.

When I was able to calm down, I described the book I had seen, then asked, "Lindy does it ring a bell to you?"

"Maybe." Her head was crooked at a strange angle like an owl studying something I said. "I just ..."

"What did you see that upset you though?" Owen asked.

I just looked at CJ for a moment before saying slowly, "Nothing, let's keep going. We have to be getting close." I didn't let go of CJ's hand as we strode down the hall.

We turned the corner and walked through a doorway to a room the size of a football field. In the center, mist... just mist. It filled the entire room, and we couldn't see any farther than maybe 15 feet in front of us. There was a rolling metal sound behind us and when I turned, I saw a metal rolling door slam shut, blocking our way out. I sighed.

"We can't progress if we don't go through it." I said stepping forward, but I hadn't taken more than 10 or 15 steps into the fog, when I saw myself at work all those years ago.

No.

Please.

Please don't make me relive this.

I continued to pick up the phone in slow motion as my heart dropped and I felt the tears already falling from my eyes and down my cheeks.

"Ms. Megan Keller?" The officer said.

"This is her." I said half listening.

"This is Officer Thom Melati. I just spoke to your parents," he said gravely, "They asked me to call you about your brother Matthew Keller?"

"He's dead." I said barely above a whisper. I vividly remembered my heart stopping at that point. The water bottle in my hand falling and splattering all over the floor as I stared off into space. The heavy feel of my tongue as I said, "Drunk driver."

"Excuse me ma'am?" Officer Melati said.

"Green Audi sedan. Personalized California plate read "ZOOMIE"." I said without thinking, barely above a whisper. I had watched it all play out again while on the phone with him. I knew that the woman who hit him had bright red-dyed hair, up in a bun. I also knew that she had mascara running down her face like she had been crying for hours before the wreck. I wasn't supposed to know any of those details.

"Ma'am. Can you please come down to the station? We would like to talk to you."

"I'll be down in a few minutes." I said just putting my phone down. After a few moments, I watched myself send a text to Amber, one of my best friends, who picked me up and drove me down to the morgue. I had cried the entire time in the car.

"They said they couldn't identify the body." Officer Melati said when I asked my why parents couldn't be the ones to come down to handle this.

"Take your time Ms. Keller." Officer Melati said when we walked into the room that smelled too much like some high-grade antiseptic.

When I looked down at Matt, a painful knot sat in my throat. He laid there, ear missing, nose bent to the side, cuts all over his body and his wrists had clearly both been broken in the crash. His broad chest was slightly caved in where someone had been doing CPR to see if they could revive him. I looked back down his broken body and my eyes stopped at his leg. Was his leg even attached, or had they placed it back up his pants to give him a semblance of looking normal?

"It's Matt." I croaked around the lump in my throat.

I was gently led into another room.

The scene stopped and faded away when another figure took a couple of steps forward.

"Megra." The figure said, calling me the pet name I hadn't heard in years. I froze.

He was dead.

I had identified the body. I saw the leg, connected, but not connected.

I just kept looking at him. How could he be standing there? Just as I remembered him before the crash. I shook my head, tears flinging from my face. It couldn't be.

"Megra." Matt said reaching for me and smiling brightly. I instantly stepped back.

"Is that really you?" I said.

"In a matter of speaking." He smiled brighter, spread his arms out wide, and said, "In all my glory."

"Matt your dead, you can't be here." I was shaking my head back and forth, and I felt wetness run down my cheeks.

This can't be real. This isn't real.

This. Isn't. Real.

"Yes, I am dead." He lowered his arms, but then looked at me with sad eyes. "You know it wasn't your fault."

"My visions.... You knew they were real; you knew...." I cried."Yes. I was just hoping for once you'd be wrong. Why couldn't you just have been wrong about this one?" He said with a giggle, and then seriously he added, "Let's sit down and talk."

I took two hesitant steps deeper into the fog, not daring to take my eyes off Matt. There wasn't a scratch on him. His body was ... whole.

"Megan. Seriously. I'm not going to hurt you. Please sit down. Let's talk." He said softly.

I sat down on a bench that reminded me of the ones we used to sit on out by the beach to watch the waves crash. Matt on the other hand walked to stand before me, crouched down and put his hands on my knees. I could see them there but couldn't feel them.

"My death was not your fault." He said. I felt my heart try to shut out his words, but he said them again, more forcefully. "My death was not your fault."

"How are you here?" I asked him, reaching to put my hand on his, but I stopped before touching him and pulled my hand back.

"I... I don't know..." He said hesitantly. "One second, I was there. Then I was here."

"I miss you." I said.

"I know. How is Melissa? Does she know how much I truly love her?" He asked quietly.

"Of course, she knows that you love her. How could she not!! You little brat!" I said just like nothing had changed. I sighed though because of course, everything had changed. "She moved back to Andorra to help out her parents with the resort. Last I talked to her, she was still struggling, but was working through it."

I stopped then asked, "You said you were there, now you are here. What is there?"

He opened his mouth, but then stopped. "I can't explain it to you. I don't have the words to."

We sat there in silence for a bit before I sighed. "Mom and Dad..."

"Yeah, I know" He interrupted. "I was filled in once I got here. Suddenly I knew why I needed to be here."

"I'm sorry. This is all my fault." I said.

He grabbed my hands and they felt so warm, so, normal. "Megra! It's not your fault. None of this is. And I know you question your visions, you always have. Your visions are a gift and a curse."

"What if Dad is right though? What if because I see these things, they come true. That means I'm responsible for you dying." I croaked past the lump in my throat.

"You know that isn't true." He said scoffing.

I looked at him evenly.

"Hum." He pondered. "Well, apparently not. That's why I'm here."

He stood and turned away from me for a minute, then walked over and put his hands on my shoulders. I could feel the warmth of his love, but I couldn't feel him. Matt looked me straight in the eye. He must have found what he was looking for.

"Megra, you have to accept the fact that you are not responsible for what happens in your visions. They are what they are. No, you won't be able to change them. Good or Bad. They will all happen. You have a wonderful gift, and you are using it for all the right reasons. Trust it. Trust in them." Matt said jerking his head toward the exit of the fog.

He pulled me up and embraced me in a huge hug. It was just like the way it used to be when we were kids. He squeezed me tighter and I could feel his arms around me. I held him tighter, and I felt something that was splintered inside me be pressed back together.

"Trust. Trust in that family, Megs." He whispered.

"but ..." I said letting tears I didn't know I was holding back slide down my face.

"No buts. Trust them. Trust CJ. He will help you through this. Hell, he will be the best part of this. CJ is your beacon. Follow it. It will save you."

He just held me for a long time. When he pulled back, that part of me, that part that had blamed myself for Matt's death, had been fused together with love and forgiveness. Forgiveness in myself.

"Thank you, Matt. You're the best brother anyone could ask for."

"I know." He said owning it. "OH, and tell CJ that if he hurts my sister, I'll haunt him till the day he dies, and even then, I'll find a way to torture him." Same ol' Matt. I started to laugh.

"I love you Zombie Bait." I said.

He let out a huge laugh and said, "Love ya too sis. Now get a move on. You may have to wait for the others. Give them time. One will take a while. She has a lot she has to work through before emerging." And then he disappeared.

As I walked out of the fog, I saw the next door and sighed. I turned to look for the others but only saw the fog. What was the deal with the fog anyways? Why hadn't I seen or heard the others?

"CEEJ!?" I yelled out.

"Owen? ... Jean? ... Lindy? ... Clarice? Where are you?" Then I saw movement on the left side. It was CJ. I ran to him and bounced in his arms.

"OH, BY THE ANGELS! Megs!" He looked at me and checked me over to make sure I was ok. "Are you ok? You hurt? What happened to you?"

"Yea I'm fine. What about you? What did you see in there?" I said pressing a quick kiss to his cheek.

"You... you ... you told me that you never wanted to see or hear from me again... that you never loved me, and that ... well... for a time in there... I thought I'd lost you." CJ forced out.

I looked at him plainly, "Cory James. You know better than that!" and just to prove my point I swung my arms around his neck and kissed him. He picked me up and kissed me back, hard deep, and full of a need that we couldn't give each other right now.

"I know you do babe. That's how I was able to walk out of there. The first time, I just looked at you and told you, you were full of shit. I know how much you love me. That I know it like I know my heart beats every second. I just had to keep explaining that to whatever that was in there."

Just then Lindy came out, her face wet and her hair was sticking to it, but when she looked up at us, and as CJ put me back down, she smiled. Then she walked over and gave us both huge hugs. There was a new vibrancy in her step and her eyes seemed to light up that much more.

After a few minutes, Owen came out his syth's in hand dripping with blood that slowly vanished. We asked if he was ok, and he just nodded and went to sit down against the wall. He looked shaken up, but he was here.

I sat there thinking of what Matt had said to me. I did feel a little stronger and lighter inside. Is that what this fog did? Make us address our greatest guilt. Our largest fear? I sat there mulling it all over when something else Matt said made me laugh.

I whispered so only CJ could hear me. "CJ honey, I have a message from Matt for you."

He raised his eyebrows. "From Matt?"

"Yup. That's who I had to face in there." I said gesturing to the fog. "He told me to tell you, and I quote, *He hurts my sister, I'll haunt him till the day he dies, and even then, I'll find a way to torture him.*" I tried to use my best Matt voice, but it just came out corny.

I looked at CJ and he was trying hard not to bust up laughing. I smiled and we both erupted in laughter. Lindy and Owen looked at us like were crazy, but then I caught Jean walking out of the fog, and we jumped up.

She walked out, screaming "Mickel!" as she stumbled and held her stomach. Owen rushed to her and made sure she was okay. I hadn't even seen or heard him move. She was white as a ghost, and it took her a few minutes before she was able to pull herself back together.

"Where is Clarice?" Jean asked when she and Owen got back to where we were.

"She hasn't come out yet." I said quietly.

"Clarice!!!" Lindy yelled but there was no response.

We waited and waited for Clarice. Lindy and I kept yelling for her occasionally, but there was never a response, except for Jean who just told me that while in the fog we couldn't hear anyone. She explained that after I had disappeared inside the fog, they called for me before following me in. I couldn't bring myself to tell them that I had spoken to Matt while in there.

After about an hour, Clarice came crawling out. Lindy rushed to her. "Clarice, open your eyes, it's ok, it's over. Look at me. You beat it."

"No. It's not something that can be beaten. I have to accept it. Someday, I will just have to accept it. I won't have the choice." She whispered shaking her head back and forth. We just looked at each other, none of us knowing what she was talking about.

"Open your eyes, Clarice." Lindy put her hands on either side of her face, trying to get her to focus. "Focus and open your eyes. Center yourself." After continual coaching from Lindy, finally Clarice was able to open her eyes, but it took a while.

"Let her rest." CJ said.

"How long was I in there?" she asked panting.

"Don't know sweetie. At least an hour longer than the rest of us. We were starting to get worried you weren't coming out." Jean told her.

"Didn't feel that long. Felt like only about 20 minutes." She said.

The last thing I wanted to do was sit around and wait any longer, but I knew she needed to rest. Her mind had been torturing her for a while, and she needed to re-align herself with whatever it was that she faced in there.

I sat down and played with the electricity in my cocoon watching CJ pace. I stretched and twisted that power letting it slowly thread out of its cocoon and fill my body. I worked on keeping it centered and prepared for the fight I knew to be on the other side of that door.

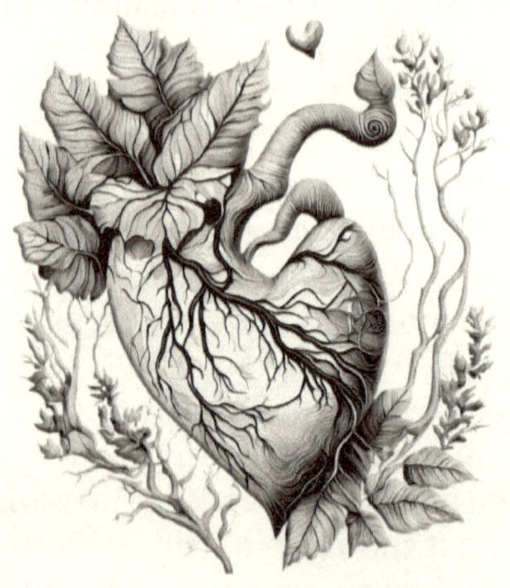

CHAPTER 38

CLARICE OPENED THE DOOR, and even though I knew it was *the* room, my heart, along with any confidence, sank. Knowing and *knowing;* are two different things. I clinched CJ's hand as we continued into the room.

The second all of us had crossed the threshold, the creature I had seen so many times in my visions sprang in front of us. The shoulders on this thing were at least 15 feet high. Its head was one of a bobcat, the body of a cheetah, claws like a raptor, and its coat was a deep red. Blood red. I groaned at the irony of it.

It didn't attack, just stood there, daring us to pass.

"What is it?" I whispered. CJ stepped in front of me and pulled me behind him.

"It's an Asmita Gonda." Owen whispered back.

"But aren't they usually brown or tan ... and docile?" Jean asked looking at the beast. No one but CJ had moved an inch since it stood in front of us.

"The tan and brown are, yes. The red ones, well let's just say they are the most vicious kitty cat you will ever meet. It had been rumored that red ones had been killed when born." Owen explained.

"Obviously, not." Clarice said pulling her whips out and placing them at her side. The Asmita Gonda noticed right away and let out a deep growl I felt deep in my chest. Before the growling had stopped, two more came to stand just behind it.

Clarice cracked her whips, hoping to scare them off, but all it did was anger them. They pounced.

I threw up a wall to protect us, but when they lunged, we all scattered. CJ had ahold of my hand so he came with me, but Clarice and Lindy went off in the other direction, with two Asmita Gonda right behind them. Owen and Jean somehow ran between the legs of one of them and ran toward the center of the room.

CJ and I ran through rows and rows of bookcases. I heard Clarice's whips cracking and the sounds of battle from everyone else but couldn't find them. Being separated was NOT a good thing.

As we ran through the stacks, I saw a glimpse of my parents and I felt panic rise in my chest. CJ screeched to a halt before me and before he could look down the row, I turned him toward me.

"CJ, this is the room." He looked at me like I had rocks for brains.

"What do you mean the room? What room?" He said panting.

"This is the room that we, I ..." I couldn't say the words. I saw the realization of what I was trying to say cross his face though.

"Oh." I just nodded my head. He reached down, kissed me hard, and held me tight. "Just remember I love you and nothing will change that. If we can't have this life together..."

"STOP! DON'T EVEN TALK LIKE THAT." I hissed at him, not daring to scream it for fear of my parents finding us.

"No. I have to say this. I ... I will find you in the next life and we will have our lives together." Before I could say anything else, he kissed me again. I melted to his touch, and vowed to myself once again, I would have my happiness with him. My parents would fail, I would save him, and life would be wonderful DAMN IT! But our moment was cut short when I heard a short curt giggle. I slowly turned to face her.

"Mother." I said with more bravado than I was feeling. I felt the jump and crackle of the electricity at my fingertips. I didn't even try to coil it back in.

"Megan. CJ." She said. "So nice to see you two again."

I passed all the protection I could to CJ and silently told him to stay close. No matter what she threw at me, I was going to keep him safe. I felt him slowly slip one of the syths from their sheath at the small of my back.

I took a deep breath to center myself and I could see Lindy and Clarice's embers burning brightly. Clarice was limping a little bit, but I could see her put an end to the Asmita Gonda she was fighting. Lindy was still working on hers and I flinched when I saw the tail swing around toward her. I felt out for Owen and Jean, but Jean was lying on the ground, not moving in the middle of the room. Owen was fully engaged with my father.

As I looked closer at my father's ember, it was darker than my family's, but it was still much brighter than my mother's. I turned all my attention to my mother and studied her ember more closely. It didn't act as any of the other embers I had seen before. Even darker than what I remember seeing when we were in the meadow in the Manusia. The center was a lot like my father's, but it pulsed erratically. Her eyes were that deep fire red, that flashed in my visions.

Symatha turned her head sideways, a predator assessing its prey, gave me an evil smile as pain twisted through my stomach and pressure built upon my chest. I looked down and saw nothing.

I threw a wall up close to my body, just to get the pain to stop, and then threw it back to her. When the wall hit her, she stumbled and then she …

"Did you just growl at me?" I said puzzled. Her ember pulsed as she bared her teeth at me and lunged. When our syths met, I felt the reverberation all the way down my arm. I pushed some of my power down my syth and I smelled burning flesh. Her hands were smoldering, but she just looked at me.

She threw a punch with her other hand connecting with my wrist that made me relent. She came at me again and again. I did everything I could to keep CJ from being hit, but occasionally I would hear him hiss through is teeth.

CJ grabbed my arm and pulled me back a few steps just as Symatha's arm swung directly for my neck. I threw up a wall and engaged her again. I saw the knife he had taken from the small of my back in CJ's hand behind me and his eyes flickered to something just above my mother's head. I wasn't sure exactly what he was trying to tell me, but I focused on keeping Symatha's attention solely on me. A split second later the syth flew from his hand and cut the rope holding the tapestry above her head, which landed perfectly over her.

I looked at him. Then at the tapestry. Then at him again.

I wondered when CJ had learned to throw a knife like that. That wasn't an easy shot. The syth would have had to hit at just the right angle.

The tapestry started to smoke, then burst into flames. Symatha stood up, sighed loudly, and dusted the ashes off her arms and legs. She looked up at us, amusement in her eyes. "Well, it seems Megan isn't the only one who has been training."

"No. Just a lucky shot." CJ said.

She growled again at us and lunged. I ducked but CJ grabbed her wrist. In a move that looked like he had been training in hand–to–hand combat for years, twisted her away from us.

I looked at CJ in astonishment. "Ceej. How did you...?"

He looked at his hands. "I..."

The next thing I knew Symatha grabbed my arm and it felt as if she had gripped my head in a vice. I couldn't help but press my free hand to my eyes. When the pressure released and I was able to open my eyes, it was just like in my visions. My mother had a tight grip on my arms, and no matter how hard I tried to get out, I couldn't.

She had been toying with us. Delaying things.

CJ had disappeared. *Please tell me he ran. Please tell me he ran.*

I frantically searched for Owen and saw him standing straight as a board as if he were bound in a straitjacket against a pole, but his focus was on Jean.

Where are Lindy and Clarice?

A row of bookshelves came crashing down, and Lindy was still fighting the Asmita Gonda. She jumped onto its back, and when she used one of Clarice's short swords to decapitate it, its head rolled onto the floor. As the body collapsed to the ground, she focused her attention on my father and her hands flew up like she had claws.

"Don't do this Ansel." Lindy said through her teeth.

He laughed mockingly. "Are you so sure you'll be able to stop me this time." He tusked as I saw hatred flare in her eyes.

I've never seen that from her before.

"I survived the Mirror. Now for the Angel of Love, I need my daughter's heart." He turned to face me and with a voice, I would have never expected to hear from my father, he spat the words, "Apparently your mother and I were not the only ones keeping secrets all these years. Were we Megan? "

"I don't know what you're talking about." I said struggling to move out of my mother's grasp.

He wiggled his fingers and CJ flung into my view about 4 feet off the ground, a black rope circled his body binding his arms to his sides, and then he was flung through the air to my father's side. "CJ owns your heart and now you will pay for Matt's death."

"I will pay for Matt's death? Matt was killed in a car crash, you idiot! How could that possibly be MY fault!? I was at work when it happened."

"But when you see it, it will happen my child." He said anger flashing in his face.

"BULLSHIT!" I screamed back to him.

He shrugged. "You will see. Your visions have the power to shape the future. I'm sure you've even seen this." He gestured the area around me and then looked me straight in the eye and said, "Now, I'm taking CJ with me."

I didn't see where she came from, but Clarice flew through the air and slashed him across the back with her whips. She was still in the air when my mother knocked her back against the wall where she slid down into a heap on the floor.

There was just enough of a break in everyone's concentration that I was able to free myself and CJ. We ran for the stacks. I heard Lindy fighting them both, but I would have to come back for everyone else, I had to get CJ safe.

What I didn't expect was to round the corner and run into Symatha. She tusked and used her power to throw CJ back into the center of the room, back into my father's grasp.

I was so focused on CJ that I didn't see my mother vanish.

I centered myself and threw all the power I could summon at Ansel. Symatha flashed in front of him, and all my power just dissipated to dust. With a simple flick of her wrist, Symatha lifted me from the ground, where black mist ropes bound mid-air.

I pulled thread upon thread of that electrical current from my cocoon and tried to find the right angle to throw it at Ansel, but no matter what CJ was always in the path or could be in a split second.

A light whisper in my ear, "Let him go, Megan. I promise your father will not hurt him! I will see to it." Her voice was mocking. I struggled against whatever it was that had ahold of me. I thought through every incantation I could think of to get free, nothing seemed to work. I could feel my power stirring, and I tried to push against the ropes. I threw whatever electricity and power I had into those ropes, but it just sizzled out.

Symatha reappeared a few feet in front of me and slowly sauntered toward me. Her face was twisted in a venomous smile. "Oh Megan, I didn't realize you were such a fighter. You were so passive as a child."

"There's a lot you don't know about me." I said growling the words. Just as she took a step closer. I kicked hard and my foot landed square on her jaw. Blood splattered everywhere and she screamed in pain.

"You want to kill him you evil bitch! You lay a finger on him, and I will hunt you down and kill you." I screamed.

"Ohh, Megan. You're so vindictive." She said with twisted pleasure in her voice.

"Vindictive. That's funny coming from you." I said through my teeth. "I promise you. If you hurt CJ, I will kill you."

"Kill him? No. We just need your heart. We don't have to kill him to get that. We could keep him alive if we were so inclined. Maybe we will, just so you will have to live with knowing you left him as a vegetable for the rest of his life." She spat as she wiped the blood from her lip and jaw. "Come on Ansel. Let's get going. I am tired of these games. Time is running short."

CJ was struggling to get away, but our eyes locked just as blue smoke engulfed him. I was instantly freed from the invisible restraints and dropped to the floor.

I ran straight for where they had been standing.

"No. No. No. No. No." I said over and over no louder than a whisper.

I saw flashes of white, red, blue, purple, and orange. They flashed before my eyes as everything inside of me shattered. I tasted metal in my mouth and the smell of dust and burnt plastic filled my nose. I couldn't see anything, but those flashing colors.

I faintly heard people screaming at me, screaming my name, but it was as if there were cotton in my ears and I was underwater.

CJ.

He was gone.

Lindy rushed to me and put her hands on my shoulders. She shook me but I didn't respond. I knelt there, still staring at the spot where he was, flashes of color still dancing in front of my eyes.

"Megan. Megan. Say something." Lindy said, but her voice as if it was behind a thick layer of plexiglass.

CJ was gone.

I hadn't been able to stop it. I thought I could have prevented this one.

Lindy put my face in her hands and started slapping my cheeks. "Megan. Please say something."

"CJ is gone." I whispered, looking at her but a little bit through her. "I wasn't able to stop it." My voice hitched when I heard Owen scream for Jean. Owen had rushed over to her and started chanting, but nothing was happening.

I forced myself to look at her ember and it was steady. She would be ok.

"Megan, are you ok?" Lindy asked. I nodded my head. She knew I wasn't, but that wasn't really what she was asking. "CJ is still alive. We will get him back."

Lindy kept repeating it until I was able to breathe normally again.

"We good?" She said when my eyes met hers.

I just nodded my head and she got up and went to Clarice.

I concentrated on Clarice's ember, and it was flickering in and out. I shook my head trying to temporarily push my personal panic attack aside to help Lindy with Clarice.

"Owen, Jean will be fine, her ember hasn't flickered at all. It's strong. Just give her time. She will come back." He nodded and I turned back to Lindy. "I need your help with Clarice."

I walked over and took Lindy's hand and placed my other hand over the Sa Ra. "Lindy put your hand on Clarice." We started chanting. I really had to concentrate on not letting my mind wander to CJ.

All I wanted to think about was if CJ was ok, if I would ever see him again... Of course, I'd be able to see him again. My visions came true right? That meant that I would see him in Noctulanar. I shook my head. Clarice. FOCUS ON CLARICE.

Through the gaps of space and time;
We ask the Angel of Healing to bind...
Through the gaps of space and time;
We ask the Angel of Healing to bind...
Please Angel, I can't lose her too ...
Through the gaps of space and time;

We ask the Angel of Healing to bind...

Clarice thrashed at whatever the Sa Ra was doing to heal her, but after a few more moments, Clarice's ember started to stabilize.

I got up and separated myself from them and sat back against the wall. I looked at my family. They were battered and bleeding, but they would be okay. They would be okay.

They would be okay.

CJ.

CJ was gone.

He was in the hands of my parents who were going to... going to...

My parents were going to take my heart and ... and ...

My power jumped to my skin making it sizzle in my ears. I started hyperventilating again and as flashes of light started to dance in front of me again, I put my head in my hands and started to cry.

CHAPTER 39

I WOKE UP THE next morning or maybe it was later that night? I shook my head, looked for a clock, but when I didn't see one, flopped back on the bed.

After it was clear I wasn't going back to sleep, I sat up and looked around the room. It was so quiet. Not a sound except for the blankets moving around me. I vaguely remember arriving in the residence where I had stripped out of what was left of my clothes and just let them lay where they fell. They were ruined. The shirt was just strips of fabric and even my bra strap was sliced through. Hell, even my underwear was a lost cause. I didn't recall how or when any of that had occurred, I had just stripped it all and climbed into bed.

All the strips of fabric were still in a trail from the door and my syths, belt, and one of my short swords laid on the floor. I just stared at them. Where was the other sword? Owen would surely yell at me for not properly putting them up last night.

I sighed. I'd have to ask the guard, who I'm sure was stationed just outside, to have fresh clothes brought to me.

My eyes burned and I wrapped the blanket tighter around me, and just sat there for a long while. I didn't look at anything in particular. I just saw Ansel and Symatha take CJ away in that blue smoke. That damn misty, dusty, ocean blue smoke. How dare it be the color of the ocean I loved so much.

ANGELS. CJ, please hold on. I felt drained. My power danced around my chest and rested at my fingers; a small glow encircled them. Nothing special. No strings of electricity, just a small faint glow. I had hardly used any of my power in that fight. When I threw that batch at the ropes holding me, I hadn't thrown everything at it because I knew that if I could get loose, I was going to need it to fight Ansel and Symatha.

"Hold on CJ. Just hold on." I tried to push to him. I couldn't feel his ember. I couldn't feel anyone's ember outside my room. Julian must have a guard stationed outside my room, but I couldn't feel him out there.

Slowly, I slid from the bed and walked through the living room to the door. As I went to turn the handle, I saw my hand. It was cut up and as I looked up my arm, bruises were forming on my arms.

I furrowed my brows. Bruises. I don't get bruises. Not with the...

My hand flew to the base of my neck and found nothing. Nada.

No. No. No.

I ran back to the bedroom and threw off the blanket to the bed, frantically searching.

No. No. No.

No. No. No.

I can't have lost it last night. If they got the Sa Ra, then CJ was ... I couldn't let myself think that way. I had to find it. Panic flooded me. What little power I had, zinged across my skin and zapped everything I touched.

I tore apart the bed and found it sitting just next to the pillow CJ would have used last night. The flood of relief in me was enough to let tears slide down my face. The chain had broken and the medallion sat there taunting me. I wanted to take the pillow and tear it apart with my bare hands.

I stopped. Took a deep breath and grabbed the medallion. I unthreaded one of my laces from my boot, threaded it through the loop of the Sa Ra, and tied it around my neck. It hung a little lower now, which was probably a good thing. This was at least easier to hide under my clothes.

I felt for the cocoon of my power to start coiling it back in, but found the spot where it once was, empty. In answer, my power jumped up and down my back as if it were laughing.

Laughing at me that it had escaped. I groaned.

I flopped myself down on the floor and started to recreate the cocoon.

Breathe in.

Breathe Out.

Cocoon and coil.

Breathe in.

Breathe Out.

Cocoon and coil.

Breathe in.

Breathe Out.

Cocoon and coil.

It took longer than I anticipated, but it was going to be a long day, and I needed to make sure I don't lose it. Having all of it out of its cocoon was not going to help me keep my head cool. It was only going to charge my emotions.

When I finally gained my composure again, I wrapped the sheet from the bed around me, went to the door, and opened it. Sure enough, there was a guard standing duty. He jumped imperceptibly. I tried not to smile at the redness that rose to his cheeks as he saw me wrapped up in nothing but the bedsheet, which at that very moment slipped lower across my chest.

"Can you have some fresh clothes sent in for me?"

"They are already on their way Ms. Megan." He said with a small nod and pointedly not looking anywhere south of my eyes.

I thanked him, closed the door, and headed for the bathroom. When I stepped into the shower, I turned the heat up as hot as I could stand it. I ran my hands over my face and pulled them away staring at them. They were shaking. I tried to pull myself together, but just slid down to the floor and cried again.

When I felt like I could control my emotions, even just the littlest bit, I started scrubbing the dirt, grime, and blood from my body. Under my nails were black and even though I had had my boots on, my feet weren't much better. How did I get so dirty? This couldn't be just from the fight. At least I had the luxury of being able to wash it off. Who knew when my next shower was going to be?

Once I had scrubbed every inch of my body and was as clean as I was going to get, I reached for the towel and realized just how big the bathroom was. It was the size of my bedroom back in the Manusia and the whole thing was done in white marble. Pure, nearly flawless white marble. The sink even seemed to float above the counter with the water flowing straight out of the wall with just a small faucet to guide the water into the sink. And the towels... oh the towels were so soft, I just wanted to curl up in them.

As I stepped back into the main room, I noticed someone had come in and picked up the shredded remains of my clothes, and started the fire. I sighed. I really had liked that shirt. It had been a Christmas present from Annie, CJ's mom, last year.

My syths, short sword, and the Calling Stone were neatly lined up on the freshly made bed and when I checked the closet, there were fresh sets of clothes and new clean boots on the floor. Even the sheaths for my weapons were hanging on a hanger next to the clean set of clothes.

How long had I been in the shower?

Shrugging it off, I got dressed and steered my thoughts to strategy. CJ was my number one priority, but we need to keep my parents from getting the rest of what they need.

Beauty, they have the flower, however, it is going to start wilting soon.

Love. I winced.

Remembrance, well, that's a lost cause.

Healing, I have the Sa Ra, so they will need me eventually, but having CJ ensures I'll go to them.

Finally, Death. The Book.

There are a bazillion books in any given universe. Hell, just in what we've seen in the Nalrin Library Archives, there had to be millions of books just there. How are we going to be able to find out WHICH book we need? I headed to the door to go and talk to Lindy, but when I opened it a Council runner was standing with her hand poised to knock. Once she recovered from the shock of me almost running straight into her, she bowed in respect.

"Ms. Megan, the Council wishes to see you. The rest of your family awaits your arrival." She said quietly.

"Ok. Ummm... how do I get there from here?" I stammered.

"I can show you, Ms. Megan. Follow me." She said.

I grabbed the jacket hanging on the back of the door, slid my syths on at my thighs, and followed her. The guard raised an eyebrow and acted as though he was going to say something but decided to keep his mouth shut.

She led me down three levels, and through the main courtyard. The reflecting pools, which were even more spectacular at night captured my attention and I stopped to listen to the sound of the water which released some of the tension from my shoulders. The Council runner was kind enough to just let me take it in and wait patiently. I knew I was only putting off the inevitable and continued to the council chamber.

As we walked down the halls, I heard the murmurings of what we had endured. The rest of my family must have already told the council everything that had happened down in the library. Word spread quickly it seems. When we passed one particular couple talking, I slowed my step to listen more carefully.

It seemed the Council had either started to head to their own designated territory or were in their private residences.

That was fine with me. The last thing I wanted to do was show my defeat in front of the Nalrin council, let alone the

ENTIRE NALSAR COUNCIL. Bottom line... that's what I've done. I knew it. I've let everyone down by not stopping them ... once again.

When the runner and I arrived, I was led inside. The silence was deafening.

I could hear every step my boot made as it connected with the floor.

Clomp.

Clomp.

Clomp.

There were only a handful of people in the chamber now. I tried to keep my head high and looked at Julian who had a small smile on his face. The last time we were in this room before the Council we had agreed to not discuss our trip into the archives, what we had seen, and anything we had done. Which seemed a bit ridiculous when everyone was already gossiping in the hallways.

A dignitary behind and to the right of Julian started to remind us of our vow of silence on what we had seen when I huffed, rolled my eyes dramatically, and crossed my arms in defiance.

"We all but signed away our firstborn with Penny before we headed down there. We know we can't talk about it, but it isn't us you need to worry about. Your hallways are buzzing with gossip." From the corner of my eyes, I saw Lindy's jaw drop in surprise at my attitude.

A man who was on the far right stood up and yelled "Yes Ms. Megan, you had. However, considering the slaughter your family caused on a batch of Asmita Gonda, which we won't be able to be repaired for some time now --"

"They would have killed us. Then we wouldn't have even been able to attempt to stop Ansel and Symatha." Jean interrupted him.

"Which you failed at, along with losing one of your own it seems." He spat. And now he had just totally crossed the line with me.

"Listen here you LIMP-DICKED prick!" Owen tried to stop me by whispering something about remember who I'm talking to. "AND NO, I DON'T CARE WHO IN THE FUCK YOU ARE. You are talking about my heart they have just taken. You know the story of the Five Angels. You know that they need my heart for this. IF you think for one DAMN FUCKING minute that I'm going to let that happen you can think again!"

"You have already failed, what twice now?" I flinched, which he took delight in. "What makes you so confident that you will succeed at all?"

What he said was true. I couldn't deny that, and I didn't really have anything to say. I remembered back to one vision I had had. I hadn't told anyone about it. I didn't want to put false hope into their minds. However, standing there looking at the prick who was more worried about his precious creatures instead of Nalrin, I straightened before saying, "CJ and I will be married. Julian will preside over it."

Lindy, Owen, and Clarice's head swung around to stare at me. The Council just stared at me, but that didn't stop him.

"Girls fool wish. Your love is blinding your reason." He said with a scoff.

"No, she has had a vision of it." Jean said as she took my hand. I hadn't told them, but she backed me up anyway. Her confidence was reassuring. "She had also seen that they would take CJ and that yes indeed Ansel would walk away with the crystal."

"And you believe these foolish visions?" he said.

"Yes... every single one has come true." She said with a great amount of pride.

He was pissed now. "Then why did you come and tear up our library. Slaughter the Asmita Gonda, and create such havoc and destruction when you knew all of this would happen? Why not just stay away and save yourself the heartache of losing your "heart"?"

The gesturing of air quotes around *heart* did it.

"YOU SON OF A ..." I started to lunge toward him, but Jean had a firm grip on my arm while Owen had one hand over my mouth and one on my shoulder holding me back faster than I had seen him move even in a fight. It took everything I had not to lick his hand so he would let me go.

Lindy was the one they probably should have held back. "So, you expect us just to sit back and let them have it so easily? What if we can change what she sees? Do we believe in them? HELL YES! We wouldn't have gotten this far without them. Do we want to change some of it? Again, YES! But has she seen them create the weapon in full?"

Julian spoke faster than she could finish her thought. "Sit down Malikal." He didn't show that he was upset or frustrated. He just made the command and it happened.

Julian turned to us. "So, Ms. Megan, have you seen Ansel and Symatha complete the Five Angels destruction?"

I looked to Owen, and he slowly removed his hand from my lips. I almost licked them this time, just in a show of defiance, but didn't.

"No, Julian I have not." I said in a low voice. "but that doesn't mean they won't." I had to admit that even if it didn't help our cause.

"I understand that Ms. Megan, but I will take comfort in the fact that you haven't. Now I have a couple of personal questions to ask you."

"Excuse me?" I said shocked.

"Yes. Please meet me in my office in 20 minutes. I need to finish up with the council and I will meet you there."

"Yes, sir." I said hesitantly, bowed and we were escorted out.

Once the doors closed, I blew. "That FUCKING JACK ASS! Who in the hell does he think he is? Doesn't he think we have thought of all of that before? Does he really think we just wanted a joy ride down through the deepest depths of the library for FUN?!"

"Malikal is the animal caregiver of the Nalrin Library. There is a lot at stake down there, and we just killed 3 of his most precious beasts." Jean explained to me.

"But he ... UGGGG never mind. Doesn't matter." I was so emotionally charged, anyone who said a cross word to me was going to get both fists aimed at them. I turned to the guard who was standing outside of the Council Chamber, "So where is Julian's office? He asked me to meet him there."

He bowed.

"This way Ms. Megan." When we were out of earshot of anyone else, he whispered, "And for the record, I think what you are doing to save us is most noble."

"Well noble or not, doesn't mean we will live through it."

"Either way you will go down in Nalrin history."

I stopped dead in my tracks and turned to him. "I'm not looking for notoriety. What my parents are doing is wrong and someone has to stop them."

"Agreed Ms. Megan, but your family is the only one doing anything about it. In fact, I think they are happy that you are handling it so they don't have to appoint someone. The Council is too wrapped up in its own politics and want for power that no one else is willing to stand up and try."

"Well, that's not exclusive to just this dimension. Power and Politics corrupt. Once power is received, it isn't given away freely. Wars are fought all the time over who has the most power, or better religion. History is re-written for personal or political gain. Both fight for what they believe in or what they want to protect. My reasons for war against my parents are simple... survive. They broke the laws." I saw him start to say something but I continued on "Even if those laws are written by powerful and corrupt politicians, religious committees and council members. What they are doing is wrong. Period."

He nodded in agreement, and we walked the rest of the way in silence.

"Here we are, Ms. Megan. If I may ask a favor of you?" He asked when we arrived at the large double doors.

"If I can I will." I am not about to promise anything I can't deliver right now.

"I would appreciate it if you did not mention our discussion to anyone. Strictly speaking, runners and guards are not to talk to guests or dignitaries."

"Secret is safe with me." I smiled and returned his bow as he opened the door to Julian's office for me.

When the door closed, I paused. The office wasn't what I had assumed it would be. I had thought that it would have been opulent and decorated with the finest of furnishings. Instead, I found a simple wood desk that had the seal of Nalrin carved on the front of it and a couple of modest couches that looked quite comfortable.

I walked out to the balcony where there was a simple stone bench sitting on the patio with a few plants decorating the area across from the bench. I shook my head smiled and looked up to the sky.

The first moon seemed to be doubled the size of what I was used to back in the Manusia. I felt like I could reach out and touch it. The second was faded off in the background and I took a long deep breath, trying to will myself to try to relax.

Memories of CJ flooded my mind. The silly simple stuff. Memories of when he lived just a few blocks away and he would get up in the middle of the night to help settle me down after a vision, which there were many. All the times we were just sitting in the living room laughing, or when he helped me through my math test. Like when I missed the bus and he had to drive me home, only to royally piss off my dad, who happened to be home that day. Then there were all the times we would hang out with friends at Russo's or out at a club.

He was always there for the heavy stuff too. He never left my side after Matt died because he wanted to be there to "catch me when I fell." He wanted to make sure I was okay since I had to shoulder it all since Mom was trying to hold Dad together. Not to mention how he was there at my bedside the entire time after my parent's death in the Manusia. CJ has always been there for me. I can't think of one happy memory where he wasn't present.

Then there were the more recent things. Sure, the sex was great, but the look in his eyes when he kissed me or the most innocent of touches that just drove me crazy. That undeniable need in his eye. It's not something you fake. It made me realize just how much he was holding back in the Manusia. Most of all, he stayed. Just to be with me. Not to mention his total acceptance of all that has happened in the last few months. This is straight psychoville.

It is no wonder things moved so fast with us once we "officially" got together. Though I guess since neither of us has seriously dated anyone for years, it's almost as though we had been dating each other. We talked all the time on the phone, traveled to each other whenever we could, and when we were in the same city, we were always together. Joined at the hip as they say. Maybe we had been dating for years without even realizing it. I shook my head and smiled at all those memories.

"Beautiful isn't it." Julian said from just next to me making me jump.

"It is. The moons don't get this large in the Manusia. Nalrin is so amazing. I hope that CJ and I will be able to enjoy it someday." I wiped a tear from my cheek, not realizing I had even started to cry, and then realized my manners with Julian. I instantly stood and bowed.

"Please your family should not bow to me Megan, at least in private. I will allow it while in a public setting, because well, appearances do have to be maintained." He raised just one corner of his lip as he raised a hand to stop me, "Your family is doing so much to protect and save our world."

"But it is also my family that is seeking to destroy it." I said looking down at my hands.

"This is true." Julian said it so matter-of-a-fact. No judgement.

"So, it has to be us to stop them." I said looking at him with a questioning look in my eyes.

"Others would not be so brave." This time, there was a twinge of frustration in his voice.

"Well, maybe they should be."

"But you are one with special abilities to help you along Ms. Megan."

"I'm glad you believe in them because there are times I sure in the hell don't."

"I'm not the only one. Your family does as well."

I knew that, but I just looked up to the moon. "You said that you had some personal questions for me Julian?"

"I do... the first of which is how does your Maltal feel?"

"Fine. Why?"

"Owen had said that after your parents left the library, and you had helped Clarice, that you broke down." He paused, studying me a moment before continuing. "That your maltal glowed so brightly that it was almost blinding, waves of color pulsed from you, and ..."

"and what?"

"Megan. Why hasn't your family reported that you have electric power?" He said smoothly.

"Umm. Ahh. Why..." The look he gave me was answer enough. "How did you find out?"

"Owen let it slip that lightning erupted in the room, and there may be unexplained burn marks in that particular room." He said easily.

"I don't remember that." I said. That answered why my cocoon needed rebuilding this morning and why it was so drained.

"How do you keep it controlled?" He asked quietly. He wasn't judging me. He wasn't acting like it was something huge and special. Just a simple question.

"I figured out how to create a ... cocoon for it to sit in." I said looking down at my naval. "I coil it up in there and pull just the threads I need. I had to recreate it this morning."

"So, you don't feel weaker or drained?" he said tilting his head to the side.

"Of course. I just spent I don't know how many hours busting my ass and apparently erupted my power out. Then slept for only a couple of hours. A couple of hours of sleep is not going to wash that all away."

"Agreed." He smiled and giggled. "The next question I have is really personal, and if you don't wish to share it, I do understand."

"Okay." I said drawing out the word.

"What did you encounter in the fog?"

Well, that isn't what I expected him to ask. I looked up at the moon again, took a deep breath, and after a minute said, "Matt."

"Your brother?"

"We sat and talked and when he thought he had said what he needed to, I walked out. Why?" An over-simplification of what occurred, but I was still processing it all myself. I couldn't tell Julian that.

He paced across the balcony. "Interesting... very interesting."

"It's never good when someone says it like that Julian."

"The fog is supposed to make you face your greatest fear... or your biggest regret. And since Matt is your brother, I don't think that he would be your biggest fear... however, if he is your biggest regret?"

"My greatest fear or regret? I'm scared to death of failing and my parents destroying this place or losing CJ forever. There are so many things that I'm scared to death of, why did the fog choose Matt for me to face?"

"That's the interesting thing. The fog must have chosen Matt because you need to get past the guilt you carry in order to deal with what needs to be done. Do you blame yourself for his death?"

"Yes... no... I'm not sure anymore." I said with a sigh. "CJ told me that it was never my fault and just because I saw it happen so often in my visions, doesn't mean I'm responsible for it. Matt basically told me that he was just hoping that my visions were wrong for once, but that I didn't kill him. It wasn't my fault."

"That is true. You should not carry the weight of his death. That weight is to be carried by others. Not you." He said meekly.

"How do you know so much about the fog?" I asked after a moment.

"I placed it there of course!" He said with a giggle. "Now what is the next step in your journey?"

"That would be getting CJ back, finding the Book which I need to speak to Lindy about, and finding the circular room in Noctulanar Castle." I told him as we made our way back into the main room.

He froze mid-step. "How do you know of the circular room?"

"I saw it in a vision." I told him with question in my voice. "I saw CJ tied to a circular stone table with 12 pilla..."

"STOP. Don't tell me anymore." He said waiving the information off. "No one knows what that room looks like. I only know it exists and nothing more. Do not burden me with that information."

"Oh. okay." I said hesitating.

"No one should know what that room looks like. Even as council members, even though some of us know of its existence..." he trailed off lost in thought.

"Like Lindy...." I suggested.

"Like Lindy. She knows more than most of the current or past, council members." He sighed and then looked at me "Considering her past history with the council. She knows more than anyone on the subject on The Five Angels. I'm sure she has been of great value to you in all of this."

"She has, but she seems to think about things a lot before she answers." I said.

"There is a lot of information for her to sort through before she can answer one properly. She and Auturno were–"

"Auturno?"

He stopped and looked at me carefully. "Lindy's husband."

"And my father's brother."

"Yes." He nodded. "I wasn't sure how much you knew."

"She's told me a little, but I know there is still a lot that she hasn't." I said looking at a painting of a lake on his wall. Maybe in time. Maybe never, and right now, I was okay with that.

"Anyways, as I said Lindy and Auturno were incredibly gifted at translating those scripts and scrolls. When he died, it hurt us all. ... but Lindy saw Ansel kill him. That is a pain that I hope no one else ever has to endure."

We stood there staring out at the moon and over the reflecting pools for a long time. I looked over at Julian and he was deep in thought, I wondered what tortures he has had to endure in all of this.

The longer the silence hung in the air, the more I thought of CJ. Flashes of my previous vision of CJ bound to the center stone table in Noctulanar, the room, and then my mother taking the book off of that pedestal flew through my mind.

We need to find out more about that book. Where do we even start? Sighing at the realization I was going to have to spend more time in a library, but, "Julian, I know this is not usually permitted, but I require something from the Council." I said hesitantly.

"Whatever you need, Ms. Megan." Julian said, straightening.

"We are going to need access to those scrolls and scripts on The Five Angels." I said before I could chicken out.

"Now Megan."

"We need to figure out what Death needs. We know it's a book, but nothing else. We … I really need to be able to stop my parents. They are probably already heading to Noctulanar Castle, and I think they already know where it is. We need to be able to get to it first. I saw it in a vision, and it was leather-bound with some etching on it, and the inside was completely done on papyrus like paper."

I could see him thinking. Why was he taking so long to approve this? "This is a no-brainer. You know you need to let us in there. Stop being stubborn Julian... this --"

"I know what's at stake Megan. But to allow all of you in there to read what we protect most. It's ... It goes against everything the council has sought to protect."

I thought of that for a minute. Lindy and I need to get down there and find out where we need to go.

"Just Lindy and I then. The rest can stay up here and rest. I need to be down there because I've seen what we are looking for and if there are any drawings then I'll be able to identify it. Lindy needs to be there because she already knows what is down there. Please Julian." I was almost begging on my hands and knees.

"Wait here." No sooner were the words out of his mouth, he was gone. What was his problem? Why couldn't he just allow us to go. I even offered for it to be just me and Lindy... I don't get it.

I took another a deep breath to try and relax. I had to remember that I was talking and dealing with Julian, the HEAD of the Nalrin Council, and if I wanted something, it had to go through him. Best not to make him mad.

A few minutes later Julian returned with Penny, who looked totally exhausted. Did he get her out of bed? "You and Lindy may have access, but only you and Lindy. The others have to stay here. Penny will lead you down to those archives."

"Thank you, Julian." I said bowing to him.

"What did I say about bowing to me." He said raising his eyebrows.

"Sorry." I said with a smile. "So, when can we get in."

"First thing in the morning. You need some more sleep, and Lindy is already settled for bed. Meet Penny at nine in the morning at her office."

"Is nine okay with you Penny? We could meet you earlier." I asked her.

"No, nine is fine. I can go back to bed and get another few hours' sleep." She said not making eye contact with me.

"It's you I'm more worried about. You haven't gotten more than maybe 4 hours sleep." Julian said.

"I'll be fine." I tried to convince them. I wasn't fine. Every muscle in my body ached, and I wasn't sure how I was even standing. Even my power felt unstable. "But I agree Lindy should get some more sleep. I'll see you in the morning."

"Good night Julian. Ms. Megan." She said bowing as she left.

"She looks exhausted Julian." I said hesitantly.

"Penny was really worried about you guys down there. She didn't sleep till you all... well when you came back up."

I knew why he paused, and my stomach felt like a hollow endless pit because of it. I could feel the tears gather in my eyes, but I willed myself not to cry again.

"I'm not sure I trust Penny." I said quietly. "I think she delayed us in getting to my parents. When she closed the door before she left, she kind of gave us an evil smirk." Julian gave me a surprised look, but I continued, "I can't prove it. I know you need proof for an allegation like that, but I will be taking my weapons with me in the morning."

"I'll look into it." He said twisting one of the ends of his beard braids.

"Julian, is there someone who can take me back to my room?" Suddenly realizing I had no idea how to get back.

"ANGOLIS!" The door opened and a woman who looked to be about 35, but I was sure had to be older, opened the door. "Can you please take Ms. Megan back to her room?"

"Of course." The guard said.

I couldn't help but think about if CJ and I stayed here. Would the age, looks, and longevity of this world affect us too. Hell, even though I knew Julian was well over 200 years old, he didn't look much over 50. People back in the Manusia would kill for that kind of "fountain of youth".

First CJ and I have to get through all of this. How will I look in 50 years? Would I age slowly as CJ continued to age? Not high on the priority list of thoughts right now Megan.

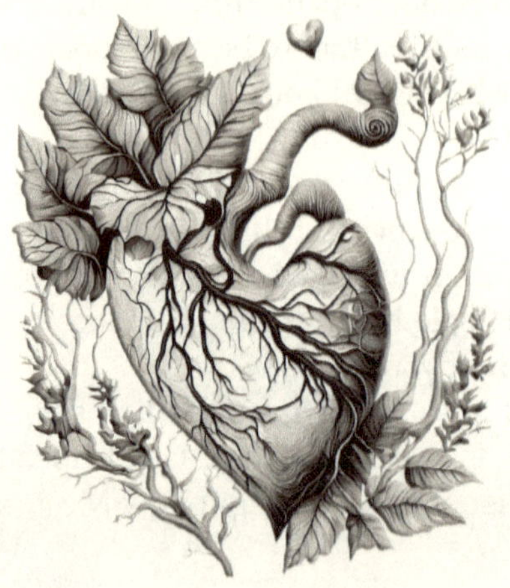

CHAPTER 40

IT SURE DIDN'T FEEL like it took longer to get to my room. We didn't even go outside past the reflecting pools. I flopped on the bed and thought about CJ, but the next thing I knew Lindy was knocking on my door.

"Megan? Are you ready? I'm sure you are going to want to get some breakfast before we meet up with Penny. Megan?" She finally just let herself in. "Megan, wake the Underworld up! I've been banging on the door for over a minute straight. The guards were getting ready to take the door off."

I grumbled.... I couldn't believe how tired I felt. "Ok... ok... just give me a minute. Let me at least brush my hair and clean up a little bit, okay?"

I was brushing my hair back into a ponytail when she asked what Julian had wanted in the private, so I explained to her what we had discussed. Then I told her how I practically had to get on my hands and knees begging to get access to records, that we all knew that Lindy had already seen, we just had to find out the particulars.

Once I was ready, headed down to the dining hall, had some breakfast, and set off to meet up with Penny.

She led us down hallway upon hallway. Once again, Lindy knew the way better than Penny did. Lindy even rolled her eyes at me a couple of times and when Penny had to look at the map for the third time, Lindy suggested that we head off to the right.

I shook my head. There was something about Penny that was really off. She looked paler than she had the last couple of days, and her eyes were super glassy.

When we got to the door, I just looked at it then looked at Lindy with a questioning look, and back to the door. It looked more like a janitor's closet door, or simple bedroom door. Penny not only had to unlock it, but she also ran her hand along the door jamb softly whispering, *"Bilitous artuious cotim salas vindicum"* over and over until she had circled the whole door. The lock clicked and the door swung opened.

"You expected something more for the door hiding the biggest secrets of Nalrin right?" Lindy said with a smirk on her face. There was a memory that flashed through her eyes at that statement, but she didn't elaborate.

"Yeah." I said astonished.

"Exactly why it isn't. Anyone else would have walked right past it, not thinking twice about the door." She said smiling. "Let's start over there. If they haven't changed my organization too much, Angel of Death should be there."

"I'll be right here by the door if you need me" Penny said. "I'm not really authorized to see these documents."

Lindy nodded to her and we headed to the stacks.

"Does Penny seem a little bit ... more off today?" Lindy asked.

"Yea. She didn't seem so ding–batty, yesterday ... day before yesterday? Whenever it was that she led us down." I said, but Lindy just shrugged.

We walked through a huge room that was filled with stuff I only could wish I had time to study. There was a statue in the center of the room that gave off a beautiful golden light.

The center sphere moved and swirled like lava that never really cooled. The outer layer wasn't static either. The sphere just rolled and swirled on itself. I reached my hand out to touch it, but Lindy grabbed my hand and shook her head.

"The last person to touch the sphere was never seen or heard from again." She said with a very stern expression on her face. I just nodded my head and pulled my hand back looking at the silver ironwork holding the sphere and smiled.

There were five faceless statues joined at the hands, that I immediately recognized as the Five Angels, holding up our light, our power.

"Beautiful, isn't it?" Lindy whispered.

I nodded. I was completely at a loss for words.

"Come on, as you said before, we are short on time." Lindy said pushing me further back into the massive room and stopping at three large tables set up between some bookcases.

"Stay here a second." Lindy said as she disappeared into the stacks. I worked on cleaning off the layers and layers of dust that coated the tables and a few minutes later she dropped some books on the larger of the three tables.

"Come with me." She said clapping the dust off her hands. "There's a lot more where those came from. Oh, and be careful with what boxes you open. Somethings in here are sentient."

"Sentient?"

"Yes. As in, they must stay in their boxes. Understand me?" She said finger pointing at me.

"Yes, ma'am." I said pinching my lips together and putting my hands firmly at my sides.

Laughing, she went through and grabbed a few stacks from different places shoving them into my arms.

"You said it's a book, right?" She said and I nodded. "Then let's start here in this section. If we don't find it here, we will just work further down this aisle."

THE FIVE ANGELS

We had been looking through books and more books, scrolls, and even more scrolls for hours. There had been references to a book of leather that never aged, but not much more. Often chalked up to myth. Nothing more.

I was reading a scroll about leather books touched by the Angels when my vision went fuzzy.

Lindy and I were exactly as we were now, hunched over the desk with a bunch of documents all over the table, our hair an absolute mess and we looked tired. But there were just a bunch of jumbled images like if someone quickly flipped through a photo album. There were scrolls everywhere, then I hyper-focused on a particular scroll with a bright blue ribbon on it, a syth flying through the air, screaming, and then I was looking at the desk again.

I looked around to see if I saw Penny, and she was still sitting by the door reading a book. She was chewing on her thumb and looked up at me and our eyes met. I thought I saw them narrow slightly, but then she smiled and I turned back to the documents in front of me. I shuffled through the stack of scrolls I had and searched to see if I could find a scroll with a bright blue ribbon. It was the only thing that I really saw. For the Angels, it could be completely unrelated to this anyways. Could be something years from now.

I ran my hand through my hair, my fingers getting caught in the leather strap for my ponytail, pieces of hair getting caught in my ring. I pulled my hair out, and was putting my hair up as I walked down an aisle looking for something similar. There, near the bottom of the pile on the second shelf up. Three scrolls bunched together with bright blue ribbon. I unrolled them and was speechless when I looked down and saw it. I walked as quickly as I could back to where Lindy was and sat down across from her.

"Lindy, I think I found it!" She was too far engrossed in what she was reading so I sent a spark of my power and she jumped and rubbed at the spot on her arm where it hit her. I looked up and Penny was still by the door. I didn't want to risk her seeing us. *Come here, but quietly.* I pushed toward her.

The scroll said the Book of Death rested on a pedestal that looked like a tree trunk in the center, with the roots and leaves intertwining like Celtic knots intertwined on each other, forming a circle around the tree trunk. The book was in a hidden garden in the southwest lower portion of the castle and being held in place on a tree like pedestal with twig or root like fingers. Underneath were the instructions on how to get the book.

"A sacrifice given, but life not taken." I whispered, "Only this will release the hold of the book." When I looked up to Lindy, I saw Penny sneaking up behind her just as she released a shock wave toward Lindy. I threw a wall up to block it, but it knocked us back too. When Penny stood up, she turned to me, smiled, and said "Symatha will be so very thankful for this information."

I drew my syths and lunged. Penny's were in her hands before I reached her, and when our syths clashed together, I threw my electricity down the blades. Penny hissed at the feel of her syth heating. I could smell the sizzling flesh, but Penny didn't relent. I heard the soft whine of Lindy unsheathing her syths and narrowly missed a syth flying through the air. Everything slowed down as I watched that syth fly past me.

Penny ducked just as Lindy's syth flew just past her head and embedded itself into the bookcase behind us. I swung and punched Penny in the jaw as I jumped back. Penny stumbled back a moment and spit blood. She smiled, blood coating her teeth as she said, "This is fun. I haven't had a good fight in a long while."

She whirled and flung one of her syths at Lindy, which skimmed her arm, a bright red line of blood welled up. I looked back to Penny just in time for her to kick my ribs, making me stumble back a few feet into an adjoining shelf where several artifacts fell to the floor releasing a high-pitched scream. I covered my ears to the noise and closed my eyes.

I heard both of Lindy's syths clash with Penny's now drawn cutlass. I pushed a wall between them that Penny waved off quickly. Blood ran freely down Lindy's arm as Penny smiled with gritted teeth. Penny's ember mostly looked normal, but there were flickers of darkness flittering around the edges. I reached down for the throwing knives, which I had specially made with no hilt, stayed low, and flung them at Penny.

I barely heard them fly through the air, but Penny was quick. One caught her in the back of her calf, and the other, which I aimed for her shoulder flew past and skittered across the floor.

Shit! I ducked as she swung her cutlass toward me.

Swing. Step back and dodge.

She swung for my head and I stepped back realizing, I was being cornered against the stacks. Lindy took an opening to slice her syth along her left side, Penny growling in response.

In the seconds that Penny was concentrating on Lindy, I climbed the stacks and flipped around the other side of Penny flinging the leather strap out of my hair wrapping it around one of her wrists.

Penny turned to me and laughed.

Lindy and I froze.

Her laugh was maniacal as she slowly faded away into a white mist.

"What the?" I looked at Lindy. Other than the gash down her forearm, she looked to be alright.

"I ... Don't ... Know." She said confused.

"Her ember was not the same as it was yesterday. There was an edge of darkness to it. It was starting to look like Symatha's when we were in the Garden of the Angel of Beauty. How do you think Penny got wrapped up in this mess?"

"I don't know. Come on let's head up and let them know what we found. We need to arrange for transportation to Noctulanar... and quickly." She said not fully explaining herself and half lost in thought.

I headed over to where the scroll was. I wanted to read over it again, but when I got there ...

"Lindy! IT'S GONE! The scroll. It's gone. Penny must have taken it."

"Julian is going to kill us for letting a piece out of here." She said with a heavy sigh.

"Well, it isn't like we meant to. And it certainly wasn't our fault that Penny turned out to be a spy." I said with a sigh. "Well let's head up. Nothing else we can get down here."

"We suspected she was a traitor though. He will tan our hides for still allowing her down here."

"I mentioned it to him last night. I told him I suspected but didn't have any proof. He may still yell and scream, but I don't' think he will actually skin us alive." I said.

"Good thing you did." Lindy said, but then she asked, "How did Penny just disappear like that? You can't dimension travel right now." Lindy said.

"Why not?" I asked.

"It's completely locked down." She said accidently kicking a box on the floor that screeched in protest.

"Oh shut up. *Blinkal chakble*." She said and the box went motionless and silent.

I just looked at her in question.

"One of the relics you aren't supposed to know about." She said with a smirk.

I nodded then asked again, "Why is travel locked down right now?"

"Remember when we taught you how to dimension travel and we said it was very strictly against the rules to travel within the same dimension that way?"

"Yes."

"When Ansel and Symatha took off with CJ yesterday, dimension travel was locked down for the time being. No getting in or out of Nalsar right now. No transporting of any kind, not even within the same property is supposed to be able to work. Ansel and Symatha broke a law that goes beyond just the Nalsar dimension, Megan. The Heads of all the realms are now involved. Julian had to bring them up to speed as you would say, to what has been going on here the last few months." She said seriously then added with a laugh, "I'm sure Julian has enjoyed those conversations."

As we closed the door to the room and Lindy replaced the incantation to lock it, my mind started to race. There was so much I still needed to learn. So many political entities. So many things that were just beyond my comprehension.

About halfway back, I started to concentrate more on the book and the Angel of Death. "Lindy, why does the Angel of Death refer to so much life? Life or the reverence of life was continually referenced in all those books and scrolls. Doesn't Death take away life? And yes, I know how silly that sounds, but you know what I mean."

She giggled a light sound. "The Angel of Death represents LIFE, Megan. When you die, it's not the end. You continue on. In death brings life. There are variations from religion to religion, or even a life belief, on what happens after death, whether you go be with a God, Gods, you're reincarnated, or even at the most basic of understanding; When you die, your body will either be buried, cremated, or laid to rest in some part right?" I nodded and let her continue as we picked up the pace down the hall. "Well parts of you, are absorbed into the ground, and as gross as it sounds, you become nutrients for other life forms. Ashes to Ashes, Dust to Dust."

"So just because he's the Angel of Death, doesn't just mean he's all dark and gloomy. That explains why he isn't depicted in any of the statues as a hooded grim figure or anything like that."

"I never understood that depiction by the human race." She laughed.

Making our way back I mulled over the instructions on releasing the book *"a sacrifice given, life not taken."* Did it really matter? Even if we did figure it out, I had already seen Symatha get the book already, so she's obviously going to figure it out. How are we ever going to stop them? Book or not. I can't lose CJ. I let out a big sigh at the thought.

"Don't worry sweety. We will stop them. You and CJ will be together again." Lindy said. She knew me so well.

"I hope so." I said sighing my fingers going to play with the ring on my finger.

"We will. Have a little faith." She smiled big as she said that. She was really trying to cheer me up, so I forced a smile and just shook my head.

CHAPTER 41

WE WERE SITTING IN a waiting room of sorts while Lindy talked to someone here in Nalrin about transportation to Noctulanar. When we met up with Jean, Owen, and Clarice, we had filled them in on what had happened downstairs with Penny.

I sat there playing with the electricity through my fingers as the others tried to figure out just how Symatha could have gotten to Penny within the city center, which was tightly locked down. It was clear to me. She had been helping them from the start. Long before lockdowns happened.

"One thing doesn't make sense to me though," Clarice said. "Why is it we had to fight through all the barriers to where the mirror was held, and fight off the Asmita Gonda, but Symatha and Ansel didn't? If that was the only way down, why wasn't the potion puzzle and the Asmita Gonda already taken care of?"

"The potion puzzle reset immediately after we passed. I thought I heard something growl in that corner, so I looked back

295

to the table as we were walking out, but the sound was just the puzzle being reset." Jean explained.

"and what about the Asmita Gonda?" Clarice asked.

"Penny was in from the beginning. She fed them the information. Penny also gave Ansel and Symatha the back door entrance to the Mirror of Remembrance. It's just that simple." I mumbled and brought my knees up to my chest wrapping my arms around them protectively.

"Megan! Megan!" I heard in a faint voice. I raised my head quickly, but everything went fuzzy and out of focus again. I moaned and put my head on my knees.

"Megan!"

"CJ?" I shout back. I could hear the others come and stand next to me. Someone's hand was on my back and someone else, I think Owen, hand his hands on my knees. I could faintly hear them asking what I was seeing.

"Megan! Megan where are you! Come to me!" CJ was yelling.

"Where are you?" I shouted. I was standing in the swamp again. Once again, I started running through the trees screaming for CJ. I felt my breathing getting more labored, but it was getting harder to breathe. It was like running in a swimming pool and inhaling water.

I was pulled forward again and just like last time, I wasn't able to move my feet. This time, however, instead of going from the forest to the circular room, I stopped in front of Noctulanar Castle. Only this time I wasn't really me. I was looking down at the scene before me, instead of being part of it. I saw myself standing before big black iron gates and a stone wall with a plaque on the stone. As much as I tried to focus on it, I couldn't read what it said. The gate had a black barrier to it, and around the edges of that barrier, there were thin black finger like strings that seemed to flicker.

I watched as I walked up to the gates, blood dripping from the syth in my hand, and pressed my palm to the lock. The gates creaked and hissed open as I was pulled forward and back into the circular room.

Everything played out as it had every single time before, except that this time, I wasn't able to look away from CJ, covered in blood, on that table.

It was like there were firm hands on either side of my head making me watch the scene in more detail. In a voice that was many voices, whispered in my head, "What do you see?"

Once it all played out, I was back in the room with my family. My head throbbed and everything faded to black.

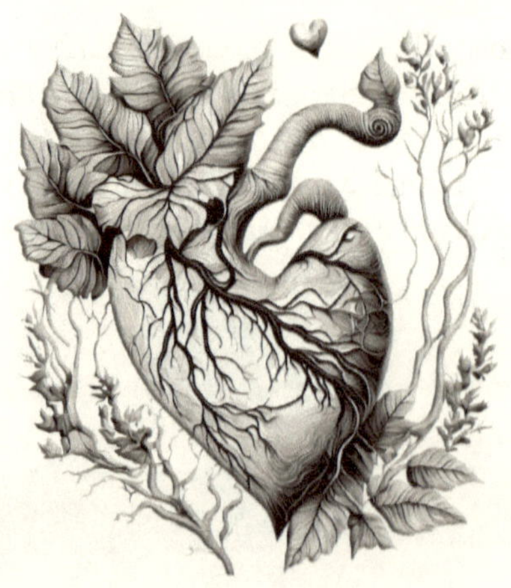

CHAPTER 42

Tick. Tock.
Boom.
Tick. Tock.
Boom.
Seconds rolled by in my head as the boom would thunder through my head. Once it faded, it would start anew.

I could hear Jean and Owen talking about how we had to hurry, while Lindy was trying to explain to someone that some of my visions just affect me in strange ways.

Holy Death. My head hurt like hell.

I forced myself to open my eyes and try to sit up, but the room decided to spin a couple of times, so I put my head back down. Jean was sitting at my feet with Owen on the other side.

No one really said anything, but everyone looked at me. I looked around the room and there were a lot of people there I didn't recognize. Angels, I hated being on display. "Go away." I tried to say, but it came out as a mumbled, "mum awmmay".

Clarice was talking to Julian and another man with skin the color of caramel, who was dressed in a beautiful jade green robe with silver corded hooks on the front with a Mandarin collar, but it went down past his knees, with four splits in it from his hips to the floor. There were also three women with Lindy who were dressed similarly, only theirs were bright blue.

"How are you feeling?" a voice to the left of me asked. I looked up and saw a woman with brown hair and the lightest grey eyes I have ever seen. I must have taken too long to answer, because she repeated, "I said, how are you feeling?"

"Um, a little bit of a headache, but that's happened before." I managed to say as I tried to sit the rest of the way up. "Who are you?" I asked.

"Hurgo, Head Physician here in Nalrin. I was asked to come and see you because your family was concerned." She said with a highly intelligent assessment.

I looked at Jean and she looked a bit sheepish. "Jean?"

"Just before you passed out, your ears started to bleed. You hadn't done *that* before. Hurgo was already in the building, so she got here pretty quick." She said trying to sound sorry.

"Well other than the headache, and a little thirsty, I feel fine." I told them slightly annoyed. "I think ya'll overreacted a little."

"Bleeding from one's ears, no matter the being is always a cause for concern." Hurgo said with a curt smirk, "Oh don't look at me that way. If I had a coin for each time I've said that I wouldn't need to work. Regardless, I'll get you something for the headache and some water."

I watched as she took quick clipped steps and left the room. Just who in the underworld... I sighed and leaned my head back. My head hurt too much for this crap.

"Ms. Megan, please tell us what you saw." Julian asked gently, but I knew it was an order. One does not refuse the Head of Nalrin.

"Noctulanar again." was all I could manage to say. My family nodded in understanding while everyone else had huge questioning looks on their faces. Well except for the man who was standing next to Julian.

"Noctulanar Castle?" he shouted with his face contorted in a mix of surprise and anger. "That is where you want to take them? Julian, you can't believe I would agree to this?"

My head shot up, and I just stared at him. Who in the hell is this guy?

"Quiet, Kalit." Julian commanded.

"But…"

"I said quiet. We will discuss this after we hear from Ms. Megan what she saw." Julian said even more forcefully. It amazed me the presence and force a 5-foot-tall man can command. The man named Kalit pursed his lips and looked at the ground in front of him.

"Ms. Megan, I can see your family understands, but can you please elaborate for those of us who do not?" I know his words themselves could have come out crass and rude, but Julian had a way about him that made them sound understanding. Perfect speech presence.

"I saw us at Noctulanar and … in a specific room" I looked to Julian and silently pushed *'the circular room I'm not supposed to talk about.'*

"Then why speak of it, Ms. Megan?" Julian said out loud.

"Speak of what?" Jean said.

Julian looked at me. I cocked an eyebrow and told him silently, *'I didn't say that out loud.'*

"Ahhh. That we will speak of later." He said giving Jean and Owen a look that made them both flinch. "Please continue Ms. Megan." Julian said, but I could see Lindy trying to suppress a smile. She knew exactly what was going on.

"Anyways, I was in that room again with my parents and CJ. This time though I saw us standing outside the gates of the castle and…" My head was still pounding and there was a slight ringing in my ears too. I massaged my temples and continued, "We were standing at the gates of the castle and there was a plaque to the side of the gate. The gate was iron I think, but it had a black barrier to it so I'm not sure."

I didn't want to elaborate too much on the gate. It gave me chills and even the thought sent a shiver through me.

It seemed Julian knew what I meant though. "The barrier. Did the edges seem to finger off?"

"Yeah." I looked at him very carefully. "How did you know?"

"Ms. Megan you aren't the Head of the Nalsar Council without knowing certain things." He said with a hint of humor. There was a quick glance at Clarice who didn't pay attention to him.

I waited to see if he would explain further, but when he didn't it was Jean who spoke up. "So, what is it?"

"Death. Darkness." Julian answered evenly and there was a look in his eye that seemed personal. I think Jean noticed too because she eyed me and started to open her mouth to say something, but I shook my head cutting her off.

"So anyway, once we got past the barrier I was pulled to the same room as before and it basically played out the same. Just this time it was like I wasn't allowed to look around the room. I was totally fixated on CJ."

As I said his name my heartfelt heavier and sank a little more. I wish I knew how he was doing, how he was holding up. I don't even want to think about what my parents could be doing to him. What kind of tortures they were putting him through?

The door swung open and Hurgo came through with some water and a couple of small pills in her hand. I took it, threw the pills back in one quick motion and downed the bottle of water she had given me to help wash it down.

"Ms. Lindy, let me look at that arm." Hurgo demanded.

"It's fine." Lindy told her moving her arm further behind her back, but Hurgo was already standing next to her grabbing it.

"How did that happen?" Owen asked her.

"Penny got me before she disappeared. Don't worry about it." Lindy said and then turned to Hurgo, jerking her arm away from her. "It's nothing."

That seemed to piss Hurgo off.

"Well, if it's nothing then why after a couple of hours is it still bleeding through your wrappings?" She put her hands on her hips and by Lindy's silence knew she had won and grabbed her arm again. "Just let me fix it up and it will be nothing, but if you continue to be a pain in the ass then it will be a whole lot worse by morning."

Lindy looked totally pissed and dumbfounded. It made for a very funny facial expression, and I tried very hard not to laugh, but a few spurts of giggles passed through my lips. She looked up and glared at me. I just stuck my tongue out at her.

Hurgo sprayed something on it, which must have stung because Lindy winced a bit and hissed through her teeth. A few seconds later green goop started to ooze out of the wound. Hurgo wiped it out as quickly as she could, but it took a few more sprays before she was satisfied and re-wrapped her arm.

"Now it's nothing, and it should heal properly." She said with a bit of sass and a smile on her face. She faced Julian. "May I be excused please sir? There are some patients I need to get back to in the PW."

"PW?" I asked.

"Physician's Ward." Jean said patting my knee. She was trying hard to comfort me.

"Of course, and thank you for taking the time to mend them." He said, as Hurgo bowed respectfully and left the room.

My head really was killing me. I played with my necklace and tried to figure out why it was so much worse than the last time I passed out. My ears bleed. But why? I mean the last time I passed out I was talking to Symatha, and in some way, I guess it makes sense since that was more than just a vision, but this was just a vision. It was just a vision, right?

"Megan, what's wrong? Should we get Hurgo back in here?" Owen asked while halfway across the room and heading back for the door.

"No, she doesn't need to come back. I just can't wait for this aspirin to kick in." I told him.

"Kelmaldin." Lindy corrected with a smile. "It works differently than the aspirin of the Manusia."

"Whatever. As long as it can help me keep a solid train of thought, then I don't care what it is called." Why was this happening? Why were my visions affecting me so drastically now? They have gone from once a week, or a couple of times a week, to every day, to multiple times a day, to ear bleeds and black outs.

"What are you thinking?" Clarice asked when she saw me make a face.

"The last time I passed out I was talking to Symatha, so that would make sense, right? Extra strain on the brain equals brain hitting the reset button. So why is it that this time, in what appears to be a normal vision, would I be affected so much worse than any of the others. It's like the more visions, the more it wears on my body."

"You said that you were practically being forced to look at the events, and couldn't look around right?" Jean said.

"Yeah."

"Well maybe there was something there that you needed to see, but you were so set on looking for other clues to help us, that the force is what caused it?" Lindy said.

I leaned back and flopped my arm over my eyes, but said, "I could hear a voice tell me to see what I haven't seen before, but I don't know what I was supposed to see. This is all just so weird."

"Yeah, because having multiple Congniti in a family is normal." Jean said sarcastically. She was trying to defuse the tension in the room.

"I've never claimed to be normal!" I groaned with a bit more bite than intended.

The man there must have been growing impatient because he cleared his throat and asked "Julian, may we finish our business so I can return to the stables?"

"Yes of course. This is Kalit. He is head caretaker of the animals and creatures here in Nalrin."

"I'm sorry. I thought Malikal was the caretaker?" Owen asked. He'd been pretty quiet since I woke.

"Malikal is the head caretaker for the beast and creatures that reside and protect in the Nalrin Library. Kalit here is caretaker of the other animals and creatures that are in Nalrin itself." Julian answered.

"The creatures in the library are of a different nature than those that are to the benefit of Nalrin. They serve different purposes and require different care and attention. So, they have different caretakers." Kalit explained.

"Kalit will be lending you a means to travel to your next destination." Julian explained. "His assistants here will be going with you so that they can care for them while you are, or shall I say until you are ready to return home."

"They will not go near Noctulanar Castle, Julian. My breeds will not be able to handle that level of darkness. The fact you are even taking them into Obsecuritan is going to be difficult on them." Kalit pleaded with Julian.

"I understand that Kalit, however, they are the fastest means of getting Ms. Megan and her family there. It is of the utmost importance that they arrive as soon as possible." Kalit opened his mouth to plead some more, but Julian cut him off. "This isn't an option. Please ready your finest and have them ready in three hours' time for departure."

Kalit and his assistants bowed to Julian and left the room.

"I'm sorry, Julian. How are we getting to Noctulanar?" I asked when the door had shut, and it was only my family and him in the room.

"Why Dragons, of course, Ms. Megan."

I blinked at him.

He smiled and I blinked again.

"DRAGONS!" I shouted sitting up and looking at everyone as the room spun a little. Each of them had a little smirk on their face. "Seriously, I'm gonna be riding a DRAGON!" I couldn't tell if I was really excited, or really terrified. Part of me was thinking "OH WAY COOL" and the other part of me was thinking "ARE YOU FUCKING NUTS?"

"But of course. It is the fastest way to get there." Julian said, but then he realized why I was so surprised. "I'm sorry Ms. Megan, I forget you were not raised here in our world and are still adjusting. Granted they are rarely used and there aren't many left after the battles of ... well never mind that now."

I looked around the room, and my family just stood there smiling.

"It's like nothing you've ever experienced Megan. Just wait." Clarice said.

"It seems just so unreal to me. Back home dragons are not something you ride. They are something of fairytale, fantasy, and usually danger." I tried to explain.

"Really? They are gentle giants." Lindy said looking very confused.

"Really! In a lot of stories, they are protectors, breathe fire, and would love to rip you apart! In fairytales, they are always on the side of evil. Yes, there are stories where they are majestic beasts who work with humans, but those stories where the dragon is the good guy are extremely few and far between."

"Dragons can breathe fire, and they are great protectors, but evil? Not inherently. They are more like giant puppy dogs. Loyal, True, and FAST! You ride duo or trio so no need to worry."

"Ok ahh... Okay. If you say so." I said still a little nervous.

"You should go and prepare for your trip. When you're ready, meet Kalit down at the stables. Lindy, I believe you know the way." Julian said.

"I do." Lindy said nodding.

"Ok. Then I shall see you upon your return. Safe travels." Then Julian bowed to us and headed out the door.

"Julian!" Lindy said urgently running out the door and shutting it behind her.

I looked to Jean and she shrugged. "No idea, but we should pick up and start packing."

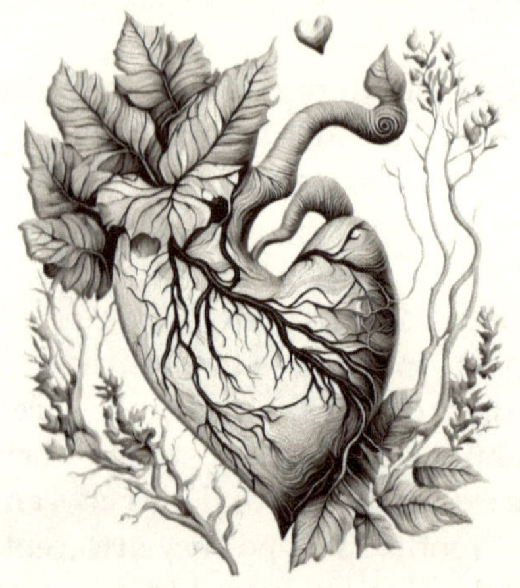

CHAPTER 43

ON THE WAY TO the stables, I played with my necklace thinking through the last vision. I couldn't figure out what I was supposed to see. Maybe it was about what I couldn't see. The flower was there, the crystal, the book, Symatha holding ... I froze.

"My necklace."

"What about it?" Lindy asked.

"In the vision, I didn't see the Sa Ra." She just looked at me a little confused. "The Sa Ra." I said pulling on my necklace to show her. "Angel of Healing... "

"Yea. I know what the Sa Ra is Megan. I'm just not following you."

"Ok from what you have said, the Golden Medallion of Sa Ra is the piece that they will need to get for the Angel of Healing. To bind all the pieces together, right?"

"Yes." she said slowly, eyeing me carefully.

"I don't remember having a vision about them ever actually getting it from me. In the vision I had earlier, Symatha was holding a replica of the Sa Ra." She still had a completely lost look on her face. "Okay. Remembrance: They have the crystal from the mirror." I ticked off on one finger.

She nodded her head. "Right. Still, really wish we could have gotten there in time to stop that."

"Yeah, well we didn't. Beauty they have the Desumo Nitor." I ticked off on another finger.

"Which will wilt soon."

I brought up a third finger, flinched, and continued. "Love: They have CJ."

"Right... and Death we just found out where to start looking for the book."

"True, but I have seen Symatha get the book and Penny was going to tell her exactly what we found out. Not to mention I've seen my parents performing the ritual in the circular room. So, we know that is going to happen."

"Which from what we have read, you can only find the actual location from the Book of Death."

I sighed. I could see the wheels turning in her head, but she hadn't gotten there. "I haven't seen anything regarding the Sa Ra." I tried to explain to her. "Nothing. I have for every other piece, except for the Golden Medallion of Sa Ra."

She thought about that for a minute. "But Symatha knows you have it."

"She thinks she has it, but we know that isn't true because we have seen this work."

"So, they must get it somehow." She paused, "Considering that you've seen them conduct the ceremony and... kill CJ."

I took a shuddering deep breath.

"I shouldn't have voiced it, but -"

"No. It's okay. It's what I've seen. Just to hear it out loud like that." I took another deep breath and asked, "So we make sure they don't get the real one? Leave it here?"

"Oh No. The council wouldn't be able to resist taking possession of it. I'm kind of surprised they haven't confiscated it already. She won't get it." She said with a swaggering confidence that I didn't feel.

"And you know this how?" I said huffing a laugh in frustration.

"I have faith." She laughed and grabbed my arm. "Come on, let's catch up with the others."

We walked down past the empty stables, and when we rounded the corner the air in my lungs left me in an exasperated huff. Dragons. Three of them. Just sitting there. Just slightly bigger than a large elephant, they were not near as big as I thought they would be. Granted, I only had what Hollywood would like to portray them as, and truth be told, shape and overall look was pretty close. The first had pearly white scales, the second was black as night, but still shimmered like glitter, and the last one was a little smaller than the others but lavender.

Kalit was standing there, securing the saddles on each with what I assumed would be his normal grumpy face until his dragons were safely back at home. When he finished, he introduced us to Sam and Jin who would be watching over the dragons while we were in "*that horrid place*". Owen just rolled his eyes each time Kalit would draw out the words.

Sam and Jin jumped up onto the lavender dragon which had huge packs on either side of the saddle and along the back edge. Sam instructed Owen and Jean to get on Blanca, the white dragon and Clarice, Lindy, and I on Jack the black one. Of all the names I was going on a Jack? I couldn't help but laugh. Clarice jumped up first, but when it was my turn, I froze.

Jack looked back at me and there was a gleam in his eye, I did not care for.

"I am not crunchy and good with ketchup." I said under my breath to him.

"Oh come on silly!" Lindy said as she practically pushed me up the dragon's side.

"I guess now isn't the time to tell you I'm afraid of heights?" I stuttered as Clarice hauled me up and onto the seat.

When we were all settled and ready to go, Sam rose her hand and commanded, "To the sky's and into Obsecuritan."

They spread their wings and lifted us up and into the air. It was smooth, but with the first booming of wings, it was like someone had suddenly thrown earmuffs over my ears. When we got high enough to clear the buildings of Nalrin, they flew full circle and bolted to the south.

It was a fairly spectacular way to travel, like flying in a plane, with more legroom and viewing area. The lack of wind was a bit surreal and but allowed you to enjoy the view of the river below winding through the forest. As we headed further south, the savannah with the abundance of wildlife was mesmerizing.

When we reached the edge of the Nalrin province, we flew over a channel of water that separated Nalrin from the Seltic Marsh, a huge peat bog that went on for as far as you could see. We veered to the right and up through a mountain range. The dragons weaved between the mountain passes with quick precision. Quick smooth movements made me sick to my stomach. I looked down at my hands hoping it was mostly visual. It wasn't. Luckily, it didn't last too long.

As we broke through the mountain pass, my hands were firmly over my mouth and I was breathing very carefully. I had never been so happy for the vast nothingness that allowed for the dragons to just glide in the currents. Once my stomach had settled, I looked out at the open expanse of black, white, and greys.

The sunlight was different here. There was really no color. The reds and oranges in the Seltic Marsh were gone. Here it was if twilight were the only time of day.

What would have been a three- or four-day trip by land, the dragons did in just a few hours. "Welcome to Obsecuritan." Clarice said darkly, as she looked to the south looking for something, or someone.

I opened my mouth to ask her what she was looking for, but Lindy, seeming to read my thoughts, elbowed me and shook her head. It was harder to let her be when I saw her wipe a tear from her cheek. I just grabbed her hand and smiled.

A few minutes later we circled around and landed on a rock ledge of the same marsh I had seen so many times before in my visions. It made my heart race. I took slow deep breaths to slow it, but it didn't work. When we dismounted, the air changed to a hot, wet, muggy world.

I slid down the side of the dragon and met up with the rest. Owen was talking to Sam and Jin and assured them that we would be back within a day or so.

How many of us would be back though? I looked at Lindy, Clarice, Jean, and Owen. Trying to keep my mind from the very real possibility, that one or more of us may not make that flight home, was impossible. My heart raced faster, my hands were trembling as I buckled my pack and my palms were sweating so much, that they felt ice cold.

"Let's go." I told them before anyone could say anything. Clarice held back a moment looking to the far south before turning her heels and stomping into the marsh after us.

"Is she going to be ok?" I pushed to Lindy.

"Yea, she will be. This has to be hard for her to come back here. I don't think she's been to Obsecuritan since she turned her back on it so many years ago." She said quietly.

"Did she read the scroll?" I whispered.

"She did and before you ask, I don't know what it said. I also don't know why she left or where exactly she originated from here in Obsecuritan."

Nodding, I focused on the route ahead.

Hours passed and the air started getting denser. Heavier. I was sweating, but cold and shivering. The coldness, however, had nothing to do with the weather.

As I looked around, there were tree branches full of leaves, sagged from the weight of the water in the air, flowers, and vines, but I think what made it feel so strange was that there was no color, well virtually no color. The closer and closer we got to Noctulanar the more even the grey went away, and things just started to become more black and white. The ground was muddy, and each step sloshed and became harder to take.

The ground was also covered in black clover, which felt as if it sucked the energy right out of you. Just like in my visions, there was the total absence of wildlife. No crocodiles, frogs, or even one mosquito. I kept listening for a bird, a bat, anything, and it was just this strange silence.

"How can it be so wet and not raining? I'm covered in sweat." I complained.

"Megan." I turned and faced Clarice who had spoken for the first time since we left Nalrin. She was pointing up ahead, where just past the tree line, you could see the outline of the castle.

I sighed heavily. "Well, here goes nothing."

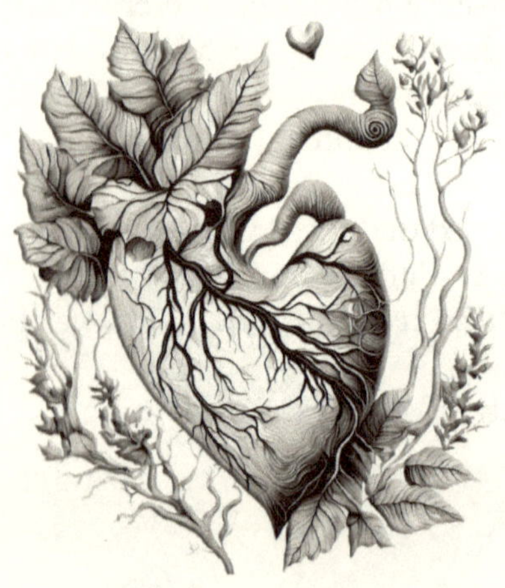

CHAPTER 44

WHEN WE BROKE THROUGH the tree line, I got to see Noctulanar in all its glory. It wasn't gothic in nature or similar to any other castle I had seen through my travels through Europe after college. It was almost contemporary in nature. If a stone, ancient castle could be contemporary. Long clean straight lines, square and rectangle windows.

Noctulanar had an entrance that was at least 150 feet wide, and each wing off to the side had to be longer than two football fields. The Castle reached to the grey sky and had no less than ten above-ground stories, based on the maps we had seen, but looking up, there were sections that had to extend more than 10 levels. We knew from the books that the number of subterranean floors were uncountable.

On the fence grew lush breathing black ivy. Then there was the gate, just as I had seen it in my vision; big, black, and made out of iron with the creepy black, barrier to it. At the edges of that barrier were those thin black finger strings flickering. Each step toward that gate felt colder than the last, and by the time we reached the gate, we could see our breath. Each breath felt like shards of glass. No ice built upon our surroundings and we all shivered and held ourselves to keep whatever warmth we had.

I felt out into the Castle grounds to see if I could feel my parents and CJ inside but, ... I blinked.

Nothing.

Absolute nothingness. Just a vast black void in the space where the castle stood.

"Great." I mumbled. Lindy gave me a look, her teeth were chattering so much, she didn't even try to talk.

I looked to the wall where I knew a plaque was placed and read it out loud:

CRUOR VITUALAMEN PLACO OBSECURIAN

"Clarice. Translation please." I through my own chatters. I didn't even try to be pleasant about it.

"The Blood Sacrifice appeases the Darkness" she whispered and blew air into her hands.

I walked over to the lock and with my syth I quickly cut my palm and pressed it to the large flatlock.

Black flickering fingers surrounded my hand, freezing my hand to the lock. The cold spread up my arm, and when it got to my elbow the lock fell to the ground. Still unable to move my arm from the darkness wrapped around my hand and forearm, the darkness retreated down my arm so, so, slowly, as if it was pained to do so, then slid off my hand. Only then did the gates hiss open. The temperature quickly rose around us to a comfortable level except for a lingering phantom shard of ice in my hand and arm where the fingers had been.

The ground was covered in overgrown ivy and other plants that all seemed to have the same dark flicker as the gates. As we made our way to the front doors, the ground cover pulled back to reveal a stone walkway. Owen and Jean got to the doors first but were unable to open them.

When I took a step onto the first step to the door, there was a harsh click in the door, that made me jump, then a shudder flowed through the building before the doors opened. I smiled slightly at the awe of the realization that the castle was alive. It explained why no one was able to map the lower levels, or why there was still so much unknown about the place.

"Eerie." Lindy said to Jean whose hand was firmly in Owens.

We entered the main room and the architecture was magnificent. There was a beauty about it. There were four story tall ceilings and two-story windows on the far side showed black and white roses, daffodils, and tulips breathing just outside the window.

Even though it should feel cold and hard, it felt warm and inviting. There was a hint of vanilla in the air like someone was baking in the kitchen. Then I felt it. A soft caress surrounded me, and I almost sagged into it. Nothing threatening. Nothing cold. Nothing dark. It was if the castle was welcoming me.

I saw Owen, Jean, and Lindy shiver a little. Clarice's reaction was harder to read. In fact, it looked like she was trying very hard to keep something at bay. Obviously, I was the only one getting the warm welcome, but I eyed Clarice a bit closer. She seemed to be assessing, weighing, judging the area.

"So where do we start?" Clarice said sighing heavily. She was looking through the walls to the maze of hallways and possibilities. We had looked at the maps a million times and knew that the direction we headed in now was going to be key.

My hand still stung where the cut was, but as I played with my necklace, I could feel the sting of it healing. I started to look around to the various doorways to different parts of the castle. I could see the map laid out like some kind of hologram that showed where every doorway lead.

I pointed to the one to the left near the front, "That one leads to the library."

Lindy pointed to the next one, "The staircase down to the dungeons."

"Kitchens"

"Main living quarters."

"Armory and main bathory" Owen said pointing to the hallway just to the right by the front doors. I smiled. Leave it to Owen to know where the Armory was.

"Guest quarters upstairs" Jean said pointing to the right in the middle of the staircase.

I kept staring down a hallway at the far end to the right of the windows. They continued to discuss where passages lead to, where they intertwined, where they lead to different areas. The castle seemed to push me in the direction of that hallway. Just a small gentle nudge in that direction. I looked down at my hand and there was a faint black haze at the line that was forming there now.

"This way." I said as I started heading down the main room. Then paused when everyone else just followed. "No one is going to ask how I know? Or why this way?"

"I was going to suggest it." Owen said. "It's the only hallway, I couldn't remember where it leads to."

"I'm already lost in here. I have no idea where to really start." Jean said with a defeated sigh.

"Okay then." I said and headed down the hall.

We walked down hallway upon hallway, and when we got to a set of stairs I paused, but the room where CJ would be downstairs, not up. Lindy seeming to read my hesitation and started heading down the hall in front of me.

I continued to rub my hand where I had sliced it open. It stung even though it had healed to a think pink line now. It was still colder than my other hand, and I wondered if it always would.

We turned another corner and looked at the staircase heading downwards for a split second before I all but ran down the stairs. The corridor was dark, but light flooded down the hall just as I made the turn from the stairs.

At the end of the corridor Penny laid on the ground, eyes white as milk, and her skin had paled. Guess Symatha disposed of her, just as she did to me.

"Oh, poor Penny." Clarice said.

"What's in her hand?" Owen asked.

"Well at least we know we are going the right direction." I heard Lindy say.

I bent down and took the piece of paper in her hand. It was old and fragile, and as I uncurled it, I realized, "It's the scroll from the library!" I handed it to Lindy. "You need to make sure it gets back down there." She simply nodded.

A voice from what seemed like years ago whispered in my head. *All is not lost. Look to the darkness and you will find what you are looking for but stay in the light and everything you hold dear will be lost forever.*

As the voice trailed off, I felt my hand sting. Looking down at it, fingers of darkness swept out from where I had cut my hand down the hall. I looked at it confused. Look to the darkness and you will find what you are looking for but stay in the light and it will lead to their success.

Listen to the darkness? Clarice had said months ago that just because something is dark, doesn't mean it's bad. That there is good and happiness in the dark, if you know where to look.

I bolted down the hall. I could hear them behind me yelling at me to tell them what I saw, but that's just it, how do I tell them that it wasn't a vision. How do I tell them that darkness is leading me?

I ran down the long hallway, but when I turned the next corner there was a door just in front of us. The door, it had the same black fingers that the gate had around it.

We just looked at the door. I knew we needed to go through it, but when Owen tried to open the door, the darkness lapped at his hand and he jumped back.

"That is the weirdest feeling. It stings but it doesn't really hurt." He looked at me thoughtfully, and at my hand that I hadn't realized I was holding out, with a thin red line welting in the center of it. He glanced at my syth in my other hand and sighed. "Megan, you don't have to do everything."

I gave him a one-sided smile and shrugged. When my hand wrapped around the knob, darkness covered my hand and lapped up the blood from the cut with more force and intensity this time. It was greedy this time and it hurt, but I just clinched my teeth and turned the doorknob.

I blinked. A lush meadow, beautiful tall flourishing trees, lush grass, the sweet smell of honeysuckle, the warmth of the sun shining, and the soft blow of a cool breeze met us through that doorway. There was a detailed rendering of the Angel of Death in wood on the left side of the meadow and I couldn't help but close my eyes and breathe in its serenity. A place like this shouldn't be in a castle where everything was in blacks, whites, and darkness.

"Megan." Jean said pulling me out of my thoughts. "Look."

My heart sank when I saw what she was pointing at. There in the center, on a small mound of rich green clovers, was the tree trunk stand. There was a bed of green and blue clovers, framed by fingers of wood which had loosened the grip on the Book of Death.

"Fuck the Underworld's Belly!" I said throwing my hands in the air and dropping to sit on the ground. This is getting old. Can't we catch a break at all? I knew that she would get the book, HECK I even thought I had accepted that fact, but actually seeing the truth of it, was defeating. I guess even deeper inside I wanted to believe I could stop her.

Even if I could have stopped her, what would happen to CJ? She wouldn't need him anymore. Would she kill him like she did Penny? At least with me, she just abandoned me.

As I shifted my weight, I felt something in my back pocket. I pulled it out, and an idea hit me like a ton of bricks.

"The Calling Stone?" Lindy asked.

"Yeah. I forgot that CJ had insisted that I carry it wherever I go. I thought he was being silly, but when we went to leave to go to Nalrin, I saw it sitting on the dresser and grabbed it."

"Try it. See if he can hear you?"

"What if he doesn't have his?"

She crossed her arms and looked at me evenly, "If he did what I told him to do, he has it alright." The way she said that made me wonder what she had threatened him with if he didn't carry it with him.

"CJ" I whispered, but my voice still sounded shaky. I took a deep breath, trying to calm myself. *I have to be completely calm. I know it works when I know people are so close, but what if he's on the other side of the castle?* The castle was a vast black void my power couldn't see through. Another deep breath.

"Ceej. Can you hear me? Use your stone if you can. Two for yes please."

I waited.

Nothing.

"Ceej. Honey. Can you hear me? Two for yes on your stone."

We waited five agonizing minutes. I sighed. Nothing again.

"I don't think it's working. Maybe he doesn't have it," I said, but stopped as Lindy shot me a look. Man, if looks could kill. "or he can't get to it." I quickly added.

I could hear her mumbling but just sat there looking at the stone. It looked so odd sitting in my hand with the light pink lines behind it. *What am I going to do? Everywhere I turn there are roadblocks.* My hand continued to sting.

I could just see the edges of darkness still there. *Yea I know. "Look to the darkness and you will find what you are looking for; but stay in the light and everything you hold dear will be lost forever."*

I stood up and looked at the statue of the Angel of Death, it looked just like the one of the Angel of Beauty in the garden in the Manusia with a few differences of course. "Asshole." I muttered.

Clarice's head whipped around to stare at me.

"What?" I said.

"Did you just call the Angel of Death ... an asshole?" She asked half incredulous, have smiling.

I shrugged, and just said, "We should move on. There is nothing here and the Calling Stone isn't working."

They just looked at each other. Sometimes I wondered if they were Cogniti too and just hid it from me. I felt a rush of anger and anxiety rush through me as I stomped out the door. Striding down the hall and to a central room, I looked around to see if there was anything that I could pinpoint to help me figure out where we are in the castle.

"Eighth level down on the right Megan." Lindy had done the same thing, and the hologram in my head instantly brought a picture of the map of the castle to where we are.

"If that's true, I don't think we are far from where we suspected the room is." The map didn't have direct connectors to the circular room, but we had made some educated guesses. At this level, there were questions as to what connected to what, and it was thought some of the connections may change.

I headed down the second hallway to the left. Stopped and felt totally lost. Letting the darkness of the castle guide me, I randomly took a couple of turns and down a doublewide stairwell at the end of a hall. I stopped when it opened up to a corridor with one single door. Precisely where the one map of the circular room we had found would have it placed. I turned to face Lindy and her face mirrored mine.

"It can't be. I just randomly took hallways. I have no idea where we are!" I said in half hysterics. "I'm not sure I would know how to get out of here at the moment."

There was a blood-chilling scream from behind that door that shred any sanity I had left. My feet were moving down the hall without thought.

"MEGAN!" I heard the others calling behind me, but I knew that scream with every ounce of my being.

I just prayed I wasn't too late.

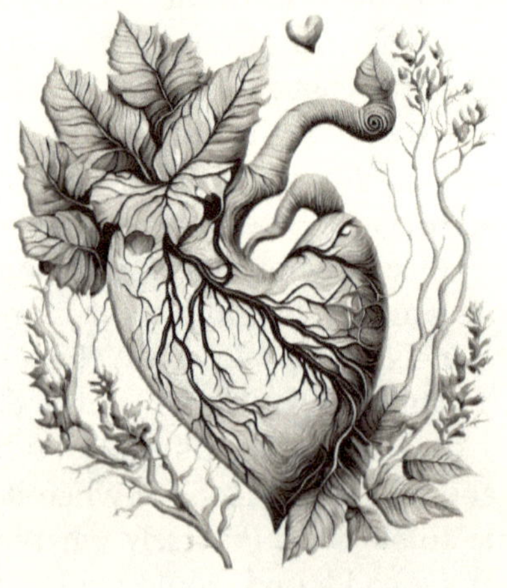

CHAPTER 45

"CJ" I WHISPERED IN horror as my heart dropped. I reached for the door and saw the darkness on the handle. Without conscious thought, I slit my hand open again and threw myself through the door staying as quiet as I could.

The room was bathed in bright sunlight. The walls around the outer circle were covered in green clover and small white daisies. The ground between the wall and the pillars was bare dirt that melded into grey stones in the center. The 12 stone pillars stood about five feet in front of me following the circular curve of the room, but my attention was solely on the round stone table where CJ laid. The air huffed out of my lungs as I saw what they had done to him. My visions had not shown me the full breadth of CJ's condition.

Long deep, precise cuts ran down his legs and arms. There were pools of blood on both sides of him, and the top of the table was slick with it. As I moved around to see if I could get a better angle to free him, I froze. There was a thick slice down his left side.

No. No. No.

He took a raspy wet breath and relief strong and fierce crashed through me. I wasn't too late. My eyes flicked to Symatha and Ansel then back to CJ.

"Ceej." I tried to push toward him, but there was no response. *"I'm here Ceej. Just hold on."*

Jean, Owen, Lindy, and Clarice had snuck in and looked about the room with a sense of awe from behind the pillars nearest the door. I however, continued to make my way around the room to get a better view of how CJ was secured to the table. I had to find a way to get him unbound. Then get him out of here.

When I heard Owen whispering, I pushed to them, *"For the Angels! Will you shut the underworld's darkness up?"*

Symatha was standing next to CJ's feet while Ansel stood near his chest holding a bloody knife. I threw an invisible wall up between CJ and Ansel, but as soon as it was there, it was gone.

I took a deep breath, concentrating and centering my power with all I had, I tried again just as Lindy snuck in next to me. Once again once it was there, it was gone.

I pulled as much of that power from my cocoon as I dared, electricity humming loud in my ears, and after a few deep breaths, threw it at him again. I saw the electricity sit over CJ for a whole five seconds before it fizzled out completely.

"It won't stay!" I hissed as Clarice came to join us behind the third pillar. They took my hand and we tried again. Once again, as soon as it formed it disappeared.

"Why won't it stick?" Clarice asked barely above a whisper.

"I tried to push them back and it won't work either." I vaguely heard Owen growl behind the fourth pillar. Jean went and joined him and they tried again, but nothing. They started trying various other incantations, but nothing worked.

"This doesn't make sense." Clarice whispered.

Lindy just shook her head in thought. "No, it doesn't"

"Remember when I said that I wanted more hand-to-hand practice?" I was staring at CJ. Clarice gave a quick nod with a questioning look.

I looked at her, waited and slowly realization crossed her face. "In case our power was rendered useless." She thought a moment longer. "Did you know then?"

"No, but" I looked back to CJ. "I have to protect him. He would protect me, even without any power."

"The wounds should be bleeding more. They've given him something to make the blood flow slower. Keep him alive longer." Lindy said, then in horror, "To make it last longer and cause more pain."

My eyes darted around the room. How was I going to stop Ansel from driving that knife into CJ? Symatha would see me coming if I launched myself out there right now. I could just see the others moving around behind Symatha swung something back and forth, and I instinctively reached for my neck.

"Megan. I love you." CJ was saying over and over again. His breaths were short, wet, and quick. He was saying it as a whispered prayer like he wouldn't let any other words be his last.

I looked back at Ansel. He was standing over CJ with both hands on the hilt of the dagger he raised it up. I was out of time.

"With the heart of a loved one, I offer this to you Angel of Love" and then swung the dagger down toward CJ's chest.

My power burst from my cocoon cracked at my fingertips and hummed in my ears as I lunged.

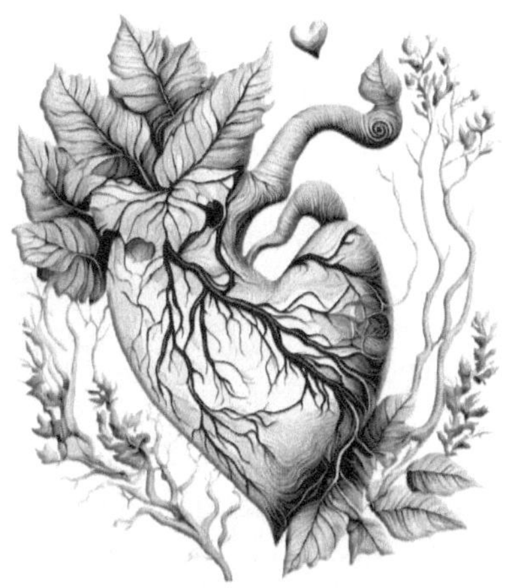

CHAPTER 46

I FROZE THREE STEPS in.

I willed myself to move.

It was happening, just as I had seen it.

The knife in my Father's hand was just above CJ's chest.

Just as that knife would have pierced his chest, an unimaginable burst of power blew through the whole room, deafening any and all sound.

Even my power heeded to it.

I tried to scream for CJ, but I couldn't. I tried to move toward him again and couldn't. I looked at my father and he was frozen too.

"Get Megan's Heart!" Symatha ordered, lips straining to move.

"I can't move." Ansel hissed through his teeth. Then the round table CJ was attached to started to rotate. Multiple voices filled the room and spoke in unison:

The pressures of time are like a clock

All the right pieces you must have
To make the pieces work in unison
Love is Strong. Love is All.
The pressures of time are like a clock
All the right pieces you must have
To make the pieces work in unison
Love is Strong. Love is All.
The pressures of time are like a clock
All the right pieces you must have
To make the pieces work in unison
Love is Strong. Love is All.
Just as the voices trailed off, CJ's chains broke.
CJ's back arched, as he gasped for breath.
CJ's wounds started to heal at a rapid pace.

Thirty seconds later he was healed enough that he was able to get off that table scrambling for the doors. He got just past the pillar that Jean was at before he too froze in place.

I tried to mentally tell him that we were all here. I tried to move toward him but was still frozen in place.

Seconds passed for what seemed like a lifetime after CJ disappeared behind that pillar. Three loud chimes sounded and the voices said one last time:

The pressures of time are like a clock
All the right pieces you must have
To make the pieces work in unison
Love is Strong. Love is All.

I felt the force holding me in place releasing. Anger surged to feed my power and I saw flashes of light, that were red, orange, and blue. All that electricity bounced back into my veins and my only thought was that Ansel, my father, had tried to kill CJ. Half a second later, the force fully released, and I ran for Ansel with my syths in my hand.

I hadn't seen Symatha leap toward me, but she pinned me against the pillar with Poseidon, the bottom of his trident poking me in my back. I braced my feet on a small lip and my hands were on her shoulders, but she had one arm across my chest and the other against my hips holding me in place. I pushed my power into her shoulders, and while her skin sizzled against it, she merely flinched and pushed it back towards me.

She looked at me inquisitively for a second before she said, "How did you find this place?"

"Oh, you know just wandered around till I found a room I liked."

"How did you find this place?" She screamed. Her eyes were glowing bright red. I could see Jean and Clarice fending off my father behind her. Where were CJ and Owen?

"Doesn't matter. We will finish you off." She said through gritted teeth.

I laughed. "And how are you going to do that without CJ or the Sa Ra. You heard what it said. You had CJ literally on a silver platter. The flower is right there, you have the Book of Death and the Crystal."

"And the Sa Ra." She spat.

"Or so you thought. Didn't you just hear? *All the right pieces you must have.* You thought you had the Sa Ra." I sneered.

She looked down and looked at the pendant around my neck. Laughed and said, "You think that is the Sa Ra? Please that is just a mangled mess!"

"What makes you so sure that what you have is the true piece?" I asked her, pushing my power back against her, her clothes burning and crumbling to ashes under my touch. I threw spear after spear of electricity into her shoulders to get her to release me, and she just stood there as if she felt nothing.

"What makes you so sure yours is?" she spat back, I groaned as she put even more pressure on my chest which drove the trident deeper into my back. Then I was falling back to the ground picking up my syths from where they had fallen. Lindy was standing about five feet from me twirling her syth in her hand, and Symatha pulling one from the back of her calf, glaring at Lindy.

Lindy motioned for me to head over to where Jean and Clarice were fighting with my father to help watch over CJ. "I have a bone to pick with her. Owen will help."

I nodded and took off for the other side of the room and heard Lindy and Owen fighting with Symatha. I ran toward the doors, and when I got to the door, Clarice had one of her whips firmly around my father's wrist while he was trying to fight off Jean.

"CJ!" I screamed.

"Megan!" CJ said with half relief and half apprehension in his voice. He ran towards me, but when he was a few feet away I saw a spear being thrown in our direction.

"Duck!" I shouted at him, but I wasn't fast enough and the spear caught in my shoulder pinning me against the wall.

"Megs!" CJ said his eyes full of panic. The pain in my shoulder was horrendous. My vision was fading in and out.

"What the fuck?" He said reaching me.

"Ceej. I'm so sorry. I'm sorry."

"It's okay. You are going to be okay babe." His eyes were bright and when he looked at me, he continued. "This is gonna hurt like a mother fucker." He put his hand on my shoulder and one hand on the spear.

I gritted my teeth, grabbed onto the Sa Ra for comfort, looked at him, nodded, and there was a flash in his eyes. "On the count of three."

"1.... 2.... 3" and he yanked it out in one single motion.

I waited for the pain, but none came. I had expected it to hurt like hell, but I didn't feel a thing. My knees gave out under me, and my head swam, but CJ wrapped his arms around me and kissed me hard. It felt so good to be back in his arms and the feel of his lips on mine. When our kiss broke, his eyes flashed again somewhere deep. I hugged him tight with my free arm and he winced.

"Sorry." I said.

"It's getting better, but considering I was a half-step from death just 5 minutes ago?" He smirked and went to tear a part of his shirt off to bandage my arm when Jean ran over.

"I'm sorry to break up this little reunion party but" then she saw the blood running down my arm, "Oh Angels! You okay?" She cocked her head to the side studying it.

I looked down to see it had already started to heal. You could see it healing. The hole in my shoulder was already filled in, and I felt nothing. I should be bleeding out. I should be in so much pain I should be passing out.

A moment longer, and it became a round pink scar that resembled the one in my hand. I moved CJ's shirt and he was completely healed as well. Just a jagged pink scar where they had sliced him open. He was standing straighter too. I blinked.

"Guys!" Clarice hollered. I looked over to where Lindy and Owen were fighting with Symatha. They were getting pretty banged up.

I grabbed my syths again and ran after Ansel. "Jean, watch over CJ."

When I got to where Ansel and Clarice were, he had her up against the wall with a syth at her cheek starting to slowly slice down from the nose across to her ear. "You won't need that pretty face anymore."

I sliced behind his knee and he collapsed to the ground, but he took Clarice with him, who grabbed his syth and stuck it just above his other kneecap. He pulled it from his leg and pounced up.

I jumped back. Someone with a syth to the knee should not be able to just pull it out and then jump up to continue fighting. That's when it hit me. "Jean, you said my father was only half Sangra! Please don't tell me the other half is indestructible."

"Not indestructible, just nearly impossible to kill." She shouted back at me. GREAT! Though considering the healing that had occurred with me moments ago, Sa Ra or not, there was something in this room keeping us alive. My arm was just a little sore at the moment, so it shouldn't surprise me he was able to get back up so quickly.

I hadn't taken my eyes off him, and he just stood there smiling, but it wasn't normal. His eyes had gotten larger and his smile wider to show more teeth. I had flashes of when I was a kid when he was mad at me and yelling. I thought I had imagined his eyes getting bigger, but I definitely had not. They were larger than that even now.

I expected him to go for me but instead, he reached for Clarice catching her off guard, and tossed her against a pillar where she grabbed ahold of Athena's spear to keep from falling. The pillar, however, toppled and fell against another one, creating a domino effect. As Clarice fell to the ground, it knocked over 2 more before it got to the one with Poseidon, which broke in half sending the top crashing down.

Clarice was quick and was already on her feet heading toward the center table CJ had been on. As she smashed the crystal and burned the Desumo Nitor. As the flower turned to ash, the Book of Death slowly faded away, and the temperature of the room dropped.

Then a scream burst through the room.

CHAPTER 47

"SYMATHA." ANSEL WHISPERED IN horror. He turned to me and growled, "This is all your fault! This isn't over child. You will pay for this."

He lunged, and my syth met his. He was spitting a string of words I couldn't understand. I brought my knee up to meet with his groin, and when he bent over, his nose break against my other knee.

He backed up a little further to where he saw CJ standing with a short sword. CJ took two long steps toward him, swung at Ansel's chest. Ansel bent backward missing the blow and brought his leg up to kick CJ in the gut. As CJ stumbled back a few steps, Ansel took the opportunity to run for the door.

Pain spiked in the back of my head. Bringing my syth up and twisting to defend myself, nothing was there. I checked to see if I was bleeding, but my hand came back clean and my hair felt dry.

The pain spiked again and if I didn't know any better, I would have thought someone was driving a hot poker through the base of my skull, from the inside out. The pain was dark and heavy as it tried to pull me under. It faded a moment later, but still hung there like a bad headache.

Ansel's lips were moving in fast succession, as he ran for the door. Just as he passed the last pillar before the open door, I saw a dagger fly through the air toward CJ.

"CJ!" I screamed.

He turned. I blinked and saw CJ catch it mid-air, take half a step and fling it back towards Ansel. I blinked again and saw the dagger land in Ansel's shoulder before he disappeared around the corner.

"Megan!" It was Lindy, but I couldn't take my eyes off CJ. What had he just done? How did he do that? He just stood there staring off where Ansel had disappeared. I took a few tentative steps toward him and when I reached out toward him, he turned his head and looked at me.

"Ceej." I said carefully.

"Oh my god. Megan. Are you ok?" He said completely changing gears and checking to make sure I wasn't seriously injured.

"I'm fine. You?" I asked as I rubbed that pain in the back of my head.

"Yeah." He gave me a quick kiss on the temple before resting his forehead on mine. "We need a real vacation after this. Deal?"

"Deal." I said kissing him quickly.

"Megan?" Lindy walked up slowly. "Come here please." I turned to her and grabbed CJ's hand pulling him with me, pain in my head easing at his touch.

I turned around the pillar and my mother laying there, Poseidon's trident pierced through her chest. Her ember was fading quickly, as her body pulsed between her Sangra form and the black mist of the demon within her. Her eyes flicked from the red of the demons to her rich brown eyes. Waves of emotion flowed through me.

Sadness.

Relief.

Anger.

Anguish.

Rapture.

I stood there looking at her trying to figure out if I was supposed to be upset that she was going to die. I should be upset my mother was going to die, shouldn't I? Just because my childhood was a lie and my life with her was a lie doesn't mean I should wish her dead. Right? The problem was my childhood was a lie. My whole life had been a lie when it came to my parents. They were trying to destroy a whole world. What about all the innocent people that died at their hands? I briefly thought about Penny and how she had been discarded like a piece of trash in the hallway upstairs.

"Megan." She whispered. I watched her as the black mist pulsing around her dissipated, the demon within her dead. Recognition crossed her face. "Please believe me when I say I love you and I never meant for you to see any of this."

"No. Instead you just abandoned me and kept family away." I couldn't keep the accusatory tone thick in my voice. I felt CJ's hand squeeze mine, probably in a way to tell me to give her a break since she was going to die, but he stayed quiet.

"I didn't abandon you. We made it look as if we had died. Children lose their parents at some point. It was supposed to be a clean break."

"Well, you didn't die. You took off to kill people, including family."

"I have no family in Nalsar. You and your father are my only family." I looked to Jean to see Owen holding her back and shaking his head.

"You abandoned me. You could have trained Matt and me." Anger was washing away all the other emotions and I tried to keep my voice calm, "Instead you were so full of hatred and vengeance that you never told us of this place or our family here!"

"After what they had done? They forced us to go to another dimension. We had no choice! Everything I've ever done was to protect you and Matt." She said and choked out a wet cough.

I sighed heavily and the anger left in a flash. "No Mom. They punished you for your actions. Dad got caught breaking the laws, they punished him for it, you took it too far. Matt and I were not even around for any of that. Yet, we have had to pay the consequences of your actions."

She looked at me like she had when I was a child, so loving, so caring and the mother I had grown up with. Only I had changed. This new life had changed me.

"Ansel will not stop. He will take revenge. He will blame you for my death." She whispered in a hoarse voice. "I loved you and Matt fiercely. Then he died, and ..." She gurgled a few words and took one last deep breath.

Her ember faded, pulsed one last time, and died out. She was gone.

Searing pain jolted through my head and grew until blackness took me over.

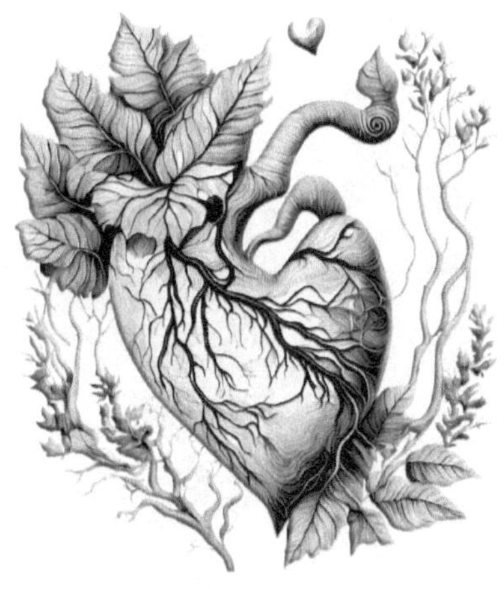

CHAPTER 48

I'M FLOATING.

Hovering over black clover fields.

"Ansel will not stop. He will take revenge."

The pain increased again, pulling me back into the darkness.

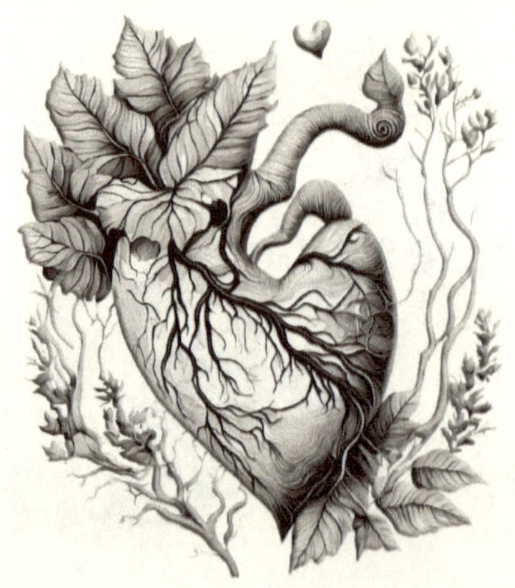

CHAPTER 49

I'M LYING IN A bed of soft grass.

My head resting on CJ's lap.

It's a beautiful spring day in Pacific Grove, California. The fog burned off early today and the sun is shining. CJ and I were having a wonderful picnic in one of the parks along the beach. Everything was as it should be.

I turned my head to have my vision filled with my father's big eyes and too-wide mouth as he screamed in rage.

I turn back to CJ. He smiles and whispers, "Megan, come on, snap out of it."

BEEP! ..... BEEP! ...... BEEP!

"Come on Megs don't make me wait again."

CJ! I felt his lips on my hand, but then he let go.

BEEP! ..... BEEP! .... BEEP!

A red-hot poker goes straight through the base of my skull. I scream.

THE FIVE ANGELS

A comforting heavyweight tugs at my mind. It's a heavy ball and chain.

Someone is pulling on the chain.

I surrender to it and fall backward into the darkness.

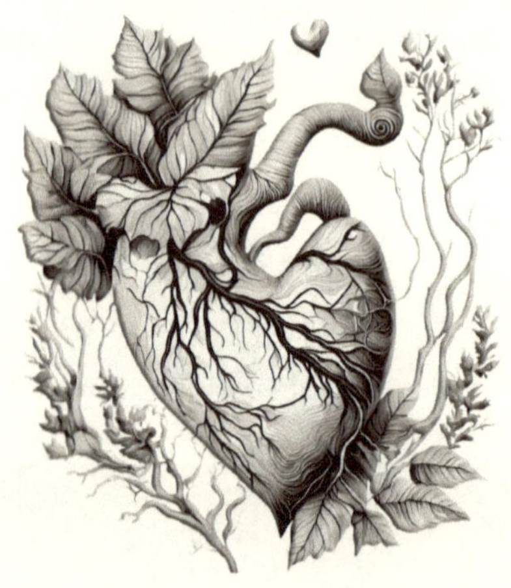

CHAPTER 50

I COULD HEAR PEOPLE talking but couldn't make out who the voices belonged to.

"She did the same thing after the explosion when her parents faked their death. She just won't wake up." The first voice said.

"Her brain activity is all over the place. One minute it is in ultra-rapid fire, other times it slows to almost nothing." Another said.

Silence.

"There is no reason for it. Everything else is normal." The same voice said. "I'm sorry Mr. Mathewson, I just can't give you any other answers."

"Please call me CJ." I hear him say.

CJ! Is he safe?

"I understand. She has been through a lot in the last year. Maybe she just needs to rest." He said quietly, as he grabbed my hand. I willed myself to squeeze it. I have to let him know I am here.

"On a different note. How are you feeling?" another voice said.

"Worried. Scared. Excited. Determined." He let out a light giggling huff. "Terrified."

"No more nightmares?"

"Nah. They are all about her." CJ said just above a whisper. I can feel each puff of breath as he continued, "At least she'll be fully protected. Though it's going to be interesting to see how she reacts to it."

It? What it?

"She'll be fine. Don't worry about that. You have a great support system here. Now get some sleep. The rest of your family will be back tomorrow to check on her."

"Yes, doc." I could hear the eye roll in his voice and that made me mentally smile. It comforted me that he could still keep his sense of humor through everything that has happened.

"Oh, and CJ. Thank you for everything that your family has done."

Silence.

After a while, I felt him rest his head on my thigh and squeeze my hand. He gently rubbed it for a while before he fell asleep.

I let the darkness carry me away too.

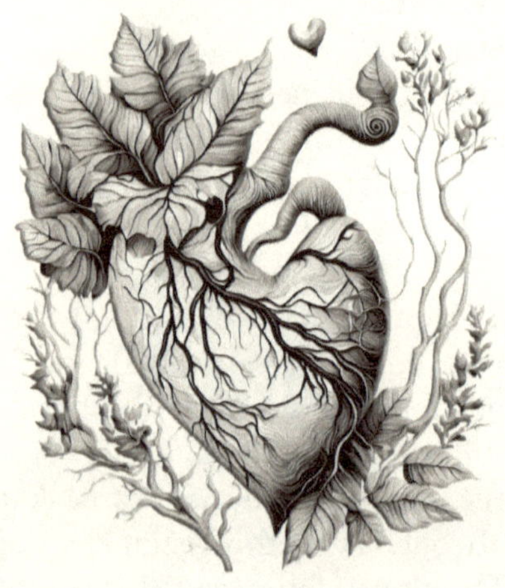

CHAPTER 51

I WAS ABLE TO determine that there were two or three someone's who rotated staying with me, but the only voice I could identify was CJ's. One would come in, then another would cover, then CJ would return. The rotation was odd. There didn't seem to be any regularity to it. CJ was there most of the time, but when he wasn't... I just couldn't figure out who the other two were.

CJ just kept trying to get me to wake up and believe me when I say I was trying. I kept refusing to let the pain in my head take me back under again. Oh, it hurt like hell, but I think I was starting to show signs of being there because when it really hurt CJ would come and hold my hand, comfort me, and tell me everything will be ok, that he loves me, and how much he's looking forward to making me his wife and starting a life here in Nalrin together. When he held my hand, the pain would disappear.

It was the other times, when he wasn't there that it was harder to keep from slipping back under. There were times I couldn't help it and that comforting silence just took over. I'd slowly come back and find that it was once again CJ holding my hand.

Slowly, bit by bit, the pain was easier to manage. I wasn't going out anymore. I had heard the doctors saying that my brain activity was getting more normal, with fewer and fewer spikes and no more low points.

One day, CJ asked if I could squeeze his hand for probably the thousandth time. I concentrated with everything I had, and my fingers twitched.

"Megs!" CJ said.

I tried to force myself to open my eyes and was only able to make my eyes flutter for a moment, but I think he saw me try.

"Megs. Come on you can do it."

I tried to open my eyes again, but nothing.

UGGG! This is so frustrating. Why can't I get my body to wake up?

I'm here CJ. Can you hear me? I tried to push to him.

"What was that?" he whispered.

I'm here Ceej.

"I think I hear you, but it's like you're muffled behind a wall."

What? Have I lost it? I reached down into my power and tried to pull a thread to the surface. It was like clawing at dust. I focused on it and pushed to him, *"Ceej."*

"Megs!" His voice cracked. "You are there!"

"Where did you think I'd go?"

"Smartass." I could hear the smile in his voice. "Try to open your eyes again."

"I'm trying. I've been trying to tell you I'm here for days." I pushed to him. I felt my electricity jump up my back but die out at the base of my neck. *"I'm not sure how much longer I can do this. My power is .... strange."*

He squeezed my hand tight for a moment before he let go. The pain in my head rose again and it took everything I had to keep the weight from pulling me back into the darkness.

"The doctors and nurses are gonna be pissed as the Underworld is black at me for putting this back on you." He took my hand after he was done placing something around my neck and continued. "Ok Megs, I need you to concentrate on healing. Nothing else."

I took a mental deep breath and even heard him whispering:
Through the gaps of space and time;
I ask the Angel of Healing to bind...
The machines went crazy.
BEEP! BEEP! BEEP! BEEP!
Through the gaps of space and time;
I ask the Angel of Healing to bind...
BEEP! BEEP! BEEP! BEEP!
Through the gaps of space and time;
I ask the Angel of Healing to bind...
People came flying into the room. Someone pulled CJ off and when his hands left mine, searing pain raged in my head. I arched up off the bed, as I fought off the pain, willed myself not to under again, and mentally screamed, "*Ceej!*"

"Megan! You're getting clearer." I heard some rustling around. My bed got pushed to the side and I heard someone hit the ground with an OOF.

I concentrated on not submitting to that weight, but the pain in my head pressed on. That ball and chain pulled hard this time, but CJ was right there.

I didn't want to go under again, not when I was so close.
BEEP! BEEP! BEEP! BEEP!
It pushed and pushed against me.

The pain was crushing me into that darkness. I fought and fought against it, but the voices in the room were getting more and more muffled. I could barely hear CJ now. I latched onto his voice like the last thread on a rope.
BEEP! BEEP! BEEP! BEEP!

"If you want to keep that arm, you are going to let go of me, she needs me." CJ roared. Seconds later his hands were in mine and the pain in my head disappeared again.

"Keep concentrating honey. *Through the gaps of space and time; I ask the Angel of Healing to bind...*" CJ was joined by another voice.

There was someone else saying something about stepping down, but I concentrated on CJ's voice. It was my thread. My tether. I held it tight in my hands and pulled on it with all I had left.

BEEP! BEEP! BEEP! BEEP!

The machines in the room continued to beep like crazy. I remotely heard one of the doctors saying he hadn't seen anything like this. The weight of it all pushed back and I slipped a little into the abyss.

BEEP! BEEP! BEEP! BEEP!

"Megan, don't pay attention to them." He said and I clinched tighter on that thread. I bound that thing around my hands so tight, it was going to have to rip my hands from my arms to become separated from me.

So, they continued...

Through the gaps of space and time;
I ask the Angel of Healing to bind...
Through the gaps of space and time;
I ask the Angel of Healing to bind...
Through the gaps of space and time;
I ask the Angel of Healing to bind...

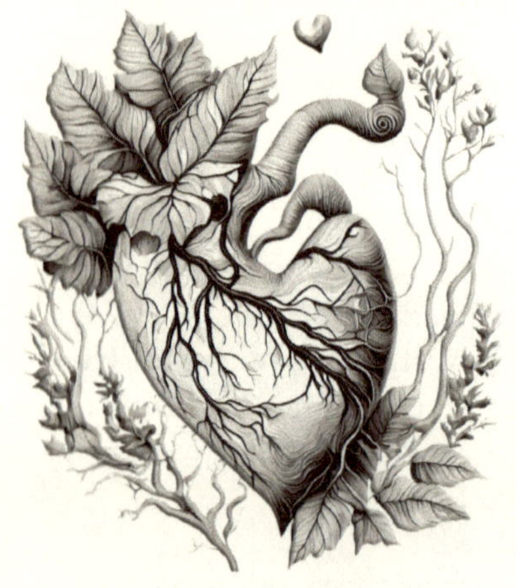

CHAPTER 52

I HEARD PEOPLE IN the room come and go, pace back and forth, doctors tell other doctors that nothing going on was making sense. All the while, CJ's hand never left mine. I thought I heard Jean and Lindy chanting with him occasionally, but it was CJ's voice that I continued to concentrate on. My power was getting stronger, and I could feel the electricity slowly start to fill my body again.

Jean and Owen tried to get CJ to get some sleep, but he refused to leave. When the last time he had slept? Part of me wanted to tell him to go and get some sleep, but I also knew that the only time the darkness and pain stayed fully away was when he was touching me.

The machines had been beeping so erratically and so loudly that the doctors finally came in and unplugged them. I felt things being removed from my arms and toes, and even when the nurses needed access to the hand that CJ was holding, he wouldn't let go, he just slid his hand up higher on my arm so he didn't stop touching me, and then slide his hand back into mine when the nurse was done.

At some point, they demanded access to my right side, so he switched over to my left, and I felt him slid something back on my hand. My ring I realized. He kissed it, kissed my palm, and started whispering things into my hand. I tried to make out what he was saying, but I couldn't.

Julian had come by to check on how I was doing after the nurses had turned off all the machines, and talked to Lindy and Clarice for a bit before asking them to let him know when I woke up.

Now, CJ was resting his head on my hip and I thought at least two other people were whispering in the corner. I felt stronger. My power while bouncy before felt solid and calming. I pulled at a thread of it to spread the golden glow over his fingers.

Imagines of the two of us in Pacific Grove, Seaside, San Francisco, Chicago, Disneyland for Grad Night, and our Florida vacation, that somehow was just the two of us, flittered through his mind. Some of the memories were when we were with friends, but most of them just the two of us. It was like he was concentrating on all the happy memories of our past. There was even a tone of happiness to some of the so-called fights that we had had when we were younger.

"CJ, I love you." I pushed to him during one of them.

"I love you too babe." He said out loud, but then he jumped awake.

"Megs?" He asked hesitantly.

"I love you." I pushed again.

"I heard you clear as day."

I fought to put a smile on my face and strained to open my eyes. They hurt in the bright lights of the room. He reached over and flipped a couple of them off. I blinked repetitively allowing my eyes to slowly become accustomed to the light before quietly whispering, "Hey!"

The room was full of people, but the only one that mattered to me was CJ. I just stared at those deep green eyes and his bright smile.

"Thank you for guiding me back, again." I pushed to him. Then he reached down and kissed me. Warmth spread to places I didn't realize were cold.

"Hey." He said against my lips.

"Hey."

CHAPTER 53

THEY WOULDN'T LET ME go home for over a week, even though I felt perfectly fine, passed all their tests, and even that headache hadn't come back in a few days. The day I was finally discharged, I had just gotten dressed when Julian walked into the room. I instantly bowed.

"What did I tell you, Ms. Megan?" He said pointedly.

I giggled as I sat back down on the bed. "It is sorta ingrained ya'know."

"I wanted to thank you for everything in person. What you and your family have done is something Nalrin can never repay." He said after a few moments.

"Well, I had to do it." I said solemnly.

He nodded and said softly, "I know."

I looked down at my feet as they hung off the edge of the bed. "Julian ... Ansel said that this wasn't over. "

"Jean mentioned something about that. Seems he is pretty angry at you."

"I guess ruining his whole plan would do that." I shrugged with a smile. "But he couldn't have seriously thought no one would have tried to stop him."

"Who knows. I don't think he ever expected it to be you and the family Symatha had left here in Nalrin."

I stared at him. Was he purposely skirting the question I was really asking? "Ok, fine, I'll be blunt. From what we went through it would be quite a few more years before he should be able to get at least the Desumo Nitor, and I'm sure the Council has upped security around the Mirror of Remembrance, but what are some other ways he could enact his revenge. He isn't finished yet. I'm not sure he will be until he is either dead ... or the rest of us are." I added at the end.

"So anxious to get back in the fight?"

"No, not really. I would prefer just to go home, marry CJ, set up life in a little cottage somewhere near the beach, away from everyone else, and relax."

"Then that is what you do. Go get married. Have a life. I have some work that you can do until you decide what you want to do for your vocation."

"So, now we just wait for him to rear his ugly head?"

"The Council is working on that."

"Don't you think that I should be involved? He is my father after all." I said.

"Megan, you have just spent the last month in the hospital recovering from something no one can explain. Go home and relax for a little while. Plan a wedding. Get settled at home."

"While my father continues to act?" I said with way too much attitude.

Julian raised his eyebrows, "While you regain your strength. You deserve some time off." I was about to interrupt, but he pressed on. "Let the Council take care of Ansel. Besides didn't he say something about you paying for stopping him?"

"In hindsight, I think it was more for killing my mother than anything, but yeah."

"Then I don't think that anything will be happening without you knowing about it." He said with a smile. "Besides, you have your family, plus the added benefit of a Vernadali to protect you." He said with a huge smile on his face.

"I'm sorry, what now?" I said my eyes bugging out of my face.

He looked at me, questions in his eyes, but he continued, "Yes, only you have an Angels Blessed Vernadali."

"Vernadali Nathanial gave me the overview, but what exactly is a Vernadali?" I asked.

"Your personal Guardian and Protector. They are from the days of old. Vernadali were always from a few select bloodlines from the oldest families in Nalrin. They start training as soon as their powers come to fruit in a compound in the Curtails of the North. They are extremely talented and powerful, and usually have a special ability that is specific to the one they will later be assigned to. There are so few of them, that unless under certain circumstances they are usually only assigned to those on the Council." He explained just as CJ walked back into the room.

Julian nodded to CJ and continued. "A bond is established between the Vernadali and their Charge. The Vernadali has an ability to work as one with its charge. There is a set path for them, that is, and forever unchanging."

"And I have one of those?" I said crossing my arms.

"You do." He said sternly.

"No disrespect Julian, but I don't want some hired hand to protect me. I don't want to be responsible for anyone else who may get hurt or killed." I said with a heavy sigh. "I almost lost Owen, Jean, Clarice, Lindy, and CJ just in the last few months. I can't chance losing someone else."

"I don't think you have a choice."

"I appreciate the honor, Julian." I said bowing formally, "However, I respectfully decline and refuse the protection of a Vernadali."

"Again, you don't really have a choice in the matter." He looked to CJ. "You haven't told her ... have you?"

I looked at him. "You knew about this?"

"Megs." He said a little fear lighting his eyes.

"Why didn't you tell me? I don't want anyone else being affected by the horrors of my family."

"I was going to tell you everything when we got home." He said looking at Julian.

"I'm assuming this Vernadali will be protecting us effective immediately?"

"Yes." Julian said a little slower than was necessary as he glanced at CJ with meaning I didn't catch.

I looked to CJ, "So you were going to tell me when we got home? What did you think I was going to think of someone coming home with us?"

"Megs. Please." He said in a whisper, pleading in his eyes. "You don't understand."

"You're right. I don't. Explain it to me, Cory James Mathewson. Who is it? Who else do we have to worry about getting killed?"

He looked at me for a long moment, stood up straight crossing his arms across his chest, and said, "I am your Vernadali."

⌘ END OF BOOK 1 ⌘

About the Author

K.M. Ringer

K.M. Ringer lives in California with her husband, little human, and two furballs, a Jack Russell mix and a Pomeranian Terrier mix. She loves providing some spice to her stories and showing that no matter what happens in your life, you are worthy of love.

Contact K.M. Ringer:

www.kmringer.com

Instagram: @kimberlymringer
Facebook: www.facebook.com/kim.m.ringer/
TikTok: @kmringer

Sign up for her newsletter on her website and receive freebies, coupon codes, and stay up to date on all things Kimberly M. Ringer and K.M. Ringer

Other Books by K.M. Ringer

Weekend Series

Weekend with Rylie
Weekend with Malcom
Weekend with Desiree
Weekend with Bethany
Angel's Shadow

The Ashstrike Sanctorum

The Ashstrike Sanctorum: Orgin Story
The Astral's Bonded
The Exorci's Touch
My Kismot Savior
The Kismot's Undesirable
My Kismot's Beloveds

Other Books

Ashes and Flame
Otter Be Saved
Under the Needle
Dedicated in Ink

Ashes and Flame

AFTER WORKING AS AN Advisor for the Roman Empire, Tiberius Maximus Vispania returned to Herculaneum in 79AD to start over. When he meets Sidonia Regilla, a fire instantly ignites between them. She would be allowed to choose her future husband. Could Sidonia be happy with Tiberius?

Just when happiness finds a way, an epic tragedy occurs and the entire village is wiped out. Only Tiberius and his best friend survive, courtesy of a curse that's provided them with immortality.

2,000 years later, Kelsey walks into his bar and lights a desire within him that only Sidonia had ever done. When their dark worlds collide, an overwhelming need to protect her takes over, and he realizes there may be more to Kelsey's ability to get under his skin than he thought. When Kelsey is kidnapped and tortured, unknown old rivals and secrets come to light.

When Max rushes in to save her, he vows that either all of them would come out alive, or none of them.

THE ASHSTRIKE SANCTORUM

THE ASHSTRIKE SANCTORUM: CREATION STORY

When the Dark Witches of Moesia go rogue, and start creating immortals, will the paranormal creatures allow the new beings to live, or will they be out to destroy them? They have tasked Benjamin, an Ovexa, with finding three of these immortals to be interrogated to determine if they can be trusted to keep the paranormal world a secret from the humans.

Jorgen Hegland has found himself newly made but quickly learns being an immortal isn't worth it. When Benjamin finds him and demands he meet with the other creatures of the world, he agrees, but it isn't until he finds his mate, that he decides he will fight for his right to live.

THE ASTRAL'S BONDED
THE ASHSTRIKE SANCTORUM:
BOOK 1

EVEN ALPHAS HAVE TO ANSWER TO SOMEONE.

It was supposed to be a simple assignment. Astral Jade Romero was supposed to fix the werewolf problem at the Porter Ranch.

Only there was a problem, she hadn't prepared herself for, the human foreman Kolton Webster. He occupied all her thoughts and sucked her in like she never had been before.

When the wolves attack and Jade is injured will it be Kolton or the wolves that destroy her?

THE EXORCI'S TOUCH
THE ASHSTRIKE SANCTORUM:
BOOK 2
WHAT DO YOU DO WHEN YOUR ASSIGNMENT DOESN'T DIE.

Exorci Jesse Westbrook can't touch anyone with his bare skin. If he does, they die. Such is the curse of an Exorci, the executioners for the Ashstrike Sanctorum.

His job is as simple and complicated as that. Receive the name and location of the person, and with a simple touch, the extermination is complete.

Jesse's life isn't all death and destruction. He has Maddie Taylor. The woman is his forever, but he's never dared to truly touch her. When her brother dies, her life spirals out of control, to the point she pushes Jesse from her life. Now... Now she's his next assignment.

MY KISMOT SAVIOR
THE ASHSTRIKE SANCTORUM:
BOOK 2.5

Angelica's life has been nothing but hiding from her parents and trying to make ends meet. It's been hard, but worth the freedom it afforded her from her family.

Morgan would have never guessed he would have found his queen just walking down the streets of Carmel, California, but there she was, arguing with the most despicable of women.

When Morgan intervenes, chaos ensues and Angelica and Morgan's secrets come to light quickly. Only Angelica seems to have one more...

<u>THE KISMOT'S UNDESIRABLE</u>
<u>THE ASHSTRIKE SANCTORUM:</u>
<u>BOOK 3</u>

Masen Cartwell was the son to the pride's king. It was his responsibility to ratify the treaty by marrying the Los Padres pride's undesirable, Veronica Aktins. There is something about her though. Something that pulls at his protective instincts and calls to his tom.

Ronni was the daughter of traders to her pride, an outcast, the Undesirable. Used and assaulted by the princes, the King has demanded that she marry the rival pride's prince and kill the Ventana Prides ruling family. Only, when she meets Prince Masen, his possessiveness over her and the adoration he showers her with sings to her heart.

When Prince Edwin steals Ronni, Masen will do anything to get her back. He had promised to protect her and keep her safe from her old pride.

Masen Cartwell won't let anything happen to what is his, and will stop at nothing to have his Queen back.

My Kismot's Beloveds
The Ashstrike Sanctorum:
Book 3.5

Leo Banks has watched his best friend and his prince find their mates. As hand to the crown prince, he was okay with that. They found their happiness and now his princess, and a woman he considered a sister, was pregnant with twins. He vowed to be her protector through the troubled pregnancy. He was happy with just being Uncle Leo.

Then when her pregnancy takes a turn for the worse, Dr. Marie Fuller and her nurse, Hadrian Fuller, come to Landow to care for her. When they arrived, Leo was not expecting to find his mate, let alone a queen and tom.

Can he balance the stress of protecting his princess, and welcoming his mates into his life?

WEEKEND SERIES

BY K.M. RINGER

WEEKEND WITH RYLIE
Book One

Luci's whole life changes in one weekend with her boyfriend, Rylie Allen.

Of course, there was the mind-blowingly good sex. It always was, but then there are secrets revealed, and a new job opportunity that would change everything between Luci and Rylie. When her ex-boyfriend comes back to haunt her, it threatens to throw their lives into further upheaval.

WEEKEND WITH MALCOM
Book Two

Malcom Henderson has been obsessed with his Project Foreman for months. When she's disrespected at a bar he steps in and after an enjoyable night, he hopes to have it turn into something more. The next morning, she's convinced that as much as she wants him, it was only a one-night stand, and tries to protect herself by kicking him out. A torturous week pulls between them when unexpected problems are occurring on the job site that ends up being tied to the Chicago mafia families, and it's not long before Malk and Raquel find themselves in the middle of a brewing war.

WEEKEND WITH DESIREE
Book Three
With threats against the Don Supreme and his family lurking around every corner, Jensen Maloy, the most feared man in all Chicago, has been working overtime to ensure everyone stays safe and alive. Desiree Hernandez loves and trusts Jensen with every fiber of her being, and while she understands the reason, they need to live in lockdown, it doesn't mean she's happy about it. Even if she

is living with her best friend and honorary sister, and her fiance.

Jensen and Desiree aren't used to being apart for such long stretches of time, and despite all the support from friends and coworkers, tensions rise, and morale drops to an all-time low. When the enemy takes drastic actions to finish the deal, they forget to factor in two very important things. Desi is not to be underestimated, and Jensen will stop at nothing to make sure his Princess is safe and in his arms. Who will still be standing when the dust settles?

WEEKEND WITH BETHANY
Book Four
Her strength will save them all.

Weekend with Bethany is the explosive conclusion to the Weekend Series. The war between Dallas and Vaux has become deadly, and no one is safe. When Beth is captured, she was shocked to learn that her Wes was the one and only Wesley Backnoff. Sure, she knew the name. Who didn't? Can she reconcile the compassionate man with whom she fell in love, with the killer who stands before her?

After rescuing Bethany, Wesley Backnoff, second to the Don Supreme of Chicago, can't hold back his feelings for her any longer and is bound and determined to keep her.

Old secrets come to light and threaten to destroy them all. Who will pay the price? Will Beth and Wes survive the night or has their time run out?